SLAYERS INC.

THE CRIMSON LINE

KENDRAI MEEKS

The Crimson Line (Slayers Inc. #1) © 2025 by Kendrai Meeks

Print ISBN: 978-1-953073-23-5

Book Cover by **MIBL Art**

Edited by **Chantell Reid**

Interior and Ebook Design **by The Last TK**

DEDICATION

At the age of seven, I wrote my first book ever: a language arts textbook for my dolls to study. (I believe I wrote the title on the front as "Langawge Arts.") My grandmother read it and declared it superb work.

When I first published professionally twenty-five years later, I wrote romance. *Steamy* romance. She wanted to read that too, because I wrote it. Nervously, I said "Grandma, it has sex in it." She looked at me deadpan and said, "I've had four children. I know what sex is."
She loved it. Or so I was told; I was never brave enough to discuss the "naked people" books with her directly.

I dedicate this book this book and the fact that I had faith in my talents

to become a writer to my first reader and biggest fan, Mary Ellen "Molly" Malvitz.

I hope she wouldn't mind that this book does *not* have sex in it. I think she would, however, appreciate that my spelling has improved dramatically since my first work.

FROM THE NEW DIARY OF AMY POPOWITZ

I don't know why I've waited so long to start a diary again, but it's not like I had a lot of time over the last two years to sit down and think, let alone write anything. Also, I was, at times, literally *running* for my life, and how could I know I hadn't died and was stuck in some kind of hell loop? After all, I wasn't exactly a model person up to now. Hated my parents, slept with anything that made googly eyes at me and had a decent bod, pissed away a college education getting a degree in a field with little to no job prospects...

To serve up a plain bagel: it's been weird, like some stupid reality show where I'm being set up to be punked. At any moment, I expect some B-lister celebrity to walk into the room and be like, "Fooled you, dipshit. Like vampires and werewolves actually exist. I mean, come on, you honestly believed your college roomie was some kind of supernatural ninja or something? Just how blonde *are* you?"

But either I'm currently in a coma and having the longest dream ever, or it is real. It's like I went to sleep one night and woke up in a cult horror franchise remake of every Disney princess movie ever, only with worse clothes and straight princes. Also, the princes have fangs or howl at the moon, and the princesses have swords.

Some of them also try to kill you.

Though I guess it's possible I could still be in a coma, and if so, I hope my dad is wracked with guilt for all the time he wasted treating me like I was shit just because I dared to survive my childhood.

Once upon a time (and living in real life fairy tales as I am now, that phrase will forever make my eyes roll), I asked my surprise supernatural roommate, Geri Kline, AKA a descendant of both the real Red Riding Hood and the Big Bad Wolf, why she ran away from her little bum-fuck town in Northern Michigan. "Because you have two chances at having a family," she'd said. "The one you're born into and the one you choose for yourself. I'm here looking for that second one."

Which, I guess, I understood, even if I didn't agree with. I mean, I ran away from New York City to avoid the family I'd been born into, but *I* came to Chicago for three reasons: great shopping, great food, and an airport big enough to let me escape anywhere without connections. But why did Geri decide Chi-town was her escape?

She'd thought about that for a moment before giving the most practical answer in the history of man. "Because I didn't think my truck could make it any further without breaking down."

So, that's her world. Grab at every possibility... as long as it's within a drivable distance. She dreamed big but still managed to be pragmatic, doing what she could with what she had available. Kind of inspirational, right? Of course, back then, I had no idea that Geri had just broken up with a werewolf or that the whole "supe" world was on the edge of an open war with Dracula (yes, *the* Dracula, Vlad Tepeş.) If I'd been Geri, I'd have run away from that too. Instead, she ended up meeting another werewolf in Chicago who needed her help finding his kidnapped mate. Unfortunately, when Geri found Tobias's mate, it was too late. And then... Tobias became my roommate too.

Of course, when all that went down, I was still in the dark. I just thought Geri was stupidly friend-zoning a hot widower, not sheltering a broken werewolf. I mean, not my type, but yeah, Tobias was raging hot if you like that whole "grimes up good" thing. And, honestly, I did make me feel a little safer knowing there was a bulky big man taking care of the woman who was becoming my best friend, even if it was (according to her at the time) COMPLETELY PLATON-IC.

But the question remains: did Geri get her found-family? Well, a year and a half after "The Battle of the Tahquamenon" where Vlad Tepeş (again, yes, *the* Dracula) finally bit the big one, she's shacking up with the hunky English werewolf and living her best life. They even adopted a kid which... sounds like a stupid thing for a twenty-something newlywed to do, but whatevs. Geri, Tobias, and Little Mina seem happy in their bubble of domestic bliss.

They just rented a little house outside Marquette, Michigan. Geri's hoping to start a Master of Education program at a local college up on the edge of civilization next fall, and even I admit that chubby-cheeked pup with whom they formed the world's weirdest pack made my biological clock tick for a nanosecond.

Of course, I quickly came to my senses and made sure my IUD was still in place, because me, a mom? Fuck. No. I am never having kids. NEVER.

So, yeah, Geri's dreams came true. But mine?

HA! Hardly.

First, I'm STILL IN CHICAGO. By now, I'd thought I'd be the hot arm candy of some ancient Californian billionaire with a heart condition. Granted, I do have a job that pays me way more than I'm worth and a pimped-out apartment with a great view, but that view is *Chicago*. And worse... I have a roommate: my ex-roomie's ex-boyfriend.

Who is also my boss.

And hot as hell, but also, a total male slut and a little bit of an arrogant, party boy prick.

And my boss.

Yup, that's right. I, Amy Popowitz, not only ended up living with Caleb

Victor Helsing, but wait, there's more! I'm also the den mother to his small court of sun-throwing superheroes-in-training, the Reclaimed. And listen, I get that it isn't the slayers' fault that they're so unfamiliar with how the human world works. Before they were rescued from the fanciest prison ever, most of them had never been around hueys. So now, these potential undead assassins are developing skills and common sense most people learn as kids.

Sergei struggles to understand the concept of money, most of all why each country needs a different kind. Teiko needed lessons on how to wash dishes. And don't even get me started on personal hygiene. Oh, no, it's not that they're *unclean*. Quite the opposite; they're a race of neat freaks. But somehow, I was the one who ended up teaching them all how to shave because in their Club Fed vampire prison, they had attendants to do their dirty work. It was crazy: twenty of us in the training gym, reviewing the basics of soap, lather, rinse. Of course, I forgot to distinguish the *regions* of shaving for men and women in the huey world and ended up with some extremely smooth-legged men the next day.

Overall, things could have been worse. What else was I going to do? Head back to NYC to be a professional gopher at my dad's law firm? Join my mother researching rooftop bars (and reverse-tipping the servers like she was still my age)? No thanks. Yeah, Caleb does grate my nerves, but at least I feel more like we're in a battle of wits than the target of a nuclear assault like I am with my dad. But I'll be damned if what I do should be called "assisting."

Caleb is supposed to be the leader of his community, and yet, it always seems I'm the one they all come to with their problems. He clubs all night and sleeps all day. But shit needs to get done, and guess whose job that ends up being?

She's got two thumbs pushed into her big knockers and her name is Amy Popowitz.

Fuck my life. Fuck my boss.

In fact, just plain fuck me.

ONE

Amy didn't have to wonder why her dipshit boss was a no-show for the third time this week. The lacy thong discarded on the floor outside his bedroom door told the whole story.

Unbelievable. The so-called leader of the Slayer race and new shadow CEO of White-Whitman Labs, skipped out of the Board of Directors meeting... to get laid.

Again.

Had they not just discussed *why* he needed to grow up and focus? Yes, they had, and the text conversation had gone something like this:

> Hey, asshat, turn the tops of every toadstool in Chicagoland if you want, but remember the Board is as pissed at you right now as I am right now. BE AT THE MEETING.

> Seriously? They're vampires. They live for centuries. So what if they wait? Besides, shows them who's boss if I ignore them and get away with it.

IF.

Caleb?

CALEB!

Sorry, phone call. You need something? Thought we were done.

Look, I don't care if you go out six nights a week and lay waste to every woman on the Magic Mile, just be at the BOD Meeting on the seventh. DO your job, not some girl. I swear, it's like talking to a caveman with you.

grumble grumble *hits chest with fist* me horny and want to get drunky but if make you happy, me will come back to cave with buffalo and throw on stone table for pointy-tooth monsters

Okay, that last part *had* made her laugh.

Then.

With a direct threat issued by Raquel de la Vega herself involving her fangs and Amy's neck, Amy wasn't laughing now.

She pulled her phone from her pocket and hit the third name in the favorites. Though, given that Caleb was in the first position due to the need of frequency, she didn't think that was a good name for the list.

Gabor picked up before the electronic ringing had a chance to go off, but he still wasn't fast enough to beat Amy, the Blonde Huey, jumping into a conversation.

"It's me. I need help here. I have reached the docks and have confirmed that the sun is still below the horizon."

"Miss Popowitz, hello. I must tell you again, there is no need for code."

The man on the other end sighed, and she could picture the Mayan-fisherman-turned-vampire pinching the bridge of his nose. "I'll let the members of my team know that you've tracked down the Solari in his own apartment. As usual, they will be impressed at your huey capabilities."

Huey. That's what the supernatural set called mundane mortals like her. She didn't know if the term predated its association with a precocious cartoon duck often in trouble due to his youth, inexperience, and incompetence, but it wouldn't surprise her. Despite the probable sarcasm, she wouldn't be distracted. She leaned into the door to see if she could hear anything. She wanted to be sure she didn't catch the leader of the Slayer race *in flagrante* when she kicked it in. No plopping, grunting, mattress spring creaking...

But Amy could smell a brand of perfume that she was both too picky and too young to wear.

Amy cupped her hand over the receiver. "He's in his room, and I don't think he's alone in there."

Her own bedroom was on the other side of the building, despite being a part of the same spacious luxury unit. Turned out to be a perk of being CEO was the penthouse suite. A consequence of being his personal assistant was sharing it.

Amy wasn't sure if Caleb's bedroom turned into an EDM act when he had a hook up. Something told her he was a loud lover, and that he loved to pick up screamers. He'd want a woman who could give him lots of positive feedback. Either she'd been completely wrong and he was a mime in the sheets, or the slayer and his woman du jour were still asleep an hour before sunrise.

Which also meant she would have been in there since the night before.

While Amy was on the other side of the penthouse, changing out batteries, grabbing a steamy romance book, and questioning her life choices.

Gross.

Pinching back her nausea, the blonde huey turned on a heel and made her way toward the kitchen. "Update: the seagull is still circling. I repeat: the seagull still eyeballing the man holding the hotdog on the beach. I need the weatherman to come and blow the clouds from the horizon."

"And again, *again*... if I'm just going to wipe the memory of yet another huey woman, there *is no reason for code.*" This time, Gabor sounded like one of her high school teachers giving her a well-worn lecture. "Go ahead and accuse them of having intercourse at the top of your lungs. It doesn't matter."

"Oh my God, *intercourse?* The only person I ever heard use that term outside of a classroom was my high school art teacher, and even he only ever did it ironically." Amy dropped her hand. "Just how ancient are you?"

"I will be three hundred eighteen, next month."

"I was being facetious, Gabor." Her fault for asking. "Look, your own security team drilled into me that it was *muy importante* to be careful what I said around humans. That's all I'm doing, okay?"

The human, who they must thought *didn't* listen, pushed a fist into a cocked hip and glared at the doorknob. No, she wouldn't do it. Even if a small part of her *was* curious if Little Caleb lived up to the hype, Amy didn't want it confirmed.

"Gabor, please get your ass down here. Caleb was supposed to be in that meeting..." the clock hanging over the kitchen counter struck the hour and truth, "... ten minutes ago. If I walk back into that conference room without him, the chairperson is personally going to fang me."

The voice she expected to come through the receiver spoke immediately behind her.

"No need to worry, Miss Popowitz. I am already here."

Amy turned, the phone slipping from her hand as her arms instinctively shot out to her side in surrender. She hadn't even heard the penthouse door open, though she did hear it *close*. But only after Gabor was already standing beside her, a dull, unamused expression on his face and her way-too-expensive phone in his hand, saved from certain broken screens by the grace and agility of vampire reflexes.

"Gabor!"

Amy lashed one hand over her cleavage, the feel of her heart a jackrabbit beneath her fingertips. Try as she might, she still hadn't been able to bust herself out of the PTS-fueled reaction every time a vamp took her by surprise. And that was like, hourly.

"How many times have I said: only come into the penthouse like that if it's an emergency?"

"My apologies, Miss Popowitz." The hint of a smile flashed on his face before evaporating. "But you were speaking in code despite my repeated efforts to encourage you otherwise. I could only assume you were being held hostage or were somehow otherwise under duress."

"You did? Oh, yeah, I guess..." Her voice tapered off and she schooled her own body's reaction.

She was *not* about to die.

Amy let her head fall back against the wall and drew a few quick, deep breaths to reset herself. Gabor had a presence that made you respect his size while still thinking he might be a big old teddy bear deep down. The kind of man who bought balloons for children, then drove across town to rip out someone's spine. Looking into his sharp features, umber skin, and somber gaze, she could easily picture him stroking her check moments before breaking her neck. She knew in principle, however, that she didn't need to be afraid of WWL's Chief of Security.

"You needed my assistance, Miss Popowitz?" The vampire inclined his head after she'd been silent for several moments. Moments that must have seemed longer to him.

"I did. I *do*." Her heartbeat was slowing now. Until, that was, she remembered why she'd called Gabor to begin with. Potential heart attack averted, Amy crossed the room, pulling the old vamp by the hand. "Caleb *must* be at this meeting. I can't make any more excuses for him. I know he's got someone in there. I need her vacated, both physically and memory-wise, so I can drag his ass upstairs. Open the door and take care of it."

The vampire straightened. "Miss, I would never presume to encroach upon the Solari's private chamber except in matters of life and death, and most certainly not when he's entertaining a paramour."

"I don't think she's handicapped, and even if she is, I don't think that changes anything." She got behind the vampire and attempted to launch him into battle, despite his utter immovability. "And it *is* a matter of life and death: mine. If he's not up in that boardroom in ten minutes, Raquel de la Vega said she would eat me."

"Perhaps she was trying to woo you, Miss?"

Amy stopped her useless pushing as her face screwed up. "Raquel is gay?"

"Vampires don't like to use such labels. But if you mean does the Chairperson of the Board prefer the intimate company of beautiful young women over that of young men, it has been my observation that, yes, she does."

Amy didn't think that's what the words *I will take my capable fangs to your throat and drink you dry* meant, but she'd heard worse pickup lines.

Hell, she'd *fallen* for worse pickup lines.

"No, I think she meant as food. Look, are you going to help me or not?"

"Of course, Miss. I only ask that *you* be the one to breach our mutual employer's bedroom door. If I, one of the stronger and more senior vampires in Chicago, were to enter unbidden it might trigger a slayer to act as instinct demands. It would only take one solarium aimed well to turn me to ash."

"What do you think it's going to do to me, give me a healthy glow?" Amy held out her arms akimbo. "In case you haven't noticed lately, I'm human. A *huey,* as you guys call me. And all hueys have a severe allergy to getting hit by a supernatural ball of solar energy."

"All the same, this is a boundary over which it is not wise for me to step. At the very least, because I wish to maintain my *job and my life.*"

Two balled up fists planted on her hips, Amy plastered on her best "you got to be fucking with me" glare.

The vampire remained unchanged, something they were really good at.

"Fine." She shook out her aggravation and her hands as she approached her boss's door. "But I'm not getting you that nice Christmas present I had picked out."

Two

S leepless and growing more annoyed by the moment, Caleb lay in place where he'd awoken: his left arm wrapped around the previous evening's distraction, his percale bed sheets twisted around both of their ankles. Outside his bedroom door, his chief of security and his assistant conducted a verbal thumb war. It didn't matter who opened the door, really. In the end, it wouldn't change the truth.

Caleb Helsing's life was fucked up. And now, *at last,* he was out of time and worse, excuses for why he couldn't unfuck it.

Michelle (that *was* her name, right?) stirred, a coquettish smile bubbling on to her face when their eyes met. "Hey."

Caleb pulled in his hand enough to lift the stray hairs covering her face, tucking them behind her ear. "Hey back."

Michelle looked out the wall of windows, taking in the pre-dawn soft glow of the Chicago landscape as seen from over a hundred meters off the ground. In the distance, Lake Michigan's ice-crusted depths sank into the blossom of a sunrise.

"It's so early. Why are you awake?"

"I haven't slept at all."

He withheld "because I'm a supernatural being who is genetically prone to being nocturnal." It raised questions, ones he'd be perfectly willing to answer since Gabor was standing by to rewrite any of Michelle's memories that a huey shouldn't have, but he wanted to hold on to this escape a little longer.

Last night, this king mattress had been a canvas he'd painted a masterpiece using the leggy brunette beside him as the brush. It had been fun. *Had been.* But as Michelle relaxed into a semi-boneless existence and drifted off, sated and exhausted, *Caleb* stared at the ceiling, mentally sparring with his ever-present anxieties. Even fantastic sex couldn't divert his thoughts for long.

With a little purr, Michelle tucked her head into the crook of his shoulder and snuggled into his body. For warmth, Caleb presumed as he kept his suite at a temperature Amy described as "frigid as fuck." (She tended toward drama.)

A slayer was always a warmer than a huey. Despite not understanding the science behind it, it made sense for a supe whose defining ability was hurling balls of solar radiation about. This side effect of his heritage had often come to his advantage when entertaining members of the opposite sex.

Caleb reached out, angling the sexy minx's chin and dotting a kiss to her lips before he spoke. "Last night was awesome, but I think I'm late for a meeting I promised to make."

"A meeting? Now?" The odd statement took her eyes to the teal glow of the alarm clock on the bedside table. "It's six-fifteen in the morning."

"I know. That Board always schedules these damn things at the ass crack of dawn. It's... weird. I think they just like watching the sunrise in safety from the TK floor."

WWL's cash cow, so-called Athenian glass, took care of that. The shit was as expensive as hell, but it managed to block out the exact wave lengths vampires were allergic to. While the executive offices were subterranean to avoid daylight, the whole boardroom was wrapped and gave a view of the city skyline even a bloodsucker could enjoy without turning into a pile of dust.

"Believe me, I don't *want* to go," Caleb admitted. It was the most open he'd been with her since they'd met twelve or so hours before. "But I don't think I can get out of it any longer. I'm sorry."

Just at that moment, he heard Amy repeat a threat handed down from the chairperson of the board, and his urge to protect kicked in. Caleb's muscles clenched; his grip on the woman beside him intensified by instinct. Michelle must have thought she was getting an aggressive hug because she threw her arm back over him and squeezed back.

"Oh, did you want to have a little morning cap before you head off, then?"

No, he did not. He wanted to show Raquel the business side of his solarium. Honestly, he doubted the chairperson would make good on her threat. Caleb had spent the last year letting everyone know Amy Popowitz was *his*. Not in a sexual way, but in the ways a vampire could lay claim to a human who tickled his fancy, so he, a Slayer, made it well known around the halls of the Walt Whitman Labs that you didn't touch the blonde huey unless you wanted to chance being ashed.

If they were going to respect him, he had to back up that claim with action. "I really should get up and go," he said through clenched teeth.

But the brunette countered, "I thought *you* were the boss. CEO, isn't that what you said at the bar last night? Just tell them you'll be there in an hour."

"There might be... consequences."

And that wasn't limited to having his assistant being used as a blood bag. The Board could take this all away. His lux townhouse, sizable salary, his fancy corporate title...

Did they not know how limber Michelle was?

Whether they did or not, Caleb could hear that the conversation outside his door had reached its crescendo, and footsteps were turning his way.

"Michelle, I think we'd better get up before..."

If you wanted to tempt fate, point at it and laugh in its general direction.

The door burst open, and Caleb pulled himself up. He yanked the bed sheets along for the ride, covering up the parts considered unprofessional to show a woman who worked under you in a professional capacity while also respecting the privacy of the one who had worked under him the previous night in a more casual way. His back pressed against the cool metal frame. From a break in the curtains, an orange-red beam of sunlight shot and illuminated the tip of Amy's blade.

Fucking *Hitchcock* couldn't have designed it better himself.

"Amy." He said her name as part acknowledgment, part accusation. "You're looking well this morning. Any particular reason for the knife, though?"

Before Amy could answer, the trembling brunette came up to speed with the scenario change. Wearing nothing but a confused expression and the most adorable lacy pink bra, she cowered into Caleb's side, one hand full of sheet and the other pointing at the possible murder weapon.

"C... C... Caleb, She's got a... a... a... knife."

The slender blonde dressed in a black pencil skirt and sleeveless white blouse rolled her eyes. "Oh, my God, Buffy. I think your Friday morning special is about to piddle in your bed."

Well, no one ever said Caleb didn't listen to his assistant at all. Or that he didn't care about his linens, even if a man in his position and with the kind of wealth he'd inherited could afford to have them replaced easily.

"Michelle, baby, it's okay. Amy's not going to hurt *you*. If she fillets anyone, it'll be me. Give us a few minutes to clear up any sort of... confusion."

There was something about assuring a one-night stand that she wasn't about to be murdered that let her focus on more immediate issues. Michelle found her backbone and her feet in the same moment, her pallor going from bleach white to crimson red in the space of a minute, just like her hands went from out at her side and ready to defend herself, to crossed over her chest and cupping her generous breasts... for the sake of modesty? Seemed a little late at this point.

Still, lucky hands.

"When I asked you last night if you were in a relationship, you said no, asshole," she shrieked. "So why is your girlfriend—"

"Whoa, toots, I am so *not* his girlfriend." Amy's words were as sudden as they were biting. She was so precious when she tried to look all tough. "But then again, neither are you. And if you think you were ever going to be, your tits are bigger than your brain." She side-eyed Michelle for a moment before scowling. "Actually, that's probably true anyway."

Well, fuck. As much as he loved the idea of a cat fight, he should probably diffuse the situation before the woman with a knife had a reason to want to carve up the woman *without* a knife.

Caleb lowered his lips to press a kiss to the quaking woman's forehead. "Michelle, go in the bathroom and get cleaned up. My security chief is waiting outside to take you home as soon as you're ready."

"What, you're just going to throw me out of bed in the morning, and that's that?" Michelle bolted out of bed, taking the twisted sheet along with her, exposing Caleb's second-best asset next to his ability to throw balls of solar energy. "How about you get rid of your crazy ex first?"

That would be the next likeliest role for Amy, wouldn't it? But even Caleb was getting eager to get on with this already.

"Amy is not now, nor has she ever been, anything romantic to me. She's only my..." The fingers of his right hand swirled the air. "... flatmate slash assistant slash pain in my ass." He swung his legs off the side of the bed and grabbed a towel off the floor, wrapping it around his midsection as he stood. Not for Michelle's sake. She had seen his manhood from the inside three times in the last six hours. He would, however, like to avoid a sexual harassment lawsuit if possible.

Besides, even a thin layer of Turkish cotton between the knife and his manhood made him feel just a little bit better.

Caleb put a hand to Michelle's back and shepherded her towards the ensuite. "Go. Please. This is weird enough for the two of us already. I'll deal with the crazy woman."

If he had thought getting Michelle out of earshot and eyeful would have calmed Amy, Caleb was immediately proven wrong.

The blonde huey cocked her hip and glared. "*Deal* with the crazy woman?"

"At least with her potentially lethal weapon, yes." He pointed to the sharp pointy object still clasped in Amy's right hand. "You know, you'd never have a chance, right? I can run faster than you can stab."

Not like she needed the display, but Amy might do with a reminder. Just because Caleb avoided his office and anything to do with it with zeal didn't mean he lacked ability.

In a swish of movement, the slayer was before her with his hand cupped around hers. A little squeeze, which probably felt like a vice to the huey, and Amy's fingers opened, her hand instinctively pulling back from pain. Not that it could have hurt that much. Caleb was gentle and, while Amy *was* annoying, he'd never hurt a woman just to make a point.

The knife dropped, and just to complete the demonstration and to keep her toes from potential harm, Caleb caught it by its hilt and tossed it on the bed behind him.

"Now that *that's* out of the way..." he said, adding a cocky grin. "To what do I owe this impressive wakeup call?"

Amy huffed. "Remember when you were heading out to the club last night, and I stopped you by the door and told you 'Hey, jackass, don't miss the Board Meeting if you want to live?' Why is it that I seem more interested in you doing your job than you?"

He turned to find some clothes, even as the shower came on in the bathroom. "Job?"

"Yeah, you know the one where you're supposed to run this company?"

"It rings a bell." Caleb pulled a pair of briefs and socks from his dresser before heading into the walk-in closet. "That's the one I get paid a shit ton of money to do, isn't it?"

"Theoretically." By the sound of her voice, she was following him in. "We were supposed to meet an hour ago in my office to prep for the board meeting, but you never showed up."

"As you can see, I was busy doing something."

"Some*one,* Caleb. Some*one.*" She came to a rest outside the door. Though Caleb couldn't see it, he could picture Amy, her back against the wall, her arms crossed over her chest.

The view in his mind's eye was... inspiring. Not that he thought of Amy in that way. As the best friend of his ex-girlfriend and his employee, she was off limits with a capital O. Still, as last night and frankly, most nights proved, Caleb was a hot-blooded and virile male. Besides, Amy would probably castrate him if he ever actually came on to her. Well, came on to her *again*. But the one time they'd kissed wasn't because of some kind of attraction. Caleb had been trying to make his ex jealous. Given the fact that Geri Kline was now Mrs. Geri Kline-Somfield, mated to a werewolf and legally wedded under the huey laws of the great state of Michigan, it hadn't worked.

Amy's voice dragged him from his reverie. "You can't miss another meeting. Vega told me if you don't show up this time, she's opening my vein and drinking slowly until you do."

"There isn't a vampire in this building who would dare, not even her." He hunted through the racks of clothes with more labels than a soup factory. Money was a good thing. A lot of money was a very good thing. "I'd ash any that tried. Raquel was bluffing."

"Threatening," Amy countered. "She was *threatening* me. And you promised me that you'd never put me in a situation where I had to feed a vamp, Caleb."

The shower shut off, and Caleb knew they'd only have a minute or two to speak openly before Michelle came back in. Not much time to relieve Amy of her concern.

"Do you remember what happened the first time we came here together?" Caleb asked, emerging from the closet while straightening the blue-and-pink silk tie. It matched well with the pink linen shirt and cobalt blue suit.

Her eyebrows lifted at the change in direction and maybe, his appearance. "You mean that time we showed up in the middle of the night and you blew up one of the members of the board, proclaiming yourself Big Boss and Lord of All? Rings a bell."

"I *ashed* a member of the Dracule bloodline and *informed* the board of Inga Rosethorn's death, adding that I was her heir and CEO Designate." Nuance wasn't the blonde huey's specialty. "I didn't kill that vamp just because he was plotting against the interests of this company and me personally. I did it to show that I was someone you don't fuck with. No vampire at WWL is going to fangrape you, Barbie. They know that you're under my protection, and I don't just *threaten*."

"You say that, but it's hard for them to remember that you even exist when you never show up for anything. Besides..." she shrugged, "... there's developments that I can't deal with, even if it doesn't result in me being down a pint."

"Developments?" He sat on a bench and pulled out a pair of matching shoes. "What developments?"

"Why don't you show up and find out?" Amy's eyes cycled, looking, he assumed, at the shapely brunette who walked out of a bank of steam pouring out the bathroom door and back into earshot just at that moment.

"Caleb?" Michelle's tone lifted.

He waved Michelle in, keeping eyes on Amy. "It's okay. Amy is disarmed, and she was just on her way to turn on the espresso machine."

"I am?"

Two little words that, translated from Amy to English, meant *Who in the hell do you I think I am, your waitress?*

"Yes, you are," he said, nodding. "Because if you expect me to be at my best with the Board, I'm going to need caffeine. Now, go, you harpy." With a jerk of his hand toward the door, he shadowed the command with a direction. "I need to talk to Michelle for a moment."

His Thursday-night entertainment visibly relaxed when Amy turned on heel and went back from whence she came. Wrapped in a towel and wet hair sticking to the side of the face, the lady before him had lost a little of the painted-on charm that had caught his eye in the piano bar the night before. No matter. She was still a knock-out, and he didn't want her to think her time and efforts hadn't been appreciated.

"That was fun, Michelle." He leaned in, his hands bracing her shoulders and his lips dancing over hers.

"After I get dressed, can you... will you walk me out?" She looked up at him from under a curtain of hair. Then, her smile broke, and she rolled her eyes to the side. "Sorry if I sound like a little girl, but waking up to a crazy blonde wielding a knife isn't how I usually start my day. I could use some..." she ran a finger down the center of Caleb's tie, "... *comforting.*"

The playful, slightly teasing tone was familiar. Many of his conquests employed the gentle lilt that balanced hope with promise. But the last thing Caleb wanted after he'd had a woman was the woman he'd had.

"No. Like I said, meeting." He pulled away and dropped his hands to his side. "Besides, we're never going to see each other again."

Her smile dropped, as did any pretense at foreplay. Michelle pulled back, her spine straight and her glare, burning. "Excuse me?"

"Ah, sweet Shelly. How can I explain this?" Caleb tucked his hands into his pockets and took a step back. "Look, you're smart, pretty, and damn, so amazingly limber. But the truth is that we're never going to speak again. In fact, I'm probably not even going to remember your name in a few hours."

"Um... okay?" She blinked her surprise. "Not like I was expected to pick out furniture and meet your parents, but when did you turn into such an asshole?"

"I was already an asshole when you picked me up. But you liked the size of my wallet and my, well..." His eyes did a quick visual acknowledgement of his crotch. "And believe me, I'd *love* to see you again, but it's a security thing. Don't worry, you also won't even remember my name in a few minutes."

Nesting a hand at the bottom of her back, Caleb guided Michelle toward the door, using his other hand to pick up the pile of her clothes from the dresser as they passed. It didn't matter that she was cold and almost naked. A few enthralled suggestions from Gabor and a warm robe from housekeeping, both issues would be null. They'd make sure Michelle was well fed and groomed before filing her back into her life without any memory of the crazy night she'd just had.

"Hello, Mr. Helsing."

The security chief stood in waiting right outside the bedroom door. Not surprising. Pretty sure Amy had his digits engraved on the back of her eyelids.

All vampires were fierce, but Gabor also looked like it too. Six-two with broad shoulders, biceps the size of bowling balls, and fists that could crack coconuts, he nonetheless had a reverent, peaceful demeanor about him. He was one of the few vampires Amy felt comfortable around, probably because anyone who took the time to know Gabor discovered he was more teddy bear than grizzly.

Gabor nodded to them both as they emerged into the kitchen. "Mr. Helsing, good morning. And Miss Carrow, how do you do?"

Michelle froze in place. "How do you know my name? And did you say... Helsing?" She turned to Caleb. "I thought you said your name was Musk."

"I did. I lied."

Did she expect him to go around using such a famous name?

The one that actually belonged to him, that was?

"Helsing?" Her eyes sparkled in the way eyes always did whenever some huey discovered Caleb's family name. "Like *Van* Helsing? Like in *Dracula*?"

The slayer closed his eyes and exhaled with gusto. "No, there's no *Van*. Stoker made up the part about my family being Dutch. Guess he wanted his eccentric hero to be foreign but, you know, not *that* foreign. And just so you know, it used to be Hellsinger, but the name gave us a reputation."

"Let me guess, as vampire slayers?" Michelle's eyebrows arched.

"No, as bad vocalists." Caleb blew across the surface of his espresso. "The vampire slayers part is something we're kind of proud of."

Her face went blank as she tried to work out if he was joking. Few hueys could immediately wrap their heads around the fact that supernatural beings existed, let alone that Caleb was one. He wasn't sure why his performance in bed last night wasn't proof enough. Could a human move like that, let alone three times in a row?

To skip to the end of a potentially and absurdly long back and forth, Caleb held up his free hand and poked up an index finger. With a split second of intention, his power lit. The tiny bead of solar energy, a ball no bigger than a marble, suspended in the air, just above his fingertip. In a moment, the brunette's mouth went agape.

Oh, that look is familiar, Caleb thought.

"I use these to kill the ones who go bad." Moving the solarium a little higher in the air so Michelle could see better, he also commanded the ball to ascend, coming to eye level. "Wooden stakes through the heart or brain work too, of course, but they're so messy. Plus, you have to get closer to a vamp to use them than I like being."

"And he doesn't really kill that many of them," Amy piped in, bringing a package of chocolate chip scones to the table and sitting. "As a backup, he'll also just yap on like this until they want to die."

With an assistant like this, who needed an enemy?

"Anyways..." Caleb rolled his hand back into a fist and extinguished the energy. It puffed out with a flicker. "Amy and I have work apparently, so I'm going to ask Gabor here to get you dressed, put you into a car, and alter your memory so you have no recollection that I exist or remember anything you just found out. Gabor?"

"Wait, what?" Michelle's face curdled. "So you're all just nuts, then? Or is this some sick joke for getting rid of the women you fuck?"

"You say joke, I say unfortunate but necessary solution." Caleb ignored Amy's disgusted glare. "What, you think I wouldn't want you to remember how hard I made you come last night, or how many times? Do you have any idea how much easier it would be to hook up with women if I could build up a reputation to do half the work for me? Like I said, it's a security thing. The wrong vamp picks you up and finds out you have a connection to me, there's no telling the torture you'd endure. So again I say, Gabor?"

The hottie didn't know if she should be more scared or angry but instead tried to be both at once. The war he saw play across her face didn't exactly lack entertainment value. She both wanted to run away and to lunge out and strangle him all at the same time.

That was until she locked gazes with the security guard.

The solemn vampire stepped forward. "Miss Carrow, come with me, please. I want to make sure you get dried and dressed before you catch something. It's going to be very cold out this morning."

Before any further attempt to insult and or reject could take place, Michelle grew very still and very quiet. Gods, Caleb was so jealous of the vampire ability to enthrall. Thank God he had this one at his beck and call to do the deed for him. Prior to coming to WWL, Caleb had had to make up long, lingering stories about who he was and hope he never ran into one of his conquests again. It was the reason he'd done most of his booty hunts in the bars of hotels near airports. Women who were only in town for a few days and likewise preferred a quick fling with no future intention had been his target demographic.

"Of course." Michelle's dreamy voice perfectly matched her relaxed features. She looked like she was walking on a cloud as, with Gabor's hand in hers, they left the kitchen.

Once they were alone, Caleb pulled a scone from the plastic clamshell and took a bite. "So, you were saying?" he mumbled around chunks of pastry.

Amy gave him "the look," the one that admonished his actions and called him out over every single insult without saying a word. Normally, this was the part where she would have lectured him about how women weren't things to be used. (Forget that until she'd moved in with Caleb in the WWL tower, she'd been the one to let herself be *used*. Frequently, from what he'd been told.)

"The Board is breathing down my neck, Caleb. And since they're all vampires, that isn't a metaphor, and it doesn't stop at creepy stalker vibes. You can't miss another meeting."

She said all this as she went to the fridge and pulled out the ingredients for her dawn smoothie. Amy had given up coffee after a month of living nocturnally. It was great at keeping you awake, she'd said, but it also made her heart pound. The last thing you wanted when you were a tasty morsel surrounded by the befanged was to advertise a healthy pulse.

She slumped down into the chair across the table from him. "I promised Vega you'd be there tonight. I staked my reputation on your disreputable ass, and you made me look like an idiot when you were a no-show. But more than that, the Board needs you there."

"Right. Developments. You said something about developments. But didn't I give you my proxy already? Just do what you think best. You know I trust you."

She grimaced. "Yeah, for signing off on things like sales reports and supply orders and stuff. But, hey, guess what? Turns out the one thing vampires hate more than having to report to a slayer is having to deal with his pet human instead."

"One man's pet is another man's protégé."

"Not if you're the man in question." Amy rolled her eyes. "Look, Caleb, I understand why you hired me to be your assistant... if the way I came to be here could be called hiring. But, seriously, why am I here? Yeah, the pay is great. The townhouse is great. But what is the point of my presence except sheltering your ass from what you're supposed to be doing yourself?"

He'd put up a hand before she was even halfway through her statement, but proved at least enough of a gentleman to wait until she was done. "We both know that if you weren't here, you'd probably already be working through the estate of your second very wealthy but very elderly husband."

She blinked her confusion. "Why would I need a second one?"

He ignored the quip and moved on. "If I hadn't enlisted you when I did, you were going to get your ass kicked to the curb by the supernatural in-crowd. It's hard to go back to a mundane existence after you've seen 'behind the veil.' You never would have been happy again. And don't act like your life isn't a lot more interesting since you found out your best friend is a descendant of Red Riding Hood and that her boyfriend is an actual vampire slayer descended from the most powerful line in history."

"I think you mean her *ex*-boyfriend. She broke up with you, remember? Married a werewolf named Tobias? Has a happy family, an adopted daughter, and a small mortgage on a big house in the middle of nowhere?"

He did remember those things, each and every one of them, with excruciating accuracy.

"And don't act like *you're* the one who saved *me*," Amy went on. "If I hadn't been here this last year doing the work you refuse or seem unable to do, this company would have kicked *you* to the curb already."

He chortled. "Let them try. Inga Rosethorn deeded fifty-one percent owner-ship to me. We supes might not be able to use huey courts, but a vampire would sooner die than get earn a reputation as a flouncer. There's nothing they can do about me being CEO."

Amy's lips wrapped around the straw sticking out from her smoothie as she kept her gaze locked on his.

A colony of bugs woke up in Caleb's stomach. "There's nothing they can do, right?"

She sucked so hard her cheeks went concave.

"Amy?"

God, the sound she made was annoying.

"Amy!" The plastic cup went flying as Caleb smacked it from her grip, leaving the straw hanging in space from her mouth.

Lacking any urgency or an ounce of reaction, Amy reached up and took it between two fingers. "The Board meeting resumes in five minutes." Then she put the straw down on the table and stood, heading for the door. "Come and ask them yourself."

THREE

T he retina scanner did its thing, and the doors to the elevator parted. Security at WWL took on both old forms, a la kindly henchmen and men in suits with guns at the street level entrances, and more modern ones, like this kind of tech that still felt like something from some spy flick Caleb had watched once. That described WWL by extension. Vampires as old as four hundred years populated senior suites, while R&D dished out beyond state-of-the-art products thanks to vamps born in the last century staffing.

And here he was, in charge of them all, unchecked and unchallenged. Or so Caleb had thought. What had Amy meant by ask the board? Wasn't being the boss supposed to mean that he answered to no one? If anyone deserved a little R&R, it was the guy who helped kill Dracula and squash his sycophants. Those motherfucking vamps owed him for saving the goddamned supernatural world.

Ungrateful leeches.

Agitation festered as Caleb looked down to see his fingers curling, his upper arms tight against his frame. Why was it taking so long to go between the penthouse and the floor where the executive boardroom was located?

Time to give Raquel a piece of my mind, he thought as the numbers on the display went down. Had she forgotten how he'd started his tenure at WWL:

dusting one of her fellow board members in front of everyone? Screw anyone who thought they were going to take anything away from Caleb Helsing.

By the time the heavy wooden doors that led into the executive board room opened, Caleb wouldn't have been surprised if *he* had sprouted his own pair of fangs.

"What the fuck, Raquel?" Who needed to exchange meaningless pleasantries when you had profanity in your tool belt? "After everything I've done for this company, what kind of shit are you trying to pull?"

Raquel wore her chestnut hair tied up in a tight bun he was pretty sure he could bounce a penny off. Her human years had been spent as a sickly prostitute in the Yucatan barrios, leaving her thin, gangly. Expensive clothes hung off a frame that lacked curves and appeal, and her glare shot out of humorless eyes. Despite what some might dismiss as a lean-and-hungry look, she was still a vampire three hundred years into her afterlife. Being of old stock, she'd been reared on formality and decorum, even amongst rivals.

Even if she was clearly pissed off that Caleb had decided to do fuck all with formality.

"Mr. Helsing." Somehow, whenever she said his name, it sounded like an insult. "How nice of you to join us. *Finally.*"

Caleb scanned the seats around the table for Amy, hoping to goad her into repeating what she'd intimated up in the penthouse they shared. His brief survey left the blonde huey unaccounted for. That was until Raquel, seeming to understand what he was searching for, pointed into the upper corner of the room. Caleb turned to find his huey assistant stationed at his five o'clock, a legal pad on her lap and her eyes fixed there like she was purposefully using it as an excuse not to look up.

Well, that wasn't going to do. Had she been sitting off to the side of the room during all the meetings he'd skipped? No wonder the Board didn't take her seriously. Someday soon, Caleb was going to have to educate the blonde huey on how cowering marked her in the vampires' eyes as a scared animal, not demanding respect.

"*Miss Popowitz* has my proxy."

Caleb backstepped to wrap a hand firmly around the huey's bicep, pulling Amy to her feet before depositing her into the brown leather seat at the head of the table. She'd be pissed at him later for manhandling her. (Frankly, she looked pretty pissed at him now.) But the move served as a display to the board: this was Amy's proper place in the room. In the captain's chair, so to speak. To reemphasize, Caleb took a position right behind her.

"A CEO is a busy man with a lot of things to do. You can't expect me to just show up here whenever you think it's convenient."

"If by things to do, you mean hot flowing blondes and brunettes... yes, I've heard how *busy* you've been." Raquel looked down at him in more ways than one. "And while we respect Miss Popowitz's contributions, as well-intentioned as they've been, at the end of the night, she is *still* just a huey. Some matters require the personal attention of the CEO, even if he is only a slayer and *not* a vampire."

"The Slayer Solari, and the one who saved your fucking asses. Or did you forget how I solved that little Dracule problem that threatened to set your kind off into a civil war?"

"That title has not been used in a century," Raquel noted. "And it is one that must be earned, not handed out by a lot of Stockholm suffering sycophants. Yet, according to my reports, you haven't spent any significant time with the Reclaimed since you *accidentally* exploded the executive swimming pool."

He was never going to live that down, was he? "Like I said, *I've been busy.* And in case you've forgotten, not only did I rescue all those 'sycophants' from Dracula's dungeon, but I also managed to wipe out hundreds of Tepeş's loyal soldiers single-handedly. How much more do you expect me to do to 'earn' my title?"

Raquel folded her hands and placed them on the table. "Mr. Helsing, rest assured that the Board recognizes your generous and sizable contributions at the Battle of the Tahquamenon which aided in the defeat and death of Vlad Tepeş. It also feels, however, that some of the credit should be given to the multi-tiered supernatural forces that fought the Ravens that night. You were simply one person on the battlefield. Without the efforts of the Grand Matron of the Wolfsretter and her daughter, Gerwalta Kline, the victory may have never come."

Caleb tried not to flinch. He had some righteous indignation built up during the elevator ride up, and he didn't want it pissed away because he got mopey hearing his ex's name.

"Yes. Well, still..." Arms against his sides, Caleb's voice stiffened. "The point is, this is bullshit. I am the CEO of this company. Inga Rosenthorn left all her shares, fifty-one percent of the company, to *me*."

"A controlling share, indeed, which would, in normal circumstances, firmly secure your position."

The stitch in his side that had struck earlier with Amy's tease came on again. "These aren't normal circumstances?"

"No, Mr. Helsing, they are not. *You* are a slayer. This corporation was founded and has been led by vampires for the last forty years. While your deal with Rosethorn did leave you in charge, she had the foresight to know that a young slayer might not be the best choice as corporate head. Or maybe her lack of faith was because *you* were the slayer in question."

No need to remind Raquel that, at that time, Caleb had been the *only* slayer in question. Outside of rumors, to the best of everyone's knowledge, he'd been the last slayer at all until it was discovered that Tepeş had twenty-two of them imprisoned. He and his elite generals, the Ravens, used Caleb's kind as their personal wet bar and fountain of youth.

Caleb clicked his tongue. "No need for personal insults, Raquel. Did I say anything about your resemblance to the scarecrow in *The Wizard of Oz*?"

The vampire ate the insult with a haughty jerk of her head. "I could cite the provisions in the transfer agreement word by word, but in summary, it comes down to this: We can do nothing about your ownership, but we do have options about your leadership. The Board has the right after a trial period and annually thereafter to conduct a vote of no confidence and remove you from your position. And let's just say, with one month left to go of that original trial period, our confidence... is not strong."

The air seemed thicker than it had been a moment ago. Caleb struggled not to choke on it. "So you've been evaluating me... without my knowledge or consent?"

"You're not a child, Mr. Helsing. We don't need your consent. And as for knowledge..." Raquel's eyes beamed in Amy's direction, "... *she* knew. I had thought her reluctance to tell you was an unspoken agreement we had reached to let you run yourself, if not this business, into the ground so we could remove you without conflict or remorse."

"*Ammmy?*" Caleb's chair squeaked as he swiveled. "Did you believe you and *Miss Vega* had an unspoken agreement to let me fuck myself over?"

For a moment, the blonde huey kept her eyes forward, her jaw grinding hard enough to powder walnuts. Finally, the weight of his stare broke her, and Amy in turn snapped the pencil fisted in her hand.

"Look, when I started here, Corporate sent a whole bunch of things to my office. Binders and files and, hell, I think there were even some papyruses in there."

"It's papyri," Raquel said down the table.

He ignored the grammar nazi and focused on his glitzy, red-cheeked assistant. "And what did the *papyri* say?"

Amy's face screwed up. "I don't know what they said. It wasn't English or, hell, anything written in a language I could recognize. It looked like a chicken had run all over the page."

Caleb buried his chin into his chest. "Sanskrit, Greek, or Amharic?"

The question, of course, was not for Amy. If she didn't recognize the scripts of other languages, she probably couldn't distinguish if the accused running chickens had been from India, Europe, or Africa.

"The collection was extensive," was Raquel's reply. "But the documents that dictated the terms of your inheritance and the boards' rights regarding it were typed, placed in binders, and presented in Greek, as was Miss Rosethorn's preference."

Well, fuck. Caleb couldn't really be mad at Amy on this one. He'd never told her that, among vampires, contracts and agreements were drafted in one of what vamps considered "the mother tongues." And it wouldn't be like he'd understand it either. He could wrap his tongue around many things; those languages weren't any of them. Caleb spoke English of course, having lived in the States since he was a teenager. Turkish came from his mother's side, and Hebrew from his father's. He'd picked up a little Tagalog once while traveling through Asia, but none of the things he knew in that language were appropriate for the current situation.

Or any situation in which clothing was worn.

"Yeah, so, I tossed most of the binders out," Amy continued. "I thought they were takeout menus."

"Takeout menus!" He ran a hand through his hair. "Amy, why would Corporate send you take-out menus?"

"Same reason they would send *me* anything. Because *you're* never in the office to receive anything."

Well, she had him there. And so too, it seemed, did Raquel.

"Mr. Helsing, this is just one illustration of the many disappointments you've given us since your somewhat explosive arrival here."

"I didn't explode Hoffman," Caleb protested. "That would have been messy. I *ashed* him. Still messy, but not so, you know, blood-and-gutsy."

The chairperson closed her eyes and clenched her teeth before she could resume a professional demeanor. "I would have the room now."

Caleb was relieved to see that he wasn't the only one confused. He looked around at the other members of the board. Nine vampires from different bloodlines, each with his or her own story that brought them to this time and place, none of them grasping what was going on, or who made a move.

Amy, on the other hand, was busily gathering up her notepad and half a pencil. She couldn't seem to move fast enough.

A fact proved a moment later when Raquel extended a finger the blonde huey's direction. "Not you, Miss Popowitz. I think it best that you, the woman who's been doing her best to save this man from his own incompetence for far too long, stay."

His assistant's face screwed up, no doubt concerned about what fate might befall her. Nevertheless, without a word otherwise, a feat that was probably tougher for Amy than anything else, she lowered back into her chair.

"Well, anytime now." Raquel grew restless, and took to fixing an acidic glare on each of the board members in turn. If she'd had Godzilla's powers, they'd all be melting in their seats. It did the trick, however, and in a short space, all that were left in the room were Raquel, Amy, and Caleb.

The chairperson pushed herself away from the table, rose, and fixed her gaze outside at the sunrise lifting the edges of the horizon, the Athenian glass keeping her safe from harm.

Sadly.

"When Inga told me a few years ago that she'd chosen you of all supes as her heir, I thought she'd gone as moonmad as a lone werewolf," she started.

Caleb's shoulders tensed, and he pulled himself to the edge of his chair. "I didn't think anyone knew about our deal until I announced it after her death."

"*I* knew." Raquel planted balled-up hands on her hips and turned his way. "I had to put on a show in front of the other members of the Board that I was just as surprised as they were, but *I knew.* Inga was my friend. I don't have many of those, Mr. Helsing, and that may be why I was willing to hear out her reasoning instead of acting rashly."

Reasoning, it seemed, Caleb was about to hear by proxy. Suddenly he felt like he was back in school, getting lectured by Miss Duncan about how important it was to respect the teaching staff, even if they did have impressive knockers.

"Anyone else might have thought her decision an apostasy," Raquel continued. "Especially after your little stunt when you assumed power."

"Hoffman was a Dracule. He was literally their spy inside the company," Caleb protested.

To his surprise, Amy piped up right after him. "And an internal investigation after the fact turned up evidence that he'd been tasked with taking over the company on behalf of his bloodline *if* the CEO position opened. Tepeş wanted to use WWL as a piggy bank. Luckily, Caleb got back here to claim it before news of Inga Rosethorn's demise reached the Dracule."

Raquel put her hands up, palms facing them. "I'm not criticizing what you did," she said, perhaps with a little more emotion than they typically expected of her. Lowering her hands, she continued. "Hoffman had to go. Still, you can imagine how the rest of the Board felt seeing a fellow member so dramatically and, well, *permanently* dismissed without a chance to defend himself. Even most hueys give their criminals a chance to mount a defense, no matter how blatantly and obviously guilty they are."

"Surely you're not saying we should start acting like hueys." Caleb managed to look sheepish as he turned to Amy. "No offense."

Seemed the lone huey in the room was gaining some gusto without the larger audience. Amy lifted a hand, plastered on an acidic smile, and extended a middle finger.

"Of course I'm not," Raquel continued. "There's something you should know, Mr. Helsing. *Some* of the Board believe a slayer might be just what we need. Not just at WWL, but in the vampire community on the whole. Without your kind, bloodline power struggles are breaking out all over the globe. I had hoped your demonstration signaled a willingness to bring the more rebellious of our society to heel through an *appropriate* application of your abilities. But so far, you've failed to show that you have any concern for this company's work, ethics, direction, products, or clients, let alone for performing your sacred duties outside of WWL."

Caleb's head cocked to the side. "What am I, some kind of slayer chosen one? Who died and made me the grand poohbah for an entire race?"

"Modify your vibe, asshat," Amy said, suddenly reasserting her backbone.

Were... two women... ganging up on him? He had to admit, it was kinda sexy.

"Did you bring the Reclaimed here so I can babysit while you're off getting your Johnson waxed every night?" Amy continued. "Or was it so they'd be safe while they learned to assume their roles? Don't think I don't feel sorry for them, but the fact is, you're the only fully-awakened and trained slayer known of. So suck it up and start acting like you're someone who can save your whole civilization, because, sadly, you are."

By the time Amy finished her rant, any sexy potential was gone and the seeds of doubt had already started to sprout. Who in the hell was she, a huey, to dress down a supe... even one as self-centered as Caleb Helsing? But just to prove you're not safe from surprise until you're dead, Amy went rigid as Raquel came to stand beside her, even going as far as to put a hand on the blonde huey's shoulder and squeeze.

"Well stated, Miss Popowitz," she said. "If there is one credit I can give you, Mr. Helsing, it was in hiring this huey to be your assistant. Anyone else would have ingratiated themselves to you for your approval."

Caleb's face blanched. "Hey, I would never sleep with an employee, even if she is hot as fuck."

Amy rolled her eyes as Raquel pulled back. "She means they would have kissed your ass, idiot. Whereas I don't really give a damn about calling you an asshole when you're being an asshole."

"That *is* another way of saying it." Raquel turned toward the door, taking their eyes along with her. "At the end of the night, it comes down to this, Mr. Helsing. In a month, the Board will hold a vote on whether you should be allowed to stay in your position. From where I sit right now, I can only see one direction for that vote to go."

FOUR

A s slow as the elevator had been on the way down, it managed to move twice as slowly on the ride back up.

Amy kept her eyes on her phone, giving Caleb time to eat his own liver and brood uninterrupted. She was sometimes sweet like that. The only problem was, he could have hours and come back to the same place he started when he'd woken up tonight. Vampires were low-handed, dishonest creatures who couldn't be trusted.

His dad had been right. There was a reason the world needed slayers to kill the rattiest of those rat bastards. He wondered what Moshe Helsing would have thought of the shit show his son had cast himself into. In his mind's eye, Caleb pictured his father, all wavy gray-black hair and a permanent five o'clock shadow. *Serves you right for forgetting what else your ana and I taught you.*

Growing up, his parents had always told him that they were the last of their kind. He hadn't been sure if Mama and Papa Helsing had actually believed that, or if it was their attempt to keep their only child from openly searching for others. What Caleb did know was that, although a slayer was gifted with the ability to conjure solar energy to destroy a vampire, your run-of-the-mill vamp would always have an advantage over your garden-variety slayer.

"It's not just that they've had years, sometimes centuries, to learn and perfect their skills," his Dad would say. "It's that they've had that long to learn how to outsmart us. Never trust a vampire, on the battlefield or anywhere. Deal with one as much as you need to. Being an asshole—and they're *all* assholes—isn't reason enough to kill one. Sometimes you can even use one to your advantage, but always keep a professional distance."

Letting Inga Rosethorn, the previous WWL CEO, to suck off his neck to keep herself alive long past five hundred couldn't really qualify as "professional distance." Especially not when she repeatedly told Caleb that she'd be open to sucking other places too, with or without the fangs. He generally took all women who showed an interest, but he drew the line at vamps.

Yet somehow, Inga *had* managed to fuck him... and from beyond the grave at that.

"It's really not cool what they're trying to do, you know."

The silence and his thoughts had grown so thick, he'd forgotten Amy was still there. Caleb looked up and over, but she still had her eyes fixed on her phone.

"Sorry?" Was he asking her to repeat herself? There was no way she could be defending him or daring her to admit that she wasn't sad that he might be kicked to the curb.

Amy lowered her phone and pivoted on one heel. "I mean, yes, you are a fuck up. Clearly."

Well, that didn't clarify anything.

"But WWL belongs to you," she went on. "Or at least, fifty-one percent of it does. They can fire you from the position if there was an agreement in writing letting them, but hey, at least you'll still own the company. You can fire the board if you want."

"So you really can read ancient Greek? That, or you have some kind of secret MBA I wasn't aware of."

Amy shrugged. "My dad forced me to work two summers in high school at his law firm. I picked up a few things. Some of them *weren't* his junior partners."

She said it with zero pride. Actually, she sounded kind of annoyed. Not for the first time, the question of what kind of life one Amy Popowitz had lived. When it came down to it, there was actually very little Caleb knew about her past before she'd been dragged into the supe world. Amy was from New York City, but you only had to talk to her for thirty seconds to know that. She'd come to Chicago to attend university and dated roughly ten percent of its single cis male population between the ages of twenty and thirty. That was based on observation and reports from friends in common. Thinking back, though, Caleb couldn't remember her saying much about her parents before.

"Your dad's a lawyer?"

Her face garbled up. She had no patience for his idiocy. "Corporate lawyer. Pretty damned good one too, if the house we lived in was any indication."

"And your mother?" Caleb asked this just as the doors opened and they entered the penthouse's lobby. "What does she do?"

"My father, when she has to. Otherwise, she spends his money and does enough charity work not to feel guilty about it, including this little boutique store of hers on the lower west side. Today's fashions for yesterday's trophy wife, or something like that."

Ah, so one of *those* marriages. Granted, that couldn't have been a very happy home, but at least Amy still had living parents. What he wouldn't give for just a few more minutes with his baba and ana.

"Point being..." Amy pressed her palm flat against a shiny black tile to the left of the door. A tiny indicator lit up, and a moment later, the locks on the door disengaged. "They can't do anything about the money you make as a majority stockholder. But if you're worried about losing this flat... well, yeah, you might. It's part of the CEO package. But with the money you'd be pulling, you can easily get another equally over-the-top ridiculous chick magnet anywhere in the city."

"I don't need fancy apartments to pick up women." Is that really what she thought this was all about? Caleb having a posh place to fuck chicks?

Please, sometimes he and his passing fling didn't even make it out of the club.

"And I'm sure you could find a vampire who'd be willing to work hourly to alter memories if you wanted," Amy continued as if he hadn't just asked her to confirm his lack of human nature.

She closed the door behind them as they made their way to the sunken living room and the black leather couches built into it. Beyond, floor-to-ceiling windows fitted with Athenian glass gave an impressive view of Navy Pier jutting out into Lake Michigan. This time of year, the waters lay pockmarked with shelves of ice that had formed at shallower depths before drifting out to deeper waters. The morning sun was up in earnest now; in the southeast, chords radiated from an orb rising with no hurry.

Damn, he loved this view. He'd really hate to lose it. Amy loved it as well. She'd never said as much, but whenever he caught her looking at this time of day, she was silent, a hint of a smile on her face.

He'd hate to lose Amy too. In a professional way, of course. Or didn't she know how many things he actually did do to assure his safety?"

"Even if I'm not CEO, I still have enemies out there," Caleb said. "I could fight off anyone who came at me, I think, but you couldn't. If one of my... *guests*... fell into my enemy's hand with full recollection of this place's layout, they could come after you."

Caleb's tongue stilled the moment he realized the bigger picture forming in front of him. Yes, he was pissed off because Raquel was threatening to take away something that was rightfully his. But he'd never stopped to consider the effect that would have on her or anyone else.

"Amy, what happens to you if I'm no longer CEO?"

To his surprise, her face curdled up. "You seriously think I'm pissed off at you because of what it means for me? Jesus, Caleb, my life only revolves around yours to the extent that you pay for it."

"But if not you, then..."

And then it hit him.

"It's about the baby slayers, isn't it? The... Reclaimed."

He'd never really understood that whole "It was the best of times, it was the worst of times" spiel that Charles Dickens had written until he'd helped discover and rescue twenty-two slayers from the Ravens compound. At first, knowing he wasn't the last one of his kind like his parents had told him was a godsend. Not only because he was crushed by the burden of that reality; he'd never ascended to his calling in any meaningful way his whole life beyond seeking revenge. It was just nice to know he wasn't the loneliest dodo on the planet. But then came the consequences.

The slayers weren't babies, even though that was how he thought of them intellectually. They'd just been isolated, brainwashed, and otherwise ignorant of reality. All but four had been born in captivity and raised with the belief that their purpose was to serve vampires. The women were both protectors of their patrons as well as their feeders. Occasionally their lovers. The men? Well, they seemed to be allowed to survive only to entertain the females, perhaps to mate with them. Problem was, someone in the Dracula camp had found a way and a reason to sterilize the men.

No more slayer breeding program, yes. But also, eventually, no more slayers. And that would have eventually meant no more Ravens, unless they had found an alternative food source.

Amy leaned forward on the couch, giving Caleb that patronizing, head-to-the-side lamb eyes look she did when she thought he was being dense. "Yes, it's about them."

"They're not my responsibility, Amy."

From lamb to a lion in two seconds flat. Amy sat bolt upright. "What do you mean, they're not your responsibility?"

"I was morally obligated to bust them out of a vampire diva's basement, but I don't owe them anything. I mean... I got them to America, gave them fake identities, food, housing... their every need is provided for. I know Raquel is a bitch, but I don't think she'd cut off their funding just because she's got some kind of beef with me."

And even if she did, according to Amy, he'd still own plenty of the company. Surely, he could sell off a little bit to keep their funding going, and...

His smirk fell away.

Amy smirked and clapped her hands. "Bravo. You finally figured it out, didn't you?"

Caleb nodded. So what if she looked as smug as a man with a ten-inch penis? She was right.

"I own fifty-one percent, but if I have to sell off any to keep the money coming in..." His voice drifted off.

"Then very quickly, you'd be a minority stakeholder, and all they need to do is pony up the money to buy up enough to take total control. Then they could get you *and* the baby slayers tossed out completely if they wanted."

If they wanted was the pivotal term. Caleb didn't like dealing with ifs, particularly when he didn't have a personal ability to control the factors that led to a solution. Even if he didn't want to be the slayer messiah, it didn't mean he wanted to see them all turned out on the streets. With so few slayers remaining, even standing together, they wouldn't have much of a chance of resisting if another group of vampires decided to set up their own blood harem.

Or just plain killed them off.

"So by firing me, all they'd have to do is sit back and wait for me to run out of money. Or die. Even if there weren't the others to worry about, I'd have to sell off some stock eventually to fund my retirement."

"They could speed things along and kill you."

Caleb shook his head. "I got too many friends in high places now. The Grand Matron of the Hoods. One of the members of the Varanasi clan. Hell, even powerful vampires. The Doge of Venice owes us a—"

In a single moment, the words died on Caleb's tongue and the solution to his problem was born in his thoughts.

"Amy, I'm not going to get fired."

She laughed and slapped in the air. "Doubtful."

"But I'm not," Caleb insisted. "Raquel said there are some members of the Board that want me here, so I already have a chance. I just need to do something to impress them enough to give me a second chance. Show them I can get the company back on track *and* be solari enough to make a difference. Then, I can get back to doing what I want to do until it's time to impress them again. Which means, I can keep sleeping with as many women as I want."

"I don't think Raquel threatened to put a stop to that. She just didn't want it to be your only pursuit." Amy balanced her chin on the point of a finger. "But I can tell, this is going to be good by the way you're shaking your tail like a little puppy."

Caleb jumped up, moving from one couch to take a seat next to her on the other. "What if instead of trying to get the board *not* to fire me, I quit?"

The blonde huey's face screwed up. "I think Vega would spontaneously have an orgasm."

"I'm talking about seducing her. And quit? No, maybe not the right word." Even being in America as long as he had been, English did occasionally throw Caleb for a loop. "What is the right one? It starts with a D."

"One comes to mind whenever it involves you."

He didn't have time for her cryptic comments. "Delegate! What if, instead of doing the job myself, I bring in someone I can *delegate* the responsibilities to?"

Amy tilted her head down, looking up with a dour expression. "That's what you've been doing with me for the last year plus, and they're sick of it."

"Yeah, but what if I brought in someone a lot *better* than you?"

"You know, I should be insulted, but part of my problem is all the things you ask me to do that I'm not qualified for. Which begs the question..." She folded her arms over her chest. "Who?"

"The Doge of Venice, of course," Caleb said. "He's always been buddy-buddy with slayers, especially with my family. My dad used to tell me he and my great, great grandfather were practically besties."

"I thought you said you didn't want his help." Amy pointed a finger up in the air. "Something about how Geri was the one to negotiate that IOU and you didn't need any hood's charity to manage your life."

"That was in my I'm-still-angry-about-the-break-up stage. Of course, I'd say that then."

Her eyes went wide. "And now is different?"

"Of course now is different. Now calling in that debt is useful to me. Or, I don't know, paying it off?"

It was hard to tell who owed who in the scenario. Back when Caleb had been working with the hoods to track down and destroy Dracula, they'd found themselves in a pickle outside London. Massimo Bruneli, the Doge of Venice, came to their rescue. All he had asked in return was a few drops of Little Mina Kline's blood.

Geri's adopted daughter had been born of a slayer mother and werewolf father. The resulting chimera of genetics resulted in Illustrian, an extremely rare form of supernatural creature whose blood was actually a cure for vampirism. The Doge, it seemed, had fallen in love with a human and had to decide to retire and live out the rest of his life as a huey.

Geri, being the genius and protective mother she was, knew that kind of power was far more valuable than a get-out-a-jam-free card. She agreed to Bruneli's proposal, with the added caveat that he had to also become a mentor to the Reclaimed. After Dracula had been put down, however, neither Caleb nor Bruneli had moved forward on closing out the deal. For his part, Caleb didn't see what place a four-hundred-year-old vampire had becoming a life coach for slayers. He didn't know why the Doge, however, had changed his mind.

He cupped Amy's chin and tilted her eyes up to his. "And the best part of this, Amy, is that you get to go to Venice."

You'd have thought she was a supe instead of a huey the way she jumped up so quickly. "You don't seriously think you're sending me into a *vampire* court to negotiate with a *vampire prince* by myself, do you? Caleb Helsing, isn't it bad enough you make me go into that office, night in and night out, and... if you think I'm going to subject myself to... the answer is no, okay? No way."

If he didn't know better, Caleb would have said that Amy was scared. Terrified actually. He didn't need the hearing of a werewolf to know her heart was racing in any event.

"Whoa, I don't mean alone." Did she think he was going to miss out on a chance to spend some time away from this place? Caleb had been stuck in

Chicagoland for most of the last five years. As great of a city as it was to live in, it was an even better city to leave. "I mean, you'll come along with me. Let's face it. I don't know half the things going on at this company that you do. I need you there to make sure I don't fuck up."

Flattery was the highest form of currency with the huey. The anxiety melted away. "Oh, well, then." She took a moment to flatten her features, then pulled away from him, stood, and rounded. "In that case, *hell no*."

"What? Why?" He blinked three times in quick succession. "Amy, it's Italy. Fucking *Italy*. How could *you* not want to go? Do you have any idea the kind of shopping there is there?"

"One, I am not the materialistic airhead you think I am. And two, it's not about me." She tilted her head to the side. "That must sound funny to you, right? The whole it's-not-about-me concept?"

"We could ask Michelle how much I *thought* of her last night."

"No, thank you." Amy's face screwed up. "What I mean is, I don't think Vega will look at you running halfway across the world to bring in a surrogate CEO as demonstrating leadership. Besides, her bigger issue was your total lack of involvement with the Reclaimed. You have to do something about that first. Not to mention, I'm not going into some foreign vampire den with only *you* as my protection. Who's going to guard me when you're out hunting Venetian floozies?"

The woman knew him well.

But still.

Caleb shrugged. "We could take them with us."

"We can't take twenty-one socially isolated slayers to one of the most politically fraught areas of the vampiric world. It will look like we're showing up with a goon squad. It's, like, the opposite of bringing balance to the force."

She had a point there. "Okay, so what would be the appropriate number be in your opinion? Seeing as you think you need bodyguards, and seeing as I don't want you seducing any of the little boy slayers and wooing them away from propagating our race someday—"

"Don't worry, not interested. Besides, I *want* a female guard," Amy interrupted. "Your little exploding-pool day may have sparked the powers of the boy wonders in the Reclaimed, but you never followed up with any training. What's the use of a bodyguard who can't shoot their gun in the right direction when needed?"

So many sexual innuendos left unsaid. Did she even appreciate his restraint?

Amy tilted her head and tapped her chin with a perfectly manicured fingernail. "I think one slayer should be enough."

He'd expected her to say four. Anytime Caleb had seen a celebrity or state leader on TV being flanked by security, that appeared to be the magic number. Thank the gods she had mercy on him. The last thing he wanted was Amy being encircled by doey-eyed Reclaimed who thought him some kind of chosen one.

"One sounds reasonable." Caleb tried not to show his relief. "I'm assuming it's going to be Keiko, of course."

Amy and the female slayer of Japanese origin had grown thick as thieves, though she'd be a good choice beyond that.

To his surprise, Amy clicked her tongue. "Probably not. Not sure who. I'll have to mull it over."

She turned towards the door, on her way down to her office in the subbasement, no doubt. All the executive suites were two floors beneath the Chicago streets, a holdover from the days before WWL's development of Athenian glass. Few places above ground had been retrofitted to allow vampires daytime use, the executive boardroom, the lobby, and select residences being chief among them. Officially, the top echelons of the company could only be found two stories underneath it.

For vampires, that was somehow appropriate.

"I'll reach out to Venice and work with travel to get things lined up," Amy said as she walked to the door. "We'll leave tomorrow night."

Caleb looked back over his shoulder, catching her eye as she turned back from the doorway. "Make it two nights from now? I already have a date tomorrow night."

She gave him the *look*.

If hueys could somehow harness the power the *look* held, there would never be another vampire or werewolf who dared step a fang out of the line.

"Fine." Caleb relented. Even though he could be a self-centered bastard, he wasn't fucking stupid. "I'll be ready shortly after sunset."

She nodded her approval behind a sweet smile. "Yes, you will."

FIVE

Amy wasn't sure what was more shocking: that she'd had the balls to text Vega and ask to stop by her personal residence well after dawn when she couldn't sleep, or that the chairperson of the board had said yes.

From her experience, Vega didn't socialize. Not with hueys, anyways. Courteous, perhaps even patronizing at times, Amy couldn't blame her for being aloof. The first time the two women had met was when Amy stood at Caleb's side, busting into the executive suites so Caleb could declare himself CEO and toast one of the board members on the spot. Not in a congratulatory way, but in a literal sense that left the vamp a pile of ash. That brazen act unfortunately was followed shortly by the self-appointed Slayer Solari doing jack all. For a year, Amy had been the Solari's apologetic stand in.

Yeah, well, don't blame me, she'd thought every time someone at work called out the company head in absentia. Amy had tried everything short of offering sex to get Caleb on the stick. Even she had limits; not sleeping with her BFF's ex was one, even if he had an ass you could bounce a moon off of.

The door to the unit opened, and an... aide? Maid? Sex buddy? *Whoever* showed Amy in. Any hope of having her curiosity sated waned when the path she was led through was a minimalistic foyer. The floorplan mimicked the townhouse she shared with Caleb. Only, where they had their sunken conversation pit, Vega's flat opened out onto one of the bigger high-rise balconies she'd seen in Chicago. No Athenian glass wall here.

Amy wasn't sure the science behind the company's bestselling supernatural-serving product. She *did* know it costs more per square foot than high quality cashmere and had special filters that made daytime sun nonlethal to vampires. Officially, vamps still shunned sunlight hardcore, which made what Amy was seeing oh, so interesting.

"Good Morning, Miss Vega." Only a small patch remained through the center of a space the size of a racquetball court, each side hosting a sea of pots and racks, with vegetation cascading down the walls and plying itself to the ceiling.

"Miss Popowitz." Raquel didn't turn in her greeting. "I can't imagine what you need so desperately that it could not wait until night. Or has Mr. Helsing finally done the charitable thing and renounced his position?"

Without disruption, the vampire attended a bowl of white, silky, heart-shaped blooms that crowned long, slender green stocks. The squat container in which the plant grew stood atop a wire stand about a foot and a half high and a hug around. In the back of Amy's mind, a blurry memory flickered. She'd seen something like this before, but the where and when of it escaped her.

"Um, no. I'm here because I don't have much time, and you and I need to do something."

The first flicker of reaction crept onto the vampire's face in the form of an arched eyebrow as Vega looked up. "When you offered your vein should Mr. Helsing fail to appear at the board meeting, something history has proven unlikely, I had wondered if it was merely pretext."

"What? No. Ew, gross." The words flew so quickly from Amy's lips it sounded like a gag. When Raquel's eyes went wide, the blonde huey realized she'd just insulted the woman she was about to beg a favor from. "I mean... I'm sure it would be an honor and all, but... I only mean that..."

"One of the few things I appreciate about you, Miss Popowitz, is your directness and lack of insincere flattering language." The vampire clicked her tongue as she worked off a pair of robin blue gardening gloves. "Please don't ruin your potential by developing the habit now. Or do I have to enthrall you to get a complete sentence?"

"Enthrall me?" The huey shrank back faster than an Instagram star from reality. Amy wilted and cleared her throat, conscious that the hard ass vampire might be borrowing patience.

"Be at ease. I wouldn't."

Vega threw her gloves aside and made her way to a small table that stood empty off to the side. As if on cue, the table was suddenly filled by a silky ball of white fluff. The creature brushed against a fist the chairperson balled up, leaving little smocks of moist dirt on her coat.

"A cat?"

The vampire passed Amy a glance through an upward cast. "I believe that's what this creature is commonly referred to as, yes. Why, is it inappropriate in your eyes for a vampire to have a pet?"

Amy thought of Tobias, her best friend's werewolf friend-turned-mate, and his uncanny ability to interact with pet dogs. Is that all the supernatural world came down to in the end? Cat people who drank blood versus dog people who, well, became dogs on full moons?

"Of course not, I just don't associate, you know, felines with... your kind."

Vega pursed her lips. "Buttercup here belonged to a friend who recently passed away. I can't say I ever would have gotten a pet of my own accord, but to my surprise, she's not totally disagreeable." She stepped away from worshipping the creature with attention, picked up a cloth towel from another table, and began to work dirt off her arm. "But to return to the subject at hand," Vega said. "Do you know why I'd never enthrall you? Because you're not afraid of Caleb Helsing, and for reasons I cannot completely understand as yet, he defers to you. He even *respects* you, defends you. You have value to him, and therefore, you also are of value to me. I might destroy that if I tampered with your mind."

Every nerve in Amy's body tripped. Not because the vampire just admitted part of Amy's worth lay in her ability to be a tool of manipulation where

Caleb was concerned. She didn't expect anything else from one of the creatures. Wariness gave way to indignation. "Who in the hell would be afraid of Caleb? Well, except maybe a nun about to take her vows."

"Yes, I hear he's quite... *prolific*." The jest pulled up the corner of Vega's lips. "But just so you know, *I* am afraid of him."

"You are?" Amy waited for the vampire to claim sarcasm, but Vega merely tucked a smile into her chest and nodded.

"It's hard for a huey to read fear in a vampire's eyes. We learn to discipline our emotions well. But amongst each other, the signs are more evident, and this I can assure you. Every member of the board is petrified of him. *Not* that any of them will admit so. A vampire will never admit a weakness to a huey." Her twinkling blue eyes lifted. "It's been a century since some of us have come face to face with a slayer, and Caleb proved that he's not afraid to use his abilities to bully us around. Why do you think they're all so eager to see him voted out of his position?"

"They are, but you're not." Amy figured if she came this far, she might as well go a little further. "You like me being direct? Fine then, let me be direct." She pinched her two thumbs with her index fingers as her topic rounded on itself. "We both know that Caleb is kind of an asshole, right? He's pompous and self-centered and plates more tail than The Crab Shack on a Friday night. But he's *also* the best shot the Reclaimed have to get out of this codependent relationship they're in."

The chairperson did her Spock, tilted-eyebrow thing again. She bent to pick up a pair of unusually long scissors and held them in jabbing position. "What codependent relationship? According to your own emails, Caleb has spent the last year trying to avoid anything but the most tangential contact with his people."

The board was reading her emails? Well, that was all kinds of wrong. But not the issue she wanted to deal with right now. Instead she said, "His relationship with them isn't the one I'm talking about."

Amy stepped forward. "The last living slayers being walled up inside of a corporation run by vampires? That's fucked up, Raquel, and we both know it. Especially since they've already spent most of their lives imprisoned by *the actual* Dracula."

Something shifted then, but Amy couldn't quite say what. It wasn't that Vega lunged at her. In fact, she didn't appear to move at all, at least not in a way the huey could perceive. But something in her gaze sharpened, and somehow, Amy perceived a nearness that wasn't physical in nature. Previously, she'd been looking at Amy like the blonde huey looked at that piece of art that was nothing but splashes of paint: not really getting what everyone else saw in it. Then a moment later, clarity.

The vampire crossed to one of the nearby rose bushes, dropping a towel on a chair first, before employing the snips and pecking out space behind its fingernail-sized pink and red buds. "What do you know about politics, Amy?"

The non-sequitur took her train of thought and smashed it into the pavement. "Did you just call me by my first name?"

"You used mine first." Raquel snipped off a spray of roses and held it up for closer examination. "According to your college transcripts... which, yes, I did get a hold of and review... you skirted through your only Poli-Sci class with a C plus, and that was three years ago. I doubt your knowledge has made any great leaps and bounds since then, but I don't have access to the penthouse. I don't know how you waste your precious huey time there."

"Are you deliberately trying to insult me?"

"And that would be your C minus in normal psychology." Raquel grinned before putting down the snips and pushing the two sprays of roses into a thin-barreled vase sitting on a low table. "I have nothing to gain by demeaning you. I'm only stating facts and suggesting that you focus more on what I tell you than what your huey education, or should I say *miseducation,* has left you with. Especially if you have any intention of thriving in the supe world."

The suggestion made Amy catch her breath. Thriving? She was barely surviving. Emotionally, if not physically.

"To return to the point," Raquel continued. "*Politics* is a system for deciding who gets what, why, and when. Others try to make it more complicated than that, but really, it's that simple. In this country, there are checks and balances so no single part of the system can overtake another. It's a brilliant system, really... when it works. I would even say it's modeled on the supernatural world. You see, that's what we used to have. Checks and balances. Hood and werewolf. Slayers and vampires."

The huey had heard all this explained before, back when she was new to all things supernatural and had to play a massive game of catch up. It still didn't explain what Raquel was getting at. "Your point?"

Raquel reached out to a different plant, one with waxy lime green leaves as long as her forearm. "When I was younger in the tooth, vampires respected slayers. Yes, they *could* kill us, but their restraint was what we appreciated. How they would only use that power to curb the most malicious elements in our community, as we did theirs if one ever got too full of himself. There were even stories of lovers, one of each kind, or patronage from a vampire to a widow whose spouse died in the line of duty."

"Yeah, a bunch of fucking philanthropists. Vampires are so known for their compassion." It was a sarcasm Amy couldn't hide. "And I assume all vampires are rich, of course."

"The smart ones are. Or better to say, the stupid ones aren't." Raquel examined the fingers on her right hand before rubbing them together. "If we ever do have a bad turn in the pocketbook, there's always a rich huey to enthrall. For a female vampire, it's even easier. Sometimes we don't even need supernatural powers." Raquel looked up, taking in Amy anew from tip to toe. "You would probably be in that lot, if ever you were changed."

Amy knew it was meant as a compliment. Still, she couldn't help but feel nauseous at the idea. Living in perfect health and never getting old? Sounded fucking fab. Except you had to live off blood. Not to mention, she so didn't dig the concept of third degree burns or worse if she happened to catch a moment of sun. There was still a bikini in her closet that needed to see Ibiza.

"No offense, but hard pass."

"When your huey body begins to go soft, you may feel differently. And I would prefer to take you when you're still firm and flexible... *if* ever you change your mind." Before Amy could fully process the offer, Raquel continued her previous topic. "When slayers disappeared, I hoped our kind could police itself, that the patrons of the bloodlines and their own self-interests would work together to keep troublemakers in check. Unfortunately, too many of us carry our worst human traits into immortality. The Dracule and their elite generals, the Ravens, proved that all too well."

The blonde huey did feel the temptation to remind Raquel that she knew the truth. Vampires were immortal in terms of the whole not dying, not getting sick, not getting old bit, but they weren't eternal. Without feasting off the blood of other supernatural creatures, they too would someday die.

Instead, she tried to stay on topic. "The 'vampires first' crowd grew a little too big, too fast, did it?"

"And how." Raquel grinned, giving Amy a creepy feeling of having pleased a vampire. "Vlad Tepeş didn't create the concept of vampire supremacy. He just returned from the pages of history just when the ground was fertile for the seed. I don't care what Hoods claim. It wasn't just the Dracule who supported the Ravens' cause, though vampires should assume control of the supe world. Many sympathizers across a dozen bloodlines, all too happy to turn the other supes into food, were fighting at Tahquamenon that night."

A constricting feeling echoed in Amy's memories, along with Caleb's concerns about her physical safety when she left WWL. "But they were beaten, right?"

"Even if they were, ideologies can't be defeated on a battlefield. You see, Amy, that's the real problem. A garden grows strong not because the plants are allowed to grow unchecked."

Raquel reached down to a small, bushy plant covered in orange and yellow flowers, her delicate fingers popping off one of the nubile buds.

"It grows strong because the overgrowth is pruned before it grows too wild to choke out its own." Raquel's eyes laser-beamed into the huey. "To truly thrive, vampires need slayers. Personally, I detest Caleb. He's the worst kind of slayer. Arrogant, cocky, dismissive... still, he *is* a slayer. Not just genetically, but functionally. So I'll choke back my disgust with his baser huey-like behavior and support him, as long as he finally gets his shit together and starts teaching his people what they need to learn. Which means, whatever you need from me to accomplish that, I'll do."

Amy grinned and put some steel into her backbone. "Funny you should say that." She picked up the tossed bud from the ground. The garden was so tidy, it irked her to see it there. "Caleb and I had a discussion after the board meeting, and he realizes he needs to *"get his shit together,"'* she said, using finger quotes along with the words. "He's planning to bring in an outside consultant to fast-track his efforts. We're going to go in person to ask for his help. I assume we have the budget for that, to bring a new high-profile employee on board?"

"I could dedicate some of my discretionary funds for the initial term." Then, with a watering can in her hands and hovering, Raquel grew still. "Helsing suggested this of his own accord?"

"Yeah, I was stunned too."

Raquel's face screwed up. Damn it, Amy had forgotten how vampires could detect lies from someone who wasn't typically a liar. Something about how it had effects on the pulse.

"I... may have... suggested to him that he needed to do things to impress you if he wanted to keep his job. But, yeah, that particular idea? All him."

Luckily, Raquel didn't call her on it. "I suspect his motivations are a little more self-serving than that. Still, it is a step in the right direction." She tilted the can again, giving succor to some wilting, white flowers. "Who is the consultant, if I might ask?"

"Some guy named Massimo Bruneli, I think?"

The flow of water stopped abruptly, though to Amy's eyes, Raquel hadn't moved. In fact, she looked petrified, but that was a human reaction, wasn't it?

"Massimo Bruneli?" The chairperson repeated the name with perfect an-nunciation. "The Doge of Venice?"

"Yeah, that's the one. I guess he owes Caleb some kind of favor, so..."

"And Helsing is going in person to seek his assistance... alone?" Raquel said, cutting Amy off. "When?"

A tinge of foreboding uncurled in Amy's inside, a wily snake wrapping around her liver. "Er, *we* are hoping to leave tonight?"

"Tonight? That's very soon." Raquel looked away and seemed to talk to herself. "But there isn't much choice, is there?"

"I mean, Caleb wanted to leave tomorrow, but I pushed him to get this going if it's the way he wants to run so..."

The chairperson swung back around. "He is most fortunate to have your good counsel."

A blush bloomed in the blonde huey's cheeks. It wasn't that she didn't know how to take a compliment. Someone who looked like Amy learned the skill young. But the shape this one came in wasn't what she was used to, and she found handling it awkward. "Um... thanks?"

Raquel set down the watering can. "I will need to work quickly today if I'm to join you."

Amy swallowed so hard, she was surprised her nose wasn't half way down her throat. "Join us?"

"If there is any kind of deal being brokered which will affect WWL at that level, I should be there to represent the Boards' interests. Also, I have a friend in the Doge's court. It may be nice to see him again after some time apart."

"*You* have friends?"

The chairperson's face spoiled.

Amy knew when she'd overstepped and overstayed. She clasped her hands and let out an exasperated laugh. "In Venice, I mean. Yes, yes! By all means, come along. It should be... well, something."

Six

> Need to run some errands. I'll meet you at the airport tonight. A car will pick the rest of you up at the executive lobby doors at 9 p.m. *Don't be a douchebag and miss it.*

As ever, Amy was a peach, displaying her varied feminine charms.

Caleb stared at the contents of his closet, wondering what to bring. Formal wear, for certain. Surely one didn't show up at the court of the second longest-serving vampiric ruler in Europe in blue jeans and a Man United jersey. Especially not the jersey. He couldn't remember how Venezia's season was going, but Caleb doubted touting around in English Premier League gear was going to win many friends at court. A handful of dress shirts, a few ties, some slacks, and some casual wear for off hours fit into a neat little stack in his bag. If he needed anything once he got there, that he hadn't brought, oh, wouldn't it be horrible to have to *shop* in Italy?

A small cache of wooden bullets and his gun tucked nicely in between an Armani shirt and a pair of Calvin Klein underwear. Just because he was on good terms with his vampiric host didn't mean he was stupid. Of course, as a full-awoken slayer, Caleb's real weapon was always cocked and loaded, but there were some situations where a gun was just a whole lot more effective, not to mention less likely to cause collateral damage.

The whole process took less than twelve minutes. It wasn't his first time having to pack fast for a big trip. The Solari had been around the world before the age of ten. Running for your life and trying to avoid powerful vampires who knew your blood could be their own fountain of youth meant rarely staying anywhere long enough to grow roots. Back in those days, the Helsings didn't have the luxury of suitcases, let alone closets full of designer threads and the knowledge that a private jet was gassing up at this very moment to whisk them away.

Again, the thought returned: Raquel was trying to take this all away from him.

Like hell.

A black limo waited, perfectly framed by the gilded doorway of the executive lobby. Night security waved as Caleb passed.

"Good evening, Mr. Helsing." A short, somewhat round huey doorman jumped to attention, opening first the building doors, then the car. "And may you have a good night."

A good night? Stuck on an international flight for nearly ten hours, longer if they had to stop to refuel, with Amy Popowitz? Caleb severely doubted it. What were they supposed to do to pass the time, glare at each other?

And that's when he saw *those legs*.

Long, lean, tan, and fully on display, the two cherry red heeled shoes were the perfect pedestal for a perfect pair of legs The rest of the body was hidden behind the frame of the car. Which of the female slayers had legs like that, and why hadn't he been made aware earlier? Maybe Amy had been right; maybe Caleb had been neglecting the Reclaimed for too long. But then again, even if he had known...

Many sage and saccharine things his parents had said remained true. Instead of his father's bass tones or his mother's birdsong trill, however, the voice in his head at that moment was an actress's line from an 80s film set in New York.

"Don't shit where you eat."

Caleb couldn't do with the female slayers what he did with huey women: woo them, seduce them, show them a great time, and have a vamp clean out their memories after the fact. A full-blooded slayer mind couldn't be touched by vampire enthrallment. What good would they be at being vampires' natural balance otherwise?

Still, maybe one would be interested in just having a little fun. After all, he'd once gotten away with a one-night stand with...

"Tina!"

The slayer in question leaned into view, looking at him from the seat that lay beyond the set of wonder legs. She grinned, all brown curls, Grecian features, and devious plots.

"Caleb." She gave some kind of muted salute, index and middle finger flicked off her brow. An attempt to be respectful, or recalling a little bedroom banter about him being the general in charge? Maybe a little of both. "Good to hear you remember who I am. I was beginning to wonder."

Amy must still be pissed at him. That, or she was setting him up to be murdered. Further evidence in that direction emerged when the owner of the legs, Caleb had just been picturing licking honey from, also revealed herself.

"Good evening, Mr. Helsing."

Raquel de la Vega's face remained expressionless. Caleb cycled through several expressions, none of them pleasant.

"Miss de la..." He tried to swallow but found his mouth dry. "Raquel. What are you doing here?"

"Your assistant didn't tell you?" the chairperson questioned. "Miss Popowitz requested a security detail for this adventure of yours. I volunteered."

"I wasn't aware the chairperson was moonlighting as a liaison." Caleb handed off his bag to the chauffeur standing by. "Or that I needed a babysitter to visit a friend."

"When that friend is a vampiric ruler of one of the Italian courts and a blooded sister of a Medici... well, those are some serious diplomatic waters to swim in, and I know your parents' young deaths and your subsequent life of fleeing and dodging didn't give you much opportunity for a proper education. I thought you might benefit with some guidance on proper court etiquette and politics."

Was that an insult? It felt like an insult. And nice of her to remind him of the most traumatic event of his life.

By some means, Caleb managed to get into the back of the limo without committing some form of self-sabotage. Or maybe getting in qualified. The luxurious car, well in its appointments, unfortunately still only had one long, plush bench in the back for its occupants to share. Which meant... he was in the middle. Surrounded.

"You look very..." he side-eyed Raquel, anything to avoid meeting Tina's gaze, "... casual?"

The vampire seemed too concerned by something on her phone to look up but put on a tight smile. "Do I look like some sort of video game character, Mr. Helsing? That 'chairperson' is my only mode?"

"No, but I *do* think you crawled out of your maker's creche permanently stitched into a black power pantsuit. Not that it's a bad look. Suits you, even. No pun intended."

"Nor none committed. I find suits empowering. As a huey, I was a whore. Rarely was so much fabric afforded to me. But when not on the job, I enjoy being a little more..." she crossed one leg over the other with deliberate slowness, almost like she knew what a shiny object those legs were to him, despite the identity of their owner, "... feminine."

He didn't want this conversation to go on any longer. Really he didn't. But the alternative was talking to Tina, who looked like a pot getting ready to boil over.

"I don't know what arrangement you may or may not have with the Doge of Venice," Raquel went on. "But if it effects WWL, I'm also here to make sure you don't do something... ill-advised. I did ask Miss Popowitz's blessing, as it were, before making the decision to join you."

"Yeah, well, maybe *Miss Popowitz* should learn she doesn't have Pope-like powers." Caleb flinched, as though the blonde huey could reach out and slap him upside his head in absentia. Realizing he suddenly looked possessed, he turned his attention instead to the last woman he wanted to see today—or ever—as the limo rolled out onto the city streets.

"So, Tina..." He let the name stretch. "How have *you* been? What you been up to?"

"What have I been up to?" The bite in her voice could give the vampire sitting to Caleb's right a run for her money. "Just, you know, wondering if I needed to plan a funeral. We all thought you died."

The nervous laugh wasn't so much because Caleb thought she was joking. Tina was definitely *not* joking. The nerves, though. Man, they got the better of him.

"Yeah, sorry about that." Caleb rubbed the back of his neck. "Been busy, you know, running the company and stuff."

Classic excuse. Short. To the point.

And no sooner had he said it than Caleb realized Tina knew what total and utter bullshit it was. He caught sight of Raquel in his peripheral vision, waiting to see if she called him out. While the lift of the corner of the vampire's mouth was unmistakable, she kept her silence.

Was she actually letting him get away with this? Or was this another charge she'd levy against him just when the time was right?

Amy really did hate him, didn't she?

Tina snapped. "Seriously, Caleb? Did what we share mean nothing to you?"

"Of course it didn't mean nothing." *This* was why he chose to bed huey women whose memories could be erased. "But it was one night, a long time ago.

I didn't know it had meant that much to *you.*"

The female slayer's jaw dropped. "Obviously."

Tina crossed her arms over her chest and whipped her head to the side, watching the streets of the city shrink from skyscrapers to business blocks to shopping centers through the window. Avoiding him or genuinely curious?

The Reclaimed rarely left the WWL towers. Not like Caleb was keeping them prisoner. After what they'd been through, that would have made him a total dick. Still, Security advised them only to leave when accompanied by a guard. It seemed that being followed by a vampire didn't lead to much adventure.

Caleb let out a deep sigh and relaxed back against the plush middle seat. Silence it was then. He joined Tina in her gawking without her knowing or perhaps caring, watching the limo wick away from the city he'd come to think of as home. Minutes crawled. Closing his eyes, he focused on the sound of the engine, the low hum of traffic, the leather seat heating from his proximity...

At last, the car slowed, turning through an executive service gate on the far side of O'Hare. Tina scrambled to flee. Unwilling to work his body over a vampire, Caleb slid across the seat, intending to follow, only to find the door slammed in his face.

He met Raquel's curious and confused gaze.

"I need the truth of this to know whom to defend, Mr. Helsing," she said, stating the obvious. "Why is Miss Potsia under the impression that you have jilted her?"

What the hell? His reputation was well known. "We slept together. *Once.*"

The chairperson's eyes brightened. "I wasn't aware you pursued your own kind."

"*Pursued* isn't the word I'd choose to describe it." He wrapped a hand around the handle. "It was during the few days I was imprisoned by the Ravens in Istanbul. Tepeş basically told me choose one of the slayers of the harem to bed or he was going to start killing the male slayers he had locked up in the basement."

"Because they are infertile, and you are not."

Was she stating the obvious or voicing a realization? At the end of the night, it didn't really make a difference, did it?

Caleb looked at his shoes and shrugged. "Honestly, I don't really remember much about what it happened," Caleb admitted. "I know what you think about me, Raquel, but I would never sleep with someone against their will. I did my best to block it from my memory, but I do remember Tina was willing. Eager, even. Obviously, for her, it was more than an obligation by her captors."

Again that subtle quirk in the corner of Raquel's mouth. "Obviously."

If the chairlady wasn't careful, Caleb might suspect she actually had a sense of humor. The most likely truth was, however, that she reveled in his suffering.

"Look, Raquel..." Caleb scooted back to get a better view of his seatmate. "I'm still not sure I like you being on this trip. But Amy asked for security. You may need to provide it. If I can't find a way to make good with Tina, she might look for a way to make bad with me. Let's just say she has a history of bad decisions, and I'm only one of the smaller ones."

SEVEN

Venice might carry the nickname "The Most Serene," but its regional air-port hadn't gotten the memo. It was like being stuck in some low-budget 80s movie. Speckled linoleum floors. Faded wood paneled walls. Breathe in too deep and you could still taste the cigarette smoke, ghosts of health policies past. The grimy windows weren't so bad. They blocked the bountiful sunlight, dampening the brightness of the immigration lobby. Not that the lobby could ever be truly bright. For such a popular tourist destination, it didn't look like Italy wanted to make a good first impression.

Caleb checked his watch again. The line was taking entirely too long, and he needed to piss. "I thought being first class passengers meant that we were supposed to fast-track through customs."

"We are." Amy pointed to the throb of humanity to their left, an updated reenactment of Ellis Island in reverse. "*Those* are the economy class passengers, and their lines are moving much, much slower."

"True, but only relatively."

It was one of those rare occasions where Caleb envied the vampires. Raquel had no interest in "playing human." Somewhere between deplaning and im-migration processing, she'd headed to a bathroom and never emerged. Amy reported that, while Caleb had been asleep, Raquel had told the blonde huey that she'd meet them after sunset in Venice. Apparently, she planned on smoking her way out of the airport to avoid huey contact.

Which kinda sucked, since having a vampire with them who could enthrall someone and get them VIP service would rock right about now.

"I don't understand why we came through the main city airport at all," the Solari continued. "Didn't I read in that email you sent me during the wee hours of the afternoon that Bruneli's people offered the use of the Eight Court's personal airport?"

Amy pulled her passport from her carry-on as they took another step toward the security check. "They did, and it is private. But it's way out in the middle of nowhere and we would have had to drive in from there."

"So what? We can afford the taxi fare, Amy."

Supernatural hearing meant her teeth grinding was audible to his ears. "And if this all goes south for some reason and we need to get away quickly..."

Well, that shut him up. Had Amy assumed so much of his job that now she was actually thinking like a slayer? One of the earliest lessons he'd been taught by his parents was never to enter a room with a potential enemy without having a plan that included two possible exit routes. On an island, maybe one exit route would have to suffice. So was Amy suggesting that the Doge was an enemy then? Why? He'd been the one to broker this deal to begin with. Why would they need to escape from him?

Or was there something Amy wasn't telling him?

Suddenly, the weight of the deepfreeze case at his side containing the samples of the blood felt heavier. Without Mina's blood, the deal with Massimo never would have been struck to begin with. Without Massimo, Caleb was actually going to have to stand up or get out where WWL was concerned.

"Besides, our plane is already on the way back to the US," she added. "Brunhild Kline is on some kind of winning-back-the-masses tour with Geri, Tobias, and Mina. They want to show the Asian blood lines that hybrids are nothing to be afraid of."

His ex, Geri Kline, had turned out to be the greatest rarity of all in the supernatural world. A woman who held slayer, hood, and werewolf lines. What her blood could do, beyond rejuvenate an injured vampire, was as yet unknown. Both her mate and her adopted daughter were also cross-blooded, Tobias having some hood ancestry but raised vampire. Little Mina had been born to one of the Reclaimed, with an unknown werewolf as father. Unfortunately, her biological mother had died in childbirth, which was part of the reason Mina now belonged to Geri and Tobias.

Not that Caleb didn't see the benefit of the supernatural world building bridges, but there were still certain formalities he felt should be addressed. "I didn't authorize that."

"You did. I have your proxy, remember? But I didn't think you'd mind. Besides, they're going to have it back next week and I figured we weren't going anywhere so, what's the harm?"

"The harm?" Crossing his arms over his chest in mock petulance, Caleb turned. "Have you seen the stewardesses that work on our private jet? Let's just say their ability to serve a drink ain't the only thing they got going for them. And we'd be trapped in the same confined space with them for hours. Hours, Barbie! I could have—"

Suddenly, Tina, mirroring his mannerisms, leaned into the space between the solari and huey, cutting off his words, looking like she'd try cutting off something else of his if he finished that sentence.

Caleb cleared his throat. "I could have made sure everything is running tip-top, and oh, look! They're ready for us."

The custom agent, a man with a long hook nose and tiny eyes set behind chubby cheeks, looked up from his computer monitor expressionless. "One at a time, unless you are a family."

Caleb reached for his passport, but Amy managed to whip hers out before the others. How could *she* be faster than a supe? Must be something about it being daytime.

"All others step back, *per favore*." The agent looked up and down a few times, both to make sure his orders were being followed and to compare Amy's face to the one in the passport he now clutched. "Amy Tempest Popo... Popo..."

Tina pulled herself off Caleb's side to peek around his assistant. "It's pronounced Puppy-Guts."

Shit. Okay, now that Amy looked like she was going to hit Tina, the sexiness was gone. Caleb pulled his slayer back by the arm. "Not now, dear," he said just as Amy turned back to the agent.

The agent showed no interest in their squabbling. "Why are you in Italy?"

"Visiting a friend in Venice."

He nodded. "You are from Ohio?"

"No, I'm from New York. Live in Chicago now. I was just *born* in Ohio, but there's not much I could have done about it, is there?"

A moment more, and the agent waved her through. Amy spared a moment to look back over her shoulder the way a frustrated mother would. The intent was simple to interpret. *Be on your best behavior or else.* To have lingered might draw attention, so she didn't. Instead, his assistant proceeded through a wall of doors behind the immigration stands that appeared as if they'd been lifted from some Stateside store ending in "mart."

The agent curled two fingers up in the air as he briefly looked at the couple before him. "Prego."

Caleb put his hand on the small of Tina's back and pushed her forward. "Don't make a sound, okay?"

Tina's grin radiated lust. "You know I have problems being quiet."

The agent grimaced to see them both at the desk when he looked up again. "Family?"

They definitely weren't siblings. They might both have dark hair, but Caleb's sandstone skinned took on a darker hue when standing next to the Russian female slayer's ivory complexion.

"We're I—"

His hand hooked around her hip as he pulled Tina back into his chest. "Engaged, actually. I hope it's okay to do us both together? We hate being apart for even a second."

Tina started to laugh at that, but a quick, sharp pinch on her hip shut her up. Eye rolling wasn't the best thing to get from a uniformed border agent, but it would do. Caleb had been globe-hopping and pub crawling on WWL forged documents for years, but always in a vampire's company. On the rare occasion when questions about his papers had been raised, there'd always been someone with him who could bend the mind of the one doing the raising. That wasn't an option now. Luckily, Caleb also knew from many fruitful experiences that unhappy people detested being around couples unafraid to engage in PDA.

Signore Agento d'Italia did *not* look like a happy person.

Suspicious eyes went from their documents to their faces several rounds as Caleb nuzzled Tina's ear, each time the agent's scowl becoming more pronounced. His eyebrow arched as he examined Tina's shiny new American passport; Caleb notched her chin and drew her mouth to his.

"Where are you from?"

It was unclear which of them the question was for. Caleb leaned forward, leaving Tina frowning. "Both of us born in Turkey, but neither one of us is Turkish. Ethnically, that is. We're both US Citizens now."

Technically that last part wasn't true. Neither of them appeared in any US Government computer that WWL was aware of.

"I'd like Miss *Portokalos* to answer for herself, please."

Portokalos? Who came up with that ridiculous name?

Caleb pulled back. "You English pretty well."

"Yours could use a work, *Signore...*" the agent held the passport out at arm's length, "... Odinson?"

"Just like that hot guy in the movie Amy made us watch." Tina turned to Caleb and gave him an assessment. "Doesn't fit you at all."

"Gee, thanks, *honey.*" The last word pushed was through clenched teeth. "Go on, tell the man where you're from yourself."

Oh, that grin. She knew she had power in this, that she could blow their cover with ease. Leverage. With every moment, Caleb was accruing a debt with sky-high interest. What in the hell had Amy been thinking, choosing Tina to be the slayer invited on this trip?

Finally, Tina shook the smirk and turned to the agent. "I was born in Istanbul, but only because my mom was held prisoner there. She was from Moscow, by the way. You didn't ask, but since you seem to be nosy about other stuff, I thought I'd throw that in."

The agent's stoicism broke. Three parallel lines appeared on his forehead. "Excuse me?"

"*Nosy,*" Tina repeated, careful to overaccentuate the sound of it. "I think I got that right, didn't I? English isn't my first language either, but I think it means you're asking about stuff that's none of your business."

Caleb placed himself between his nightmare wannabe-fiancée and the counter. "Tina, what are you doing?"

She could conjure up doe eyes so innocent she'd con the smartest buck. "What? I only answered the man's question like you asked me to."

Behind, the agent had lifted the phone and was speaking rapid-fire Italian to whomever was on the other end.

Great, just great.

His finger shoved into Tina's side, below the viewpoint of their interloper. "Remind me later to discuss airport etiquette with you before we fly back home." Then, turning to the agent, Caleb started in on the only other thing he could think to do.

Beg.

"Sir, I'm so sorry about that. Tina can be, well... a bitch. This is her first time in a while traveling internationally, and she doesn't know any better, or how wrong it is to be rude to you, and I'd really appreciate it if..."

"You can go."

The words were so unexpected, they temporarily rendered Caleb mute. "Sorry?"

The annoyance flashed across the agent's face so quickly, a slower creature would have missed it. "I said *go.*"

Never one to look a gift horse in the mouth, Caleb wasted no time in hooking Tina by the arm, palming their freshy-stamped passports, and getting through the turnstile as fast as, well, a human would have been able to, at least.

"See, I told you." Tina radiated smugness. "You just have to talk down to these hueys, then they respect you."

"Respect had nothing to do with it. Not for you. Certainly not for me." Through the security doors, into the baggage claim area and among the general population, Caleb scanned the vestibule. The carpet matched the drapes. Literally. Their moldy presence continued the dated motif from the arrivals lobby. "Now, where is Amy?"

"Puppy-Guts?" Tina ripped her hand out of Caleb's, and it was only then that he realized he'd been squeezing. She rounded on him, placing herself between the solari and the rest of the lobby, graceful arms woven over her perky, perky chest. "Probably ran off to get our bags like the good little serf that she is."

"Amy's not a serf. She's an employee."

The female slayer nodded slowly. "I know I'm new to the mundane world, but isn't that like, the same thing but with better pay?"

"And the choice to stay or go." For a moment, the idea that Amy *could* leave if she wanted slapped him in the face. Gods, what would he do without her? She'd been the one running the company by proxy for the last year. He didn't even know where to pick up his dry cleaning alone.

Only then, across the lobby, their eyes met. Amy picked up a hand to wave, then returned to talking to... another nice-looking package, truth be told. Tall, creamy-skinned and long, dark, red hair. The fact that this mystery woman stood there in broad daylight meant she wasn't a vampire, and the lack of a stick up her ass or broad shoulders meant she likely wasn't a hood or a werewolf. One of the Doge's human staff? Most vampires of influence had them. Even a supernatural household had the need for daytime operations. This one looked a little older than Caleb's typical mark, maybe bordering forty? But in Caleb's experience, the saying about women and wine had proved to be true, and he'd be the first to admit he liked to be overserved.

Suddenly, the solari found himself walking a little straighter, strutting across the lobby, with Tina shuffling behind, forgotten. Caleb locked eyes with Red, and he'd be damned if there wasn't a spark between them instantly.

Well, this coerced trip to Venice certainly just took an exciting twist. Speaking of twist, he wondered if Red was bendy.

"Miss Popowitz?" He came to a stop before them, unbuttoning his suit jacket. "Make a friend already? Do share her."

Amy, for her part, rolled her eyes. She did that so much in his presence, though, Caleb was surprised she hadn't developed a permanent case of vertigo.

But much to his delight, Red took the initiative, sticking out her own hand. "Oh hey, there. You must be Caleb. Welcome to Italy."

Her speech was clear, precise English. Not Italian. Not even European then. Even for those who picked up near-native ability, the accent of emulation was British. This woman's accent was maybe American West Coastal, as opposed to the east, where both he and Amy had been raised in their formative years.

"I'm happy to be someone else if that's what you're after." Caleb winked as he leaned over, pulling up Red's hand and planting a kiss against her knuckles. "Maybe your next mistake?"

The huey flushed even as Tina, catching up, hip-checked him. "I'm Konstantina Potsia," she said. No hand held forward, no sign of softness. Amy's lessons of huey conventions needed to be stepped up if his cadre of slayers were ever going to fend for themselves in the mundane world. "And just so you know, I'm Caleb's lover."

Red's face screwed up, and who could blame her?

Before he knew what was happening, Caleb's mouth began to vomit words. "She's not.... *we're* not. Anymore. Not that we were ever really... it was one time and..."

Fuck. He had to fix this fast, or this conquest was going to be over before it started. Better to press forward than be mired in the muck.

The solari shook off his sputtering and focused on the beauty before him. "Sorry, I think I missed your name?"

"I'm..."

Her eyes lashed between Caleb and Amy. She was surprised Caleb didn't know.

"Portia Kepler, of course."

Obviously, she expected him to know that. Should he have known that? *Did* he know that? Desperately, Caleb turned to Amy, his eyes begging. Was this one of his employees who happened to be in Italy? A lover he'd forgotten about? Someone he met at one of the few corporate meetings he'd actually shown up for? Unlikely. Those were the kind of hips a man didn't forget.

Amy wore the kind of glee in her eyes little kids had in those Christmas movies when they saw all the presents they'd gotten. Oh, this was going to hurt.

"You know," the blonde said. "Portia Kepler, aka the Dogaressa of Venice and Massimo Bruneli's wife."

Eight

P ortia led them past the small cadre of executive and sports cars parked curbside, and to an outdoor walkway ringing the edge of the passenger facilities. The sights and sounds of a technically non-smoking terminal gave way to cracked cement walkways, jet fuel fumes, and an undertone of salt marshes.

Caleb scented the air, thankful that slayers didn't have it as badly as werewolves where certain heightened senses were concerned. "Are you sure we didn't land in New Jersey? Smells like we did."

The blonde huey's eyes burned fire as she rounded on her boss. "It's called the Garden State, you know. And it's fucking beautiful. People got to stop thinking all of New Jersey is East Newark."

"I know that. I lived in Jersey. For, like, a month, but still, my fault for asking a New Yorker such an inane question, but..." He came to a stop, surveying the post-industrial plebian landscape before them. "After all the things I've heard about the glories of Roman architecture and Renaissance art, I expected Venice to be a little more... fancy?"

"It's an airport, Buffy. Do you think Chicago is O'Hare?"

Portia proved to be a consummate host, allowing them their bickering without interfering, until she jerked her head to the right. "The docks are this way."

Despite the frequent accusations muttered by his assistant under her breath, Caleb was *not* a fucking idiot. He *knew* Venice was an island. Actually, many islands, and most of them artificially engineered a thousand years ago. That crossing water to get to the court of Doge Massimo Bruneli would be necessary at some point wasn't a surprise. When he'd checked the map on his phone, however, there was clearly a perfectly good bridge from the mainland to the city's eastern point.

"Mrs. Bruneli, I'd prefer to go by car, if possible."

"It's Ms. Kepler. I didn't take my husband's name." The Dogaressa turned back over her shoulder, wearing an amused grin. "Don't tell me you're afraid of the water, Mr. Helsing?"

At the end of the dock, a boat the size of a van and outfitted with the poshness of a Mercedes waited, its motor giving off a steady purr that suggested many, many horses under the hood. *Did boats have hoods?* Portia and Amy came to a stop on the ramp that led down to the vessel. Caleb and Tina stayed five steps back.

The solari shook his head. "Not *afraid*. Just... cautious."

"Me too." Tina's lips curled in disgust, though Caleb wasn't sure if that was from the idea of skimming over a body of water in a glorified minibus, or because the air suddenly smelled—and tasted—of rotten fish.

Amy bit her bottom lip as she cocked her head to the side. "All of your superhuman abilities, and it doesn't include swimming?"

"Of course, we *can* swim," Caleb shot back. "But *people* like Tina and me..." Not slayers, because who knew who might be within earshot nearby. "We hate open water. How can you have lived with me for over a year and not know that?"

"I suppose because we live in a skyscraper and not on a trawler on Lake Michigan. What else am I supposed to know, your favorite kind of mushroom?"

It took only a moment, or maybe it was just the sensation that he'd been thrown off kilter. A wave hit the dock, and Caleb felt himself tipping. His hand shot out, seeking purchase on the only thing near enough to grab. That turned out to be Amy, who he'd neared without him realizing it. Fortunately, it was her arm and not one of her... other places. Much to Caleb's surprise, instead of screw up her face and insult him per protocol, Amy reached back, steadying him.

"It's okay, Caleb. I got you."

No sooner had he balanced himself than Tina jerked him up and out of Amy's hold, almost like a child saying "mine."

"Whoa, there." Tina gave him a moment to find his balls and stand alone. "You okay?"

"Just lost my footing. Thanks for the help, both of you." Only with a nod of thanks and air of competence did Tina let go. "As I was saying, Amy, we *don't* like open water. We can't... do our thing... if we're standing in water, remember? I mean, I'm not a fan of swimming pools, but at least I can get out of one easily enough."

"I guess you've never showered with..." Amy caught herself in the nick of time. "...*one of them*, then."

"Except for feeding Inga Rosethorn every so often, I've never *anythinged* with one of them."

One of Amy's eyebrows rose suspiciously as she adjusted the strap on her travel bag. But gods bless her, she chose for once just to let it go.

"I have," Tina volunteered unsolicited. "I've *everythinged* with several."

Both Amy and Caleb leaned over to look at the female slayer.

Tina pushed a thumb into her chest. "Senior member of the Ravens' harem, remember?"

If there was a way to make him feel like shit, that was it. Caleb cleared his throat. "Sorry, I didn't mean to bring up bad memories."

"Bad?" Tina's face screwed up and she blew a raspberry. "If you'd ever actually been with a vampire, the last thing you'd call it is bad."

"She's right." This time it was their hostess chiming in again, but she was doing it from the deck of the boat. "But that fact won't get us to court any quicker, and I *do* want to get back quickly. I apologize, Mr. Helsing. I wasn't aware of your... preference for land. But believe me, going over the water is much quicker and more comfortable, so if you all wouldn't mind boarding?"

Still shell shocked, Caleb shook his head. Tina let out a cackle of indignation before making her way down the rest of the dock. In her wake, the solari lifted a hand and pointed.

"Of all the options you had, Tina?"

"Yes, Tina. Of course, Tina."

"Why 'of course?'"

"Because I want to see what she's like out in the wild. Because I don't know if I want her coming back home, and it will be much easier to manage that away from the others." Amy spoke into her shoulder, having learned over the last few years of the acuity of supernatural hearing. "You may have rescued the Reclaimed the Ravens' harem, but in some ways, Tina's still there, and I'm not sure she wants to be anywhere else."

He cocked his head to the side. "I don't understand."

"You will." Amy's grip on his shoulder was incredibly firm for a huey. "I'm no fan of vamps myself, you know, but I think you both would benefit from seeing how the good ones are."

It was easy to see why so many fell in love with Venice the closer they got, Caleb thought. It was like stepping back in time, falling into a novel, and being part of a work of art all at once. From the middle of the lagoon, the mobs of tourists thronged in St. Peter's square, moving like warring masses to get hither and yon. The chilled air didn't appear to damper anything, and he credited it with suppressing the fishy flavor in the air once they'd gotten to deeper waters.

Above their heads, the red-brick campanile that defined the Venetian skyline pinned the city in place. At intervals, spinning neon swirls soared into the sky as street vendors selling tourist trinkets plied their wares. In the rare moments the throng quieted, a splash of guitar or accordion or violin from one of the many buskers would rise above the chatter and float out over the water.

"Wow, that's really just... wow." Amy was like a kid looking out from her Manhattan apartment at a passing parade, her hands pressed flat against the cabin's windows and her head on a spindle.

"Yes, I have always said that Venice is one of my favorite cities."

Amy twisted, surprised as they all were to see Raquel de la Vega sitting among them.

"And just where did you come from?" The blonde huey asked the obvious.

Raquel uncrossed her legs and stood. "I have my ways of getting around." She turned to where Portia sat, eyes wide, face white, and bowed. "Signora Dogaressa, I am Raquel de la Vega of the Xochi Bloodline, Chairperson of the Board of Directors at Walt Whitman Labs, and a friend to His Excellency's second. It is a pleasure to be in your city."

Portia had the look of an actress trying to remember her lines. "Ms. Vega, you are well met and welcomed to our court. And yes, Pavlos is looking forward to seeing you again."

"You've been here before?" Amy questioned, ignoring the ceremony.

"Once, about seventy years ago." Raquel paused long enough to rise. "I had no business with the Royal Court; it was a purely social visit. Of course, as is wise in lands still regulated by a vampiric monarch, I declared myself upon arrival. At the time, I was no one of consequence. Consequently, I've never had the honor of making His Excellency's acquaintance."

Past the square, the craft banked a gentle right. Palaces rose along the edges of the Grand Canal, the wide waterway that cut a crescent across the main part of town, tokens of the splendid past they hueys here had once claimed. No fan of or expert in architecture, Caleb still recognized legacy when he was so heavily slapped in the face with it. His ancestors had walked these streets centuries ago, when Venice had been one of the great ports of power in the Mediterranean and the Eight Vampiric Courts had been an alliance that challenged both Istanbul and Vienna alike.

Now it looked more like a theme park, thronged by outsiders and the towns-folk forced to bend to their demands just to keep their ancient jewel alive.

"This place is unreal."

Tina had lived in Istanbul all her life before being freed from the Raven's grasp, but how much of the city had she seen outside the view of the Bosphorus from the harem's windows? It took a moment for Caleb to identify the tingles he felt. He was... giddy. To watch someone take so much joy in a novel experience was surprisingly uplifting. They weren't here to play tourists. His focus had to be calling in Massimo Bruneli's marker and getting him to take over at WWL. But maybe there should be a little free time?

"We'll try to find a chance to look around, but we can't stray too far from court," he found himself saying even though it would mean spending time with the slayer he least wanted to. "The last thing we want to do is cause a panic among the vampire population here, making it look like two slayers have shown up to patrol the streets."

"Why?" Tina's sweet, innocent smile dropped away. She turned steely eyes on the solari. "That's what our kind is *supposed* to do."

"*Your kind* is supposed to inspire security, not mistrust."

In typical fashion, Raquel didn't feel the need to look at them. She kept her eyes trained out the boat's windows, taking in a wide survey as it maneuvered out of the Grand Canal, and into a humbler path of water on the left, and shortly thereafter, an even narrower stream to the right. Here, the craft barely cleared the walls, but the unseen driver had skills to meet them... by *not* meeting them.

Finally, they slowed, and the porter who'd handled their luggage at the airport docks appeared from above on the main deck of the boat, speaking Italian to another man who appeared on the banks, holding a heavy rope.

"Raquel, what are they saying?"

"I'm Mexican, not Italian, Mr. Helsing. I speak *Spanish*."

"Come on, really?" Caleb whined. "They're like, eighty-seven percent the same language, all of it descended from drunk Romans."

Now the eyes did peek up, just long enough to shoot him daggers.

"He says they received instructions from their dispatcher to take us to a back entrance to the building," Portia said, inserting herself in the conversation, her brow creased.

So Massimo didn't want two slayers to be seen arriving like honored guests, and that surprised the Dogaressa. In a city where the ruler was supposedly well loved and respected, why would that be?

Something strange was happening in Oz...

NINE

A djusting for the fact that the alley through which they passed still looked like the background to a historical drama crime scene, the hallway was, well, boring as fuck. White, undecorated walls. Low-level fluorescent lights buzzing down on gray linoleum floors. The occasional modern metal doors on either side of the long hall before them.

The smell of fish was back now that they were back in the shallower canals, but now it had taken on a defiantly culinary flavor. Evening was coming, and with it, the locals and tourists alike were coming to tables with empty bellies.

"Pavlos!" Portia's face broke into a grin as a vampire up the hall came into view, his suit and smile both a million dollars. After a brief survey of the party, Caleb noticed his eyes lingering on Raquel.

Hold it. Not lingering. *Indexing.* As a womanizing bastard, Caleb recognized one of his own ilk.

"*Dogaressa serena.*" Pavlos's formal greeting paired with the briefest of bows so shallow it was practically a nod. The accent wasn't Italian, but it *was* an accent of some kind. "Honored guests, welcome to Venice."

Portia turned on the party. "This is my husband's personal secretary and closest aide, Pavlos Katsaros. Pavlos, may I introduce..." Portia took out a folded-up paper from her pocket and opened it. *Such a huey thing.* "The Slayer Solari, Mr. Caleb Helsing, his personal secretary, Miss Amy Popowitz, one of the Reclaimed, Miss Konstantina Potsia, and—"

"Doña Raquel de la Vega." Pavlos slid up to Raquel, taking up her hand and pressing the dainty but lethal digits to his lips, his eyes looking at the chairperson in a way that suggested...

Well, to put it bluntly, that these two had definitely fucked at some point. Or were going to.

Possibly both.

"Pavlos." For the first time that Caleb could remember, Raquel's voice held a tiny bit of honey instead of the basket of nettles he usually got when they spoke. "Haven't you done well for yourself? The first aide to the Doge of Venice."

Pavlos cracked a grin and buried his head in his chest as he dropped Raquel's hand. "I've only held the position for the past decade. Signore Bruneli honors me greatly."

Their gazes held each other's, unspoken memories passing between, clouding the air around the others with awkward tension. Figuring it was as good a time as ever to establish himself as a slayer who didn't need to defer to vampires and the fact that he *still* needed to piss, Caleb cleared his throat.

"Mr. Katsaros." The solari was sorry to have offered his hand as soon as Pavlos's cold but smooth flesh pressed into his palm. "It's nice of you to host us on such short notice and to be awake to welcome us personally so close to sunset."

Flattery and formality. Vampires loved that shit.

"Of course, Signore Solari." Then, turning to Tina, Pavlos repeated the kissing-hand routine, this time without the lingering lustful gaze. "*Thespinis Pótsia, eEneh polee oreo poo gnorizo enan seempatriotee mo.*"

An uncomfortable half-grimace, half-smile flitted across Tina's face. "Sorry?"

Pavlos lowered her hand and took a step back. "My apologies, Signorina. I assumed, based on your name, that you were one of my countrymen. There was once a time in Thrace when mention of the Potsia slayer bloodline could send a chill down any vampire's spine or so I've been told. I was only turned during World War II. I'm still quite short in the tooth."

Greek! Ah, so that was the accent. Caleb knew it was familiar, but that sort of identity quirk wasn't his specialty, especially when speaking a non-native tongue.

"I... didn't know that," Tina said, then shrugged. "I've never been to Greece. I was... um, born and raised in Istanbul."

The air thickened, as did the silence in which, somehow, the words "in Vlad Tepeş's harem" still could be heard. Luckily, Amy broke the tension.

"Hi, there. I'm Amy. I'm the one who reached out to arrange our visit. I'm also the only human... Sorry, *huey* here, and as much as I hate to admit it, I really need to use your restroom."

Caleb huffed. "Oh, Amy, *please*, be a little grown up."

Did teasing his secretary for saying the very thing he was thinking make him an asshole? Yeah, probably. But at least it bridged them away from an awkwardness based on the remembrance of horrible tragedies to one based on the tragedy of the huey biological system.

Pavlos rubbed his hands together. "Of course, Miss Popowitz, how rude of me to overlook your needs." He turned, motioning them up the hall. "Allow me to show you to your rooms so that you may rest after your long journey. A servant will collect you thirty minutes after sunset. His Excellency looks forward to enjoying your company at dinner."

TEN

Tina was the last to be deposited into a holding. Or, sure, it may be a golden cage—the walls were adorned with frescoes, the canopy bed a work of art as much as a place to sleep, the smell of the flowers in vases brightening the air with perfume—but she recognized a prison cell for what it was. She'd been born into it. Grew up in it. Eventually, thrived in it by learning to acquiesce in just the right way to her captors.

When Caleb Helsing had been pushed into the harem that night, the first new slayer introduced into their population in a decade, she knew what she had to do to please her masters: seduce the male slayer, take his seed, and grow them a son.

It wasn't like it was the first time she'd used sex to make the vampires who kept her happy. Given her easy nature, Tina was a favorite among them. She'd even been called occasionally into Vlad's chamber in lieu of his other favorite, Alexandra. When miraculously Alex had revealed she was with child, and Tina witnessed Vlad spoil the mother-to-be wildly, even allowing her to leave the compound at her own will, as long as she was accompanied by guards, she had decided that her path forward lay in seizing the first opportunity to follow suit.

Caleb had come to bed that night willing to perform. She'd ignored the emptiness in his eyes as he went through the motions, sharing his body but no part of his heart or mind with her. It had been the first time she'd felt as though she'd been the one using someone else, and to her own surprise, that made her care about him.

At first, when they'd been freed, she made efforts to show Caleb that she was sorry about what she'd done to him. She was sorrier still when she learned she wasn't even with child following the act, surely he'd want to see her then. She'd wanted to reach out to him, to build a connection, to heal what so obviously was lost in him.

Then, for over a year, he'd spurned her. Not only her, truth be told. Caleb ignored all the Reclaimed. Oh, sure, he gave them a place to live, provided for their upkeep, even helped a few who were so inclined to find employment or seek higher education. They could even come and go as they wished; the vampiric guards were said to accompany them "only for protection." They'd exchanged a palace on the Bosporus for a steel tower in the sky. Still kept, still tended. Only now, there was no system Tina could exploit to get ahead, no relationship she could massage into improving her situation. She couldn't even speak with Caleb, let alone develop what they shared into something both could embrace.

The only contact she had outside of huey housekeepers was Amy Popowitz. *Puppy Guts.* While at first, the blonde huey seemed sympathetic to the slayers' situation, she'd proved unable to do anything to advocate for them. No matter how much Tina begged or threatened, and she could *threaten*, Puppy Guts never proved successful in bringing Caleb into the picture...

Until yesterday, when, at last, Tina had gotten the news. Her wait was over. Her suffering was being rewarded. She *alone* had been chosen from among all the Reclaimed to accompany the Slayer Solari on a highly critical diplomatic trip.

It was the opportunity she'd been longing for and one she wasn't going to let go to waste.

Tina knew what she had to do, and she didn't have much time to do it. She knew a way to a man's good graces was to make him feel both as big as the sky and as small as a drop of rain. She needed to pump out Caleb's ego, all while inserting herself as the critical element that would allow him ultimate success. She needed to seduce his ego and his heart, and when possible, his body. She needed to be his before this trip was over, and also, needed him to be worthy of being hers.

She needed to be both his master and slave.

Tina laid across the luxury bedding and closed her eyes.

Finally, her moment would come.

Finally, her prince would actually save her. And as soon as they joined together as a team, she'd become his and the mother of his child.

ELEVEN

An opulent display of Baroque art and architecture, the dining room looked more like a movie set than any place a modern person lived. Frescoes decorated everywhere, from the ceiling to floor, giving Caleb a heavy case of the jellies, as Amy might say. Seriously, he could do with a few more chubby cherubs and Grecian warriors on his own bedroom wall. Looking at the furniture, the solari wasn't sure if he was about to have dinner or see a Shakespeare production.

The enormous chandelier overhead must have been that Murano glass he'd read about in the airline's onboard magazine. Supposedly, *it* was what put Venice on the map. Like, literally. The islands were built up in part so the glass-workers could practice their craft away from curious eyes. The piece hanging from Bruneli's ceiling had shades of blue and pink woven together like the thing was made of cloth. Some parts of it resembled flowers or ocean spray or... was that a dolphin or a dick? The flickering "candle" bulbs were obviously electric, but a clever imitation.

Behind the couple waiting to greet them was a lavish buffet spread across the longest dining room table he'd ever seen. Seven place settings had been arranged with fine China, silver, and linens. Finally, someone who understood how to treat the guest of honor right.

The vice-doge cleared his throat as Caleb entered, Amy, Tina, and Raquel flanking him. Hard to tell which of them seemed the most pissed off. He hadn't meant to sleep more than a few minutes when he'd laid down. How "a few" turned into "we've been knocking on your door for twenty minutes, and now we're late," he didn't know.

"Yeah, hi," Caleb greeted, clearing his throat and giving a weak ass shake of his hand. "Sorry, I... not important. I'm here."

Even Pavlos grimaced. Boy, he was just pissing off all the people today.

"Very well." The vice-doge shook off his disgust and nodded to the sharply dressed couple standing to his left. "Signore Helsing, allow me to present Massimo Bruneli, Vampiric Doge of Venice, and his wife, the Dogaressa, the Lady Portia Kepler-Bruneli." He indicated the couple. "Your Excellencies, now that the Solari has arrived, allow me to introduce our guests formally."

Caleb cocked a hip. "This all seems a little unnecessary, doesn't it?"

The Doge's face screwed up, while Portia's went white. Luckily, her husband was more focused on his guests than his own wife's reaction to catch the unspoken plea to not say anything. Why didn't Portia want Massimo to know she'd met him at the airport?

Raquel stepped forward in a repeat performance of her earlier court dance. "Your Excellencies, I am Raquel de la Vega of the Xochi bloodline, daughter of Mehean Ixtal. I am honored to make your acquaintance."

"The *Balam* line?" Massimo and his second exchanged amused grins before the former motioned for Raquel to rise. "This court has not welcomed many in this part of the world. I was beginning to think they may have died out."

"There are no more makers in my line in over a century. I may be among the last born to its lineage." She tilted her head ever so slightly. "I understand His Excellency's line is in similar decline."

Caleb wasn't sure if it was considered rude to tell someone their bloodline was going extinct. In fact, he wasn't sure he'd ever actually heard of something like that happening. Too bad the Dracule couldn't have collectively curled up and died.

He watched with measured concern. Would tensions be ratcheted up, or had Raquel just made a casual remark?

It seemed the latter as Massimo nodded. "Yes, I am, as far as I am aware, the last of my bloodline reborn," he said. "At least one other survives, my older sister, the Duchess of Florence. We've heard rumors we may have a sister between us in the Americas, but most of the old families of Italy have someone in the Americas. Why should vampires be different?"

Caleb couldn't be sure, and it certainly wasn't the time to ask, but he could have sworn Pavlos's expression faltered. Was it the reminder that his master, even if Massimo stayed in Venice, was running out of time? The conversations that weren't being had were outnumbering those that were.

Caleb turned his study to the Doge. They'd met briefly once before when Massimo had helped rescue friends in London from a Dracule trap. That hadn't been more than two years ago, so that Bruneli looked about the same didn't surprise. Then again, allowing for the Armani, he probably looked more or less the same two, three, or even four hundred years ago. Dark hair with flecks of gray at the temples, muscular build, intense eyes. He'd been turned later in life than most vamps, probably in his forties. As a mortal, he had likely been a man of some influence and power then. Younger hueys were easier to control as young vamps, and the advantage that the vitality of youth gave one in the hunt couldn't be denied. Maybe the perception of his being older by default had been the reason he'd maintained control of his region for such a ridiculously long time.

But it wasn't Massimo who was capturing all his attention.

Caleb, however, couldn't take his eyes off the Dogaressa. Portia was attractive in a bookish way, slender with laugh lines around her eyes. Pleasant looking, but not the type to inspire a centuries old vampire to give up his power and immortality for her. So what was her deal? Some undefinable air surrounded her, like a secret he couldn't uncover. Reports were that she was a huey woman who'd come to Italy on vacation and ended up betrothed to the vampire prince.

Most tourists just bought keychains.

What was it about this woman that would get a supernatural sovereign to trade his power, prestige, and immortality for a chance to live out a quiet huey life with *her*? Was she *that* good in bed?

"Your Excellency. Signora Dogaressa." The solari dipped his head. *Best behavior now,* Caleb internally chided himself. He needed the Doge to agree to take over his job, after all. "Thank you for welcoming us into your home."

Portia's expression balanced sour and sweet. "Please, no titles. Call me Portia if you don't mind. I know Pavlos is doing things the vampire way, but I have a feeling slayer etiquette isn't as rigid. Or at least, I'm really hoping so."

Caleb didn't miss the way Massimo's brow furrowed.

"My parents didn't get a chance to teach me, one way or the other." Caleb grinned, even as the traces of kindness turned as Portia lowered her gaze. "I was raised feral and can scrape my knuckles along the ground with the worst of them. But you're saying it's okay if I don't genuflect and kiss the back of your hand?"

The Dogaressa shrugged. "Not much for being bowed to, and my husband *is* a vampire. He might kill you if you tried to kiss me anywhere."

"And wouldn't that be an awkward way for us to kick things off?" Massimo stepped forward, offering a hand to the Solari. "Good to see you in good health, my friend. And Venice welcomes your retinue as well. You are all honored guests."

Honored guests that had to be shepherded in through the servant entrance, Caleb thought. Something wasn't following there. But any growing suspicions that there may be more at play here would have to wait until he had a better understanding of what.

Dropping Caleb's hand and having nodded to each of the women in turn, Massimo stepped back, gesturing at a table laden with food. "May we?"

He nodded. "Of course. Amy? Tina?" Caleb's right eyebrow arched. "Raquel?"

It wouldn't take a rocket scientist to know Raquel wouldn't appreciate the familiarity. But being as vampire royalty outranked a corporate chairperson in setting the tone, she only closed her eyes and mewed rather than attempting to shout down Caleb for such insolence.

Venice was going to be fun.

In short time, they had each taken a chair, relaxing into pleasant chitchat. At the head of the table, Massimo sat with perfect posture, one hand covering Portia's on the table, leaving the poor huey woman with only the other hand free to feed herself. Pavlos was the Doge's right-hand man, literally as well as figuratively.

Servants whisked in with trays, despite the amount already present, and gave each person their own plate.

Amy stayed mum for some time, watching the two vampires opposite, sampling from their portions while pushing her own around with a small spoon, before her curiosity got the better of her. She leaned over to Caleb and whispered. "I thought vamps couldn't eat food."

"*Don't* is a better term, but they still have tastebuds. In fact, huey food tasting parties were all the rage back in the day, from what my parents used to say."

Caleb dabbed his mouth with a linen napkin, wiping away traces of the black risotto, and dashed a look at Massimo just in time to see the vampire slide the tip of a fork from his mouth. He was unusually rigid for a creature normally composed of supernatural grace. In fact, if Caleb didn't know better, he'd have said their host was nervous. The undercurrent of tension that had walked into the room with him earlier was becoming more prominent.

"The residence of the palazzo has overwhelmed me in the best possible way, Your Excellency." Raquel proved that she could break the ice with the best of them. "Classic and a tribute to the city's style, and yet, updated in the areas where it best makes sense. My compliments to the lady of the home."

As a human, Portia could still blush with ease. "That's very nice of you to say, Miss Vega, but I'm afraid the only place in the palace I've done anything is in a music room on the fourth floor. I turned it into a painting studio. Everything else in the residence and in the royal court below..." she motioned to a pair of double doors, highly ornamented and colored over in black lacquered paint to resemble the top of a baby grand, behind the dining area, "... is all Massimo's doing."

"And therefore, *I* thank you, Signora de la Vega," the Doge took up. "Please feel free in your leisure time to explore the palazzo at length. Outside of our and Pavlos's private apartments, it is open to you. Also, in your honor, we have a ball planned for a week from tonight, a formal welcome to introduce the Slayer Solari as a guest of honor amongst us."

Caleb swallowed. His goal here was to get Massimo to agree to run off to Chicago and play CEO. That was going to throw the locals into disarray for a while, no matter how smoothly he went. He wasn't sure having all the vampires of Venice know his face was such a good idea.

"So, Caleb..." Portia took a sip of her wine. "White Whitman Labs. A company that creates products specifically for supes. That sounds quite... intriguing."

Caleb sliced into something that was either pork or beef but was definitely way too saucy and smelled like fish. "Yeah, well, you know. Underserved audience and the like."

"I guess so." Portia traded out the wine flute for a fork. "But I keep trying to figure out what that would mean. What kind of things do you guys actually make?"

He took a quick glance at Raquel, hoping she might take the statement and run with it, but no such luck. Her critical eyes were on Pavlos.

"Oh, you know," Caleb winged. "A little of this, a little of that. Light-weight modular weapon handles for hoods that work well for silver grafting."

That had been his ex's idea, and he'd hoped its rapid development would have wooed the red hood Geri Kline. Never mind that that made him an asshole because she was now happily married and had a kid. The point was moot, as all she said when he'd presented it to her—in person even—was *"thank you* and not *Oh my God, I was so wrong to break up with you and please take me back. You're the only one I've ever really loved."*

He shrugged. "I *think* Athenian glass is one of our biggest sellers. I don't really pay much attention to the numbers."

Amy set down her fork and steepled her hands. "Athenian glass," she start-ed, using an air of professionalism Caleb couldn't recall hearing her use, like, *ever*. "Accounts for half of WWL's off-the-huey-books revenue. Something that shields a vampire from the worst effects of the full sun while allowing them to enjoy daytime practically sells itself. But our second bestselling product the last two quarters has been a werewolf energy drink."

"Werewolf energy drink?" Massimo took a moment from cracking an oyster to look up in astonishment. "I've rarely met one of the creatures and found him lacking. If anything, a sedative might be more in order."

"Yeah, well, you probably have only seen them at night," Amy remarked. "And I'm willing to bet there's not many of them running around the halls of Venetian palaces to begin with, are there?"

What had suddenly gotten Amy's goat, with that sly undertone? Probably the fact that Massimo had referred to wolves as "creatures." Seeing as Amy's best friend was mated to a wolf and her goddaughter was half-wolf, she was quick to rise to the race's defense.

Caleb chewed slowly. How to step this back a bit to avoid further awkward-ness?

Luckily, Raquel came to the rescue before he could think of anything. "It's actually quite an ingenious solution to a problem I hadn't even been aware of," she said. "Most wolves live in suburban or rural locations, where their only opportunity for employment is in huey industries during the day. It's as difficult for them to work while the sun is up as it is for a huey to endure through the night. Doable but challenging. Because of their supernaturally enhanced metabolisms, however, most of the huey energy drinks had to be ingested in such great quantities that there were... other side effects."

Portia smirked. "Yeah, I know when I get too much caffeine, I get jittery."

Raquel clicked her tongue. "No, the caffeine wasn't the problem. In fact, most huey versions only have one-third the amount ours does. Even then, they might have gotten by on the mortal drink if not for their highly efficient bladders."

"I don't see how that…" Then understanding spread across the Dogaressa's face. "Oh. I think I get it. Seems that could be dangerous in human hands. How does a wolf go about buying it, then? I doubt it's something you can ship to a gas station. You're definitely *not* openly selling it on your website."

Portia had looked through WWL's website? Caleb made a mental note of that for later.

"Of course not," Amy snapped. "That would be a lawsuit waiting to happen if some huey like me drank it, not to mention kicking off a possible blood vendetta. I've learned that you supes really still embrace that kind of thing."

A truth Caleb could attest to all too well. Most of his adult life had been lived to avenge his parents' murders. So much so that now, with the task done, he wasn't sure what his purpose was anymore.

Suddenly, everything in his head felt way too serious. His throat tightened. His pulse ticked up. The vampires, those supersensitive oximeters they were, all dragged their eyes to him.

He had to pull the attention away from his mini-emotional crisis. What was the last thing Amy said? Oh, right! Lawsuits, not distributing. He could follow that.

"So how do we do it then?" he asked, maybe a *little* too rushed. "How do we make sure this thing only gets into the hands of wolves?"

"Actually…" Raquel paused a moment to take a sip of wine, smacking her lips in the wake. Was she purposefully being slow? "Miss Popowitz solved that problem."

All eyes turned to the blonde huey slurping up a particularly saucy line of pasta. Well, that worked. Amy dropped the fork and dotted a napkin to the sides of her mouth. Then, leaning forward on the table, she splayed the fingers of her right hand.

"So, you know how the public part of WWL, the one hueys buy stock in and stuff like that, is a pharmaceutical company? Well, I remembered my friend saying that the hoods have this database of all the werewolves and their own kind in the world. I figured there had to be a few of them that went to medical school.

Or at least, veterinary school."

Caleb pulled a face, and as he looked around the table, he saw that he wasn't the only one.

Immediately, Amy put up both her hands by her ears. "Whoa, *I* am *not* saying a werewolf is an animal and, therefore, has to go to a vet. I know they're sensitive about that *shhh*—" She blanched, and her mouth tightened. "*Stuff.* But they live out in the boonies, right? Which means some of them are farmers, and farmers need vets for their cows and chickens and... whatever animals you grow on a farm."

As each member of the party relaxed, except Portia, who, it seemed, didn't understand what had just happened, Amy continued, "Point being, my hunch was right. There were some wolves in jobs where they could write prescriptions. So we formulated a fruit-flavored and a mocha-flavored syrup with a concentrated time release stimulant and used WWL's huey pharmaceutical distribution channels to get the product out to authorized facilities. All a werewolf does is mix the syrup into their coffee or some other drink, and they get four to six hours of wakey-wakey juice. Not only does Klaw work great, but most of the time, insurance even picks up the tab."

"That's stupendous!" Massimo clapped twice before turning on Caleb. "Well done in securing such a capable second, Mr. Helsing. She is truly a credit to your team."

Caleb didn't miss the way that, like de la Vega, the Doge maintained formality. Massimo would have to adapt to being a little more personal when he became a human again. That, or become either a butler or a hotel concierge.

Speaking of which...

"So, Your Excellency..." Caleb cleared his throat. "You're probably wondering why we're here."

The Doge paused in pushing food around his plate. "Actually, I'm fairly certain that I know."

Pavlos clearly didn't. "You do?"

Not for the first time, Caleb had to wonder exactly what Amy had communicated to them before their arrival and if that had anything to do with how their presence was being given the downlow treatment. As his "capable second" and Geri Kline's best friend, she'd already known about the deal Massimo had made in London two years ago. In exchange for helping save the motley band of supernatural crusaders from a Dracule plot to entrap them, Geri would allow Massimo a draw of her adopted daughter's blood. Mina was an Illustrian, a rare child born of both wolf and slayer heritage. That adorable little half-cub's blood, it turned out, could cure vampirism and leave its imbiber human once more.

Geri had proven to be an expert negotiator by getting Massimo to agree to serve his first ten years back on the huey rolls in an advisory position to the slayers. Caleb was a lucky bastard that Geri had had the foresight. Or had she known even then that post-revenge Caleb would turn into a directionless manwhore who'd need a guiding hand?

In any case, as far as Caleb knew, Raquel wasn't in the loop, and there was no way he knew for Tina to be.

Massimo lifted his hand in his aide's direction. "It is a personal matter between me and the Solari." His polite smile faltered. "Mr. Helsing, perhaps we could discuss this in private later?" His dark eyes flicked in turn to his wife and to Pavlos.

Portia looked between her husband and their guest of honor with growing concern. "Solari?" she said. "What's that mean?"

Massimo pulled a bit of something tan and wet-looking off his fork before twirling it in the air. "It's a term for a slayer sovereign or chieftain. Seems Mr. Helsing has resurrected its use."

The Dogaressa tried to bury her emerging laugh into her chest. "Sovereign? That seems a bit of overkill, doesn't it? I mean, there's only him and Tina. *Miss Potsia*," she quickly corrected when Tina, who had been raised by vampires and very much expected to be treated like one, gave her a dirty look.

Caleb's own fork paused halfway to skewering something resembling a slice of chicken on a halved seashell. "I, um, didn't choose it. It was foisted on me by hood politics and the Reclaimed."

Portia's brow furrowed. "The Reclaimed?"

Tina, who had yet to eat a morsel on her plate, grabbed the glass of red wine in front of her. "Yes, the Reclaimed. The slayers like me, whom Caleb supposedly saved from Sultan Vlad's estate and since, has kept us warehoused in his Chicago glass castle."

"Warehoused?"

"Sultan Vlad?"

"Slayers?"

Caleb, Pavlos, and Portia's voices overlapped in a cacophony, but it was the last who drew everyone else's attention.

"You... do... know... about *slayers,* don't you?" Amy's question may have meant to sound gentle, but it was never considered not rude to put your hostess's ignorance on display.

Portia pushed herself away from the table but remained seated. Her eyes focused on her plate of half-eaten food. "I... *do.*" The word sounded more like a question. "But I thought they were all dead." She looked up at Caleb. "Well, all except you, of course."

"That's what I thought too for most of my life after my parents died," Caleb acknowledged, though truth be told, his thoughts were still on *warehoused.* Was that what it was called to pay out of your own expense accounts for a bunch of people you owed nothing to live in some of the priciest real estate on the magnificent mile? *How ingrateful.* "But when we were hunting Vlad Tepeş a few years ago, we discovered that the rumors about his private harem of slayers he and the Ravens used as livestock-slash-batteries were true."

"Livestock? Batteries?" Apparently, that hadn't cleared things up for the Dogaressa.

"Yeah, you know." Amy flicked her index finger over the table. "'Cause vamps die after five centuries, but they can keep going indefinitely if they have a steady supply of other supes' blood to live off of."

"Oh?" Something weird was happening to Portia's face. It managed to be both barn red and pale white at the same time. Her eyes looked up to Tina. "And you were one of these slayers held captive?"

"I was."

Tina's defensive tone made Caleb begin to see what Amy had been talking about.

"I see." Portia's hands flattened on the table. "And what, Mr. Helsing, does that have to do with why you're here?"

Uh-oh. *Mr. Helsing.* There was only one reason why a woman who'd told you to fuck protocol and call her by her familiar name reversed course. Because she was pissed off at you. Though, frankly, Caleb had no idea why she would be. *He* hadn't been the one keeping her in the dark. That had been her sainted husband. Though fat chance Caleb was going to start throwing down shade in that direction. Obviously, Massimo hadn't let his wife in on all of what went down in London, and fuck all if Caleb was going to piss off the man he needed to manipulate by spilling the beans.

But Portia was looking at him. Glaring, really, and he needed to say *something.* Putting two and two together on this one, if she had, would be like, well, putting two and two together. Whatever. That was Massimo's business. But it did seem weird you wouldn't tell your huey wife you'd brokered a deal specifically so you could grow old *together.*

"I... um." Caleb stammered. "I have... business... with your husband."

"Business that is obviously none of mine." Portia turned to the Doge. "If there's *something else* you need to discuss with the Solari, Massimo, I can leave."

All it took was the teeniest hint of *you've fucked up* for Massimo to show that being a centuries-old vampire prince gave you no advantage when you'd pissed off your wife.

"*Tesoro*, it's not that it's something private. It's that you and I haven't had a chance to discuss the details and full ramifications of this decision. It should be something we approach united, not because the Solari shows up."

"And yet, here he is." Portia pushed herself away from the table, all the way this time, and stood. "Caleb, Amy, Tina, and..." She paused, seeming to reach for the name, "Miss Vega, my apologies. I hope we have a chance to talk later when my husband isn't being so cloak and dagger."

Before any of them could manage to chart a response, the Dogaressa turned and left.

Caleb didn't have a chance to brainstorm his next words before Pavlos dropped an unused napkin on the table.

"I think," he said, rising as well. "That I will also take my leave, Your Excellency. It seems there are topics afoot to which I'm not privy." He took a step from the table and locked Amy in his gaze. "My compliments on your acumen and utility, Miss Popowitz. Mr. Helsing, it must be convenient having an assistant so versed in the minute details of your business."

Pavlos hadn't known? *Pavlos hadn't known?* Nerves about telling his wife that he was about to transfer teams and hit for the hueys was one thing. Massimo not telling his second, with whom he seemed on good terms, was another.

Caleb's eyes did a quick scan of the room, wondering how many bedrooms were in the Doge's private apartments and if any of them had a couch Massimo could sleep on come morning.

This thing was already going off the rails, and he hadn't even been here long enough for anything to be *on* the rails yet.

"*Dio...*" Alone on his side of the table, Massimo tapped his fingers on the tabletop. "That did not go as well as I may have hoped."

Tina leaned over the table. "And just what did you hope for?"

"For more than a day's warning before two slayers showed up at my door, perhaps?" Massimo smiled while laughing under his breath. Then, his face sobered. "There is... a certain *unease* in Venice at present. In several of the Italian courts, actually, that make the timing of your visit *inopportune.* Tensions are already high among our society, what with the rumor of slayers and maybe... *other things...* out in the world again."

Caleb met Amy's apprehensive gaze down the table. There were undercurrents here they didn't fully understand. Until he did, he wanted to keep this thing contained.

"Raquel, Tina, can Amy and I talk to the Doge alone?" he asked.

"The *huey* gets to stay?" Tina pushed herself away from the table but didn't rise. "If you're going to be alone with a senior vampire, *I* should be here to back you up."

Raquel, on the other hand, did stand, her hand cupping over Tina's shoulder and encouraging her to do the same.

"Miss Potsia." The chairperson balanced calmness and insistence with impressive measure. "I think you'll find that, when it comes to negotiating with royalty, Miss Popowitz is far more equipped to aide Mr. Helsing."

"Like hell. I was one of Sultan Vlad's *cariye...* one of his favorites. I was *raised* in a royal vampiric court!"

"You were a concubine and a blood slave brainwashed to see Tepeş as both god and father." This time Raquel's hand tightened with just enough force to make Amy wince. "Negotiation was not a skill you were allowed to develop."

"Tina, please." Caleb figured he'd better step in before his one-night stand blast from the past remembered she held the ability to lethally strike down either of the vampires in the room. "I promise I'll tell you what this is all about as soon as I can. But Raquel's right. I really need Amy here right now. This affects the company and everyone knows she's better than me at that stuff."

Tina crossed her arms over her chest. "She's not one of us, you know," she spat out. "She can never be the kind of woman you need. She's a stupid blonde bimbo and everybody knows it. Not to mention, she's a *human.*"

Caleb's fist balled as he felt the power of his weapon gathering. Even though it wouldn't have any mortal effect on a fellow slayer, it'd still hurt like hell.

For Tina.

He was pretty sure it would make him feel great.

But this wasn't the time or place to cause a scene for many reasons, not the least of which was that Caleb was pretty sure that unleashing a solarium here would turn that fancy chandelier into a pool of molten glass.

"Konstantina Potsia!" An undercurrent of rage boiled in his tone, but Caleb kept his voice steady and low. "As the Slayer Solari, I *command you* to leave now and not approach me until such time as I summon you again."

Both women before him blinked their confusion. Yeah, he'd done it. He played the "I am your supernatural superior, and you will obey my command" card for, like, the first time ever. Thing was, Caleb wasn't sure it was true. Tina may be two-thirds bitch, but she also had the potential to be one hell of a warrior.

If he trained her.

He should have trained her.

"Tina, come." Again, Raquel pulled at the female slayer's arm. "We can sit and talk. We've never really had a chance to do that."

This time, fortunately, the slayer capitulated.

Both of Amy's hands were flat on the table when Caleb turned back like she'd been about to jump up to her own defense before he'd gone all Boss Man. Caleb shook out his nerves, forcing the tension from his body. The blonde huey did too as Caleb took a seat.

The Doge hadn't moved an inch, still as the dead.

Fuck vampiric formality. No need to stand on protocol now that they were alone. "So what's really going on, Massimo? I expected you to come calling the second we won the Battle of the Tahquamenon. Geri made it sound like you wanted to go all Team Huey in London."

"As I said, there are... issues that have arisen. Ones I could not have anticipated." The Doge leaned back in his chair, his face growing somber. "Mr. Helsing... *Caleb*, I thank you for the services you have rendered and justice you have done on behalf of all supernatural beings alike, but we can consider my contribution to your success a debt paid. I renounce my claim to the Illustrian's blood. I will remain a vampire and, more importantly, in Venice, where I belong, as its ruler."

TWELVE

S ilence and Tina rarely kept company, and that was even more true when she was pissed off. She prided herself on always speaking her mind and held her opinions as superior to the other *cariye* in the harem. They had been brought there as children, sometimes even as young teens, and had had to learn the ways of their new home to *adapt* to it. Tina had been raised in Vlad's palace. She knew that that was expected, that that was forbidden, and that which was merely tolerated. She knew when to be obedient and when she could push for favor and, more importantly, power.

She knew the world around her and had felt comfortable in it and hadn't had a desire to leave.

Until Caleb had been pushed full-frontal into the harem one day and showed her there was a whole other way of life outside her own, one where slayers could be more than servants battling for a vampire's favor and used for their blood. They could be a force unto themselves. Further, as the last known male raised in slayer traditions and in command of his power, the title of Solari defaulted to Caleb. Eventually, he'd need to take a *Solara* to provide him a legacy. For over a year, she waited for him to pull his priorities in line and come claim her.

She was done with waiting.

"I'm telling you again, we shouldn't have left."

Raquel de la Vega was about five inches away from a painting, examining...
something in the background. For her part, Tina found the human-sized canvas
uninspired. The Renaissance woman standing in it had more angles than curves,
and the baby she held was, frankly, ugly. *Huey babies,* Tina thought. Everyone
knew they were hideous. Just because she'd never seen one in person was no
reason to doubt that.

"Your Solari commanded you to leave," Vega said without moving her gaze.
"True, you aren't a werewolf. There is no supernatural alpha's prerogative com-
pelling you to comply. Nonetheless, if you do indeed recognize Caleb's position
and his counterbalance to vampire authority, your only choice was to obey."

"I thought the whole point of his busting us out of the harem was that we
didn't have to *obey* anymore. That we would be free."

"Freedom is a fantasy," Vega sighed dismissively. "A concept only poets and
Americans believe in. Everyone obeys someone or something, whether they
know it or not."

Tina cocked a hip. "Yeah, and who do *you* obey?"

"It's *whom.* Or I suppose, in my case, what." The vampire showed a queer
grin as she turned Tina's direction. "I'm more concerned right now with *whom*
the Doge is acquiescing to. I thought it may be his new huey wife, but she
seemed as surprised about our business here as Pavlos."

"Pavlos?" Tina quirked her head to the side. "Not Mr. Katsaros? Is he your...
spouse?"

Tinges of embarrassment brightened her cheeks when Tina realized she
didn't have English vocabulary for relationship roles. Oh, she'd learned the ones
hueys used from watching their TV programs—boyfriend, husband, sweet-
heart, bae... Those didn't fit in with her understanding of vampires. Given their
long, long lives, vampires could form deeper bonds over centuries, not decades.
Sometimes with multiple lovers. Or sometimes, their entanglement skimmed
across the surface of their souls, being intimate without any intimacy.

Had the Doge's secretary and the chairperson of the board had either of those?

Straight-faced Vega gave little in the way of clarity. "We have history. In fact, you might say I'm part of the reason he is where he is today."

The slayer dressed down the vampire with her eyes. "*You're* the reason he's vice-Doge, or whatever?" She miffed. "I doubt that."

"You're wise to do so." Finally done with the painting, Raquel stood erect and began moving toward the wing of the residence where they both had been given guest suites. "If you truly wish to be the mother of the Solari's children someday, as I believe you do, you'll need to prove wiser still."

Ah, there it was. The vampire's pivot from obtuse to pinpoint. The slayer refused to cough up some kind of pitiful attempt at meekness. *No, I would never think myself worthy. I should be so lucky as to have Caleb's heart. I'm honored just to be here.* There was only one solari in the world, and he would have only one official mate. Tina planned to be that mate. Not only because she was the strongest among the women rescued from the harem but because she'd already seen enough of Caleb to know he wasn't man enough to be the solari without a tough female slayer behind him providing him a backbone.

As for love, who needed that when you had power?

The question before her now was why the vampire had introduced the thought between them. And if Vega was going to be blunt, so was she.

"Do you support my ambition?" Tina asked. She took a step forward, closing the space between them. "Will you back my campaign to become Solara and do your best to influence him to go my direction?"

"I may." One corner of Vega's mouth quirked. *She* took a step back. "From what I've learned, you may be the best suited among the Reclaimed to the task. That is why I asked Miss Popowitz to invite you along on this trip, to give me a better opportunity to measure your worth. Believe me... the task was *not* easy. I even had to break one of the Solari's edicts and... encourage her."

And why Vega had seized an opportunity now to talk with her alone. Also, Tina realized the vampire was extending her some trust by giving her an exploitable fact, or hadn't the chairperson just confirmed she'd enthralled Caleb's precious little pet? Implied it strongly, at least.

"But as for influence..." the vampire continued, tapering off. "I'm still learning what I can and cannot expect out of Mr. Helsing. And if you're to prove yourself worthy of him to any gain, he must first prove himself worthy of his position with us."

"As CEO of WWL?" Tina had overheard the gossip that the Board had brought down its collective foot, telling the Solari to shape up or be shipped off. "I can aid him in that."

Vega's eyebrows arched. "How?"

Both Tina's voice and her manners spoke of determination. "I'll start by finding out what's really happening in this court. There was more unsaid at dinner than said. The Doge mentioned something about '*other things.*'"

"I picked up on that too, but that could mean anything from a shakeup in huey compatriots to a downturn in the Venetian economy. This is a tourist town, and most of the vampires who live here avoid the complication of maintaining long-term bleeders by only eating off temporary residents."

"I don't think he would have mentioned anything so plebian as that," Tina said. "No, I think there's something more supernatural at work. And once I find out what it is, Caleb will understand the worth and capabilities I bring to the table."

Thirteen

O nce, and he couldn't exactly remember when, Caleb had watched a documentary about the Hindenburg disaster. He didn't remember a lot about the why or how that the film explained, but the image of that magnificent airship, the pride and promise of a generation of German engineers, bursting into a fireball and falling into pieces on the ground was one he'd never forgotten.

And that's exactly what his strategy looked like right now. A massive conflagration, his perfect plan to have all the benefits of being CEO of WWL without any of the work plummeting to the ground.

"We weren't exactly being magnanimous, Massimo." Caleb's teeth clenched only *a little* when he ground out the words.

What was he talking about, remain a vampire and stay in Venice? Did Massimo think he could pull off a supernatural version of paying it forward? *Be selfish like the gods-damned bloodsucker you are,* Caleb wanted to shout. That and a thousand more words, most of them four-lettered, longed to leap from his tongue. He somehow managed to bite back the worst of them and *tried* to sound professional.

He went on, "You helped get me and the others out of a tight spot back in London, but what went down wasn't charity. It was a transaction. We got rid of

Old Drac, but the bill's still unpaid. I can't have it getting around that I don't pay my debts."

Amy, as always, showed him up by being a fucking adult. "Hold on, Caleb. Let's hear what's going on first." She leaned forward on the table, her brow furrowed. It was a move he'd seen many times in negotiation with the women he'd pick up. It was the 'I think what you're laying down is bullshit, but I'm going to pretend I have deep sympathy to see if we both can still get what we want out of this' move. "You say there's been complications. What complications? Maybe Caleb or WWL can help."

With a heavy sigh, Massimo nodded. "As you may know, there are eight official Italian vampiric courts, though, in truth, only five centers of power remain. Florence, Rome, Naples, Milan, and my own Court here in Venice. The other three exist now only with proxy sovereigns who owe their allegiance to a higher seat. Bologna to Venice, Palermo to Naples, and Genoa, to Florence."

Amy's eyes scrolled to the ceiling. "And where does Sardinia fall?"

"Historically, it has existed as the supernatural equivalent of an autonomous region," Massimo said. "In any case, of the substates, Genoa has always been the most difficult to keep in the fold. Peace was managed only by way of marriage, and barely then. However, my blooded sister, the Duchess of Venice, recently lost her husband, the Prince of Genoa, to a royal challenge."

Caleb leaned back in his chair, lacing his hands over his stomach. "Well, obviously, *you* should go either kill that asshole or force him to cede to the Duchess."

Massimo's face remained flat. Emotionless. Poignant. In silence, the answer to the obvious question cried out.

The solari sat bolt upright. "Holy shit, *you* are that asshole, aren't you?"

"He was plotting to overthrow her court and plotted to destabilize mine and seize it as well," he said. "I assure you, his death was the best solution to the situation, though not without consequence. As I said earlier, Patria is also my bloodline sister. My *elder* sister. While I may have yet another fifty or even a hundred years, *she* may only have a few decades at best. No one doubts her capacity to rule, but her throne is only secure because I still sit on mine. I must remain in power until she's managed to make a new match, or at the very least, named a successor capable of maintaining peace. She was counting on her youthful husband to be that man, and he let us all down. She cannot meet the sun in good conscious without knowing that Florence is in good hands."

Meet the Sun. A nice vampire idiom for death. Hueys had their own and for the same reason. It didn't matter that vampires could live five centuries after being turned. Everything that could love feared losing.

Caleb's jaw tightened. "My sympathies for your sister's loss, but it isn't like all these things popped into existence yesterday. You were planning on leaving when you made the deal. You must have had some kind of exit strategy in mind."

"No one takes the throne without a plan for how to leave it with their head intact. No one wise, anyhow."

No doubt Massimo *was* wise. He'd been the ruling monarch through epochs of history.

"But I need more time to consolidate faith in my chosen successor as well, to make sure his foundation can hold up hers, if necessary. It shouldn't take more than..." the corners of his mouth dropped, and his right hand pancaked the air, "... a decade at most."

A decade? Not many years as vampires thought, but Caleb didn't even have a few months. He needed to impress the Board so they wouldn't vote him out immediately. But maybe if he couldn't guilt the Doge into his plan, he could manipulate his emotions another way.

"And what about the human you wanted to spend the rest of your days with?" Caleb asked. "You don't seem the two-timing or quick-to-love type, so I'm assuming you were talking about Portia. Doesn't your wife get a say?"

"Of course she 'gets a say,'" Massimo snapped back. "If Portia told me to walk naked into the sun until she said when, I would, but I haven't stayed in power this long without practicing a bit of *real politique*. The truth is, *she* is in greater danger than any of us. Anyone who wanted to threaten me could do so much easier through her injury. Do you not think I am more able to protect her as the vampire that I am now instead of becoming some weak human?" In a momentary display of guilt, Massimo bowed his eyes in Amy's direction. "No offense intended toward you, Miss Popowitz."

Caleb's eyes flashed Amy's direction, praying she wouldn't make one of her sarcastic quips and fuck everything up. Instead, the huey's face flatlined. She leaned back in her chair, slouching, putting her hands on the table, and twiddling her thumbs.

"None taken, Your Grace," she said. Then, sitting up, she stuck one index finger up in the air. "But counterpoint. If you *ceased* to be the Doge and a vampire, wouldn't you also *cease* to be a threat to anyone? Then, you know, since vampires think my kind are piss-poor weak and unthreatening, it might give both of you a chance to breathe a little easier at night." She lowered her hand and shrugged. "Or do whatever you want at night... as loudly as you want without worrying who's listening."

Shit. Was that taking it too far, or had Amy just earned her pay and then some?

Without moving his head, Caleb's gaze carried between the two, looking for a crack. Finally, it was Massimo who broke.

"That's... very true, Miss Popowitz. Only, when I struck the deal in London, I was drunk with love and only thinking of myself. I didn't consider the questions that would follow. A vampire of my notoriety suddenly rendered a huey once more." He let silence and contemplation have a space. "I believe Miss Kline is your friend, is she not?"

"She is my *best* friend." Amy's expression fell. "Mina is my goddaughter."

"And I would assume, therefore, that you hold the welfare of her ward in highest consideration." The Doge allowed a moment for her to object, knowing full well she couldn't. "Not all vampires have my honor," he continued. "Nor do all embrace the consequences of a supernatural existence. To protect the innocent, I am forced to accept reality."

The Doge rose, buttoning his sleek dinner jacket. "Now, if you'll forgive me, I need to find my wife and... what is it the hueys say, Miss Popowitz? *Grovel*?"

When they were alone, Caleb turned to Amy. "Do whatever you want at night?" He pivoted in his chair. "Amy, you can't just... *rib* supernatural royalty about their sex lives." Even if it had been a brilliant move.

"Why not? I constantly *rib* you."

"Yeah, well, I'm not royalty."

Amy's mouth dropped into her chest. "You *seriously* didn't just say that, did you?"

"I seriously just did." It didn't make a difference, and it wasn't the most important thing right now. "I never thought of the danger to Mina this deal with Massimo might have. He has a point there."

Amy crossed her arms and nodded. "It's a point. But it's a bullshit point."

"Amy! Do you kiss your mother with that mouth?"

"No, and *ew*." Her face screwed up. "What I mean is, unlike you, Massimo isn't a manwhore. I did the research... the dude has ruled Venice for centuries *alone*. Yeah, he had lovers but never a wife until Portia. I don't think he was so desperate to be human again willy-nilly. When he was trying to find ways for his mixed marriage to work, that must have seemed the most obvious solution to him, as dramatic as it was. Now, something's changed. Like you said, this situation with his sister didn't creep up out of nowhere. Patria de Medici is a queen bitch. No one's going to cross her."

Caleb cursed himself for underwriting Amy's insights. Maybe he should listen to her more. She wasn't half bad to listen to when she wasn't screeching demands from the end of his bed with a knife in her hands.

"Well, that's easy," he said. "Slayers are back, and things are out of balance."

"I thought the whole purpose of there being slayers was so things would be *in* balance."

Caleb shrugged. "Everyone except the Ravens assumed we'd gone the way of the dodo. It gave the vampires time to find a new kind of normalcy, one that didn't include us. If we want to be part of this world again, we're going to have to worm our way in."

"Yeah, but it's not like the Reclaimed are out there kicking asses and taking names," Amy countered. "Hell, *you* don't even do that." She bit her lip. He hated to admit it made her look adorable. "I feel like there's something else going on here we're not getting the 4-1-1 on."

"4-1-1?" English may be Caleb's second language, but one he spoke with near-native proficiency. That was, until he'd met Amy and couldn't understand what she said half the time.

"Yeah, the 4-1-1. The *information.* Information Massimo isn't dishing, that we're going to have to find out for ourselves." She stood. "I'm sure a few of my fellow humans here speak English or maybe even French. Hopefully, at least one is into chicks and thinks they might stand a chance with me."

"If your reputation has proceeded you, they'd all think that." Caleb quirked an eyebrow. "You'd use your body to manipulate people for information? Isn't that very anti-feminist of you?"

"Is it?" She shrugged. "Don't really care. In my opinion, as long as it's my choice, it's my prerogative. But speaking of using what your momma gave you..." A whimsical smile unfurled across Amy's face. "Portia seemed to have her eye on you on the boat ride over from the mainland."

The comment lingered in the air for a moment, more a question than an answer. Until, that was, Caleb put the clues together and felt his insides twist.

"No way, you... and I say this with respect... crazy bitch. I'm not going to try to seduce the wife of the very powerful vampire I'm here to—" He managed to cut himself off before giving away his plan. "Recruit into our cause to impress the board," he said instead.

"I'm not saying bone her, Helsing. I'm pretty sure the Board's impression of that wouldn't be great for you. All I'm saying is that you have a particular set of skills. Skills that make it very easy for a man like you to beguile a woman like her."

"Are you quoting Liam Neeson right now?"

"I don't think so," Amy said, neither admitting nor denying that she might have watched a certain set of movies he'd been on her for weeks to watch together that she called "stupid male fantasy fulfillment." "Look, you're a master womanizer. Use that ability for good for once and find out what she knows. And if Massimo catches you, I'll rise to your defense and say you're just like that with all women, that Portia is nothing special."

Caleb frowned. "Yeah, because *that* would go over well."

FOURTEEN

U nlike the huey from which they ascended, a vampire's power only increased with age. That was until they turned to stone without warning
one day. There was no predicting the exact moment it would happen. The only
indicator was time. Five centuries, give or take a decade or two on either side.
Massimo still had time before he fell into that window of his ultimate doom.
Until then, he grew increasingly strong, quick, and wise.

And despite this, he couldn't seem to catch up with his mortal wife fast
enough.

"Portia, please..."

She rounded with the surefootedness of an assassin, and her pointed finger a
blade pushed in the air in threat. "Don't you 'Portia, please' me," she said, her
tone more biting than her husband in the hunt. "How could you not tell me
there were other slayers besides Helsing? You said they all died!"

The Doge avoided her glare, training his eyes instead to the floor, his hands
folded before him. "There were *rumors* of captive slayers, and rumors only. I
cannot chase down every whisper that reaches these walls, and our kind have always spun such tales. By the time news reached Venice, confirming the rumors,
not only had Helsing and the others been freed..."

"You, what? Thought I might go chasing after them?" Portia leaned forward intently. She crossed her arms over her chest. "That I would leave my husband to go find him?"

An inkling of the thoughts that had plagued him just minutes before returned. "I think you mean *them*? Or does your interest in slayers extend only to the Solari?"

Her face flushed. "Seriously, Massimo? You think I have something going on with Caleb Helsing?"

"He is handsome, intelligent, and a well-known philanderer. And you went to meet them at the airport without letting anyone in the palace know."

She blanched. "You knew about that?"

"Portia, *nothing* happens in Venice involving dark ones without my eventual knowledge." Feeling more sure-footed suddenly, he shifted balance from one side to the other. "Helsing is a well-known rake, and you are a beautiful woman."

"I'm also your wife, and I only love *you*." Somehow, she managed to bend her tone to make the word sound like a curse. "Be serious, Massimo. You know how hurt I've been by others who've cheated on *me*. I would never inflict that kind of pain on you."

It was true. The very reason Portia had come to Venice when first they met was to distance herself from the wounds afflicted on her by her Canadian ex-husband. Still, Massimo wondered if there hadn't been some interest in his wife on the Solari's part and how the slayer may mete out that attraction. True, Portia was nearing the end of her reproductive years, but it wasn't as though he could say definitively that she, like other hueys, wouldn't be able to carry a child at this point. The fact that Helsing's legacy and his race could only be secured by his reproducing was the loudest unspoken fact he'd heard in some time. Who knew why he'd kept staring at Portia over dinner? That possibility couldn't be ignored.

Many moons had passed since the Doge had been jealous of anyone. Since discovering that an inceptor had been born, Massimo couldn't deny he'd watched the huey families in his city with a growing sense of envy. In other circumstances, he would have taken a moment to tell his wife that, for his part, he had wanted the inceptor's gift to allow them that chance. He wanted a child with Portia. But now, how could he drink the Illustrian's blood and be cured of vampirism? As a huey, how could he protect her from his enemies?

All considerations would be irrelevant if he managed to drive her away. Massimo knew what he had to do. As the hueys said, eat crow.

"I should have told you about the slayers. It is a truth that was not mine to withhold. I take your aspersion and make it my shame." He broke into what he hoped was a sheepish smile. "As for Helsing, I apologize for even implying it. Of course you would be curious about him. He is the first slayer you've ever seen."

"He and that horrible woman, that *Tina*." A momentary frown blew into a gentle smile. "I'm not a fool, Massimo. I know there are things that go on in Venice that you don't tell me. That, for whatever reason, you *can't* tell me. But why did you want to keep this, of all things, from me?" She narrowed his gaze. "Who is Caleb Helsing to you? What is this deal you have, and why was it so important for you to play nice with the CEO of WWL?"

"How did my sweet huey wife gain so much insight into court intrigues?"

Portia grinned. "I've watched *Game of Thrones* three times now."

He bit his lip, nodding. "You're right. There is something I've been hiding. A reason I was hoping Helsing would never show up at our door."

He mirrored his wife's act of a few moments before, taking her cheeks in his hands and pulling her in for a kiss. It renewed that promise, as did every kiss they had. But even as Massimo delighted in the feel of his wife's mouth on his, the truth nagged at him. For four centuries, he'd managed to keep this city in check, assuring the vampire population was protected from the radical elements of both their own kind and the hueys while also guaranteeing the mortals of the city were at no risk from his court's existence. He'd never doubted his ability to maintain that balance and keep all safe. Not until he had something that meant more to him than the city itself.

And that was why he should leave.

And that was why he couldn't.

Venice was more than a domain. It was a shield against his enemies. Actions had consequences. Even though he'd killed his sister's husband-by-law in rightful and legal combat, it didn't mean there wouldn't be those seeking vengeance. All these thoughts passed in a moment, the supernatural mind racing as it always did.

"Helsing isn't a vamp," he continued as he pulled away. "He can't enthrall you. But he's cunning and charming and could trick the information out of you. The slayers are not our enemy, but that doesn't make them our friends. Helsing is here because *he* wants something. And the deal I made with him?" He shook his head. "Once, I thought I needed help to protect you. But now, after seeing where Helsing prioritizes his time, I know any affiliation with him will only put *you* at greater peril. So the details of the deal don't matter because I have backed out. I will play host, as is my duty. And I do truly believe it must be known and welcomed that slayers have returned to take up their mantle and that I support them. But I don't want anyone out there who may come after me for it to catch you in the crossfire."

"Massimo, if all I wanted was protection, I would have asked you to enthrall me and make me forget everything. But what I want more is your support, to help me discover all about this world you live in and where my place in it lies. I accepted the risk of being..." she conjured her most ridiculously accented Italian. *"La Dogaressa, amatissima da Sua Eccellenza e consorte al trono!"*

She rumbled off her official title with a smile, which in turn made the Doge laugh. He stopped, however, when she drew his hands to her lips and kissed his knuckles.

"I know you'll do your best to protect me," she said. "But don't do it at the cost of my growth. No matter what I am to you, I exist within myself *first*. I'm still learning what that is, what my *nature* is."

His eyes cast to the floor. "I understand."

"Good." After a moment of silence between them, during which mountains could be lifted on the strength of their gaze, a coquettish expression turned up the corners of Portia's smile. "So speaking of enthralling... I don't suppose you'd be interested in... *convincing* me of something before going to bed this morning?"

"Convincing you of—" His words cut off as she rolled up on her tiptoes and began to suckle his earlobe.

Massimo didn't often use his supernatural abilities in his wife's presence. It put distance between them, reminded each of the imbalance in power and strength. But there was one trick he had which always succeeded in bringing them closer together.

Even if it involved a lot of screaming, and ultimately, a shower.

FIFTEEN

C aleb would credit Massimo and his house staff. The light-blocking curtains in his suite were primo. Unfortunately, as a supe whose nature was tied to the rising and setting of the sun, he didn't need his eyes to know when dawn hit. Sleep and he remained estranged despite his best efforts. Caleb wasn't sure if it was something inside the palace walls or out in the Venetian streets —*canals?*— but a high-frequency hum permeated the air, keeping him wide-eyed.

Or maybe it was just that it was a strange bed, and he thought the time in his life when he woke up in one of those had come and passed. Without a woman, anyway. His youth had been a circulation of houses and hovels, his parents dragging him from one city to the next, all trying to outrun detection. Truth be told, Zeynep and Moshe Helsing were slayers who rarely slayed. When you were the last assumed member of your species, you didn't draw attention to yourselves. He still had no idea how the Ravens had found his parents back in New York.

And if there was *anything* that was going to keep him from sleeping more than that infernal racket, it was turning over the events of that horrible day on Long Island when he watched their murder.

A few hours into the day, Caleb gave up. Maybe he could walk himself into sleep? It was worth a try and would leave less stains on the Doge's high-end sheets than the alternative.

Clinking silverware drew Caleb down the hallway towards the grand dining room, the site of his first failure of diplomacy. Familiar ground, he supposed. But unlike the first ill-fated meal, he found no human servants, no table full of amazing delicacies, no audience. Instead, the Dogaressa sat alone, wearing a navy blue sweatshirt with the letters UBC boldly stitched in white floss across the front.

His insides squirmed, remembering what Amy had suggested. Had she set this up? How would she be sure he'd be awake? Was Amy a witch? No, that was silly. Witches were a story supes told their children to scare them.

Portia took turns poking at a bowl of fruit before her with a fork in her left hand and gliding a pencil in a gentle arc across a sketchbook with her right. Her hair looked damp, her red locks glistening in the sun that streamed in from a window whose curtains had been pulled back.

"Um, hey?"

She was startled as Caleb made his presence known, and he again felt like a bastard.

"Oh, my God." Portia pushed a hand to her heart, the pencil falling to the table. A smile blossomed between pink cheeks as she attempted to recover. "Sorry. It's silly. I live with vampires, but I'll never get used to how you supes can sneak up on a girl."

He often forgot how silent his movements were to a huey, especially since he spent most of his time making them scream. *Not a thought to have right now, Helsing.* Portia was not a target of conquest. She was the wife of the man who could save his ass and keep him from being kicked out of the WWL penthouse.

"Yeah, Amy says she's going to sue me when eventually give her a heart attack." Which she could only do if he still had something left to win. "Sorry. I should have made some noise when I saw you alone and concentrating. I could have gone back up the hall and stomped my way back in." He motioned to the table. "Since I'm here, is it okay if I join you?"

"Of course." Portia shook off her nerves and motioned him to sit. "Would you like me to call the kitchen? Usually I just pick up myself something at the café down the street and bring it home to eat, but someone might be on duty there."

His eyes narrowed. "I'd have thought your kitchen had ten chefs, given the spread we had when we arrived."

Portia shrugged. "Massimo owns a couple of restaurants around town. They cater for us when needed. The kitchen here is more of a cafeteria for the huey staff, and, well, *me*, I guess. We weren't planning on serving breakfast for you and the others until sunset, but they can bring up some pastry if you're peckish."

The smile on his face appeared for a moment and it was gone. "No, thank you. I try not to eat past my bedtime. I just couldn't sleep."

The statement dripped into silence as Caleb wondered exactly which direction to go. It would help if he knew what the hell he was trying to find out. But then, he supposed, he wouldn't need to have a conversation at all if he already knew. If his goal was to get into her pants, his next move would be routine. Getting into a woman's *thoughts?* Not so much. "So, the Doge doesn't spend mornings with you before going to bed?"

"You mean Massimo, the four-hundred-year-old vampire?" Portia smiled. "Oh, we spent some *time* together," she said suggestively. "But no. Right after we were married, he'd stay up with me after sunrise. He'd sit right where you are now, poking at food and putting on a good show. Then I found out that vampires have a hard time digesting too much solid food after they're turned, that they really only *taste* things, not eat them." She shrugged delicately. "I told him 'til death do you part' didn't have to include breakfast."

"I bet going nocturnal has been a flip. Amy's almost got it down now, but I know for a fact she takes an hour nap in her office after her lunch break around one a.m." *And drinks more energy 'smoothies' each night than a long-haul trucker,* he added in his thoughts. As an espresso addict, however, Caleb couldn't really criticize. "Has it been hard for you?"

It seemed an innocent question, one that, for some reason, made Portia's eyes wide. "I expected it to be different for someone like me, but part way is as far as I've gotten."

He nodded before wondering aloud, "Someone... like you?"

"You know, a huey."

Did Portia think Amy had been raised as a squirrel? Whatever the case, Caleb didn't miss that she was avoiding his gaze. A classic sign that she was being less than honest, if not outright lying.

"I'm a creature of habit," Portia went on, bringing her eyes back. "I'll be up until about noon today, then sleep until an hour or two after sunset. I usually spend the mornings in my studio. I suppose it's just like any painter who works into the wee hours, just flipped."

"So you're an artist." Had he known that? Was it important? Why was it so hard to have a conversation with a woman when the goal wasn't to get into her pants?

"I mean, not professionally. I dabble. But whoever said you had to make something you love your profession?"

A crude observation he heard once played in his thoughts. *Whores never fuck for love.*

"Still," Caleb cut in, picking at the threads of the conversation. "As a huey, you must miss the daytime. It's my first time in Venice, but I spent a little time in Tuscany once. The art and architecture seem to be a giant collective frame to accentuate the beauty of sunlight."

"But a slayer can carry the sunlight into the night, can't he?"

Something nagged at him. An elusive hunch that there was *something* she was trying to say without actually saying it. Caleb studied Portia like he was trying to see past her.

"Not carry it," Caleb clarified. "More like *summon* it from... I don't know, the ether maybe. Things get fuzzy when you try to explain supernatural abilities with science. When I make a solarium, it just feels like I'm *pulling* the sunlight through me, not creating it."

"Oh, I guess that makes sense." Her eyes lost their brightness. For a few moments, the Dogaressa went silent, working a pencil over her paper, until finally, she said without looking up, "So about what happened at dinner..."

"Yeah, about that." Caleb rubbed the back of his neck. "I'm not sure what that all was between you and Massimo. I'm sorry if what I said or even showing up here caused a fight between you."

"It did, but that doesn't make it your fault. Anyway," she batted the air with an open palm. "Don't worry about it. We kissed and made up."

He threw up his hands. "That's none of my business. I just hope you don't think I was... well, being a dick."

She blinked at his words. "Being a dick?" Just about the time Caleb was readying a barrage of apologies for being crude, she smiled. "I guess slayers aren't all prim and proper like vampires, ey?"

"Hard to say." He side-eyed her while squelching down a play at innuendo that was practically his conditioned response. "I've never known any other slayers except my parents. At least until we rescued the Reclaimed. *They* were indoctrinated by vampires to be proper, but I'm doing my best to be a bad example and lead them into temptation."

"Massimo says you don't lead others into temptation as much as organizing safaris to it."

Ah, so his reputation *had* preceded him. "I'm not shy and reserved if that's what he means."

"We both know precisely what he meant," she said. "And I find that... *very interesting.*"

The coquettish smile Portia flashed his way stirred his insides. *All right, all right, all right.* Only then did reality slap his animal brain and make him realize something. He was forcing himself to be on his best behavior because he really did like having his arms attached to his body. But the Dogaressa was flirting with *him.*

"Caleb?" Her big brown eyes glistened. She batted her eyelashes. "Is that true?"

For some reason, he felt the need to sit up straighter. He put his hands flat on the table and changed the subject. "We were surprised to see you at the airport."

Oh, that turned the tide. Suddenly, Portia's eyes were anywhere but on him. She sucked in her bottom lip. "Yeah, well..." A pause while she drew up a story, no doubt. "We were going to send one of the huey servants out to meet you, but I was awake, and that seemed really impersonal for welcoming the Slayer Solari."

"I thought you said you don't get up until an hour or two after sunset. We arrived in the late afternoon."

He studied her features, seeing the tale-tell signs—increasing pulse, a tick up in her breathing. She was lying about something, and she knew she'd been caught.

She gave a half-hearted laugh. "I did say that, didn't I?"

"And then at dinner, when I almost mentioned it, you gave me a look that said, 'I don't want my husband to know about this.'" Caleb leaned forward, weaving his hands together and setting them on the table. "I don't know if you know this yet, Portia, but vampires can tell when you're lying. There're certain physiological changes in a huey that give all but the most skilled away. If there's something you don't want to tell me, fine. But if there's something you're trying to keep from your husband. Well... he's not psychic, but he's going to figure out you're hiding something."

"I *am* hiding something, but not from Massimo. He already knows."

That only left one possibility as far as Caleb could see. "Then there's something *you* want to tell me that he's asked you not to."

She said nothing. Silence, in this case, meant yes.

He nodded, swallowed, and sat back in his chair. "Well, I guess that means we both are keeping one of your husband's secrets from each other."

Tit, meet tat.

But if Caleb expected the tease to get Portia to open up, he was sorely mistaken. Instead, she grinned like the cat that got the cream. "*My* husband," she started, extra accent on *my*. "Has ruled Venice for almost four centuries. You honestly don't think I assume he has many secrets I don't know about, do you?"

She stood, taking her sketchpad and a cup of coffee with her, leaving behind the pencil and her empty plate dotted with crumbs.

SIXTEEN

J ust because she'd been a prisoner all her life didn't mean Tina was without
an education. She knew Venice had once been a world power in the region.
But as she walked its streets and crossed over its canals, its only power seemed
to be an echo that drew in tourists and inspired the imagination to wonder of
ancient times.

The morning air held a chill and carried the scents of fish, coffee, and
fresh-baked pastries. Cobblestone paths slick with dew led away into an
ever-narrowing of bridges and paths. On occasion and without warning, one
would open into a brilliant but small courtyard of sorts, a conjunction of
different roads where, in ancient times, markets and meetings took place. It was
both like and unlike the Istanbul she grew up in. Much smaller in scale, and yet
obviously bearing the evidence of ancient imperial wealth and power.

Eventually, through twisting and turning, her feet brought her to a main
thoroughfare. Despite the early hour, men dressed in black pants and wearing striped shirts tended long, narrow boats magnificently decorated, holding
carved wood furniture and velvet textures. A sign gave a price for a ride both in
English and Italian. Exorbitant, but luckily, she knew from Amy's orientation
before they left that the little piece of plastic she'd been issued had sufficient

funds to back it up. In a city where the streets were made of water, a boat would be the quickest way of getting around and looking for any supernaturally suspicious behavior.

"*Buongiorno, Signorina*." The slender man of medium build tipped a white straw hat as she walked up. "*Como stai?*"

He must have thought she was Italian. Her Ionian ancestry may have been responsible for that. Genetically, the peoples of the Mediterranean basin varied little from one another. Tina may have been a slayer raised in Istanbul, but she most certainly wasn't American.

She pulled the plastic from her pocket and looked at the little symbol on the back, matching it with one on the sign. "I want to take a ride. Do you accept this as payment?"

"Of course, Signorina." The accent was heavy, but the words were crisp and, thankfully, English. He leaped atop the bow of his boat, catlike in his grace and balance. "At the kiosk over there, you pay. Then, I take you."

She followed with her eyes as he pointed at a tiny building just large enough to shelter one person in a seated position. The sign on the window gave prices in Euro. Portia presented the piece of plastic when asked and signed a slip of paper, then made her way back to the dock.

"Am I good now?" She held up a receipt.

The gondolier nodded and offered out a hand. "*Prego.*"

No sooner had Tina lifted her foot to step on than the boat bobbed, pushed by the wake from a passing motorboat. Suddenly, a vision of tipping, of being submerged in the water flooded her thoughts. Tina pulled the lapels of her coat together, backing a step or two.

The gondolier grinned. "Signorina, I am an excellent swimmer. If you were to fall, I would save you." Then, smiling, he held out his hand as if to invite her. "And if you like, we take the smaller canals. Not as deep, maybe even you touch the bottom if you fall out."

With no small amount of embarrassment, she confessed she'd prefer that, even if he had probably meant it as a joke.

They glided along, the gentle push of the boat combining with the sunrise to relax her. She was a creature of the night. Even with the time change, she *should* be sleeping now. But if she was going to find out what was happening in Venice and prove her worth the Caleb, she couldn't waste time.

"Your first time in Venice?"

"My first time anywhere that isn't home."

A smile brimmed across her face. *The first of many places,* Tina thought. As queen to the Solari, no doubt she'd be able to travel widely. She wanted to see all those places she'd only read about. China, India, Brazil, Australia... Well, maybe Australia could wait. Even for a supe, there were animals in that part of the world that put her off her tea.

"The city agrees with you, Signora." The gondolier used his full range of muscles to push at the long stick he had in his hands. The boat banked in the opposite direction of his movements, leading to a smaller canal than the one in which she'd boarded. "I can see how you smile."

"Your city is very beautiful." *Istanbul puts it to shame.* "But that's not why I'm smiling."

He smirked, straightening their course. "There is a man," he concluded. "Or perhaps, a woman."

"Man."

Tina wanted no doubt about that. In the harem, very strict rules dictated the knowledge of the flesh among women. Even though the female Reclaimed had been permitted socialization, including romance, with their male counterparts, their bodies were for service to the Ravens. There had been no female Ravens during Tina's time in the harem. In America, she'd discovered that most people accepted what had once been forbidden to her, but long-ingrained dangers of displeasing her lords still lingered.

"Do you love him?"

Her whole body tensed. "*That's* very personal."

Rather than be rebuffed by her tone, the gondolier let out a single laugh. "Not to an Italian man. We live and die for love."

"It must be difficult to pay your debts, then."

Tina settled back in her seat. She liked Caleb. Liked what they had done together during their tryst in Istanbul. But love? That sort of thing only existed in books and movies. Real relationships were built off shared ambitions and values.

"No, I don't *love* him," she finally said. "Love is a power transfer, and how can you ever be someone's equal if they hold power over you through *love*? I would be the best decision for him. He may be the only decision for me. Our... *family* needs us to be strong to survive."

"You have some kind of family business, no?"

It was as good a way of describing the current state of the slayer community as any. For over a year, Caleb had neglected his duty to his people. He kept them safe and comfortable, but slayers weren't meant to live in gilded cages. They were meant to hunt and destroy evil vampires. They were no closer to living out their natures than they'd been the day they were "rescued" from the harem. True, Caleb helped awaken the male slayers' abilities and managed to destroy a swimming pool in the process, but beyond that, he'd done nothing for his people but feed and clothe them.

In some ways, he was worse than the Ravens. At least with them, the Reclaimed had purpose. With Caleb, they were just being shelved. She would end that when she was queen. Tina would make the Solari fulfill his role as the leader of their community, and slayers would take their rightful place in the world again.

"We do. One that will not thrive if my *man* doesn't get his act together."

Ahead, another gondola approached, its hull lacquered and shiny, but its interior done up in creams and golds. The man who stood atop it tipped his hat at Tina's own gondolier. The two exchanged a few amicable words in what Tina assumed was Italian before the latter man dropped his smile and looked down at her.

It was only a momentary locking of eyes as the gondola listed ever so slightly. A glance as the other boat passed, but that was all it took.

Suddenly, she felt knotted in her skin, like hands were squeezing her. Chest tight, air fled from her lungs. Tina's pulse spiked, her ears rang, her teeth clenched. Somehow, she managed to reach out and wrap her hands around the edges of the boat as though it could steady her.

But it couldn't, could it? It was on water, not solid ground. And if she stood and tried to center her senses, she'd fall out into the canal.

She couldn't even swim.

"That's very pragmatic, Signorina." The gondolier spoke as though he didn't notice she'd just turned into a spooked cat. "And encouraging."

"Encouraging?" Tina fought against her body and its sudden panic. She was being irrational. The gondolier had told her he could swim, right? Surely, he wouldn't let a paying customer drown.

The slayer buried her chin into her chest, pulling a deep breath and exhaling as she slowly brought up her eyes. Something was different now. Their direction had changed. She did agree to smaller canals. But this one? It was too small. Too isolated. Too off the beaten—*rowed?*—path.

"Where are we going?"

Only silence in return. She steadied herself, ready to stand, even knowing she might tilt out. They'd left the canals. She looked up to see a stone ceiling overhead and saw an archway behind her. They were *inside*, even though they were still on the water.

Tina left caution behind. She shot to her feet for a second, then collapsed, her legs folded under her, as the boat rocked beneath her.

"Where are we?"

Any explanation she may have hoped for was lost the moment the gondolier sprang lithely from his perch on the back of the boat and onto a platform leading to a set of stairs. It took only a few moments for him to be out of sight and for Tina to find herself alone.

Tiny waves made their way in from the canal, lapping both the side of the boat and the masonry work of the dock surrounding it. Somewhere, dripping water added to the soundscape.

The air here was different from the outside. Musty, yes, and one would expect that in an internal cavity half-filled with water. But it was more than that. It smelled like a dead animal may be near and a garden. One that bloomed with sweet, fragrant blossoms.

Maybe this was a typical part of the trip, she thought. Maybe this was the gondolier's home, and he'd just realized he'd forgotten his phone or wanted to kiss his lover good morning. Would it be inappropriate to follow the way he went, assuming she had the right?

Tina's hands hooked over the side of the gondola as she gingerly sat, then leaned, ever so cautiously, over the edge. Maybe she could gain perspective, see into the stairwell, get some clue.

And then it happened.

The water rose up to meet her.

Heart racing, hands flailing, Tina's feet peddled, trying to find purchase. No such luck. There was nothing but water. Water and water and water... and a hand.

Pulling her under.

SEVENTEEN

C aleb had just turned up in the hall, his attention focused on getting back to his room and getting some damned shuteye, when he spotted Amy coming from the opposite direction.

She looked different in Italy. More refined somehow. Elegant. Sophisticated. All things she failed to be as she came to step next to him... and belched.

Just as quickly as the sound had erupted, she lashed her hands over a face that had turned red. "Oh my God, that was gross."

"Barbie?" He wasn't about to tell her that, as a supernatural being with a better-than-human sense of smell, she had no idea how true a statement that was. "You sick?"

"Whatever we ate when we got here yesterday. It's... not agreeing with me." Even though her face strained with effort, another croak bubbled up her throat. "In fact, I think it's filing a formal complaint."

"We could ask someone if there's an apothecary nearby."

"Nobody says apothecary, Caleb. Not unless they're playing D&D." She dropped her hands. "So, I just got done talking to a few fellow hueys I found being all *servantry*."

"Wow, that was quick." He took a few steps back in the search for cleaner air.

"Find out anything?"

"Only that Massimo and his senior staff are, like, six layers of bureaucracy above them," she said, moving her hands in a stacking motion. "They said they see Portia sometimes, but only when she's grabbing something out of the kitchen. They said she's very nice. Asks about their families and all that. Apparently, she *loves* seeing pictures of their kids."

Did it suggest that the Dogaressa, a woman who certainly caught the eye but had to be in the sunset of her baby-making part of life, was living vicariously through others? If so, *that* could be a way to woo her to his side of the argument. Surely Massimo wouldn't object to having a rugrat or two before it was too late?

But it wasn't the slam dunk he was hoping for. "That's not much to go on, is it?"

"No. Did you get anything out of her?"

Caleb shook his head. "Not really. She confirmed there's something she's not telling me, but she seemed kind of proud of the fact." Suddenly, he realized something. "Wait, Amy, how did you know I saw and spoke with Portia? And why aren't you surprised to see me asleep? You know how hard it is for me to stay up after dawn."

Especially since he didn't have access to his espresso machine here, surely the kitchen had one. Something to investigate tonight when he awoke.

A devilish grin overcame the blonde huey's face. She reached into her pocket and pulled out a tiny remote. "Let's just say I *bugged* your room when you weren't looking. Or, technically, I had one of the maids do it. Is that rude, calling someone a maid?"

"You..." No. He refused to believe it. "What? Why?"

"Because I knew what I said got into your head. I also know that, if you can't sleep, you stroll. As for knowing Portia would be up too..." She shrugged. "Call that huey intuition." Just at that moment, a rumble permeated the air. Amy's face screwed up. "Okay, I think I need to go now."

"Part of me wants to say this is what you deserve for doing something so devious. But seriously, Amy, it's nothing to be embarrassed about. Text Pavlos and ask him if there's anyone who can grab you some medicine. Maybe it would even give you a chance to ask *him* a few questions."

"You want me to parlay a request for a couple plop-plop-fizz-fizzes into espionage?" She laced her arms over her stomach as a low rumble turned into an awkward gurgle. "No, just for... *so many* reasons."

He shoved his hands into his pockets. "Did you at least get some sleep?"

She let go of her stomach, and her face relaxed. The spasm must have passed. "The only thing that sucks more than being the only huey in our little group and having to adjust to being nocturnal is being the only huey in our little group and having to adjust to being nocturnal *and* jetlagged."

"Not well, then."

"No, and not just because of my stomach or the time shift." Amy crossed her arms. "Looks like my room is next to the royal suite. Or should I say... *sounds* like it? FYI... if Massimo and Portia did have a fight, they made up. They made up... at least *three* times. I guess they figured the *huey* wouldn't hear all the moans and mattress bouncing, but you'd have to be deaf not to hear Portia when she... you know."

"Lucky you. A room and a show. I'd say the Doge is doing his duty to the crown, but vampires aren't fertile that way."

"Yeah? Try telling him that. He did his *duty* for her at least four times."

"Four?" Caleb shrugged. "Every man has an off night once in a while."

Amy's mouth dropped. "Four is a *low* number?"

"Oh, Amy, it hurts my heart that you even have to ask that." He turned to her, serious eyes contrasting with the hard-to-contain smirk. "*Super*-natural, remember? That doesn't just stop with the five senses. Maybe you should pick up one of the vamps in the accounting department for a night. See how high he can get *your* numbers."

Amy crossed her arms over her chest. "You do realize, if WWL was a huey corporation, I could sue your ass into the pavement for sexual harassment, right?"

He did. Thank the gods it *wasn't* a huey corporation. At least, not the part of it he controlled. At the same time, he'd *never* banter with most women this way. But Amy was... well, *Amy*. His assistant. His ex-girlfriend's bestie. The woman who was saving his ass on a daily basis. He needed her in this part of his life to get to the next.

Caleb dropped his eyes. "I'm sorry. I was out of line."

"I accept your apology." She let her arms drop. "This time."

On that note, Amy let out a grunt and walked away. Three steps, anyway, before turning back and looking over her shoulder.

"Really, four times?"

Caleb shrugged. "I usually shoot for a five-to-one ratio myself, but you know... married couples."

Her face went wide, but she said nothing back. Alone, Caleb finally felt the day wearing on him. Maybe if he was quiet and was willing to sacrifice one of his socks, he could find some sleep after all.

EIGHTEEN

T ina coughed, then gasped as she broke the surface. Her limbs felt like jelly, and her insides seemed to be experiencing a seismic event. Was that adrenaline or the effects of being submerged? As a slayer, she avoided water whenever possible. Her showers were quick in-and-out affairs. The only time she'd swam in a pool had been alone in the WWL building before Caleb's effort to awaken the male Reclaimed had destroyed it.

This was no swimming pool. Slowly, her surroundings took shape. She was still at the boat dock, but the doorway that connected it with the outside world had been closed. The waters around her shifted and spilled, no doubt in response to her struggling. But struggling against what? Tina looked around and saw... nothing.

But there *had* been a hand woven through her hair and keeping her head below water just a moment before, before Tina had managed to press her feet down and discover bottom, pushing herself to stand, her head and shoulders above the waterline.

"I am behind you."

She spun, and though she was certain there had been no one there before, now a woman, both sodden and sullen, stood in the water beside her, shoulders just breaking the surface. Her skin was the same earthen tone of the buildings along the canal, something between tan and pink. Bright blue eyes looked out from behind a curtain of long, straight black hair that stuck to the sides of her face. She wore a white sleeveless tee, the saturation rendering the cloth translucent enough for the peaks of pert breasts, bobbing just above the water line, to create dark circles. She held both hands up, showing them to be empty.

"Peace, I bear you no ill intent."

"What in the hell..." Tina hacked another cough and took a step back, "... were you trying to do then, give me a bath?"

"I was holding you underwater long enough to neutralize your powers and give us a chance to talk."

Neutralize her powers? This wet waif knew, then, that Tina was a slayer. How? She wasn't a vampire. Tina would have sensed it standing this closely.

Tina shivered, her skin turning to gooseflesh. "You should know, I'm the intended of the Slayer Solari. You fuck with me, you're dead."

A hint of a cocky grin ticked up the corner of the waif's mouth. "Threats do not become you, Konstantina."

Tina froze. "You know my name?"

Instantly her mind went to work. Who in Venice could possibly have that information? Someone who overheard the others call her by name their brief time in the airport? A huey in service of the Doge? There *had* been servants at dinner the previous night. But how could a huey be strong enough to hold her underwater? And would a huey know at all that that was a slayer's weakness?

The mysterious woman pressed on. "I only have a small space of time to relay a message."

"Okay, so we're not talking about how you know my name, then?" Tina asked. "A message from whom?"

"The children of the sun are few in number," the waif went on, ignoring the question. "But not as few as you think. You must seek them out and build Aten's army once more."

"Right. Got it." She didn't. This time when Tina spoke, she put some backbone into her tone. "And back to *how* do you know my name?"

The pale woman took half a step back. "I was told by one who knows."

"No kidding. And that would be..."

The other woman tilted her head, regarding Tina like a curious cat with a mouse. "Does the Solari truly wish to be a champion of your kind?"

In any other circumstance, that question might not hold context. "Why would Caleb have done that if he didn't intend to help us reclaim our proper place in the world?"

A ghostly smile crawled across the woman's face, and for the first time, Tina noticed something she hadn't before. A sore on her head, barely buried in her hairline. The blood around it had matted the hair and dried as a gluttonous, dark purple mass that even the canal water hadn't washed away.

"Good." Her gums looked unnaturally pale. "The path before him grows thick with barbs. He will need you more than he knows."

"Need me?" Tina pushed her thumb into her chest.

The woman's expression flat-lined. "Not *you specifically*. The collective you."

Tina tried not to be disappointed, then refused to be. She was still part of the community, wasn't she? In the end, the fact remained that Caleb would eventually need to claim a partner, and *she* was the only one he'd ever shown any interest in.

"Seek the other slayers," the waif continued. "Endeavor to find them all. Only then can we push forward into battle together."

"And who are we fighting exactly?"

But before any answer could come, the woman began to back away, each step taking her toward the boathouse doors. "Each ray is precious and necessary. The Doge hides his from the Solari's gaze. The Solari must free her from her captivity."

"Captivity?" Tina stepped forward. The water was rising now, both on Tina and on the woman backing away. She couldn't go much further without her feet not finding purchase, assuming it continued to go down. "If there's a slayer to be freed, tell me who. I will free them."

"She is kept in a cage made of gold and marble. Bring her to the water's edge, and the goddess will send her warriors to aid in her freedom." Pale hands with dark blue nails reached up to anchor on the garage doors. "I have given you the message. My time and purpose here are done."

"What are you.... no, wait! Don't go. Tell me—"

But it was too late. The woman's head sunk beneath the water. A moment more, and she was gone.

Shivering in her soaked clothing, Tina considered her next steps in a very literal way. Follow where the woman had seemingly swum, and she could definitely get out, but would she get carried away? Tina had no idea of the type of currents the canals of Venice had. She could get back into the gondola still bobbing nearby on the water. Its operation didn't look too complex. Maybe she could head up the way the gondolier had gone and see if she could get back into the cobblestoned streets that way. But the city was such a warren of bridges and alleys, how could she find her way back to the Doge's Palazzo?

Steps coming down the stairs arrested her thoughts.

Tina spun, meeting the wide eyes of the gondolier as he came back into view.

"*Signorina!*" He pulled the little black slip of a cap he wore from his head and wrung it in his hands once before throwing it down and rushing to the edge of the dock. He dropped to his knees, outstretching a hand. "What happened? Are you okay?"

"I'm fine." But it wasn't like she was going to refuse his help. She paddled over, deeper into the cave, and took his hand. "Where did you go?"

His eyes went wide, even as he pulled her with both hands up onto the stones. He began to look around. "I do not know where we are."

Tina bit her tongue. For some reason, she didn't think he was playing. He was honestly clueless. He'd been manipulated somehow, and a woman who'd been raised in service of vampires could recognize the signs of a man enthralled.

"It doesn't matter," Tina said. "I need to get back to where you picked me up quickly. I know how to get back to where I'm staying from there. Can you take me back?"

"Of course, *Signorina*. I am so sorry. I do not know how this happened. Getting you back is the very least I can do."

Nineteen

M assimo Brunelli was in a pickle, and the method of extrication was *most* uncertain.

Honestly, he was only partially certain he understood what that phrase even meant. The saying was one of many he'd recently picked up from Portia. Even if it was true that the Doge had been in his position for the better part of four centuries and that no vampire got invited out to coffee by another without his ability to ascertain the details, he'd admit he'd lost track of many huey idiosyncrasies through the years. For example... how did one get *in* the pickle, let alone out of it?

Pavlos knocked on the door with efficiency, a triplet of taps perfectly spaced. "Enter."

Being immortal was not being immutable. One might freeze physically in a moment of existence, but that did not mean they could not wear the worries and welcomes of the day in their visage. Pavlos appeared harried as he assumed the room. Unkempt hair and a wrinkled dress shirt. No suit jacket and his tie, present, but badly tied. Vampires could not get bloodshot eyes, but they could lack shine.

Despite presenting so, his second assumed the manners of his station. He closed the door behind him before bending at the waist and bowing his head in reverence.

"Your Grace," Pavlos straightened but kept his eyes trained on the floor. "Before the business you've summoned me to discuss, I first wanted to offer my apologies for my behavior last night. I shouldn't have shown such disrespect, especially in front of guests."

When he'd been shorter in the tooth, Massimo would have punished such insolence without remorse. In the ceiling of his gathering room was a moon portal that could be opened during the day as well, the result, a beam of sunlight in which the offender would stand and bake for whatever length of time met his offense. These days, Massimo didn't see the point in such theatrics. Corporal punishment didn't embolden his throne. More so, it gave him away as petty. In Pavlos's case, it would also damage the man who would assume its power soon enough.

The Doge set down his pen. "All is forgiven. And yet..." with a slide of his hand through the air, he invited his second to take the seat across from the sovereign's desk, "... the fact that you left in so dramatic a fashion leads me to believe you know why the slayers are here."

"I'm not certain I *knew*." A flicker of a smile lit Pavlos's face before he reigned in his expression. "I *suspected*, Your Grace, that you invited them here in some effort to vacate your throne."

"Vacate my throne?" This time, it was Massimo's wry smile that flitted away. "Did you think I'd give myself to the sun when I'm so newly married and so happily?"

"No, which is why I thought longer on the matter." Pavlos scooted to the edge of his chair. "I thought you had changed your mind on drinking the Illustrian's blood. That you no longer wished to be rendered human again."

"My *wish* for it has not changed, but the practicality of it has."

Silence bloomed until Pavlos made a motion with his hands, inviting Massimo to expound.

"Since the moment Vlad Tepeş told me the birth of an Illustrian was imminent, I have dreamed of the life I could give Portia if I somehow obtained its blood. Of the life I could have *with* her. Perhaps even a life we would *make* between us. But I was only thinking of myself. I never considered the greater ramifications."

"Such as?"

"I can't be the only one of our kind who ever had the desire to step back across the crimson line." Massimo rose then, crossing to a window that looked over the smaller canals bracing the palace. "We say 'the Illustrian' as though it's 'the dog' or 'the book.' She's not a thing, Pav. She's a sweet, innocent child who would be hunted, caged, and milked by those less honorable than I. And with her adopted family being who they are, that would trigger an all-out war in the supernatural world. We came too close to that when the Dracule tried to seize control, and Vlad Tepeş was a megalomaniac, his justifications weak and self-serving. If the Red Hoods raised their banner with werewolves at their side and waged war on vampires..." Massimo visibly shuddered. "I can not stomach being the catalyst of such an event.

"I agree that... how would you phrase it? *Regression,* perhaps? That *it* could expose the Illustrian's existence if it is done while you're still in the public eye." Pavlos joined his sovereign at the window. "Maybe the simplest solution is the best."

Massimo's face screwed up. "Keep my throne and enjoy the time I have with my wife, watching her grow old alone and knowing that any day without warning may be my last?"

Pavlos's face screwed up. "When you put it that way, it makes me wonder what difference your becoming mortal again would make." He straightened out his smile when Massimo shot him daggers. "But, no, I don't mean that. You once told me the only way you'd leave the throne of Venice would be by force, either losing in battle or to time. Maybe there's a third path... retire."

"Retire?" The Doge coughed a laugh. "Don't be silly. Vampiric sovereigns don't just *step away* from their crowns."

"Inga Rosethorn did when she ruled Venice before you under the name of

Luciana."

"She didn't *retire*. She was *overthrown*." By Massimo himself, with help from a powerful vampire and an infamous wolfsretter known to history as Red Riding Hood, but that was beside the point. "Or are you suggesting you'd be willing to overthrow me?"

"Assume the throne, *not* overthrow."

Was... Pavlos endorsing a transition? Any time before now that Massimo had suggested making a formal declaration, his second had demurred. "There's still so much I have yet to teach you."

"And there is yet much for me to learn." Pavlos sobered. He turned to his sovereign, held his hands behind his back, and nodded once. "But what better way to learn than by doing? I am ready."

"Are you?" Massimo cocked a hip. "True, you are older now than when I took the throne in 1687. But the courts are the most unstable they've been since the Consolidation Agreement of 1902 . A society is an ocean, and its tides are always rising and falling. I have always captained Venice as my one true love. Do you feel prepared to do the same?"

"As my one true love?" Pavlos shook his head.

Because his successor's one true love wasn't a city. It was a woman. One who would never be his to claim because she too, held a throne, and their official union would start a war.

"But I will dedicate my heart, body, and soul to Venice's keeping," Pavlos continued. "And once you are no longer the sovereign and living away from Venetian eyes, no one will notice if you start going gray or get a little flabby around the edges."

"I still plan on maintaining an intense physical course of exercise." He did have a wife's pleasure to see to, and without the ability to enthrall her into utter ecstasy, he'd need to rely on more mundane ways of making her body perform.

It was a challenge he was eager to take.

"But I fear any open loop will invite investigation," Massimo continued. "For a truly peaceful transition of power, I need to serve out my term, to die in office."

"Perhaps you only need to *appear* to die, Your Excellency."

Was Pavlos suggesting what Massimo thought he was? Fake his own death? True, when a vampire went into the sunset of natural causes, the body turned to stone, stone which in turn would turn to ash if exposed to direct sunlight. There would be no question if his body could not be accepted as proof. The mechanics of the plan came together at once in Massimo's thoughts. Only... it would mean deceiving Portia. She wasn't so good of a liar as to outwit vampires.

But surely, she'd forgive the ruse when the truth of what his lies bought them became apparent, would she not?

"The Dogaressa..." Pavlos said, snapping Massimo out of his reverie. "Did you tell her of the deal made in London?"

A smile cracked across the Doge's face. Of course Pavlos's thoughts would walk the same path as his own. "No. I had intended to last night, but she *was* more upset to learn that I kept the discovery of the other slayers from her. Once I smoothed that field... well, there were consequences which distracted me from proceeding." Warm, wet, fleshy consequences. "But now, if I *am* going to consider taking up Helsing on his offer..."

In the canal below, a motorboat, slow but steady, passed the palazzo. Its ripples were tiny, but there were still many lapping licks when they hit either side of the passage.

"My enemies are few, but they must all believe me dead. And Portia... she has many skills, but dishonesty is not one." Massimo flexed his hands, cracking knuckles. "And there is also the *other* issue with which we've been dealing."

Pavlos nodded into his chest. "I had wondered if that was why Helsing was coming when Miss Popowitz reached out to me. 'An urgent matter,' she called it. I've done my best to keep the discovery of the exsanguinated bodies under wraps, but I don't know what kind of intelligence network WWL or Hesling has developed. But if not the bodies, why do you think he appeared so suddenly to press you into seeing through a deal in which he is the debtor?"

The answer came to the tip of Massimo's tongue in a hurry, but he held it back. "What are your thoughts?"

His second straightened, chin pitched to the side, eyes scanning empty air. It was a credit to his wisdom that Pavlos didn't rush to answer, instead taking time to pace out the possible ramifications of either choice. More evidence that when the time came, Massimo was leaving his city in good hands.

Finally, after contemplation, Pavlos made one quick nod. "If the slayers are to ever be accepted among our kind again, then we must have trust. Otherwise, they will only be seen as an infection which must be culled from *le corpe vampirique.*"

"That's a term I've not heard in an age." Massimo cocked his head to the side. "Now tell me the argument for *not* telling Helsing."

Pavlos answered without hesitation this time. "In truth, we do not know the Solari's intentions for his people, or more importantly, his ability to be a leader to them at all. We might empower his position, only to have it usurped by an underling with more vengeful intentions. Any truth that strengthens their numbers could, in turn, strengthen any force they'd bring against us."

"Certainly, there would be some understanding if some of the Reclaimed see *all* vampires as evil," Massimo agreed. "Now liberated, will they see us as merely an oppressor caste to be conquered?"

"Your thought, Your Excellency?"

"My thoughts are... still coming together on the issue," Massimo said quite honestly. "It is the reason, however, that the female slayer is here. I asked Miss Popowitz to include in their party the one who she believes the most loyal to her Dracule captors. I was curious to know of their mindset."

"The Stockholm effect?"

Massimo shook his head. "It's deeper than that. Did you see how she lashed out at Helsing over dinner? How she demeaned Miss Popowitz, who, despite being huey, seems a steadying hand in Helsing's administration? I credit Helsing in putting down the insolence quickly and firmly, but I'm not certain it would have worked as well without Miss Vega's persuasion and ability to reaffirm his authority."

Pavlos buried a laugh into his shoulder. "Yes, Raquel can be *quite* persuasive."

This time it was Massimo who grinned. "You have a history with her."

"You might say she is the reason I am here today."

Massimo watched as memory clouded the other vampire's features. The expression that straightened his face suggested not all of it was pleasant. He wouldn't delve. If there was something Pavlos thought Massimo needed to know, he'd tell him. If not... well, there were plenty of secrets the Doge kept in his own pocket as well. For the moment, that was—as Portia would say—neither here nor there.

"I will discuss this matter with the Dogaressa in the morning to learn in general her thoughts," he said. "Needless to say, even if she seems amenable, I'll need to inform her that I've decided not to pursue the matter. Meanwhile, you and I will conjure up a way in which the matter can be resolved with as little trauma to our court or our persons as possible. Now, with all that settled, perhaps we can—"

He threw back his head and huffed as Pavlos's mobile device pinged. "If I wasn't immortal, the past few years would have aged me. Surely, this is the worst of it. "

"Sir, have you ever heard the phrase, don't invite trouble, because it always accepts?"

Massimo's head swung up to see his second staring at his phone. "What is it now?"

Pavlos lifted an expressionless gaze. "Trouble."

TWENTY

In the evening, Amy and Caleb met in his suite, which, in addition to a monstrous canopied bed, included a private balcony overlooking one of Venice's midsized waterways.

"It's a shame we're not here on vacation," he absently said as they sat around a small round table, he sipping espresso and she sucking down some kind of probiotic grass thing that smelled and looked like compost. "I'd like to see how many would fit comfortably in that thing." He tipped his head in the direction of the bed

"I swear, all you ever think about is sex."

"Not true," Caleb shot back. "Just now, I was thinking how beautiful it is when the moonlight catches your hair that way."

"I'm not sleeping with you either."

"Come on, Amy. What happens in Venice stays in—"

His next words were halted as he shouted, *"Get back!"*

They shot to their feet, the espresso launching off the balcony as Caleb moved so quickly, Amy almost followed the arc of it as he shoved her back protectively. The tension lasted only a moment, however, when they both saw Raquel de la Vega reform from a cloud of smoke into her customary tight-assed self.

At least she'd ditched the power suit since they'd arrived. What she wore couldn't quite be called casual, but the black slacks and loose-fitted, billowy white blouse would do.

"Raquel." Caleb snapped twin solaria that had sprouted and hovered over his upturned palms. He turned, making sure Amy was okay. "You know, you might knock."

"I considered it, then I decided against it." She crossed to them, leaning against the frame of the balcony door. "I wanted to ask if either of you have seen or heard from Miss Potsia since last evening."

Ah, yes, there was another reason his evening had been delightfully quiet and pleasant, wasn't there?

"The last time I saw Tina was when she left dinner with you," Amy said.

"Likewise," Caleb added, turning up his Rolex to read the time. "I did tell her to remain in her suite until I told her she could leave. Maybe she's there, sulking. Did you try ringing her cell?"

"More than that, I tried pinging its GPS coordinates." The chairperson shook her head. "I'm not getting a response. I loath to admit my concern, but still, I *am* concerned."

Suddenly, so was Caleb. If there was any of the Reclaimed he knew well enough to know they could go off half-cocked, it was the leggy Greek. Caleb was still busy figuring out how he'd get Massimo to change his mind and come to the States to save his ass. That would be harder if Tina went out and toasted a few members of his court in some kind of "Don't tell me what to do" show of bravado.

"Okay, well, the first thing we have to remember is that just because her phone is dead doesn't mean she is," he said and turned to Amy. "Any ideas?"

"We could try *looking* for her." They were simple words, stated by Amy in a way that she might use with simple people. "Venice isn't that big of a city. We might be able to find her just walking around."

"Unless she doesn't want to be found," Raquel suggested. "Or unless she's left the city altogether. Or she *is* dead, possibly eaten."

Amy threw up her hands. "She's *not* dead. And she would never leave the city without Caleb. In her mind, the two are practically already engaged."

Both the slayer and vampire went wide-eyed, gawking at the blonde huey.

"Hey, don't blame me," Amy said. "Blame Mr. Couldn't-keep-it-in-his-pants here."

"I was *literally* being held prisoner by Dracula, and he was *literally* threatening to start killing slayers if I didn't sleep with one of them. Vlad wanted to be a Grandpapa in the worst way."

"Yeah, but did it have to be Tina?" Amy said. "The one with the biggest ego?"

"She volunteered! What did you want me to do, rape Keiko or Mahal?"

Raquel stepped in, both literally and figuratively, putting herself between them. "This bickering is not going to help us find Constantina," she said. When they managed to bite their tongues, she dropped her arms. "Now, let's think logically. A member of our party is missing. She may be out in the city, twisted in its web of canals and courtyards, or she may even be somewhere here in the palace. Either way, the best thing we can do is reach out to Pavlos."

"Yeah, but doesn't that make us look incompetent?" Caleb questioned. "Or, more importantly, me? If I can't keep track of one slayer, how is the Board going to believe I can keep track of twenty-one of them?"

"It's going to make you look more incompetent if you don't ask for help when you really need it," Amy cut in.

Raquel nodded. "Miss Popowitz is right. Particularly if Pavlos can help us to quickly remedy this situation, in which case, no one in Chicago need ever know it happened. But for that to happen, we must speak with him openly and immediately."

No sooner had the words left Raquel's mouth than there was a tapping on Caleb's chamber door.

Amy obviously wouldn't have a clue who might be beyond the wooden edifice. A huey without supernatural abilities, her perception of the world was limited to subpar senses. But when Caleb looked at Raquel, a vampire who could hear and smell better than him, if not exceed his senses in every way, and she merely shrugged, he felt the need to conjure a small solarium in one hand behind his back as a precaution.

"Um... come in?"

The door swung fully open in moments. In its frame, Pavlos bowed before taking a few steps inside.

"Damn, that was fast," Amy said. "Speak of the devil, and he appears."

The secretary's face screwed up. "The devil, Miss Popowitz?"

Obviously not a phrase the vampire was familiar with.

"Don't worry about the silly huey." Caleb stepped forward. "Mr. Katsaros, excellent timing. We were just going to try to reach out to you. We need your help."

"And I shall be happy to give it," Pavlos returned, bending briefly at the waist before jerking back up. "But first, *we* need *yours*. His Excellency would like to request your presence in the kitchen."

That was the last place Caleb would expect to have a meet up with a vampire prince. Unless Amy's snooping with the staff involved the need to sanitize some surfaces.

The buxom blonde took a possibly offensive position, being the first to ask, "The kitchen? Why? What is it?"

Pavlos frowned. "We thought the walk-in refrigeration unit was the best place to put the body for the moment."

TWENTY-ONE

A ll the tension in his body left the moment he saw the cadaver's face. *Not Tina.* It still niggled at him where his supposed clan member? Packling? What was the appropriate term for a member of the slayer community under his purview? His whatever had just galloped away without a word to anyone.

That would have to wait, however. For the moment, Caleb needed to find out why the vampiric sovereign of Venice wanted him to consult about a huey corpse.

"I'm not really sure what I can contribute," Caleb said, shrugging his shoulders. "I don't have any credentials that qualify me to examine dead bodies. My work has been mostly with living ones."

On that, he had exceeding qualifications.

Massimo dipped his head. "Your efforts are appreciated, nonetheless." He looked around the room, his eyes focusing on the hall Caleb had just emerged from. "Is Miss Potsia not joining us?"

"*Miss Potsia* needed some air. You know how women are." Caleb had learned from experience to lie to vampires by *not* lying to them. Instead, you told tangential truths. "She *should* be back soon." Hopefully, that *wasn't* a lie. "I've asked Amy to join us instead. I hope that's okay."

Like Amy was going to let herself not be a part of this. As soon as Pavlos had left the room, giving the guests a few minutes to freshen up before making their way to the kitchens, she'd practically bounced on her heels. "This trip is finally getting interesting! A mystery, a body, court intrigues?"

Caleb had lowered his head to his steepled fingers. "Amy, there's no court intrigue. And only you would think this is entertaining."

"Are you kidding? It's like an Agatha Christie novel, only with vampires and better clothes!"

In the present, Massimo shook his head. "I intended that your assistant be present as well. She has proven herself quite resourceful beyond her mortal status." His gaze narrowed in on the huey. "Do you recognize this woman, Miss Popowitz?"

Amy's face screwed up. "No, why would I?"

Massimo's expression shifted to one of disappointment. Caleb didn't have a chance to ask why before Raquel interrupted.

"Do the local police often release bodies to you without question?" The chairperson asked as she finished a finite examination that had been done without a single touch of the corpse. Her body hovered over the victim's surface, her eyes fixed on the pale flesh as she spoke.

Across the table, Massimo grimaced. "No, but they do release some to us with *many* questions," he said. "Whenever a death cannot be explained away in a manner the huey mind appreciates, they call Pavlos. As you might expect, we maintain communication with trusted select members of the human authority."

Raquel stood, her hands laced behind her back. "And they trust you not to mete out justice if one of your own is to blame?"

"A member of my court in good standing has not killed a huey in this city in over fifty years. But the occasional tourist with extra teeth, shall we say, thinks he can have a bit of sport while vacationing. In those rare cases, I have dealt with the scourge with haste."

Raquel seemed satisfied, though if it was the words or the tone, Caleb couldn't say.

"I don't know that I can add much to this situation either," the chairperson said. "I concur, The death appears to be supernatural. Although I am not a physician and do not know all the ways a human can die, I've never heard of one of their kind that suffered exsanguination naturally."

"You mean... drained of all blood?" Amy's gulp was audible, even without supernatural hearing. "I thought you guys didn't do that. That you only needed a few mouthfuls at a feeding."

Pavlos's features softened. "That is true, Miss Popowitz. There's simply too much blood in the average adult body for us to consume. However, some of our kind feed in groups, in which case, it's been known to occur." His chin cupped in his balled-up right hand, he nodded and stepped forward. "But that's not the case here. There are no fang marks, let alone the type of violent rending of flesh that would be required for a body to be emptied simply by bleeding out. In fact, I wonder how it looks so *appropriately* plump."

Amy huffed. "Are you seriously body-shaming a corpse?"

Caleb's fingers flexed as he hoped that the vampire side-eyeing his assistant didn't take offense. Luckily, a moment later, Massimo used his authority to make things certain.

"He wasn't trying to offend, but the deceased's condition isn't consistent with what we would expect to find," the Doge said. "When a human body is pulled from the canal, even when the victim died by natural means, the corpse becomes bloated beyond recognition. This woman is simultaneously lacking bodily fluids while also being remarkably unchanged after floating for hours in seawater. It's like she passed away after somehow giving up all her blood and then decided to go for a swim moments before she was pulled out. Not only that, but this is the third body this month to be sent to us in such a condition."

"I would say we have very odd serial killer on the loose, except I'm not certain this woman *was* murdered or if she simply expired." Pavlos leaned down over the body, looking intently at the dead woman's face. "One also has to wonder if, perhaps, this woman was supernatural herself."

Something happened at that moment, one that left Caleb confused. All three vampires stood up straight, shared a look that seemed to say, "well, you know what we must do," and then lashed their eyes all in different directions. It reminded him of the time he was briefly in a public school in New York City, and the kids who didn't want to be called on to write the answer on the board became spontaneously interested in the Famous Mathematician posters on the wall or the words etched into their desks.

That left Caleb playing the role of teacher. "Mr. Katsaros," he said, not picking a favorite so much as picking the one who he could most afford to have pissed off at him. "Is there a way to tell if a body is a supe?"

"There is, only..." Pavlos's face curdled. "While we need and thrive on living blood, a vampire does not necessarily appreciate the taste of flesh. The only time we do it habitually is as part of the rebirthing process, and the flesh is that of our maker."

"Oh? Oh." Even the Solari's stomach gurgled at that notion. "Huey's skin *tastes* different than a supe's, then. And to tell you'd need to..."

"Take a bite out of her, yes." For once, Raquel couldn't force stoicism. Caleb swore he heard her suppressing a gag. "I'm certain the authorities would not appreciate us handing back the body with more damage than we received it."

"Jesus, you guys make things so complicated." Amy stepped forward, pushing one of her perfectly manicured red fingernails into the dead girl's chest. She fixed Pavlos in her sites. "If you can't see what killed her on the *outside*, then obviously, you should have a look at her *inside*."

"*Inside*?" Pavlos shook his head. "We don't have the facilities for that sort of examination. Besides, I'm certain an autopsy will be the huey's next move, and they will tell us if they find anything that requires attention."

"The previous two bodies proved inconclusive, but as the proverbial saying goes, perhaps the third time is the charm. But I believe Miss Popowitz wasn't suggesting anything to do with a scalpel," Massimo said. "I think she is implying that one of us should *smoke* ourselves in and inspect the corpse from that perspective."

Raquel threw her head back and chuckled. "It's one thing to speed through the ducting system of the WWL Building. Human capillaries are an entirely different matter. We'd explode a body if we made the attempt."

Amy cocked a hip, arms crossing over her chest. "Do I look exploded to you?"

"You don't mean to say that a vampire journeyed *inside* you?" Raquel blinked.

Amy's nod and tone was all business. "That's exactly what I'm saying, and I don't mean in a fun way."

Caleb wouldn't have said it in the current circumstances. He thought it, but he wouldn't *say* it.

Amy went on. "It's how I found out about vampires. One of the Ravens smoked into my lungs and tried to suffocate me. Hell of an introduction, I tell you that much."

Pavlos shook his head. "If this is an ability our kind has, it is not one I know of and certainly not one I can perform."

"It's something that's gone out of fashion these days but entirely possible," Massimo said. "Like the Hoods no longer blood-claim silver by running it through their veins, as it's seen as too difficult and unappealing a task. Only the most skilled and powerful among us can achieve the feat without entirely desecrating the body." He stepped forward. "I believe I can manage it."

News Caleb welcomed, even if the concept threw him for a loop. "Do you, like, have eyes when you're smoke? I can't help but remember the Groucho Marx line, 'Outside of a dog, a book is man's best friend. Inside a dog, it's too dark to see.'"

All three vampires sneered, obviously not fans of early Hollywood humor. Or maybe it was the comparison to dogs that they didn't like.

"I will attempt to be quick," the Doge continued. "But I will need to exercise caution. As Miss Vega said, I'm likely to crack the body open from the inside if I do not. As a precaution, I would advise all of you to stand back."

The Doge took time to remove his jacket, then his dress shirt, and then his shoes.

"I thought your clothes just kinda magically traveled with you when you guys became smoke," Amy said.

Obviously, Caleb wasn't the only one wondering how far this strip show would go.

"They do." Massimo didn't stop to look at the blonde huey as he undid the button holding his slacks up. "That doesn't mean they don't pick up odors or sometimes even physical particulate as we travel. This suit was far too expensive for me to carry it along."

As he pulled down the zipper, giving everyone present the knowledge to swear in a notarized affidavit that in the boxers versus briefs debate, Massimo was completely Italian, Amy gasped. Hell, even Caleb, who considered himself straight as a razor blade, had to admire —maybe even slightly be envious of?— the view. The Dogaressa was a lucky woman.

Finally, left only in socks, a banana hammock, and a pure white undershirt, Massimo nodded once to Pavlos as though handing off power in his absence. For a moment, nothing happened. The Doge stood with arms akimbo, his eyes fixed on some spot in the middle distance. Then, as though a cloak was being thrown over him from behind, the edges of his form went fuzzy, then semi-transparent, dissolving into a gray-black cloud of smoke. Massimo's formless entity funneled forward, the cloud gathering over the corpse like a thunderclap, before extending a straw-thin trio of fingers that channeled into the body through the victim's mouth and two nostrils.

The others grew silent. What was there to say? In Caleb's opinion, a lot. He'd seen vampires take their smoke form on the regular. It had never occurred to him to think about it too much, however. Suddenly his mind was filled with questions. Could a smoke vamp feel pain? Be killed by a wooden stake? Perform an enthrallment? Another time, he'd need to fill in this serious hole in his knowledge if he was ever going to be the greatest slayer who'd ever lived.

And he did want that, didn't he?

Oddly enough, Raquel began to talk... to Amy. "It's upsetting for you to see this."

"Um, no, not really." The blonde huey shook her head, even though her eyes remained fixed on the corpse as though she expected the young woman to sit up and start playing pattycake. "I mean, of course this makes me remember... *vividly*... what happened to me. But I'm blocking it out. I don't let my past control me."

Any further conversation ended as the miasma circling over the corpse began to lift, thickening as the Doge withdrew himself.

Then, what happened next happened way too quickly.

Massimo reformed, his body prostrate on the ground, coughing. Pavlos flew to his side as Caleb called out. Amy went suddenly white and fell limp into Raquel's arms. The Doge's secretary leaned over, preparing to help his ruler to his feet when it happened. A heavy, single thud of a heartbeat that hadn't been there before.

At first, Caleb thought it might be coming from the corpse because it certainly couldn't be coming from the vampire. But when a second, strained *lub-dub* clashed with the rhythm of those in the room inflicted with a pulse, it became all too clear to whom it belonged.

The Doge.

TWENTY-TWO

M assimo would have liked to say that it was the first time he'd smoked into some poor huey's body. In truth, it was the third. But it was true that it was the first time the person had already been dead when he'd done so.

The other two soon after were, by design. It was a horrific way to die, a punishment visited only on his worst enemies. Barbaric in its approach and gruesome in its execution.

The slayer had asked Massimo if he could see while smoke. He could. He could also see quite clearly while solid. Helsing was after something. The position he was in, the Solari should be a monolithic figure amongst supes. But since doing his part to defeat Vlad Tepeş and his allies, Helsing had petered away his influence and power in self-indulgence and retraction. With the boldness the slayer had shown in London, Massimo would have sworn Helsing would have proven to be a natural-born leader. In the end, perhaps he'd merely been trying to do then the same thing he reportedly did now, impress females to woo them.

"Your Grace?" Pavlos remained frozen, his hand unstretched but unseized. The two words seemed to be as much "May I help you?" as "What the fuck was that?"

Massimo, eyes wide, face flush, buried his chin in his chest. He shook his head.

To what? Pavlos's offer of aid? To the fact that he'd just felt his own blood warm in his veins for the first time in over four hundred years. To the possibility that it could be happening at all?

A deep breath in, a deep breath out, and just as suddenly as it started, it was over. Massimo rose, his face again pale, his shoulders square. The pulse he felt in his chest... gone.

Pavlos backed away before extending his hand and giving two quick snaps. From seemingly nowhere, two men dressed in gray suits stepped forward. The palace guards. They had been instructed to remain outside the kitchens and only to emerge if called upon.

"The Dogaressa is out about in the city. Find her at once and summon her home. His grace is..."

"No!" Even with no pulse to race, Massimo felt his metaphorical heart leap into his throat. "Do no such thing. And swear to secrecy about what you've seen! Breathe a word, and I'll see you meet the sun."

His guards knew well enough to know that Massimo did not make idle threats. A man didn't stay in power for centuries by not carrying out the occasional dark promise. The two men nodded, aggressively even, before being dismissed from the room.

The Doge accepted Pavlos's pull to help himself to his feet. But now that that matter was dealt with, Helsing couldn't hold his tongue. "Okay, so..." The Solari stepped forward, an index finger pointed in the air. "What in the hell just happened?"

Massimo ignored him. He turned his tongue to Italian. "Pavlos, advise the *polizia* that we will *not* be giving the body back. She was a vampire in life. Inside, I could scent it." How her body did not turn to ash in the sunlight despite floating in the waters near the city, he knew not. "I want it taken from the city and burned immediately. Offer our assistance if they need aid erasing the edges of her disappearance from any huey's mind."

Apparently, Helsing was not a man given to being overlooked. "Sorry, but are you planning on talking to me, or should I go back to my room and wait for a memo? Also, are you going to tell us what you saw and why you wanted us here to see it to begin with?"

But Miss Popowitz proved once again that, while the physical inferior of everyone else in the room, her mind could compete. "He wanted to see our reaction to the body," she said, more to the room at large than anyone in particular.

Her voice was raspy, her breathing shallow. She hadn't fainted, it turned out. Only lost her wits for a second. PTSD? If so, she should have therapy back home. He'd need to mention it to Helsing, who was either too blind or too close to see the truth of how overwhelmed the poor huey had been.

Amy went on, "You know... if we recognized her. To see if we had slayers spies out in the city in secret. Since I'm a huey, he'd be able to tell if I was lying when he asked if I recognized it."

If this blonde huey was not already associated with the Reclaimed, Massimo would make a serious bid to woo her into his administration. She'd make a fine vampire.

"Slayer spies?" Helsing blew a raspberry. "Why in the world would we be spying on Venice?"

"Because he has a secret he's hiding from us." Again, the huey could see what the slayer could not. "Remember, he said this is the third body they found like this. Then we just happen to reach out out of the blue? He wanted to see if we were coming here to clean up a mess or cause one."

Massimo flattened his expression as he turned. "It was a possibility. Not one I gave much weight to, but now one I can dismiss wholly." He decided to distract any resentment or accusation that admission could brew by turning back to the elephant in the room. "Let me tell you what I saw inside. At first, nothing, absent the absence of blood, seemed unusual. She hasn't the superfluous mammary glands one would expect to see in a werewolf, and I couldn't perceive any presence of silver, as would be found with a hood."

At first, when he'd tasted gold, he thought the corpse may have been a slayer. Massimo prayed she wasn't. *That* would bring about several questions he was either unable or unwilling to answer. The only other thing he knew of that would have gold in its insides would be a vampire, one who'd been attacked by the substance. Though the reaction wasn't as intense as when a werewolf touched silver, the element did have a negative effect on a vampire. Not lethal, but still incapacitating. Slayers of old used the technique to gain physical proximity when hunting with wood instead of solaria. But when Massimo had journeyed deeper into the cavity and discovered the lack of liver, intestines, stomach, and lungs, he knew this vampire's fate had been delivered in a different way than he'd ever seen.

Then, another twist. The speck of shiny metal along an intact but shrunken heart. Massimo had reached out a smoky finger, prodding the object. It had been a terrible mistake. In a flash, lightning lit. Electricity sparked. He needed to exit. He *had* to get out, or he'd materialize inside. The cold cement floor of the palace kitchens told him he was flesh again. The lack of corporal miasma strewn about him told him he'd gotten out in time.

Nothing explained the sound of his own pulse spiking inside his ears. Two distinct beats, life—and death—running through his veins. But just as soon as it started, it stopped.

He was getting too old for this stuff.

"She tastes of vampire," he continued. "But never mind that. There was something very peculiar I found in there... or rather, something I didn't see, which concerns me far more."

"Something you *didn't* see?" Pavlos asked aloud the question they were all thinking.

"Organs," Massimo said. "Some are missing. Not all. Also, something small and round and made of gold near the heart."

"Gold?" Amy's eyes brightened. "Maybe some kind of medical device? My dad had to have a stent put in after a heart attack last year. If gold was an option, he got it."

Helsing cocked his head to the side, his face screwed up. So not only did he ignore his assistant's best attributes and most pressing needs, he also wasn't intimately involved in her life at any level. Who raised this so-called man?

"A stent?" Massimo tried to place the word. Possible he knew its Italian equivalent, but also possible he didn't know the term at all. "I am no expert in modern huey medicine, but whatever is in there seems to be... *attached* to the tissues near the heart. Also, there is no reason of which I can conceive for a vampire to have any medical device."

Popowitz's eyes started doing that left-right scan hueys did when giving something extensive thought. "Maybe she choked on something? Girl in my high school did that. She had some kind of oral fixation, always putting her jewelry in her mouth. Then finally, she accidentally swallowed one of those gaudy-looking crucifixes. They had to rush her to the hospital to cut her open and get it out."

Massimo was about to follow up on that when they all picked up on footsteps coming up the hallway and into the kitchen. All except the huey, that was, who turned only to that side of the room after all the others had. But it was the huey who was the first to address the woman who walked in.

"Tina?" Popowitz took a few steps forward, then froze. "Oh, my God, your hair... what happened?"

Whatever it was, the Doge thought, it wasn't isolated to the female slayer's head. Miss Potsia looked like something that just fell out of an animal giving birth. Hair matted and disheveled. Clothes smocked with dirt and grime. She smelled like a cup of milk left out in the sun all day long. Her olive skin had paled, and superficial but undeniable scratches raked across visible patches of skin.

"Seriously, Puppy-guts, my hair?" Potsia reached up, running the ends of her dark locks through her fingers. "I went for a walk. I... fell into a canal."

"You what?" Helsing pulled a face, though given the stench, he couldn't be blamed. "Why were you outside? Where were you going?"

"I was just looking around the city. And, by the way, *I'm fine*. It wasn't that deep. It—" Suddenly, Potsia cut herself off, her eyes focusing on the scene around her, falling lastly on the dead body. "Why is *she* here?"

"She?" A peculiar way to say *what is a corpse doing sitting on yonder kitchen prep table? Even for a vampire's house, that's weird.* But then again, Potsia, like Helsing and Pavlos and Vega, even like Massimo himself, wasn't a native English speaker. Sometimes the words went their own way.

"A body found floating in the canals today," Vega supplied when Helsing didn't speak right away. "She appears to have been a vampire."

"No, she wasn't."

They all narrowed gazes, and the pressure forced Potsia to continue.

She crossed an arm over her midriff; her eyes went unfocused. "I mean, why do you think that? If a dead vampire was out in the sunlight, it would have turned to dust."

"True, but this one is also drained of blood even though she doesn't have any wound marks on her body." Helsing's head jerked in the direction of the corpse. "Massimo smoked inside and looked around. He says it's a vampire. Or was. He reemerged right before you walked in." He left unsaid that the Doge had come out sounding like the drum solo of some minimalist musical act.

"He what?" Potsia asked. "He could have exploded it that way."

Helsing shrugged. "Amy's idea. Not sure if it's anything more than a waste of time, though."

"Hey, I'm standing right here, fuckface."

The Solari turned to his red-faced assistant. "Such a mouth in front of our hosts?" With a grin, he swiveled back. "Seriously, Barbie, they're going to think we're a bunch of goddamned yokels."

"What is a yokel?" Pavlos asked, inkling his head in Vega's direction.

"A dismissive huey term for outsiders who know something." The chairperson's eyelids lowered. She let go of her breath before turning her eyes on the female slayer. "Miss Potsia, do you recognize this woman?"

Potsia nodded almost imperceptibly. Her voice sounded flat, distant. "I saw her earlier today when I was... *walking* around."

"I take it she was alive then?" Pavlos asked.

The female slayer's eyes flashed anger. "Of course she was. Don't you think

I'd start with that fact if I'd seen a dead vampire lying about on the streets?"

"Tina, watch your tone." The Solari's rebuke calmed his supplicant for the second time in as many days.

While the bickering that when on between Helsing and Popowitz sounded foul, Massimo recognized it for what it was—banter that underlaid friendship bordering on familial. But the Solari's treatment of Potsia... there was animosity there. True dislike that made Massimo wonder if he'd been wrong to ask the most combative Reclaimed to be invited. Or was his suspicion that amity still existed for their captor among some of them proven by this outlandish behavior?

The palazzo still had a dungeon they could make use of if so.

"Massimo?"

The Doge wasn't sure if Helsing assumed such familiarity because he was a slayer, or because he was ignorant, or because he was asserting his dominance, but as Portia may say, it was beginning to tick him off.

"You were saying there was something gold?" he continued, motioning to the corpse. "Like, what exactly?"

"Yes, in the chest cavity. I couldn't wholly perceive its nature." Massimo too, looked at the body. "The second I touched it, something... *happened*. It felt both like I was falling through the sky and being pushed into the heavens all at once. I couldn't get out of there fast enough."

And given him a pulse, even if only momentarily. He refused to acknowledge the obvious. For a few seconds, he'd been human again. True, there had been just as much of an interval between contact and conversion, but that's where he had ended up all the same. In fact, if he reflected on the facts, it seemed to Massimo that the duration of his digress had equaled the duration of his impress.

Luckily, the sole huey amongst them had the advantage of ignorance and the tenacity not to hide it.

"I don't get it," Popowitz said. "Do you mean to say that there's something... magical in there?"

"Amy, seriously?" Helsing immediately dismissed his assistant. "Magic isn't real."

"I'm sorry," the blonde protested in a tone that made certain she was *not*. "But did I or did I not just watch a five-hundred-year-old vampire become a pillar of smoke and perform an autopsy from the inside out?"

"No, you did not. I'm not even four hundred and fifty yet." The Doge turned. "And we're no closer to knowing what killed this woman. I can state only for a fact that she was supernatural, and whatever is in there may be as well. Even someone as old as I, who should have been alive long enough to know all that is and is not, can be surprised on occasion." His wife's existence had proven as much. "I think our best course of action at this point would be to extract the object and *examine* it outside of the body."

Potsia stepped forward, pulling a knife from some concealed spot on her person. "Sounds like a good idea to me."

Some of them gasped, some of them called out for her to stop, but neither made any impression on the slayer. For Massimo's part, he welcomed her forthwith attitude. It was what a slayer should do in a situation like this, the type of action he'd been counting on Helsing to take.

With the body having arrived exsanguinated, no blood oozed out as Potsia plunged her blade into the humble breast of the victim and followed that with a perpendicular slash, making an X. As soon as the chest cavity opened, the slayer put down the blade and replaced it with her right hand.

"Let me see." The slayer's sandstone eyes turned to the ceiling. The tip of her tongue peeked through her lips as her hand, wrist, and half of her forearm disappeared inside the victim. Popowitz finally proved human, slapping hands over her mouth and belching before skittering out of the room, flushed.

Helsing caught Miss Vega's eyes. "Raquel, would you..."

"Of course." The chairperson nodded once and turned in pursuit of the blonde huey. "I'll make sure she's okay."

"You're right," Potsia went on, either unconcerned or unaware of Popowitz's strife. "It's both surprisingly dry and somewhat empty. Not just drained of blood. Feels like someone put her in the oven for a while to dehydrate her." Tina maneuvered around the body, changing the angle of her exploration as she did. After a few moments, her eyes went wide. "Got it!"

A sick, gnarly rip accompanied the yank of the slayer's hand. All gathered in, Pavlos, Massimo, and Helsing, examining the trinket Potsia held in her outstretched palm.

"It's a... an insect?" Helsing turned a sweeping glance around their circle, looking for confirmation and, maybe, clarity.

Massimo nodded, removing a kerchief from his inner pocket and using it to pull the object into his own grasp. "A beetle. More specifically, a scarab. And it's coated in gold, if not made of it entirely."

"Gold?" Potsia's face screwed up. "That's important?"

It didn't surprise Massimo that a person held captive by vampires since she was a child didn't know one of their lesser weaknesses.

"It is," Pavlos said. "It means whatever put that in her, and whatever its purpose was, it wasn't done by a vampire. Gold has a similar but lesser effect on vampires than silver has on werewolves, except we're lucky enough that the slayers can't wield gold into weapons and whimsies the way hoods can with silver to harm us."

Lifting a hand to the level of their eyes, Potsia swiveled her wrist clockwise, and a pea-sized solarium burst into being. The ball of solar energy shocked the vampires into taking a step back, though such a tiny representation of the slayer's power wasn't enough to injure by proximity.

Potsia sneered. "I don't know about that. *This* little golden ball can do a hell of a lot of damage."

Only when the Solari reached up, closing his supplicant's hands with both of his, did the sickly smile drop from his face.

"Tina!" Helsing barked. "Seriously, are you insane?"

She looked as shocked as the rest of them. All the arrogance she'd shone through with a moment before evaporated. "Come on, Caleb, I was only—"

He snatched the scarab from her hand and encircled her other wrist, using the leverage to turn her out from the gathering. "You were *only* doing the slayer equivalent of holding a knife to a huey's throat. Not to mention being fucking rude."

Her fingers snapped shut, snuffing her weapon, but her glare was twice as deadly and pointing solely on the Solari. "I'm sorry, but did you or did you not rescue us from the harem so we could *be* slayers and not slaves?" Potsia lifted a hand from which sprang an accusatory finger. She lashed it in the Doge's direction. "*He* is a vampire, and *he* was implying that *we slayers* can't keep his kind in line. I was well within my rights in reminding him just who he's dealing with."

"Who he's dealing with is a basket case." Helsing's jaw ground. Taking two steps forward, his face was so close to Potsia's, he was either going to bite her or kiss her. "If you ever pull shit like this again, you're out, okay? I don't care about sacred duty or what you've been through or if you really feel like you need to show you got the biggest swinging Richard in the room. *You* are out of line."

With each word, the poor young woman's face fell. "Out of line? But as your intended, it's my duty to show how strong your side is."

"As my..." The sound that came next from Helsing's mouth was something between a laugh and a cry. He turned, running his empty hand through his ebony hair. Six steps away, then six heavy steps back to resume the same position he'd been in before.

"You are *not* my intended," he growled out. "You're not my anything. We slept together one time. ONE. TIME. And only because we were forced to. So unless we somehow get taken hostage by an immortal megalomaniac who demands we bang bits, or he's going to start killing people again, give it up. You and I are *never* going to happen."

Massimo studied the scene with interest. It was funny. Within moments of having sat down at the dinner table with the Solari, he was positive that Helsing had no merits as a leader, that the bravery he'd witnessed in London two years ago had been either a one-off or bravado to impress a woman. While this situation was mired with emotions on Potsia's part, it still called upon Helsing to lay down a line... and lay down the line he had.

Though perhaps it could have been done with a bit more empathy for the poor woman's heart, a thought that Massimo had only moments before the female slayer, biting a bottom lip, turned from the room and stormed out for the second time in as many days.

"You do seem to have a knack for driving women away, Mr. Helsing."

Helsing's chest rose and fell in huey time. The ire he worked himself into struggled to ebb. "Actually the problem I usually have is getting them to leave." He straightened, pulling a deep breath in through his nose before pushing it out of his mouth. He turned to face Massimo. "Your Excellency..."

Oh, he must really think himself in trouble if he was falling back on formality.

"I believe your wife should return home immediately," he continued, "This may be the third body you found, but I refuse to believe the fact that this vampire crossed paths with Tina today before being found in this state is a coincidence. I think whoever did this might have eyes on the palace and be following whoever leaves."

The slayer was right.

Massimo bobbed his head. "I'll go to wherever she is and escort her home myself immediately."

"I'll come along."

The Doge had barely had time to turn to leave when he was forced to pivot back. "Mr. Helsing?"

"If there's some rogue, psycho vampire out there killing other vampires, I need to find it and..." Helsing's face screwed up. "Well, do what I'm supposed to do."

"I wouldn't object, but what makes you think this was done by a vampire?"

Helsing's face screwed up. "What else would drain a victim of all her blood?"

"I don't know, Mr. Helsing, and in this city, there are not many things that I do not know," Massimo admitted. "At the same time, I've never heard of one of our kind who also extracts the organs of its victims in the process, and that without any scars or incisions." He turned and reached out the scarab to his second. "Take this. While we're gone, see if you can find out anything about it.

Short message me if something turns up."

Pavlos took the piece and bowed. "We just call it texting now, Your Excellency."

TWENTY-THREE

S ome diplomatic and/or pompous ass had bombed Amy's suite with lilacs. She'd never really been into flowers, but at least they were pretty. Or so she had thought when she'd first opened her room to find herself in a pseudo-spring garden. Now, their sickly-sweet smell was the last ingredient needed to bring acid rushing up her throat.

Amy barreled in, dashed through the bedchamber, and into the bathroom so fast, even she wondered if supernaturalism was contagious. No sooner had her knees met the cool tile than the contents of her stomach roiled up her throat.

The sounds were horrible. The stench was worse.

It seemed like one never questioned their life choices more than when worshipping at the altar of the porcelain god. As she regained control over her esophagus and fell back, her shins down on icy tile as her arms anchored over the toilet seat, the self-reflection started... and not just in the water in the bowl below.

What in the hell am I doing here? Most people would have been nearly murdered by a vampire in public and counted their blessings that they'd survived, swearing to stay away from the creatures forever. Not Amy. No, she went all "Well, obs the universe has chosen me to ascend to a higher plane" and dove into the deep end, blindfolded and with both hands tied behind her back. The blonde huey had always prided herself on her street cred. She may have grown up the spoiled, privileged daughter of a New York City corporate lawyer, but she'd never thought for a second her daddy's money could stop a bullet or make a knife miss your arteries.

Living in the supernatural world was going to be the death of her.

Amy's stomach finally stopped trying to forcibly eject itself through her throat just in time to hear someone knocking on the door.

"Miss Popowitz, can I come in?"

Shit, what was Raquel doing here? The last person Amy wanted to see moments after reverse-eating was the picture-perfect vampire who detested her huey frailty.

A moment of silence stretched as Amy decided what to do.

"Either you're ignoring me, or you're dead." A few more taps accompanied the stepped-up-in-volume voice. "If it's the first, don't. If it's the second... well, there's nothing to be done for it now, so just let me in."

That was a non-choice choice, wasn't it? "Fine, but I warn you, it isn't pretty. Just give me a sec."

Without looking, Amy stretched out her hand and grabbed a wad of toilet paper from a roll next to the toilet. She dabbed at the corners of her mouth as the suite door opened and closed, followed by the sound of a disgusted grunt.

"Miss Popowitz. *Amy.*" At least Raquel's voice was nonchalant. "Are you okay?"

The swirling in her head was still too formidable for her to look at her guest. Amy hung on the toilet like some kind of blond-haired ground sloth.

"No, I'm not." How quickly could she get rid of Raquel so she could brush her teeth? "When Tina cut into the body..."

"I understand that might have been upsetting." Raquel's brown eyes softened. "Is there something I can do, or would you prefer to be left alone to recuperate?"

"Left alone?" Amy pushed herself up, using the rim of the toilet as a tool.

"You came all the way here just to see if you should leave?"

"Mr. Helsing asked me to check on you. And to tell the truth, I was concerned as well. I've never taken you for the type of huey who would run at the sight of blood. Not that there was any blood to be seen."

Amy rolled her head to the side, taking in the chairperson's sincere expression as she trudged toward the bed, lowering herself on it gingerly. "Seriously? Have you met me? I get nauseous seeing extra saucy pizza."

Raquel smoothed down the black button-up dress shirt she wore as she passed further into the room, coming to a standstill about five feet away from the bed. "In that case, I hope for your speedy recovery."

The chairperson looked around in a slow sweep. Amy thought she might be checking for interlopers stashed into corners or behind curtains. But when she spotted a chair nested under a writing desk, she took the liberty to pull it over and seat herself beside the huey's bed.

"What are you doing?" Amy asked. "It's not like you get tired standing around."

"I thought it might make you more comfortable if I was at eye level and not looking down on you." Raquel crossed one leg over the other. "Hovering over you while we talk would make me appear like a predator."

"Talking? About what? And how would that change anything? You *are* a predator. You're a vampire."

"And you fear us. You fear *me*."

Amy wouldn't deny it. At the same time, she wasn't exactly thrilled about having it stated so plainly. She suddenly had a lot more empathy for that darned Emperor parading around in his birthday suit.

Raquel went on, "Please don't misunderstand. I'm not calling you a coward. Our abilities allow us to pick up on the physical responses of a frightened huey. Every time you walk into that boardroom, your heart races, your eyes dilate, and your skin blanches. You're terrified. Still, you do it. Your mind forces you forward even though your body is telling you to run away. To put it quite plainly, the Board, myself most of all, are in awe of your courage."

It was like being slapped, then told how beautiful you were. "Um, thanks?" But that didn't mean she was going to be distracted from the greater truth. "Look, Raquel, no offense, but I'd really appreciate it if you could, you know, get to the point of why you're actually here."

The other woman dared to appear confused. "Sorry?"

"No, you're not," Amy shifted, pushing herself to a straighter position. "You've been looking for a chance to corner me. I know you think I have some kind of sway over Caleb. Because, for some reason I can't quite pin down, you *want* him to meet the challenge and get his shit together. But this thing between him and Tina? They need to work through those issues themselves. Hopefully, they do it soon, and without causing an international incident."

"I would never ask you to do the impossible." Raquel moved to the edge of the seat. "I *would* ask you to encourage him to be more respectful toward the Doge so vampires of power like Massimo Brunelli can trust the slayers to do their duty, not be dramatic divas fighting in front of strangers. I know what it looks like when dangerous vampires go unchecked, and I also know what it looks like when we must police our own and the consequences it brings."

"Massimo seems to handle it fine." Venice wasn't overrun with out-of-control creatures of the night.

Raquel made a quick dip of her chin. "Yes, but Brunelli is a four-hundred-year-old vampire with a thousand-year-old throne and political system behind him. Even Vlad didn't dare challenge him when he resisted."

"You know one thing I've noticed about you, Raquel? You love formality. *Vampires* love formality. It doesn't really line up with modern American culture, but whatevs, I respect it. But whenever Dracula comes up, it's not *Țepeș*. It's *Vlad*."

A little grin appeared, and Amy would have sworn fangs peeked out from behind it.

"I don't like despots, and I don't like bullies," Raquel said. "That's why I want to see Mr. Helsing become a proper leader to the Reclaimed with access to all that WWL provides. We need him, and he needs us, and *he* needs someone like you beside him to do it."

"Me? A huey who throws up when she hears flesh being sliced?" As if to remind them both that Amy's stomach wasn't appreciating the conversation, it chose that moment to erupt in a loud gurgle. "Why am I so special?"

"Because for some reason, one I can't explain fully, Mr. Helsing *cares* what you think. And more so, because I think *you* care about him and everyone else at WWL. And just to show you how much I respect and value you, I'm going to do something most vampires never would."

Without delay, Raquel reached into a pocket and withdrew a tiny tin container, one barely larger than the pad of her thumb.

Amy instinctively pulled back, her face elongated as she eyeballed the pillbox. "You're giving me drugs?"

"It's not huey medicine." Raquel pinched the tin between two fingers and gave it a little shake. Inside, something pinged like glass being tapped. "It is my blood."

The nausea caused by little human dissection was nothing compared to the nausea caused by the *worst kind* of beverage.

"Um, no, thanks." Amy shook her head, remembering a time a few years before when she'd specifically been warned *not* to allow any blood to cross her lips. *It could start the change,* the hood with her had said. "I, um, don't want to be one of you. Like, ever."

Arm and container dropping to her side, Raquel frowned. "I'm not a maker, Miss Popowitz." Stepping forward, Raquel pulled Amy's hand up and deposited the pillbox into her palm. "The only effect of drinking a small amount is medicinal, a temporary relief of your illness."

"Vampire blood heals hueys?" The temptation was evident in her arched tone.

Raquel's head swayed from side to side. "Not always, and not every illness. And over time, with repeated use, your body would build up an immunity to its effects. But yes, I believe it can make your... *achy tummy...* better."

Hardly believing her own actions, Amy steadied the pillbox and twisted off the top. The glass vial inside held a liquid, but it didn't look like blood. The expression *blood is thicker than water* had always seemed more metaphorical, but not in this case. It couldn't be more than a teaspoon in the vial, and it was so dark it was blacker than red. Could such a small amount do anything?

Then she remembered how tiny a cyanide pill was.

"*You're sure* this won't turn me into a vamp?"

"If turning were such a simple feat, the world would be overrun with vampires." Raquel's eyes narrowed. "Has it never occurred to you to ask Mr. Helsing how a mortal crosses the crimson line?"

Amy's face screwed up. "I've never been a football fan."

Raquel rolled her eyes. "No, Amy. Crossing the crimson line, It's a more poetic way of saying, when one dies and is reborn vampire."

"Oh, that? No. I know it involves drinking blood. Beyond that... I guess I just assumed it's the way they show it in movies," Amy said. "Bite on the neck, and Bob's your vampire uncle."

The corners of the vampire's mouth flinched. Now Amy knew she was hallucinating. Raquel de la Vega had no sense of humor, let alone the ability to laugh at a joke.

"That *can* be part of it," the chairperson conceded. "But it's not essential. The bite can be anywhere on the body, but it's the same as when we feed. It's called the maker's bite, and the gift to perform it is rare among vampires. So rare, in fact, that when a vampire is reborn with the ability, it is the beginning of a new bloodline."

"New bloodlines?" No one had told her that was even a thing. "Does that happen often?"

Raquel shook her head. "There hasn't been one in my lifetime that I know of. Some bloodlines have even died out in recent centuries, though it's also true that some have grown exhaustively large."

"The Dracule were pretty large." Amy shrugged. "Until the Battle of Tahquamenon, when Caleb and the hoods killed a few hundred of them."

"Yes, well, the Dracule have *always* been one of the larger lines. Some think, perhaps even the first. That's because they have a unique genetic quirk. For some reason, every Dracule can administer the maker's bite."

When Raquel drew silent, Amy's curiosity got the better of her. "So a maker's bite, and *then*... Uncle Bob?"

"No. The bite floods the recipient with a biochemical catalyst that affects the human body on many levels. It's a euphoric experience, but not without its downside. Like a transplanted organ, some human bodies reject the process, and the recipient dies a slow and agonizingly painful death. For those who survive, they must complete the initiation by feasting on the flesh of their maker."

Amy almost dropped the tin onto the frilly lacework stitched into the comforter. "Okay, seriously, that's disgusting. I mean, drinking blood is one thing, but cannibalism? Really?"

"Becoming a vampire isn't as sexy as you believed, is it?" Raquel jerked her chin up. "Drink my blood if you like. Or save it for some future calamity. It never goes bad, and I will likely never offer it again. You have my word that there will be no negative effect. May the Solari strike me down if I've lied."

He would, Amy thought. She had a metric ton of doubt around Caleb's ability to stop serial one-night-standing or to become less of an annoying asshat, but she'd never questioned for a moment that he'd protect her. Or avenge her if it came down to it.

Amy nodded, pulling a deep breath in and out, then wrapped her hand around the tiny bottle and lowered it to her side. "I think I'm feeling better, but I think I'll save it for the next time one of Caleb's flavors du jour gets catty when I kick her out."

"As you wish. In the meantime..." Raquel's right hand fanned and turned it to the ceiling, "... as with all huey things, I would advise you to drink fluids and get some rest."

"Really? Two centuries bopping around the planet, and that's the best you got?"

"No, it's not 'the best I got.' I *could* enthrall you and make you feel better in other ways. But if I had wanted to seduce you, I already would have by now."

Raquel popped up to her feet as quickly as Amy's eyes popped out of their sockets. "I'll let the others know you need a little sleep, but you're well. Do feel free to call upon me if I can be of any assistance."

TWENTY-FOUR

T en minutes later, Caleb exited the palazzo to find Massimo a few meters
away, leaning against a light pole whose light flickered, waiting. Could
mean the bulb was going out, or it could mean the frequency at which it strobed
was one too slow for supernatural eyes. The Doge had changed out of his fine
suit, opting instead for a pair of dark jeans, a brown pullover crew shirt, and a
black leather jacket just long enough to cover up his posterior assets.

"You could almost pass for a huey dressed like that," Caleb said.

"Venice is not Milan. A finely dressed man draws eyes, and as a hunter, I
prefer *not* to be noticed."

"Likewise." Caleb tucked his phone into the back pocket of his black slacks.
His own suit, which he'd been trying his damnedest not to stain since arriving
three days ago, sat upstairs, laid out over his bedspread. His black sweatshirt,
however, still meant the Doge outshone him.

The slayer clapped his hands together and rubbed them vigorously. "So, any
idea where to start?"

Massimo pulled out a phone and held it up. On it, a map of the city zoomed
out so about half of the two biggest islands were visible on the screen, looking
like two crab claws clamping down on each other. A blue dot where they

currently stood pulsed in slow repetition on the right edge of the screen. On the left edge, a red dot did the same thing.

"You track your wife?" Massimo clicked his tongue. "That's considered a little creepy and controlling by the modern woman, you know."

"Unless your husband is a vampire prince with a number of enemies," Massimo said, pushing the phone back into his pocket. "It was actually Portia's idea and not merely for security reasons. When she first moved here, she often found the city confusing. Both Pavlos and I can locate her phone, and it's come into good use several times when she's gotten herself turned around."

The two set out, walking at what a huey would consider brisk, Massimo taking the lead. Late in the evening but still not the dead of night, they weren't alone. All around them, locals and tourists alike dashed, some with hands in their pockets, others talking on their own phones. Caleb picked up at least seven languages just a few steps from the Doge's door, Italian being only one of them. English, Russian, and German were the ones the slayer recognized immediately. The others had definite non-European vibes, but he didn't know enough to know better.

"I imagine that's not a problem for you," Caleb said as they made their way over a footbridge. "You must know these streets like the back of your hand. Or has it changed over time?"

"Yes and no, like any great city, I imagine. In some ways, Venice is more like it was now than it has ever been, and I have loved her every moment of it."

Well, that was cryptic. But then again, Caleb imagined that after the first century or two, certain details of memory, stacked up like layers of cake, began to taste the same when taken in the same bite.

"I never imagined that I might someday leave her," Massimo added a few moments later.

"Are you..." Like a dog asked if he wanted to go on a walk, Caleb's ears perked up. "... imagining that now?"

"One way or another, my time here is ending," Massimo answered, jerking his head to the left when they reached a pedestrian intersection.

"Does mean that you've changed your mind and—"

"No." The Doge cut Caleb off before the question could be fully rendered. "As I've already said, now is not the time to leave. I was hasty in London, striking deals without anticipating what lay just around the corner. *Venezia è il mio cuore e la mia casa*. Venice is my heart and my home."

They shuffled through a narrow passage only wide enough for one at a time. Caleb gawked at it all, how tightly houses were stacked next to each other. It reminded him in many ways of Jerusalem, the city to which his parents had first fled after leaving Istanbul. Caleb had been a child then, no more than six or seven. His father had hoped to find slayers in the ancient settlement, perhaps even relatives he'd left behind a decade before. They searched the city for weeks, finding only vampires. One had been a Dracule. The Helsings barely escaped capture, setting sail at dawn's first light on the back of a fishing boat bound for open water.

"I've never had a home like that," Caleb said, as much in conversation as realization. "Don't get me wrong. I've usually had a *residence*. But I don't think I've ever been anywhere I'd call *my heart*."

"You've been in Chicago now for a few years, haven't you?" Massimo lifted the phone to check on the red dot. Portia must be on the move as well. One moment they'd been heading left, and the next, Massimo pulled Caleb by the arm to the right.

"Yeah, but it's not *home*," the slayer said. "It's just a place where I keep all my stuff."

"You think home is a *place*?"

Caleb's eyebrow arched. "It isn't?"

"That can be part of it. But *home* is a feeling. It's energy and people and history and tradition. It's where you go to feel restored and where you leave to feel brave."

The vampire stopped for a moment just as they entered one of the city's many squares. At one end, a petite chapel was letting out, parishioners breaking off into small groups as they chatted. In another corner, a shopkeeper pulled merchandise off tables and moved it inside. Two children who should have been home in bed played some game with little metal orbs spinning on the ground.

"This is the city where I fell in love with my beloved first wife. Where my daughter was born. Where I lost them both, and then so many years later, found love again," the Doge said, his smile both bright and somewhat bittersweet. "A man in my position should question what the city would be without him, but truth be told, I do question what I would be without *it*."

Without movement to warm him, the chill in the air began to nip at Caleb's fingertips. He pushed his hands inside his slack pockets. "And how does Portia feel about living in Venice?"

"She is... content."

"But does that mean she's happy?" Caleb asked, sounding innocent as fuck.

"More than that, she's safe here." Massimo's back straightened as he looked off in the distance as if deciding which direction they should turn next. "My court is completely loyal to me. She is accepted among them, and they would all place themselves in harm's way to protect her, no matter what."

Caleb swore he could hear the Doge thinking aloud in the trailing silence, running through a list of "buts" that could follow that statement. For the first time since they'd sat across the table from one another and Massimo had told Caleb and Amy he no longer wished to see out the end of the brokered deal, the slayer thought there might be a road to making this happen.

"Exactly why does she need protecting?" Caleb asked. "You said enemies, but if you're so feared and renowned, who would dare piss you off?"

"No one." Massimo's eyes were wide when he turned on the slayer. "But there are those who may wish to harm her if..." He turned away again, tension coiling his fingers. "When you're introduced to my court at the ball, this question of what does it mean now that the slayers are back will no longer be mired in so many shades of red and gray."

Well, that was a non-sequitur that needed to be properly *sequitur-ed.*

Caleb was about to ask the obvious when the Doge held up his phone, muttering something under his breath that the slayer was certain was some spicy

Italian.

"What is it? What happened?"

"Portia's location," Massimo said. "It just disappeared from the map."

Twenty-Five

Not for the first time in the last two hours, Tina muttered one of the four-lettered words she'd learned from American media. In her mind's eye, she envisioned the city planners conceiving their *serene* city. They had boiled a pot of spaghetti, poured it out into a bowl, and drawn the outlines of Venice's road and canals from there.

"Okay, then." Her teeth ground as she pivoted to another offshoot of a pathway. "Let's try *this* way."

Not like she knew where she was going other than *away*. Tina had thought she'd been en route to the top of the island, the part she'd seen on a map that had busses and trains. Every time she turned that way, however, she kept finding herself pointed in the opposite direction after a few minutes. Like she couldn't escape, like the islands were drawing her back into the core.

She finally understood the true meaning of the huey term "tourist trap."

Up another street. Tina was both certain and uncertain she'd seen before. The hueys were beginning to thin out. The hour grew late, and their days were winding down. Still, odd numbers of them stood at the intersections, conversing, laughing, leering. It felt like everyone stared at you when you were trying not to be seen.

Tina wasn't sure if the Doge would be like the Ravens, using his authority as a security web to hold her in with a thousand loyal eyes. If so, the vamps of the city would be out looking for her soon. At any moment, a member of Brunelli's court could lunge out and grab her. Let them try. Power sparked on her palm. Unlike Caleb, Tina didn't give vampires the benefit of the doubt. She wouldn't kill one just because it existed, but she'd be damned if she was ever going to allow one dominion over her again.

"Tina?"

The slayer spun as if on cue, ready to attack. Instead of a vampire, however, who she saw approaching her across the square was none other than the Doge's huey wife. *Smart to send her,* Tina thought. Though hueys were also her inferior, she wouldn't attack one without a great deal of antagonizing. Did a bear kill a squirrel just because it chirped in his direction?

"Your Excellency." Tina put her primed hand behind her back, snuffing the solarium. She bowed at the waist, genuflecting enough to be proper without being obscene. "What are you doing here?"

"I went to see an evening exhibition at the museum and decided to take a walk before going home." She filed her hands into the pockets of her overcoat and pulled it around herself tighter. "You?"

"I'm..." Well, if she was going to be her own woman living her own life, there was no time like the present to start. "I'm leaving Venice."

"Leaving?" Portia's face screwed up. She looked around. "Alone?"

"I... um." She didn't owe this woman any explanation. In fact, it could prove foolish to overshare. But Tina had spent the last year and a half trapped in both a metaphorical and actual tower in the sky, and she longed for someone to hear her. "I can't stay here. I can't stay around... *him* anymore."

"Oh, dear." Portia raised a hand, but Tina took a step back before she could place it on her arm. Getting the hint, the Dogaressa let her hand fall to her side.

"I picked up on some tension between you two," she continued instead. "And based on what Massimo says, Caleb doesn't have the greatest track record with women." She softened her voice. "He didn't *hurt you,* did he?"

"Not intentionally," Tina bit out. Loathe to admit it, it was nonetheless true. "He's not the man I thought he was when we were together in the harem, it turns out. I thought Puppy Guts—Sorry, *Amy* had chosen me to accompany them on this trip because he'd finally remembered the connection we had. But here, all I seem to do is make him angry. He rejects my advances, my advice... my company."

"Well, then, I think that's his loss and proof of his emotional idiocy."

Old instincts to defend her captor may have been forced down deep, but they were still there. "*He* is the Solari and a slayer of a noble and powerful bloodline."

"Shh!" Portia threw her hands up in surrender and closed in. "Careful. You never know who's listening in around here."

That was truer than Portia realized, Tina thought, thinking back to her experience in the boat garage and the mysterious, bloodless corpse who dragged her underwater there, only to show up later in the Doge's palace. But that hadn't been what Portia was referring to. No one at the palace knew what had happened to Tina, and if the huey was to be believed, she hadn't yet been home to learn about the body.

Portia went on in quieter tones. "Look, I'm not knocking Caleb for... *his official position*. It's none of my business what is going on between the two of you or what your history is. But when I look at you, I see a proud warrior in the prime of life, ready to serve. He owes you respect for that, no matter what. If Massimo treated the members of his guard the way I've seen him treat you these last few days, we'd have a coup within a month."

Tina knew it had not been the Dogaressa's intention, but she'd just introduced a radical and delicious thought. A coup? What a brilliant idea. Why should Caleb be the solari, when he obviously wasn't a good leader? Thoughts to ponder later, but thoughts nonetheless.

"I hope you know that we at court respect you," Portia continued unprompted. "And if you want to leave, I can help make those arrangements."

"I have the piece of plastic that lets me purchase things." As if to reinforce the truth, Tina plunged her hand into her pocket and found the edges of the card.

"As long as I can use that to get to the airport and onto a plane, I'm fine."

"Right, so you also have your passport, then?"

The slayer grunted. "I forgot about those. Popowitz managed all the official paperwork. She must still have it, and she is the *last* huey I wish to tolerate."

"We have a guy that can generate very convincing fakes." Portia ticked her head to the right like she was indicating a direction. "I can take you to him if you like. He's a huey on the mainland. Usually not open this late, but I'm sure he'll answer the door when he sees my face on his security camera." She shrugged. "Sometimes it's good to be the Dogaressa."

Tina had seen Massimo's talents and how attractive his features were. She had no doubt it was *often* very good to be the Dogaressa.

"I would appreciate that."

Portia smiled. "Come on, then. We'll get a cab at the train station. It's just a few minutes' walk from here."

"I'm not certain about that." Tina followed as Portia led on despite the statement. "I've been trying to get there for over an hour, and I keep getting looped around."

"That's just the way Venice is. It's hard at first, like the people who planned this city wanted it to look like a basket of yarn played with by ten cats high on catnip."

Also an apt metaphor, one reinforced that moment as they turned a right down a wide corridor filled with shop windows, then almost immediately hung a left down an alley barely wide enough for the two of them to stand shoulder-to-shoulder. Tina was certain they were now further away from the train station than they'd been a minute ago.

"Don't worry," Portia continued. "I'm familiar with the city streets now. Massimo still likes to patrol himself a few times a week. I come along to keep him company. He's taught me how to get around."

"The two of you actually enjoy spending time with each other?"

The way Portia's face screwed up, Tina wondered if it had come across as an insult.

"Shouldn't we?" the Dogaressa asked.

Tina shrugged as they started up and over a footbridge. "I was led to believe in my studies that most royal marriages are political arrangements, not matters of the heart."

"Well, Massimo and I don't exactly have a royal marriage. Yes, he's the Doge, but me? I'm nothing special. Not royal, anyway." She was silent a moment before saying, "His sister in Florence, however..."

So hueys *did* gossip! It was what kept her sane in the harem, and Tina missed it terribly. "Yes?"

Portia shrugged, pointing with some hesitance to the right when their path dead-ended into another slender thoroughfare. "She's not married right now, but she has been I-don't-know-how-man times, all of them political arrangements. I'm worried she'll be expected to do it again soon and that she's not really looking forward to it. Weird how no one questions Massimo being single and sovereign, but for a woman, *nooo*."

"Supes aren't the best at keeping up-to-date with huey morays."

"Ain't that the truth?"

Suddenly, Portia drew to a stop, and Tina did the same. There was something different about the courtyard they found themselves in. The only path that connected with the square the size of Tina's Chicago apartment was the one they'd entered from, if one did not include the portal opposite them that was bordered by a canal. Fingers of fog rose from its bank, obscuring the borders of the path. On either side, walls of the finally carved stone and brick mortared together by long-dead men rose. No windows, no doorways. Other than the open sky and the way out behind them, it was a dead end hemmed in on all sides.

The slayer watched as the Dogaressa turned thrice, taking in each of the cardinal directions in turn. "I do believe we're lost."

Tina reached up and pulled closed the lapels of her jacket as a cold wind blew up from the water before them, porting the fog bank further onto the cobblestone street. "There's something off here."

"Off?" Portia's face screwed up. She looked around for a moment as though she meant to find something. "What do you mean?"

"It's the same air as the boathouse." Of course the Dogaressa would have no idea what that meant. Truth be told, neither did Tina, but the scent was the same. A vague hint of death and mold overlaid with a sweet floral perfume. A pang of unease blossomed in the slayer's belly. "I thought you knew this city. Where are we?"

"I do, but I..." Portia laughed under her breath, reaching into her pocket and pulling out a phone. "If only I had a magical piece of technology that could show on a map exactly where we are, right?" she joked.

Without hueys around and with no conceivable place from which they could see, Tina lashed out her left hand, sparking a solarium. The golf ball-sized sphere of light illuminated the space, making portraits of shadows. Tina faced the water and the pull in her gut telling her to beware.

"Portia, get behind me."

But the Dogaressa's attention remained on her phone. "That's weird. No signal. I've always had one from anywhere in the city. I don't understand. What is..."

They both heard the sloshing water at the same time. It didn't sound like something had fallen in, or even some boat passing by. It was the distinct sound of something breaking the calm surface.

Something coming *out* of the water.

"Portia!" Tina whipped out her other hand, putting twin weapons at the ready. "Get. Behind. Me."

This time, the huey listened. Heat spread across Tina's back as Portia flushed herself from behind.

"On the count of three, we're going to start walking backward very quickly, okay? We need to get out of here."

"Okay, sounds good," Portia agreed. Her left hand anchored onto Tina's coat. "Whenever you're ready."

"One. Two. Thr—"

Two beings stepped out of the mists at the same time, but what, Tina couldn't say. Human forms at different levels of decay based on appearance. One was male, red beard, white eyes, wearing only a pair of ripped athletic pants and missing one arm. The other, a woman, and that was based only on the fact that a black bra held the only flesh she still had. The rest of it was missing, along with large gaps of muscle and any hair on her head. Bleached bones poked out at intervals from leathery sinew.

"What are those?"

Portia's spoken question echoed the one Tina herself had been about to ask. Whatever they were, she had a sneaking suspicion somewhere in those chest cavities were little golden scarabs.

The slayer readied herself, squatting in case she needed to jump.

"Doesn't matter," Tina said. "They're made of meat. That means they'll burn."

TWENTY-SIX

Massimo came to a halt so quickly, Caleb couldn't stop before running full speed into the Doge's back, turning to take the brunt of the collision into his left shoulder.

The Doge regained his footing with impressive grace. "My apologies. I forgot that your reaction time is not as quick as mine."

Caleb cupped his pain as he rose to his feet. The force of his body hitting his had knocked him clear on his ass. "You also forgot the part about not putting full supe abilities on display in front of hueys."

The slayer hadn't failed to notice how heads turned as they whizzed past hueys still on the street so late. He'd had half a notion of stopping and doing some damage control but didn't want to be left behind.

"No huey will remember seeing us," Massimo informed him. "I alerted members of my court to assemble on the route. They will have taken care of any observers by now."

Caleb doubled over, hands on knees as he caught his breath. "When did you do that?"

"I am a vampire, Mr. Helsing. I can run *and* short message at the same time."

Well, what a wise man had once said was true. It was good to be the king. Even if one so old, you couldn't adapt to newfangled expressions like "texting."

The Doge turned to look over his shoulder. "You were exceptional in keeping pace, by the way. I was... impressed. You truly are a Helsing. You do your bloodline honor."

"Amy might disagree with you on that."

Caleb stood and pulled alongside Massimo to take in the view of the shadowy alley before them. From this position, and even with the gift of supernatural vision, it was impossible to see beyond its entry.

"I do not know this road." Massimo shook his head. "This place has never existed before now."

Caleb's insides flipped. "How... how is that possible?"

"How is it possible that a vampire without external injury is drained of all blood and has several organs missing? I cannot help but to believe that these things are connected." He jerked his chin in the direction of the darkness. "This is the last location Portia's phone pinged before the signal was lost. I believe we are meant to go forward, but something... repels me from this place."

"You mean, like, emotionally?"

Massimo scowled. "Do you think disgust would prevent a man from finding his bride?"

"Depends on the bride."

Caleb took a few steps forward. Unlike the Doge, he didn't perceive anything turning him away. On the contrary, it felt like gravity increased the closer he got. The cobblestones slanted downward, making each step more of a reaction to the pull than a decision to move. He looked behind, making sure no hueys were around to witness a solarium being born, then sparked one into being when the coast proved clear.

Massimo stepped back, raising his hands to the level of his eyes and wincing. "Definitely a Helsing."

"I do have a virile light, yes." Caleb took another step forward, hoping to illuminate the path. Instead, the darkness proved unyielding. It was as if it *ate* the light he gave it. "What the—"

His outburst was interrupted by a faint, muffled scream. Though it sounded distant, it had a familiar quality. "That's Tina!" He knew the noises she made when she was excited from experience, though the situation that produced them had been very different.

Caleb closed his hand, put out the light, and plunged into the darkness. To where, he didn't know. Forward, for now. Arms shot out, hands extended, feeling for a wall that may or may not be there. But there wasn't a wall. There was darkness only. He could still see his hands, his arms, his feet rushing beneath him, but nothing beyond the scope of his being until suddenly...

He ducked just in time to avoid the swing, and the zombie's hand found only empty air.

Zombie?

ZOMBIE?

They were in a courtyard with featureless walls on three sides and a canal at the end. Unlike Venice, there were no buildings or boats, and the water was inky black. Across the barrier of tall reeds, the shore was barren. The moon shone brightly in the starless sky. The water could be on fire and full of killer clowns. It wouldn't matter. What needed Caleb's attention right now was the dozen or so bodies in various stages of decay and tattered dress, four of whom were attempting to make for the water with Tina in tow, each of them having one of her limbs and holding her up like they were about to quarter her.

"Caleb!"

He whirled as Portia called out and couldn't believe what he saw. Two of the creatures mobbed the Dogaressa. One had his hands around her hips from behind, while another, missing half its head above the nose, crouched before her, attempting to sweep Portia's feet out from under her. Both had suddenly froze for some reason like they'd gotten ahold of their quarry then forgotten what to do about it. Portia, for her part, had a hand on each of the creature's heads, as much of a head as they had in a stretch that suggested she'd done a fair amount of yoga in her time.

Instinctively, Caleb headed for Portia. Yes, Tina was in a worse position, but Portia was only a huey. But then two things happened to stop him. First, the half dozen other creatures who'd been... he didn't know, *supervising,* maybe—sprang into action, barreling his way. At the same time, Portia shook her head vigorously.

"I'm fine," she said, her chin jerking to the space behind him. "Help Tina!"

She was fine? She was *fine?* A momentary temptation to argue back died when he noticed the two creatures still weren't moving. Somehow, the Dogaressa must have discovered some kind of Vulcan mind meld that neutralized their movements.

Caleb nodded and pivoted, coming face-to-face with six beings whose own faces were shredded and partially eaten, at best. *Ew. Just ew.* They stopped about five feet from him, like they knew getting any closer could mean coming in contact with his fist. What they didn't know was that Caleb didn't need to be within swinging distance to knock them off.

The first solarium shot out from his right hand, rocketing across the compact space and nesting at his command in the gullet of the middle zombie. The creature had time enough to look down, but how could he see? The sallow cavities where eyeballs should have been a pulpy, purple patchwork of pus and scar tissue. Caleb felt the power connect, and the energy asked for direction to burn out or blaze brighter.

With his weapon arm outstretched, Caleb's fist fanned out, a physical manifestation of the metaphysical command. In an instant, the blaze lit in the zombie's belly. One thing was for sure. It could feel pain. Something between a gurgle and a scream crawled up the creature's throat. It clawed its own abdomen, trying to pull out the pain. For a moment, it vibrated from top to bottom. Then, with one last gasp, the zombie threw its head back and guffawed before it disappeared into a cloud of ash.

A cloud of ash. Just like a...

"Zombie vampires?" He blinked in rapid succession. "*Zompires?*"

No sooner had the thought occurred to Caleb than the remaining five creatures, hissing and scratching, turned back, bearing what teeth they had left, revealing stained but very real fangs.

"Caleb!" Tina's shriek had gone from panicked to pissed off. "Get your solari ass over here and save me!"

Caleb lunged to the side, counting on his award-winning speed to get him past the wall of dead supes before him. Three or four meters away, Tina struggled, giving the zompires a good fight. Still, it was a fight she was losing. Two already had stepped into the water, and it wouldn't be long before they managed to pull Tina not only in but under. At that point, it wouldn't matter if Caleb threw a master blast of a solarium at each one in turn. They'd need only dip beneath the waves to be saved.

Every magic had its natural match.

He chanced a quick look at Portia to see if the status quo between had changed. It hadn't. Only Portia's heaving chest as she cycled quick breaths belied that they weren't all part of some Hans-Solo-encased-in-carbonite tribute. But the Dogaressa was looking pale. Her eyes were fluttering. Could the creatures drain energy somehow? Were these Zompires capable of enthralling, and doing some kind of mojo-no-no on her?

The concern and break in concentration proved just enough for Caleb to lose his advantage. He turned, ready to help Tina, when ten bony hands found purchase on different parts of his body.

He was airborne in moments, Caleb's eyes taking in the dark Venice sky, his body borne toward the water. He'd be dead if they got him there. Even if he could get free and pivot, his powers would be neutralized. But with his arms pulled out to the sides and held in place, projecting a solarium would be impossible.

From his hands, that was. With those out of service, any other slayer would be out of options. Caleb wasn't *any other slayer*. He was a Helsing, the most infamous slayer bloodline and the most respected by vampires, and not because of their devilishly good looks or great singing voices.

Only the other way was so much more dangerous. Even accounting for best intentions, Caleb was pretty sure Massimo wouldn't agree to come back to

Chicago with him if, in the act of trying to save his own sorry life, the Solari managed to incinerate the Dogaressa.

"Portia, drop to the ground! Get small!"

Caleb had to hope all those downward dogs and happy baby poses paid off. If she could curl up in a ball and luck out enough, his powers might pass clear over her and leave her with nothing more than a scorched winter coat and some fuzzy hair. Or, if not, he could be forgiven for giving her a third-degree burn over large portions of her body if she was still alive, right? A little nip of her husband's blood might clear up the worst of it if they were into that kind of thing and hadn't already abused it too much.

"What?" Portia shouted back.

The first zompire's foot splashed water. As he pulled and pushed, Caleb saw that Tina's corporeal litter was already up to the waist. He was out of time.

"Get down! Fetal position!" He repeated, hoping she listened, even if she didn't understand why. "When I say 'go.'"

"Go? Got it!" Portia called back.

Good, that was done. It was so nice when you told a woman to do something and she just... listened.

Caleb closed his eyes and tuned out the splash of the water where Tina was about to go under. He ignored the musty smell filling his nose and told himself the taste on his tongue wasn't because of all the rotting flesh vaporizing in the air. The pain in his wrist where one of the zompire's skeletal fingers had sliced it open would have to get his attention later.

He called on the solarium and the might of Atum-Re, the great sun god and father of all slayers. *"Let me be your conduit, Elohim. My body is yours, let your power be mine. Shine!"*

He breathed in—*Steady. Steady. Steady.*

"PORTIA, GO!"

Light and heat erupted from his every surface as power consumed, then overwhelmed him. In an instant, Caleb fell, surrendering to gravity, the creatures beneath him turning to dust as the whole-body solarium pushed out from his being. The water that ran up to his feet as he met the earth turned to vapor on contact. The stones directly beneath him managed to remain solid but glowed red from the intensity of his power.

A fact that would have sucked less if he wasn't suddenly completely naked and had had the air knocked out of his lungs.

"Caleb!"

His lungs ached for oxygen. His backside was getting the ultimate hot stone massage. And *Tina* was wailing for help.

Somehow, Caleb managed to roll over on his hands and knees, gaining insight into the corona on the ground beneath him. Luckily, Tina's aquatic struggles, some three feet away, caused enough ripples to wash over the stones. Steam rose as cool water met superheated rock. The Solari pushed himself to stand, feigning for a moment, overcome by fatigue. Those whole-body experiences were powerful but draining. A man could really get himself into trouble if he didn't know what he was doing.

"Tina!" His feet found a ledge a foot or so beneath the waves. Probably a step used for exiting boats at low tide. Tina struggled to tread water, but she managed to keep her head above the break as Caleb reached out and grabbed one of her flailing hands, pulling her to the ledge beside him.

"What the hell was that?" Tina scrambled to her feet. Her winter clothes, soaked by courtesy of the Adriatic canals, clung to her trim warrior figure, making her look like something out of one of his favorite anime. Oh, well. At least she *had* clothes.

No point in trying to cover up his man bits. Tina had already seen them. He shrugged and looked behind him, where the creatures that had harassed him had been rendered dust. "Zompires."

"Zompires? What are you—" Understanding dawned on her face a moment before her face screwed up. "Not those. I mean... *that!*" Her hands mimicked an explosion, balling up before dashing out in opposite directions. "It was as if you exploded."

"A special kind of solarium, unique to Helsings." He looked down at his own dripping, naked body, suddenly aware of how fucking cold Venice could be in the winter. "It has... consequences."

"I'll say," Tina took up, struggling to pull her saturated overcoat off. "Those things just turned to dust... even the ones in the water with me."

"Yeah, well, in fairness, so would most organic matter within about three or four meters of me. Luckily, you're a slayer so I knew you'd be fine. But... shit, Portia!"

He crossed the courtyard to her using every bit of speed he had left in him. Which, admittedly, wasn't much. Tina followed, pulling his arm over her shoulders when he faltered. Portia, still on the ground, rolled into as small of a form as she could manage. She'd lashed her arms over her ears, which explained how she didn't know the coast was clear.

"Portia!" Caleb took a knee at her side, reaching out and shaking her gently. He didn't want to startle her, but he also desperately needed to find out if he killed her. From his perspective, the only evidence of any harm was to her clothing. The portion of her body that had faced his blast had none, meaning her back, her shoulders, and her—fairly fine ass for an older chick—were all on display.

But they were also pristine and unmarred.

What the fuck, had her clothes been made of Kevlar?

She turned slowly, as if still expecting to see her attackers. Her features relaxed for a moment when she saw it was only Caleb. Then, quite suddenly, shockingly, she screamed, pushing herself up to a seated position before reverse crab walking to get some distance.

"Caleb?" She asked in an accusing tone. "Why are you naked?"

"Clothing doesn't do well against a full-body solarium." He wasn't ashamed of his naked body. Unlike a werewolf, though, he wasn't totally comfortable going commando in front of every Tom, Dick, and Harry.

Luckily, Tina, either jealous or maybe just a decent person, solved that. She'd managed to do something to her coat to get the worst of the waterlogging out. Now, it was merely wet but workable as the female slayer draped it over Caleb's shoulders. He now knew what the balloon at the middle of a paper mâché project felt like.

Somehow, he managed to push his arms through the heavy sleeves, ignoring how tight a woman's coat was on his male body. The garment proved long enough to cover even his lengthy assets.

Also, the cold helped keep *a certain thing* from being too extensive.

"Caleb, look at this."

Tina splayed out her hand, showing off a tiny button-sized bauble made of gold and painted over in strips of blue and red.

"That looks a lot like the one we pulled out of the body back at the palazzo." He pinched it between his fingers and held it up to the level of his eyes for closer inspection. "Where did you find it?"

"In the ash heap your Zompires left behind." She pointed vaguely in that direction. "And I bet you if we dug through the ashes, we'd find three more."

Caleb bristled. "I think you mean, like, ten or fifteen," he said. "You think it only took four of those things to outmaneuver me?"

"I *can* count, you know."

Massimo's sudden arrival finally snapped Portia out of her cower. She rolled up on her hands and knees before pulling herself to her feet as Caleb pushed the golden bug into Tina's borrowed coat pocket.

"*Cara mia*, no." The Doge managed to pull off a convincing Gomez Addams impersonation, hurrying to the feet of his woman and taking her right hand in both of his, kissing her knuckles. "Are you okay?"

"Massimo?" She seemed confused by his appearance. "You've been here the whole time?" She looked back over her shoulder to where Tina and Caleb stood before turning accusing eyes on her husband. "And you didn't *do* anything?"

"Something *blocked* my entry," he said, pulling her into his hold and pressing her head against his shoulder. "The moment the enchantment fell, I approached. I—"

His words stilled as his hands made their way down her back, his fingers flexing out when he found bare flesh.

Suddenly, Portia had been turned one-eighty, and found herself standing behind her husband, her eyes turned toward the water and the slayers. "Massimo, what are you doing?"

But the Doge now only had eyes for Caleb, and they were full of accusation and rage. "How dare you harm my wife with your power, Helsing! How dare you set your eyes on her naked form!"

Portia, realizing suddenly that the nippy night air was nipping places it had no place being, shrank back.

Caleb put up his hands in surrender, managing his feet if still wobbly. "Whoa, there, *Your Excellency.*" The term sounded mocking. "I just *saved* your wife's life. And *mine,* for what it's worth. Her... *backside* being exposed was a secondary effect. And as you'll plainly see once you get her home and look closer..." he made some vague motion to indicate Portia's portside, "... her Prada may be toast, but her skin is unblemished."

Which, now that Caleb thought about it, didn't make any sense. "Wait a minute..." he said, ticking a finger in the air. "Your wife is...."

Massimo's jaw worked over itself. "Don't say it. Not here. Not out in the open."

Well, that wasn't a fervent denial, was it? Only... "How?"

But before there could be any more threats or revelations, Portia struck out an arm and pointed out toward the water. "Massimo, look!"

They all turned, open accusations of secret supernatural existence momentarily pushed aside, and followed the direction Portia pointed. The water was different now. Definitely Venetian, and if its dull color and murky edges weren't proof enough, the smell would. Likewise, on the opposite shore, the customary earthen-toned houses rose from the ancient canal, except for a clearing similar to theirs where a man on foot could walk unencumbered to a boat access point.

There, stood a person in a sliver of light. The bagginess of their clothes, matched with a brown hoodie pulled over their face, made it impossible to say if it was male or female. Plus, as Caleb understood it, he wasn't supposed to make that assumption anymore anyway, no matter what his male brain told him. *They* struck up a hand as if to wave. Only it didn't. Instead, *they* splayed *their* fingers and then tightened them into a fist.

The "ash heap," as Tina so wisely called it, that had been the zompires began to throw up tiny stacks of detritus. Within moments, three dots of gold shot out from beneath the detritus and zipped across the surface of the canal, followed a moment later by many more breaking the surface of the water. The brethren joined in flight, landing with military precision straight into the palm of their master. As soon as the last scarab made contact, the figure closed *their* palm... and vanished from sight.

Massimo pushed his hand to his throat. "*Che cazzo è?"*

Caleb didn't speak Italian, but he was pretty sure there was an expletive in there somewhere. One that he was thinking too.

Suddenly, the Doge seemed a lot less concerned about his wife's partial dress. He pushed her gently towards the slayers. "Protect the Dogaressa with your life, Helsing."

Caleb flipped his hand through the air. "I thought that's what I just did."

Massimo didn't banter. How typical of the nobility. "Pavlos will be here momentarily. He will escort you back to the palazzo. *Amaro mio—*"

Portia cut off her husband by pressing a hand to the side of his face and nodding. "I understand. Go."

Massimo pushed a kiss against his wife's cheek one moment, and the next, became a pillar of smoke, zipping back out of the alley from which they'd come.

TWENTY-SEVEN

Amy jerked awake seconds after falling asleep, but not in time to keep herself from banging her chin on the table.

"Ow!" Pain exploded through her jaw and nose, as sharp as it was temporary. The kind of pain that hurt more because it made you look like an idiot.

She turned pinching eyes on the vampire chuckling lowly beside her. "Something funny, *Chairperson*?"

Raquel flatlined her features. Barely. "Nothing."

"That's what I thought."

Amy wasn't sure what had her so lippy. Maybe it was because the Latina tiger she'd feared for the last year and a half turned out to have a warm, fuzzy kitten side. Or, well, maybe at least a room temperature, pipe-cleaner-bristle side. A bigger factor, however, was the fact that she'd only gotten three hours of sleep in the last twenty-four, or that most of the food she'd eaten in the last two days had exited her body in a series of vile retches. Maybe it was because she'd stubbed her toe getting out of bed when Pavlos had summoned her to the dining hall on his way to run an errand *just minutes after she'd finally gotten back to sleep.* Maybe it was all of that.

Maybe it was hormones, because being a human female was just like that.

"Are you feeling better?" Raquel asked casually as Amy rubbed the hurt from her lower face.

"If you mean, am I still throwing up, no." She dropped her hands along with her hissy attitude. "But after whatever this is seems to be over, I need, like, a three-course meal, *no seafood.*"

"The Doge owns several restaurants in town, I hear. I'm sure that can be arranged." A moment of silence, until Raquel added, "Did you take it?"

"No."

No need between them to say what *it* was. They both knew.

Though the vampire didn't turn her head, Amy saw a smirk lift Raquel's features.

"Don't think I don't know why you *really* gave it to me," Amy bit out before the vampire could get too full of herself and her brilliant scheming. "You *wanted* to see if I'd gobble it down, no thought to the future. If it can really do what you say, it would be stupid to waste it on a... how did you put it, *tummy ache?* You were testing me, though what the hell for is beyond me."

"Someday it won't be," was Raquel's cryptic response. "But you're very young, even for a huey. Suffice it to say, Amy, I see a great future for you, especially with my assistance."

"Yeah, well, don't. I'm not your little human dress-up doll, and I'm sure as hell not your acolyte."

Any further bickering was abruptly cut off as the doors on the opposite side of the room opened, and —with Pavlos in the lead— Caleb, Tina, and Portia walked in.

Dressed in the gaudiest tourist trap attire Amy had ever seen.

Super starchy, bright-white T-shirts with *VENICE* or silhouettes of the city's iconic structures screen-printed across them in various styles and colors wouldn't have been her fashion of choice. Both the women wore skin-tight leggings printed to look like the Italian flag if it had been put on a taffy-stretching machine. Though, admittedly, they didn't look *bad.* Tina's natural-born athletic physique meant she could make two burlap sacks duct taped around her legs look good. Portia Bruneli, in the meantime, may be a middle-aged woman, but she did *not* miss leg day and had to be rocking Pilates. Caleb, at the rear, wore a pair of loose-fitting soccer shorts emblazoned on the outer thigh with the logo of Venice's Serie A football team.

Raquel leaned back in her seat, stretching one arm over the table. "Oh, this is going to be *quite* entertaining."

Caleb grimaced. "We needed clothes, and options in that part of town in the middle of the night were limited."

"Wait, you *needed* clothes?" Now Amy's interest was piqued. "What happened to the ones you were wearing?"

"The Solari's skills can be very..." Tina searched the air for the right word, "... *robust.*"

Was it her imagination, or had the female slayer come down a peg since Amy had last seen her? It *wasn't* her imagination that Tina was avoiding everyone's gazes like she was ashamed of something or maybe trying not to be noticed.

Caleb, however, ignored the question, focusing instead on the shiny silver carafe on the table. "Is there coffee in that thing? I *really* need there to be coffee in that thing. I'm so..."

He lunged forward. Or so Amy thought, until a moment later when he caught himself on the back of one of the dramatic chairs at the table to keep from falling forward.

"Caleb?" She jumped to her feet and circled as fast as she could, putting an arm around him to steady him. "What's wrong with you?"

A bashful smile blossomed on his face. "Me? Nothing. Just wiped the hell out. Those super-solaria things pack a punch, but boy, do they cost me."

"Super-solaria?" Raquel was on her feet now too, although she stayed standing on the other side of the table. "What is that?"

"You know..." Caleb made a motion with his hands like a bomb going off as he regained his feet, "... the Helsing Halo. The slayer's scythe. The OG Greek fire. Whatever you crazy vampire kids are calling it these days."

Portia, sensing an adult was needed in this conversation, took it up from there. "We were attacked in the northeast part of town by... what was that term you used again, zompires?" she asked while looking at Caleb.

He finished pouring himself a cup of coffee, downed it in one swig, then nodded. "Yeah, a dozen or so. Too many to fight individually, and they got the upper hand. So I did what I had to do."

"Apparently, the Helsings have some kind of special weapon that's like a solarium on crack." Amy remembered Geri Kline, her best friend, describing the Battle of the Tahquamenon and the maneuver Caleb had made to cut down a large swath of the enemy in one fell swoop... with the assistance of a lighthouse's reflecting dish, but still. "He just kind of... explodes energy in all directions, like a supernatural solar disco ball."

"I can direct it a little. Like when you put a wok on an open flame. The angle can change the distribution of the fire, but some of it still makes it around the edges." Caleb poured himself a second cup of coffee. Coffee, frankly, Amy would have drunk already if she had known it had been present. "Did the trick, though! Killed those freaking zompires on the spot. Unfortunately, now I feel like I've been hit by a bus. And my Brioni dress shirt? It and everything else I was wearing... a cloud of dust."

"Zompires? What is a..."

But Amy's question was cut off when a swirl of black smoke bee-lined into the room and just as quickly solidified into the Doge.

"*Mia bella*!" Massimo wasted no time running his hands over his wife's body, twisting and turning to examine all her curves and edges for any sign of damage. "Tell me you are well."

Portia closed her eyes and leaned her forehead against his. "I'm fine. Not a scratch. Thanks to Caleb."

The name seemed to remind the Doge that the Slayer Solari was present in his dining room, helping himself to a third cup of caffeine juice in as many minutes.

"You protected her with your life, as you promised you would," he said, turning. "You are a man of honor. How can I repay your valor?"

"Other than a few drunk Chinese tourists we crossed paths with and the formidable lock that Pavlos undid at the Venice View souvenir shop, there wasn't much to protect her from after we parted ways. But if you insist..." Caleb put down his coffee cup and motioned vaguely at Portia. "Let's start with the candy cane-legged elephant in the room. Your wife is a slayer."

Amy took a step back. "What?"

Caleb grinned, turning to his assistant. "A slayer," he repeated. "Notice how non-crispy the Dogaressa is, despite the fact that I destroyed her clothing when I released all that energy?" He turned back to the royal couple and flipped an index finger in their direction. "Her hair isn't even scorched."

The Doge's jaw went rigid. "Watch your tongue, Helsing."

"I thought you owed me?" Caleb bit back. "This is what you give me in return, Massimo. You give me *the truth*."

Massimo only had a moment to hiss and bare very prominent fangs before Portia peeked out from behind his protective stance.

"It's true," she said, stepping out in front of him. "Or at least, it's true that I'm *part*."

"*Dulcisi!*"

Portia put up her index finger, stopping Massimo's pleadings. "No, he needs to know this." She turned back to Caleb. "Yes, I'm part-slayer. But that's all I can tell you. I don't know much more than that. We've been able to figure out my grandmother knew, that she somehow managed to have my powers awakened when I was about twelve or so. We don't think she was a slayer herself, that the traits came from my grandfather."

"Good, now that we have that out in the open." Caleb crossed his arms over his chest. "Who else knows?"

With the cat out of the bag, Massimo dropped his defenses and his attitude. "Only the people in this room, and my sister, the Duchess of Florence. Portia's abilities are minimal. Her genetic disposition is weak enough that most vampires cannot sense her presence. Even I, with all my age, only had a slight inclination that she was different when we first met."

That might also be something the brainiacs at WWL could help with, but this wasn't the time or place to discuss it.

"So not your court." Caleb chewed on that a second. "That's... curious."

"Hello?" Amy lifted her hand in mock third-grader style. "Why are we talking about this right now when you guys just used the term 'zompire' like that was a thing?"

Caleb grimaced at her. "I'm not really sure what those things that attacked us were," he said. "They had fangs like vampires and their strength, but they looked like they'd been dead for a while."

"As a vampire myself," Raquel said, "I'll ask you to clarify on that."

"They were bloodless," Tina took up. "Like the corpse we examined earlier. When they first attacked Portia and me, I was able to rip the arm off one, but it didn't bleed. A human body, even a supernatural one, should spray blood like a firehose when it has an appendage ripped off."

"Corpse you examined—" Portia's voice broke off as she rounded on her husband. "I thought you burned the two bodies you found earlier this month?"

Massimo's face dropped. "A third was brought to us by the *Polizia* earlier tonight. They found it floating in the canals this afternoon."

"But a dead vampire exposed to daylight should have ashed," Portia said, lowering herself into one of the chairs. "My God, what is going on?"

Amy stayed focused on Tina. She had a sickly feeling this wasn't her first daddy longlegs-like experience, a reminder that the slayer hadn't emerged from her prison without a lot of backstory that remained to be told.

Before she could speculate on that too much, however, Tina continued, "But it wasn't just that," she said. "After Caleb ashed them, we found scarabs just like the one I pulled out of that body earlier tonight. But then, we barely had time to look at them before some figure across the water... I don't know, like recalled them all."

"Pavlos." Massimo stepped around his wife and approached his second. "Is the one we had here still in your possession? Have you learned anything about it?"

Pavlos bobbed his head. "I put it in the safe in my office after taking several

photographs with my phone. I used those to do an internet image search. I *do*
so love how this generation's technology allows for such things."

"And what did you find out?" Caleb asked the question they all were thinking.

"Nothing specific to the one we found," Pavlos admitted with a shrug. "Several results suggested it was akin to the amulets buried with Egyptian mummies,
a symbol of the deity called *Khepri,* their god of resurrection."

Amy's heart leaped, an event that caught the attention of all the vampires,
who turned on her immediately.

"That... *means* something to you," Raquel said as a statement, not a question.
"What?"

Yes, it certainly did mean something, but what? The blonde huey turned to
her boss. "Hey, Buffy, do you remember a couple of years ago when we were
hiding out at Schloss Wolfsretter?"

"Yeah, of course," Caleb said. "World headquarters for the hoods. The *wolf-*
sretter," he amended, using the more official name for the type of supernatural
creature Geri Kline and her people were. "Or at least, it was. The Dracule
attacked and destroyed it. It's being rebuilt now with a loan I was able to have
WWL back, but yeah.... what about it?"

Amy licked her lips before continuing. "Remember that time that old German lady who was like the janitor of the place took us down to their archive
room and showed us that weird piece of papyrus?"

"Papyrus?" Massimo asked. "Not many of those are still around, even during
my formative years as a young vampire in the seventeenth century. What did it
say?"

Caleb sounded dismissive. "It was some kind of origin story. A priestess
was knocked up by one of the Egyptian gods, and their kids became hoods or
something like that. Only, the hoods had it wrong. That's the *slayer* origin story.
My parents used to tell it to me as a bedtime story when I was little."

Amy snapped as if to say *exactly*. "If slayers and hoods come from Egyptian
gods, and now suddenly, we're dealing with something using scarab amulets to

magically bring the dead back to life, that's a hell of a coincidence, isn't it?"

"Coincidence is never coincidence."

Amy's head went on a swivel, looking at each of the vampires in turn as they recited the line like triggered Pavlovian beasts. "Seriously, did you all rehearse that?"

Caleb shook his head. "It's a vampire idiom. A stupid, *untrue* vampire idiom." He picked up the coffee cup again. Jeez, how much caffeine did this guy need? "Sometimes coincidence *is* just coincidence, or why would that word even exist?"

"It does seem to be an astounding..." Portia's eyes circled the air, looking for a different word from the ether, "... *fluke*, if nothing else, though, doesn't it? I mean, we're basically talking about mummies here, right? Minus the being-wrapped-in-bandages and moaning thing, of course."

"If they were fresh bodies, like the one we had here?" Pavlos suggested. "Who says a mummy needs to have been buried for thousands of years to rise from the grave? But what sort of power does that? Vampirism is one thing. It's an illness we're infected with. But reanimation? Even a maker's bite won't raise the dead."

"Oh my gods, people, be serious for a moment." Caleb had had enough of the outlandish, it seemed. "I don't really care what they were or even *who*. I want to know *why* they were trying to kill us."

"I don't think they were."

"Tina?" Caleb thumbed his nose and took a few steps toward the woman who'd spoken softly. "Something you'd like to share with the whole class?"

"I said," her words were louder now, pronounced with an edge of rebellion. "I don't think they *were* trying to kill us. I think they were trying to *capture* us."

Raquel put a hand on the female slayer's shoulder, encouraging her. "What makes you think so?"

Well, well. The Latina lynx *did* have the ability to be tender to other people too. If Raquel wasn't careful, Amy was about to accuse her of having a soul.

Tina shrugged. "Because that's what the one who showed up here later dead tried to do. Or did, really."

Massimo lifted a hand, his index finger bobbing. "Do you mean to say that the body we examined here... had approached you while it was *alive?*"

"Yes. Or no. Something like that." The weight of everyone's stares cracked her resolve. Tina pulled away from Raquel and began pacing the room. "Look, I wanted to tell you. I *tried* to tell Caleb, but he threw me out of the room before I could, didn't he, with his *the glorious vampire who deserves our protection* spiel? But, yeah, earlier that day, when I was out walking off my bad attitude—"

Unsuccessfully, Amy thought, but didn't say aloud.

"I took a gondola ride. The guy rowing the boat was all normal at first. But then we took a turn up some little water alley, and before I knew what was going on, he'd ditched me in some backwater boathouse and *that woman* leaped out of the water and pulled me in. She wasn't trying to hurt me, she said. Said she was just trying to neutralize my powers so she could talk to me without me destroying her first."

"And what did she say?" Caleb demanded.

"That there was a slayer the Doge was keeping prisoner, but if I managed to get her or him near the water, she'd pull off a rescue. Somehow, she *knew* about Portia, even though we didn't. And she also said that the Solari had to free all the slayers still in captivity so we could join some kind of battle."

"Me, keeping Portia prisoner?" Massimo said. "Surely you know it's quite the opposite. *I* am *her* slave. She owns my heart."

Portia was too practical to be wooed. "But at the same time, I keep my heritage a secret here only because you want me to. Maybe that's what she was talking about."

Before her husband could rattle off any sort of justification, Portia put up a hand. "Look, I'm not saying I want to put it on a T-shirt and run around court. I understand why we have to be careful. But from an outsider's perspective, it might not look that way."

Caleb shook his head. "Let's focus on the part where somebody did know, and I'm supposed to be on the lookout for more slayers so we can go off fighting... who exactly? And why?"

Tina shrugged. "Look, that's the message I got. And I agree, Portia is obviously *not* a prisoner. *I*, of all people, would recognize someone being held against their will... even if I do think we should be asking why a vampire as powerful as Massimo wants to keep her secret, especially if he's throwing us a ball and doesn't care if everyone knows who and what *we* are."

Amy could see a high-pressure system forming in the room, Tropical Storm Tina at its center. She needed to diffuse this and get them back on track. "Okay, for reals, Tina? Because you, of all people, know what vampire extremists are like. You and the other Reclaimed were the fuel cells that kept Fuhrer Tepeş's troops gassed up. Of course the Doge wanted to protect her. Now that you and Caleb are here, it's much harder to bully three people than one."

Massimo's ire, visible in the way his face had looked like a balloon about to pop, deflated.

Amy pressed on, "But to take us back to the top of the hour on this convo, *I* don't think it's a coincidence. That scroll we saw said an Egyptian god was the father, or maybe it was the mother, of all supes. I did a little research into it once, but Egyptian mythology, it turns out, isn't exactly black and white. The gods change names and powers over the centuries. I never ran across what's-his-face-it—"

"Khepri," Pavlos inserted.

"Right, Capri." Amy knew her pronunciation was off but didn't care. "But it did mention a sun god, and when you think about it, that makes a lot of sense for the slayers. Aten or Ra could match that. Sometimes in history, that's different dudes. Sometimes they're the same thing. Sometimes, they're enemies."

"And both were represented by the sun disk," Caleb said. He lifted his hand and invoked a pea-sized ball of energy. "Sorry, it's so small. I'm still pretty wiped out from what I did down by the river. But I think y'all can see the connection."

The vampires couldn't. They all had either turned or, in Massimo's case, lifted his hands to cover his eyes.

"Sorry." Caleb closed his hand, extinguishing the power. "I was just trying to illustrate my point."

"So, what, then?" Portia asked. "Why would a sun disk god *need* slayers? Surely their powers would surpass anything they handed down to their basically-huey-upgrades children."

The blonde huey stuck up a finger. "But remember, there were multiple gods, each with their own abilities. Who's to say that the one trying to recruit slayers for their army is the one who gave them their power?"

"Again, why would a god need that?" Raquel asked.

"Because the slayers have the power that god needs to defeat his enemy," Massimo said. "While the attempted kidnapping was happening, I was nearby but couldn't push forward to aid in my beloved's defense. I was kept away somehow, for some reason. I believe now because I am a vampire."

"So what you're saying is..." Caleb lowered himself into one of the chairs at the table, "... someone's gunning for vampires, and they need the slayers' help to do it. That would explain why they want me. I'm solari. You get me, you get the Reclaimed. You get an army... or at least, the start of one." His eyes pulled up and found Amy's. "We need to get home. We need to get to the Reclaimed before they do."

TWENTY-EIGHT

C aleb needed a moment to himself.

In the east, the rosy fingers of dawn had begun to tickle the horizon. A clean breeze blew in, bringing a wall of sea air. No one had told him "fresh sea air" actually meant salted fish-scented, but it did clear the lungs. He took a deep breath, wanting to trap the memory of when he gave up completely.

They were leaving without Massimo. The whole reason he'd come to this town was to trick, no. *Encourage* the Doge to fulfill his end of the bargain struck in London. For a swipe of Mina Helsing's Illustrian blood, the Italian Sovereign would be rendered human, allowing him to live out the rest of his life in tangent with his bride. In exchange, Massimo would bring his centuries of experience and library full of supernatural knowledge to WWL, where he'd serve as a mentor to the Reclaimed. And, in Caleb's mind, appease the Board enough to let the wayward CEO go even deeper into his morally gray habits.

But surprise, surprise, suddenly Caleb was so squarely on that hook, his feet were dangling off the floor. *Something's coming for the slayers.* The truth kept tickling at his fingertips, teasing his powers and his self-indulgent inclinations. He wasn't into being a leader, but the thought of his kind being targeted *again*? Like hell. They'd been prisoners and blood slaves for years. Some of them, like

Tina, their whole lives. He refused to let history repeat itself.

"Penny for your thoughts?"

He'd been so distracted, Caleb hadn't heard Amy walk up behind him. The Solari jerked to life, ripping his eyes away from the horizon and looking at the huey. "You think I come that cheap?"

"I think you'd *come* for a sip of water if the woman involved was willing."

A lightning thought passed through his stream of consciousness that, in any other situation, the woman before him might be. And like that, it was gone.

Caleb turned his head to tame his roving eyes. "I feel like we can't get home fast enough."

"We can. *We will.* We've notified Gabor. He and the rest of security are going to make sure everyone is safe until we get back. Besides..." Amy looked out from the formal entryway to the palazzo, the docks of one of the more prominent canals in Venice where members of Massimo's court entered and exited by boat. "These *zompires* seem to like water. As long as we stay away from the river and Navy Pier, we should be fine."

Caleb shrugged. "I guess you're right." He shifted his weight. "Speaking of which, I'm not sure a boat is the best way to get to the airport. Both times these things have come after one of us, it's been from the water."

"I agree."

He did a double-take in her direction. "Sorry, but did you actually just say I was right about something?"

"Broken clocks or something." Amy flipped a hand through the air. "But yeah, it's more dangerous... for us. But think about the alternative. If one comes after you guys while we're on a train or in a car, it would be impossible to keep hueys from seeing it, let alone protect them from getting hurt. Besides, if they are some kind of vampire like you said, then they can't get to us in the daytime, can they?"

"They're not gargoyles. They don't turn to stone during the day. But remember that Tina said that one did come after her with the sunup."

"Yeah, but inside a building and out of any direct light. If they really are some kind of vampire, they're weaker during the day, right?" Amy pointed to the sky, where the sun had just peaked over the horizon. "There's going to be plenty of sun, and it's only a half hour to the airport, during which time we'll be moving much too fast for even the fish to keep up."

"Okay, yeah, I guess." Caleb's eyes dropped to the ground until, a moment later, when Amy reached out and squeezed his arm.

"I promise you, Buffy, everything will be fine," she assured. "I'm only sorry this trip didn't work out the way you wanted it to. I promise I'm going to help you all through this. And if the board does fire you..." she shrugged, "... well, I guess I'll hand in my resignation too."

"Of course, you will. Nobody except me could stand to work with you."

It was obvious Raquel de la Vega's footsteps were intentionally heavy-footed as she marched into their vicinity. "On the contrary, I'd make a very good offer for Amy to stay, with or without you."

Tina, Portia, and Massimo turned. A handful of the palazzo's daytime staffers carried up the rear but stayed only long enough to deposit the leaving parties' luggage. Both vampires kept their distance from the open door, even though the sunshine had yet to angle into the adjacent canal.

The Doge rubbed his hands together before folding them in front of him. "Pavlos apologizes that he cannot be here to see you off. He's coordinating the last-minute details for tonight's gala."

"A gala thrown in our honor that we won't even be at," Caleb said. "I'm so sorry it worked out this way, after you've gone through so much trouble to organize everything."

Portia waved off the comment. "Don't worry about it. We have parties for some reason or another all the time. We can make some excuse for your early departure, but Massimo already booked staff from his restaurants and they've been preparing for a few days. There's a surprising amount of human food at these things. Even those who don't normally eat it anymore consider it some kind of cheat day. Anyway, we didn't see a reason for all that hard work to be for nothing."

"All the same," Caleb said. "I'm sorry we'll miss it. I was really looking forward to seeing Popowitz here in a ballgown."

"I've confirmed with WWL our itinerary and arrival," the chairperson said. "We'll stop to refuel in Ireland, then be home midday Chicago time. The company jet was released by the Red Matron yesterday. Luckily it was in Germany already so getting it here on short notice proved easy enough. Both it and the car that will meet us at O'Hare are outfitted with Athenian glass, so my shame will be short lived."

Amy turned and offered a pinched smile. "I am sorry about this, Raquel. It was the best solution I could think of."

Portia perked up. "What? What is she talking about?"

Massimo stepped in toward his wife. "Because of the several opportunities there would be for Raquel to be exposed to deadly sunlight, she will be concealed en route to the plane."

"Concealed is a kind way of saying it," Raquel bit out. "I am to be stuffed into a bottle like some back-alley djinn."

"Djinn?" Portia's brow creased. "Do you mean, like... a Jeanie in a bottle, little harem outfit and all?"

Raquel's face flattened. "There will be *no* harem outfit."

"I had the idea from something I was involved in years ago," Massimo said, putting himself between the two women both conversationally and physically. "There was a hood once who needed to trap a vampire here in Venice. She wielded her silver and encased him in an urn of her own making."

"Geri did that once too," Caleb picked up, ignoring the way it still hurt to say her name. "When a vamp was helping her investigate something in Austria and she had to drive during the day from Germany."

"Forgoing the bespoke silver vessels, concealment has been a form of transport for as long as there have been vampires," Raquel resumed. "Though in the age of Athenian glass, it is seen as the poor vampire's choice."

Amy reached into one of the bags the porters had deposited and pulled out a dark wine bottle, wrapped on its bottom half by straw.

One of Raquel's eyebrows rose to a cutting angle. "Seriously?"

Amy shrugged. "It was the best the staff could come up with on such short notice. Look, it's only going to be for a half hour. I promise, none of us will ever breathe a word about it to anyone."

"You won't need to. If any vampire *breathes anything* by me for the next week, they're going to smell it."

A moment passed in which no one said or did anything, until finally, Amy popped the cork from the bottle's neck and tilted it toward Raquel. "Smokey, smokey."

The chairperson scowled, turned to the Doge and Portia to make a proper bow and goodbye, and dematerialized her form. Caleb had to admit, but valuing his life, he'd never speak it to anyone, that the scene did remind him of several Hollywood takes on female djinn minus any sexiness.

"Well, that's that, then." Amy pushed the cork back into the bottle after there was no visible smoke trail before shoving it into her messenger bag.

The Doge stepped forward and handed her a small jewelry box. "The amulet, as requested."

Caleb's brow furrowed. "Why are we taking that?"

The Doge seemed confused by the question. "Miss Popowitz said you had a Varanasi on staff who might be able to tell you more about it?"

"We do?" He turned on the blonde huey too.

The Varanasi were among the oldest known vampire bloodlines, with roots in India dating back thousands of years. As a consequence, they'd witnessed more supernatural history than anyone else. Sometime around the birth of the Egyptian empires, one of them got the notion to start writing things down. If there was something to be known about the scarab, then they may be the ones to know it.

Amy's features were flat, except for her eyes which begged him to cover the lie. "Yeah, you know, Janus Souza. True, he's more of a kinda consultant, but I wouldn't expect *you* to know," she said, artfully covering up the uptick in her blood pressure with the illusion of frustration. Which, given her baseline mood whenever Caleb was around, might *not* be an illusion at all.

"Oh, right." Caleb rolled up his lower lip and nodded. "Forgot about him. Good idea. He might know something."

With that in order, Amy quickly turned on the Doge and changed the subject as she slid the box into her bag next to the bottle of Chateau d'Vamp. "I admit, Your Excellency, that I read a ton about the protocol for arriving to your court, but I'm not sure what I'm supposed to do when we leave. Do I bow or kiss your hand or something?"

Massimo put up a hand and shook his head. "We will forgo formalities amongst friends. We have weathered a traumatic experience together. Our bonds are too tight now to loosen for ceremony's sake, even in Venice."

Portia, however, came forward, arms out and heading in Amy's direction. "Yeah, well, I'm still a Canadian at heart." When she wrapped her arms around the blonde huey, there was only a moment of resistance before Amy mirrored the gesture.

"Take care of yourself, both of you," Portia said, pulling back and reaching out a hand to Caleb. Then, looking to Tina, she added, "And if *any of you* ever need a break from Chicago, know that you're always welcome here."

Caleb's face scrunched up, wondering just how close the two women had gotten during their impromptu alleyway meet up before they were beset by animated corpses. More than that, why would Tina need a break from Chicago?

Questions for a later time, he supposed. Even in the few minutes since the sun had risen, it was already gaining pavement, and the Doge retreated further inside.

"Well, then, I guess that's it." Caleb grabbed his bags and a few of Amy's and headed for the boat. "Same offer back at you, by the way. Come to Chicago. You'll love our pizza."

Twenty-Nine

T en minutes or so across the bay that separated the cluster of islands from the mainland, Amy took a seat next to Caleb inside the boat's cabin. He kept his head on a swivel, looking for any sign of trouble.

The blonde huey nudged his side. "You should apologize to her."

No wondering which *her,* the female slayer who was standing on the back of the boat out in the open air, watching the city sink into the background. Tina looked like a mopey child leaving an amusement park.

"I'd be happy to," Caleb said, knowing Tina was too close to the revving motors for even her sensitive hearing to pick up. "If only I knew what I did to piss her off."

Amy's mouth dropped open. "Seriously?"

The Solari shifted in his seat. "I mean, yeah, we slept together once, but it was *only sex.* There wasn't any emotion there."

"Maybe not for you..."

She let the statement breathe and take on a life of its own. A strange little worm too, one that niggled its way down into Caleb's thoughts until, finally and before he realized what he was doing, he was on his feet.

The cool air sliced across his face when he emerged from the cabin, reminding him of the sheer coming up off Lake Michigan during a winter storm. Caleb took place next to Tina, her gaze fixed outward.

"Hey."

"Hey."

Hands in pocket, be brave. "Tina, about what happened in the harem…"

Her hand shot up, cutting him off. "Don't."

"According to Amy, I have to." He nodded, his eyes on the waters passing below. "Okay, that sounded like I was only doing this because she told me. I'm not. *What I meant to say was,* Amy made me realize that I owe you this conversation. We have to stop *not* talking about what happened. And for my part, I wanted to let you know that I'm sorry."

Her shoulders slumped, but she didn't move otherwise. "You were a prisoner. It's not like you could have said no."

That's what I told Amy! His inner voice grumbled. While Caleb may not always agree with the blonde huey, he'd learned she wasn't totally clueless, especially when it came to emotional stuff.

"Yeah, but I didn't have to say yes so quickly. But, whatever, that isn't the point. Especially since, you know, what happened in the harem didn't mean anything."

The way Tina's head lashed to the side, and her mouth dropped reminded Caleb of the snake hair of Medusa coming to life and turning someone to stone.

"You… don't think that?"

"Well, *now* I do." Tina shoved her hands in her pockets and shifted her weight. "Gods, Caleb, you don't understand women at all, do you? For how many you sleep with, and yes, I do know about that. Everyone *knows* about that. You should have an honorary degree in female studies by now."

"I know how to please a woman *physically*." Actually, he was damned good at it. "But if you mean do I understand how relationships work or why women feel the emotions they do, you're right, I don't." He put some steel into his words and his spine. "Just like every man that's ever existed."

"Do you know one of the reasons I miss the harem?"

His eyes bugged out of his head, and he wanted to jump in with accusations, but Tina started talking before he could get his thoughts pulled together.

"It's because I knew what was expected of me, and I was valued for what I provided," she admitted. "Yeah, we were slaves, and I'm not trying to claim that was a good thing. But at least our lives had purpose. You broke us out, true. You give us the basics we need to stay alive, Caleb, but what is the point if we're not becoming something more than we were before?" She rounded on him. "I know you've your way since you lost Geri Kline, but do you have to punish all of us for it?"

Caleb's memories didn't often go back to those dark hours or the events leading up to them, but they did now. A few years ago, when he'd first met the only daughter of the Hood Grand Matron, he'd admit the attraction was merely sexual. It didn't take long for that to change. Not only was Geri a supe and already embedded into his reality, but she was everything he wanted in a woman. Brave, smart, dedicated, tough, sexy, funny, powerful... Caleb never wanted to be a one-woman man until her. After Geri, though, every other woman he'd known until then seemed meaningless.

Because they were, he chastised himself. *They still are.*

Unfortunately, the very same day Caleb had gathered up the nerve to propose was the very same day Geri had decided to break up with him. Talk about moving in different directions. Coincidentally, it was also the day he'd been taken prisoner by the Ravens. Caleb supposed part of his caveman brain had looked at what went down in the harem as a shameless "this will show Geri, and then she'll be sorry and want me back" maneuver. Because *those* always worked out.

And suddenly, Caleb realized that's why he owed Tina an apology. It wasn't the fact that they'd had sex. It was why.

He let his chin dip to his chest. "What they did violated us both, but then I turned around and violated *you* on their behalf."

"Like I said, we were both prisoners, so—"

In a sudden jolt of boldness, Caleb stomped his foot, cracking the running boards that made up the deck and cutting off her words at the same time. "Damn it, Tina, that doesn't matter."

He waited a moment to see if she'd continue to argue or give him space. Luckily it was the latter. "Yes, they demanded I choose one of you to bed, but I didn't fight it. It wasn't because I feared them. If I *had* fought, I would have given in when they threatened to hurt someone, but I *didn't* fight it. I was so pissed off that Geri broke up with me. I saw it as revenge against her. You didn't deserve that. Do you hear me, Tina? You. Didn't. Deserve. That. And you still don't."

When her lip began to tremble, Caleb thought he'd finally pushed her too far, that Tina was about to pitch him over the side of the boat.

"But you chose *me*." Her voice cracked. "There were twelve of us and *you* chose *me*. I thought *that* meant something, that you saw something in me, and you and I would be..."

Tina went silent, turning her eyes back out to the water. It wasn't quick enough for Caleb not to see her tears.

"You and I know the fairy tales hueys tell each other aren't true," she said. "But somehow, I wanted one of them to be. You were the prince who'd come to save us, and I was your sultana. Even though Vlad and the others programmed us to believe that a slayer was meant to be a vampire's servant, the ones who came to the harem a little older told me differently. They said we were meant to be free."

She lifted her gaze and turned a stony glare on him. "Then, after you freed us, you disappeared. Even when we were in the same room, you were somewhere else. You'd had my body. You had my loyalty, but that Hood bitch still had your heart."

"*Don't* call Geri a bitch." His instinct to defend the woman he still loved wouldn't listen to his voice of reason, screaming *NOT NOW*. It would be difficult enough for Tina to let go of the fantasy, he thought, especially if mixed in with the confusion of sex. Quickly, Caleb put himself and his actions back in the hot seat. "But you're right. I've been avoiding the Reclaimed because, in my mind, you all are part of my memories of her. I'm sorry. I'm not going to do that anymore. I'm not going to avoid my responsibilities."

"Responsibilities?" Her tears slowed as she sniffed.

Caleb ran a hand through his hair, scratching the back of his scalp. "Yeah, you know, being the solari?" he said, moving his hand out to make a one-handed shrug. "Shit, the whole reason we're even here in Venice is so I could call in a favor."

Her brow furrowed. "A favor for what?"

Well, if he was going to bare his heart here and try to win back Tina's respect, he couldn't half-ass it. Now that his scheme had nosedived into the ground, what was there to lose anyway? "Massimo saved our lives once. Me, Geri, and that brick-house werewolf she's mated to now, Tobias. In exchange, he wanted a bit of Mina's blood."

The Reclaimed all knew Geri and Tobias's adopted daughter well. Her birth mother had been one of them, a slayer by the name of Alexandra who'd died in childbirth. For the few months that the slayers had been drifting and homeless in the world, Mina had been their ward. What they didn't know was *what* Mina's father had been. *Who* he'd been, no one was really sure.

"Mina's blood?" Tina asked. "Why? What's so special about it?"

"She's half-werewolf," Caleb informed her. "A hybrid supe called an Illustrian. Her blood has the power to reverse vampirism. Massimo found out from Tepeş himself. And when he found out the Ravens planned to ambush the three of us in London, the Doge swooped in and saved our asses."

Not Caleb's. He'd ended up smack dab in the middle of the ambush. He'd gotten free eventually.

"In exchange," he went on, shaking his memories of those few weeks. "He'd get Mina's blood. He had just hooked up with Portia then, had this fantasy of stepping back across the crimson line and growing old with her. Geri stepped up the deal, said she would give up Mina's blood if Massimo post-rollback would serve as a mentor to the slayers for ten years. I was here because I thought he could give you guys the kind of support and guidance I so royally fucked up."

With every bit of information Caleb had added, Tina's eyes widened. He was amazed they hadn't fallen out of her head yet. He was pretty sure if he leaned to the side, he'd be able to see her brain.

"Un. Believe. Able." She managed to make sushi of the word. "I... don't even know what to be pissed off about first."

"Pissed off?" Hadn't he just told her this whole trip was an attempt to help her and the others? "What is there to be pissed off about?"

Fire flushed her cheeks and her tone. "Caleb, *you* are the solari. *You* are our leader. *You* are the one who saved us. And you were just going to pass us off to some... ex-vampire nanny?"

"To a seasoned supe... *ex-supe,*" he corrected himself before she could. "Massimo would be a better leader than me any day. He actually used to run with my ancestors, knows how that whole vampire-slayer dynamic works. Me? I suck at leading. Besides, how does helping you qualify me to be the troop leader for this whole fangfest jamboree?"

"It doesn't, but you're the one who stood up and spoken for us in Germany when the hoods tried to kick us to the curb," she said, her voice suddenly a pitch higher. "You brought us to the States, claimed WWL, and gave us shelter. If you weren't trying to be our leader, then what in the hell were you doing? What other reason would you have to protect us like that?"

Vlad Tepeş was still alive then and I needed you guys on my side if I needed to use you as weapons. It was the truth, but one he wasn't willing to share. It also wasn't the only reason.

"I kind of hoped Geri would see what I was doing and be impressed."

Tina's face curdled, going from crimson to snow. "You helped save a civilization to try to impress your ex?"

He stepped into her, his words biting. "At the end of the day, I'm an amazingly one-dimensional person."

"Yeah, well, you won't get any arguments from me on that."

Tina's hands were small, but she was a supe. Caleb had just enough time to realize she'd pushed him before his ass hit the deck.

He let the pain of his tail bone striking hard wood radiate, before looking up at her with as much acid as he could manage. "*That* is why I don't date slayers."

But the attack fell short. Something else had caught Tina's attention. The female slayer had pivoted, her gaze cast out to the distance, her hands fidgeting at her sides. "What the—"

"Um, guys?"

All words died away as Amy stepped out on the deck to join them. Not because the huey was there, but because she too had spotted a thunderhead swiftly sweeping across the open water, heading straight for them.

Caleb got to his feet. Instinct drove him to spin Amy by the shoulders and push her into the cabin. "Tell the captain to get us to land *now*."

Tina's head whipped back and forth, like she was taking measure between how fast the storm bore down on them, and their distance to the shore.

"We're never going to make it in time."

Apparently, the Reclaimed's tutoring in the harem included word problems of *a train leaves Moscow at 10 p.m. variety.* Whether or not her calculations were right, the storm suddenly wasn't the problem.

The ancient vessel moving over the water in front of it was.

THIRTY

C aleb ducked back into the cabin, bypassing Amy, and exited through the front door to the helm, using maximum speed.

"Can't we go any faster?"

The two-man crew ignored him. The one at the wheel, assumingly the senior officer, was too busy squawking rapid-fire Italian into the radio receiver in his hand.

"Hey!" Caleb grabbed the junior crewman and turned him so they could be face-to-face. "You speak English? Türkçe? Ivrit?"

"Yes, signore, English." The man's shaking voice belied the attempt to look professional. "Radio is no work."

Incorrect grammar, but not the issue of the moment.

Caleb nodded. "Are there any weapons on board?"

"This is the Doge's private shuttle." This was from the captain, who evidently had been able to afford a better ESL program. He threw down the radio. "No one in all of Venice would dare attack it."

"Yeah, well..." Caleb pointed back over the water to where the vessel leading the storm was being rowed like a bat out of hell. "I don't think these guys are exactly local."

The senior crewman evoked a select list of catholic saints, but Caleb was pretty sure they weren't the ones on the boat either. Suddenly, the ruse was up. The man put his hand down a lacquered wood panel with a single metal knob on it and pulled, revealing a hidden cubby.

"Flare guns," the captain said to Caleb's unspoken question.

"We don't need to tell them where we are. They've figured out that part."

"Caleb!" Tina's voice carried from the back deck, over the low cabin, and found him. "What the hell are you doing?"

"Improvising!" He turned back to the captain. "Flare guns? Okay, fine. How many are there?"

"Two and many flares." The captain handed one of the guns to Caleb.

"I'm good." The slayer shook his head and pushed the weapon into Amy's grip as she caught up. "Take this and get down on the floor inside. I don't want to put holes in you if Tina and I start to throw around solaria."

"Caleb, that boat is..." Her words died away, but he caught the gist of it.

Fast. Impossible. Ancient? All that was somehow true. He'd only ever seen things like it in movies. The length of a commercial airplane, the craft was completely made of wood, except for a single blood-red rectangular mass, blown full from the storm. On each side of the galleys, a handful of oars worked, pushing it faster over the churning surface of the bay. This, despite the fact that, now that it was closer, Caleb could see there were no oarsmen visible. At the front of the ship, a wooden lion masthead, mouth open and teeth bared, gained definition as they approached.

Caleb turned to the captain just as he handed his own flare gun off to the junior officer. "How close were we to land before this blew in?"

"Ten, fifteen minutes away."

He sliced the air with a chopping motion. "Well, just keep going then!"

"I can't see anything out there..." he motioned past the windshield, off the bow of the ship before pointing down at the modern instrument panel, "... or here. If we hit a boat, we drown. Currents here are very strong." The electrical instrument blinked when the captain's fingers made contact, but other than the rotating arm of the radar display, nothing was to be seen.

Caleb cupped his hand over the man's shoulder and squeezed. "Just do your best, but *keep going forward*. We *can't* let ourselves be overtaken."

If he and Tina landed in the water, they'd be SOL when it came to solaria, but hopefully, they all could swim if they were close enough to shore.

Swimming couldn't be that hard, could it?

Holy shit, could Amy swim?

The captain nodded, and Caleb turned tail just in time to see their pursuer was off their starboard stern. Two truths rattled off in his thoughts at the same moment. One, he had no idea why an ancient ghost ship was bearing down on them or what kind of supernatural had the power to pull off this kind of thing. And two, it was close enough to attack *if* there were any people on board. Where were all the people?

"Tina, solaria!"

For once, she didn't bitch. "Ready!"

"Hold on, we're going to throw at the same time." Caleb found his feet next to hers. The Solari's hands sparked with power at chest level. "Any chance you were taught the weakest part of a wooden ship in that fancy harem school of yours?"

"Amazingly, that never came up." Her head flinched, and her eyes focused on the lower front. "I'm guessing if we put a big enough hole down there by the water, that'll work?"

"Hard to argue that logic." He lifted his hand and focused on the direction they'd need to aim. "On the count of three... one, two, three!"

Dual solaria sped ahead, slicing through mist and fog, gliding over the water's surface. Neither of them had said the obvious, that to make this work, they needed to make sure their aim didn't go under the water line. Just as having their lower bodies submerged in water would neutralize their ability to fight, so would the sea eat their power if it was aimed too low.

The explosion reverberated through their boat, sending shockwaves and sea foam back towards them. Caleb flashed a look over his shoulder at the captain. The man was focused on his duty while his mate, white-knuckled and wide-eyed, stood beside him with the flare gun held in James Bond style. Inside the cabin, Caleb assumed the fetal position mass he saw on the floor was Amy.

The spray settled, and the sea became calm. The ship was no longer moving forward, and the wind had stopped. A hole the size of a compact automobile appeared where water should have been pouring in.

But it wasn't.

The slayers stood with their arms raised, prepared to take action again if necessary or if it seemed the thing to do. After a few moments of silence, they turned toward each other, observing the expressions on each other's faces.

"You're seeing what I'm seeing right?"

Caleb's nod was slow and uncertain, just like his thoughts. "Why isn't it sinking?"

Any chance to answer was stolen away by the sudden splashing they both heard. The slayers turned to observe the side of the ship broiling just below the surface. It reminded Caleb of when he used to skip stones across the surface of the Dead Sea as a child, much to his father's chagrin. Only if he had been doing that using rocks the size of his head instead of a walnut.

And as soon as it had started, it stopped. The air around them hung with tension, but not a sound was to be heard except for the gentle lapping of calm waters against the side of their boat.

Eyes fixed on the enemy, Caleb called out to the captain, "If we could move faster now, that might be a good thing."

"You think I am not trying?" The captain banged the dash. "The rotors don't turn. I have her open, but... *niente!* Probably weeds wrapped around them. I'll cut the engines so you can clear them."

The last thing Caleb wanted to do right now was lean over the side of the boat. If he wasn't already eating crow, he'd ask Tina to do it instead. Lowering his hands to the railing, he softened his knees to keep his balance and peered over. Just below the surface, he could see something. Never having really learned that much about boats, he assumed the things at the end of the stem of the engine shaft were the rotors. It couldn't be that different from his coffee bean grinding machine, right? Same basic principle, swapping beans for seawater.

"I don't see anything wrong," Caleb called out.

The captain muttered an Italian curse the Solari was pretty sure was about him. "You have to reach down and *feel!*" he growled out. "Hurry!"

Caleb's face screwed up. Of all the things he wanted to feel today, icky seaweed wasn't one. He took a moment to stand up and pull off his designer jacket, throwing it on one of the benches nearby. He didn't lose sight of the fact for one moment that being supernatural did not make him impermeable. If he did manage to pull off some of the gunk and the motor started without warning, he'd come away without his favorite hand.

Cold and wet. He only liked one of those things. But as his fingers traced down to the blades of the motor, he found nothing but metal.

"They're clean!" he shouted back over his shoulder. "Are you sure that... holy shit!"

"Caleb!"

Tina swooped in just in time to keep him from going overboard and to pull him back toward the deck. Unfortunately, a cold clammy hand that had just grabbed his wrist and tried to pull him into the water wasn't letting go.

"Pull harder!" He put all his weight into his heels, leaning back and trying to make Tina's job easier. If he could open his palm, he could blast whatever it was that had him in the face at point-blank range. Although the water would stop most of the damage, it might be enough to shock the creature into letting him go. "Or just shoot over my head and hit it at the elbow."

"I can't pull you and shoot at it at the same time," Tina groaned. "Any other ideas?"

"Yes, let me shoot it for you."

The creature's head had just broken the surface. At the same moment, a flare shot off and burrowed between its eyes. For better or worse, a flare didn't go dead just because it was wet. Caleb and Tina, free of their counterweight, fell back under the deck, smacking both their asses hard. Caleb was on his feet in moments however, pulling Tina along.

The chairperson, one eyebrow raised, glared down at him.

"Raquel?" Caleb rose, dusting off his pants. "Where in the hell did you come from?"

The vampire blinked. "Amy decided to uncork me early." She opened the flare gun and shoved in another round. "I take it we haven't made it to the airport then?"

More splashing near the bow of the ship broke the air. That drew Raquel's attention. A moment later, it also triggered her confusion as she became aware of the massive watercraft overshadowing and about to overtake them.

"Have we time traveled somehow?" she asked. "There is no crew on that ship."

More splashing. A whole cacophony of it, all of it heading towards their boat. Behind them, the crewman who wasn't the captain screamed. Caleb circled, finding the man staring down the barrel of his flare gun at a zompire. Only, the creature didn't seem to be attacking. It just stayed there, squat on the roof of the cabin, motionless.

Unfortunately, not the man with the gun. He fired and missed, sending the flare into the cabin and sending Amy screaming out of it as red smoke and flames shot out. But at least it did get rid of the zompire, causing it to leap back into the waves.

Caleb ran his hands through his hair. "I'm open to any ideas on how we get out of this."

"Any chance you could foist one of your mega solaria at them?" Tina asked.

Caleb shook his head. "I'm as liable to explode our own boat as theirs. Besides," he pointed vaguely at the gaping hole in the side of the boat. "If it's not sinking from that, I doubt me putting a few more burning holes into it is going to help."

Raquel grabbed a crying Amy by the elbow and locked her in her gaze. "I'm sorry about this, Amy. But I think you'd better sleep now."

The blonde huey's legs went out from under her. Raquel used her grip to help the huey lower safely to the deck before turning back to the others. "There's nothing she can contribute."

Caleb, not normally a fan of vampires enthralling his assistant, thought this case might be justified.

Caleb, Tina, and Raquel could see them now. A dozen corpses in various stages of decay, moving like freaking Olympians across the water. They had ten, maybe fifteen seconds before they were beset.

Raquel turned toward the cabin. "I will defend the crew. You two do your best to blast anything that comes up and over the side of this boat before it can make it aboard."

Even if they had had time to discuss the why, it wasn't necessary. Tina and Caleb could throw solaria till Kingdom come, but if they put their own boat in peril by blasting a hole through it, it wasn't as likely as the magical one off their stern to stay afloat.

Caleb put up his hands, summoning his energy. He needed these solaria to behave and follow his directions to the letter.

"Small diameter, maximum speed," he told Tina.

She blinked three times in rapid succession. "What?"

"Your solaria... small diameter, maximum speed. Throwing a cannonball didn't help. Let's try buckshot."

"You can change the size of yours?"

Now it was his turn to blink. "*You* can't?"

Tina shook her head.

Now more than ever, he wished that he would have taken the time to train the Reclaimed. Tina had been given her powers in some ritual in her youth, but she'd never been taught anything more than "point and shoot." If they survived this, and if the board didn't fire him for getting them in this situation alone, he needed to remedy that.

"It's easy. You just... imagine yourself picking up frozen peas from a plate and using a table tennis paddle to project them forward." He brought up his own hands. "Ready?"

When he turned, he found Tina in battle position. Firm stance, hands up, power ignited. She was a warrior or at least had the makings of one. If he hadn't been so self-centered and been such a dick to her, he would have seen that long ago and taken advantage of it.

Her head bobbed, her jaw tightened. "Let's do this."

"Wait until they raise their bodies above the side and make sure you only hit *them*, not the boat," Caleb instructed. "If we sink and end up in the water, we can't do Jack shit. In which case, we're all probably going to die."

"You know they're only after us." Tina turned to him with wide eyes. "We could save the others by just giving up."

"I don't think you bring a battleship just to do a kidnapping, not even an antique one."

The first arm flailed over the side. Caleb shrunk his solarium down to the size of a golf ball. Once he had a view of the spine, putting a hole through it at the base of the head should do the trick. Even if huey politicians somehow managed it, he'd never heard of a supe faring well without a brain.

It pulled itself higher, higher... The elbow, the other hand, two sets of bone and muscle fingers latched the edge until it raised itself into view and...

... it had no head.

Tina broke from her defensive stance. "Great, now what?" she barked, turning on Caleb.

All the Solari could do was shrug. "Limb by limb?"

"Seriously, that's your plan, you dumb... *muffle...muffle*"

A tremendous roar drowned out Tina's words, but Caleb was pretty sure he'd just been called an idiot.

Suddenly, they were moving, their boat spitting a fishtail of water, the other boat growing smaller in their eyes. The engine revved, reared, and repelled them away. The headless goon couldn't keep a grip as a wave filled their wake. Evidently the sight of reanimated corpses was enough to convince the captain that speeding blind might be worth the risk.

Soon enough, the clouds closed in, cutting off any view of the ancient warship. The boat rocked and weaved over the water, skipping waves and landing with tremendous thumps.

Caleb had no experience as a seaman. What self-respecting Slayer would? But he knew well enough to get down low. Tina, it seemed, didn't.

One moment she was there, and the next her head, body, and feet disappeared into the surf in that order.

"Stop! We have to turn around!" Caleb crawled like a child on all fours, making his way for the cabin. "Tina went over!"

In a moment, Raquel was back, daring the flames that had begun to eat the wood that framed the cabin. "Vampires aren't affected by water. I can find her."

Caleb managed to grab her arm before she made her way out of the cabin. "No, if the clouds clear, you'll be exposed to the sun."

"I try to dive deeper to where it does not harm me and resurface after dark."

"The captain said the currents are strong here. I'm not sure even a vampire could stay submerged all day by choice." He turned back towards the captain, observing for a moment all the movements that he made. At the end of the day, it couldn't be that hard to pilot a boat, could it? Once they broke through the cloud cover and were back out of the boundaries of whatever magic was around them, they'd signal whatever boat was in view. Caleb would transfer the hueys aboard and take Massimo's luxury taxi back out to pick up one very important passenger who got left behind.

How he wouldn't be kidnapped in the process was anybody's guess.

"Get back in your bottle, Raquel. Just as soon as possible, I'm commandeering this boat and going after her."

"I can't." Raquel's hand jutted at the cabin. "It's in there somewhere."

Caleb's face screwed up.

"Whathehellhappened." Amy's muffled words and sudden consciousness proved even vampire enthrallment had limits.

Caleb knelt by Amy's side. "Are you okay?"

She swept a hand over her forehead and back to clear her hair from her face as she sat up. "What?" She looked around, trying to come up to speed with their sudden *speed*. "I'm... fine. I'm... Raquel?"

"I'm here, Amy." The vampire was at Amy's side in a moment, leaning down and taking her hand. "I'm sorry I enthralled you. I was only trying to keep you calm while we... while we... oh, no."

There was an old saying that the best way to make God laugh was to tell him your plans.

The clouds vanished, revealing calm waters near the airport docks and a brilliant daylit sky overhead. As the captain pulled back the engines and slowed to a more reasonable speed in the crowded Venetian Bay waters, a stream of sunlight formed a spotlight, trapping Raquel in its grasp.

The fact that she was clothed slowed down the worst of it, but her hands and the back of her neck were exposed and immediately began to redden. Unlike what Hollywood movies suggested, a vampire didn't burst into flame when struck by sunlight. What they did begin to do was carbonize. A vampire in her second century, Raquel wouldn't turn to ash for at least an hour, but they couldn't get off the boat at the airport with someone who looked like a comic book villain.

Not to mention, the screaming was most distracting and coupled with the fact that a half dozen other ships were now speeding in their direction, no doubt because of the fact that their boat was very much now on fire, meant avoiding attention was going to be impossible.

Amy came alive in a way any supe would have been proud of. In a moment, the blonde Huey was on her feet and digging through her bag. She found a box and pulled it out, opening it up to reveal the tiny golden amulet she'd been presented with just half an hour before.

"I really hope I'm right about this." Amy pinched the scarab between two fingers and raised it to eye level. "Raquel, say ahh!"

"Amy, what are you—"

Without warning, the blonde huey thrust the mysterious object into Raquel's mouth and pushed her chin up to close it. The vampire's eyes went wide as she swallowed both her screams and the bauble.

"What the hell did you do that for?" Caleb demanded as he rounded on his assistant, putting hands on her shoulders and pushing her back. "We have no idea what that thing is or what it does. It could kill her."

"It's not going to kill her!" Amy shot back. "At least, not if we hurry."

What was the crazy huey talking about? How could she possibly have any idea of the ramifications? Caleb decided to focus on where focus was due for now. He swept around, ready to tell Raquel that she should make for the water and swim down. She was right, she could stay there safely until sunset. But in a moment, Caleb understood that wouldn't be a possibility. Not only had Raquel stopped screaming, but the tips of her fingers, which had already begun to turn black, had grown back their color. More than that, she was positively glowing, and the vein in the side of her neck had taken on a very uniform rhythm.

"Ave Maria," the chairperson gasped, putting a healed hand to her throat and grinning. "How is it possible?"

Caleb knew what he was seeing, but that didn't mean he believed it. He had to hear it from the horse's mouth. "How is what possible, Raquel?"

"I have a pulse." Her smile was positively infectious. "I don't know how, but I'm human."

THIRTY-ONE

T ina was on her hands and knees in a moment, violently shaking as her body wretched, purging both seawater and stomach acid. The toxic mix made her throat sore and nose burn. The smell threatened to cause her to heave again. When she felt emptied, Tina pushed herself back to sit on her heels and worked at her memory. They'd been on the boat, and they'd been under attack. By an antique one, if she remembered. Suddenly, the boat engines roared, and her balance was thrown. Or had she been pulled? It seemed that there had been something in the water there.

Either way, she'd ended up overboard. Caleb had already turned at that point to make his way to the forward part of the boat and didn't notice her gone. By the time their eyes met, it was a moment before Massimo's water taxi inked out of sight. Somehow, Tina had managed to tread water long enough to turn and see the ancient wooden ship, the hole in its port that she and Caleb caused, sucking in water. Ropes cascaded off the sides, and the loathsome creatures that had been trying to pull themselves onto their boat moments before instead pulled her up to the deck of the ship. As soon as she was steady, they sunk off below deck, leaving her alone.

The clouds closed in, and she'd lost the ability to stay awake.

So where was she now? Her eyes surveyed the space, her insides twisting when she recognized her surroundings. It was the boathouse again, the same one where the original zompire had dragged her into the water. Only there was no gondola this time. No boat at all. How she had gotten here from that mysterious ghost ship, she didn't know.

And suddenly, she knew she wasn't alone.

In a blur, Tina spun, hands raised and palms out. What had Caleb said? Frozen peas. Twin solaria burst into existence, small but powerful, ready to strike. Despite the popular maxim, Tina knew it wasn't usually possible to shoot first and ask questions later. Not if you had good enough aim.

"Don't!" The man who was across the deck from her held up two hands in surrender. "Please, you have no need to fear me."

If he was a zompire, at least he was far less decayed than the others she'd seen. His skin looked complete, healthy even. His clothes were neat and plain, a pair of gray slacks and a black turtleneck sweater. His hair lay atop his head, slicked back as though combed and not matted with dried blood. Beneath locks which fanned his head sat two black, sharp eyes. A man of medium build, he would present no physical threat. Assuming, that was, that he was a huey.

He did have one distinguishing feature suggesting there was something different about him, however. The lack of a pulse.

Now that she wasn't gagging on seawater and being mobbed by the undead, Tina began to look around with a little more leisure. She could just make a dive into the water and swim for the canal, but swimming had never really been her thing. It had been a miracle that she hadn't drowned out in the bay. She could probably run past this man and into the building atop her, but she had no idea what kind of enemies she would find there. For the moment, it may be best to just play along.

"Why am I here? What happened to the others? And who are you?" She couldn't figure out which question to ask first, and they tumbled forward like a pack of dogs escaping a pen.

He dropped his hands in a show of trust but kept his distance. "My name is Aurelio. If you mean the others on the boat, they got away unharmed." Suggesting that, as far as the non-slayers went, the plan had been to leave no witnesses. "As for why you are here, that is a very long answer."

"Seems I'm going to be sticking around until you decide otherwise," she began. "So please, feel free to explain at length. Maybe you can start with why you were trying to kill my friends."

Even as she said it, she wasn't sure that word properly defined the relationship she had with Amy and Raquel. It certainly didn't fit for the two huey crew members.

Aurelio moved his eyes to the floor. "She had no desire to kill the blonde mortal. In fact, she ordered me to take extra measures *not* to harm her. The one you call Popowitz has connections that could prove troublesome if provoked."

No doubt Caleb would go on the warpath if his pet human came to any harm. Recently, it seemed that Vega had also taken an interest in the blonde huey. Rumors always were that Amy hadn't exactly been a nun before coming to WWL. Could she be striking up a relationship with the vampire while waiting for the Solari to get his act together? An insurance policy to stay under supe protection and care?

"Puppy Guts *does* have some powerful friends, even if I don't understand what everyone sees in her." Tina could admit that, even under duress. "But the others? Why would this 'she' want to harm them? And who is *she*, exactly?"

Aurelio ignored her second question to focus on the first. "My master will favor only those who stand against the daemon."

The Classical Greek term for vampires that, like the Old German *wolfsretter* for hoods, had fallen out of use in the modern era.

"She did not expect the Solari of all people to fight her call," Aurelio continued. "He destroyed her soldiers who were sent to rescue him and aligned himself with the Doge. Though she did wish for you both to be subdued, it was only because so much is at stake. She needs to be certain you will hear her out. There are so precious few of you, and she needs each of you to wage her holy quest."

By soldiers, Tina had no doubt Aurelio meant zompires. "Holy quest? I don't like the sound of that. I was forced to study enough history to know those who claim that tend to upcycle any of their own sins as the commands of some fictional deity who can't be held to account."

"On the contrary, holding herself to account is the very reason my master seeks the aid of the slayers."

Okay, so that term was now out on the table, not that Tina had doubted Aurelio understood what she was. "Again, she who?"

He blinked once, twice. "One who now understands the errors of her ways and wishes to amend for the consequences of her creations."

A cord struck in a low, foreboding note in Tina's soul. "*Her* creations?"

"Yes. I speak of the daemon, of course."

Tina's hands struck out behind her, even though there was nothing there for her to grab onto. Suddenly the world seemed unsteady, and she needed some way to keep from falling over. Through the years, she'd heard many vampire origin theories, both from vampires themselves and from books in the harem's extensive library. The most popular modern theory held vampirism had been some kind of genetic mutation. Though she'd never thought much about it, even Tina would admit that made sense. But now?

"Are you saying..." she lifted a hand as though an accusation, "... that your master is the reason vampires exist?"

Aurelio nodded.

Tina's inner critic grabbed control of her voice. She threw her hands up in the air. "That's impossible! Vampires have been around for thousands of years, and the longest-living ones known only went eight centuries." That, only possible by feeding on other supes. "There's no way there's a creature in the world who's older than that, and nobody knows about her."

"My master is timeless. Her purpose is noble." Aurelio took a step forward, his back straightening. "She was content to stand aside and let her creation prosper, but she now believes that was an error. She stands ready to strike them down and wishes for Caleb Helsing to take up the true and full mantle of his role as Solari. He must lead the slayers and slaughter all daemon."

"Yeah, well, good luck with that."

"Meaning?"

"Meaning, Caleb isn't going to be leading anyone anywhere. Not unless there's a hot blonde at the end."

The pale man's head tilted to the side. "You're saying the Solari is unworthy of his position?"

"I'm saying he's done nothing to prove he's even interested in it." Tina shrugged. "Just look at how he's treated us Reclaimed. Sure, he'll *pay* for anything we want. College, personal trainers, fancy clothes. But his attention is never on the table."

Aurelio's jaw worked as he ate this discovery. "Then we must find another solari to take his place."

It was such a simple statement that Tina found both ridiculous and undeniable. "Again, unlikely. He might be a complete... what is that term Puppy Guts likes so much... fuck up? But the others still see him as the man who rescued us from slavery. They're not going to reject him without a good reason."

"That does hold, yes."

Aurelio tucked his chin into his chest and closed his eyes. Was he sleeping? After a few moments of still silence, Tina had to wonder. Then, just as suddenly, his eyes flew open, and he fixed them on Tina.

"*You* must be the new solari," he said. "And you must do this by killing the false solari."

This time, when Tina shot her arms behind her, she did find something. A wall. Its presence meant she didn't fall back on her ass. Instead, she pressed her back against it and slid down.

"You want me to... kill Caleb?" Her voice became frail, airy. "I can't. I *won't*."

Sure, she was royally pissed at him, at the way he fraternized with vampires and flattered all matter of huey women rather than seeking one of his own kind. Rather than seeking *her*. But kill him?

"You won't have to do it alone. My master will give you the soldiers you need."

"Soldiers?" Tina barked a laugh. "If you mean those zompire things, I think he's figured out how to overcome those now." Lots of little solarium or one of his really big ones. "The only way *I* can kill him is using a huey weapon. Solaria don't hurt other slayers. Also, he's a *fucking Helsing.* There's no world where slayers survive and thrive without his bloodline continuing."

"Then you will be the mother of his child. You will be the mother of the future of your race."

"Yeah, I don't think he's going to volunteer for *that* either."

Aurelio lifted his eyes to the ceiling, his palms facing up. "*She* can make it so."

There was something in the tone, the way he was so certain that this was not only possible but a guarantee. After a moment of letting that sink in, he lowered a hand to help her up. To her own surprise, she accepted it.

"I am her voice upon the earth until such time as she decides otherwise," he said unprompted. "When I speak, I speak for the goddess."

Tina felt her jaw drop, but she tried to recover quickly. If she was going to be the leader her people needed, she had to practice the air of total confidence. "Goddess?"

Aurelio's head dipped slightly. "And now that you have accepted her, I am also under your command."

THIRTY-TWO

M assimo's eyes had just closed when fervent knocking roused him from his day sleep.

"We were attacked," Helsing said the moment he saw the Doge standing before him. "We lost Tina, your water taxi burned and then sank, but your men are fine."

As soon as the returning party made the shadows, Massimo rushed forward, all rules of decorum thrown away in lieu of compassion and concern. He swooped Vega out of Helsing's hold and into his own. Even from a distance, he could smell scorched flesh. As soon as he held her, he could also feel her pulse. A pulse that shouldn't be there for a vampire.

Dio mio, what is happening in my city? How have I lost control so quickly, so completely? Am I too old to keep up with this? Or am I too distracted in protecting Portia? It wasn't the first time the thought had crossed his mind, nor the feeling of guilt.

But Massimo wore confidence in his words. "We will track them down. There is not a single ship or soul within fifty kilometers of Venice that can escape my reach."

"Except maybe the one that got us." This, from the huey. Amy managed to trail them by jogging to their walk. "This wasn't any kind of *normal* ship. It looked like something out of Ben Hur."

Luckily, the reference was one with which Massimo was familiar. "There hasn't been an ancient warship in these waters in my lifetime. How could something like that happen without even the huey crafts witnessing it?"

"We can't exactly explain it either," Helsing said. "Tina and I managed to blast a pretty big hole in its side, but it didn't make a difference. Not only that, but it was sending zompires after us through the water." The slayer, keeping pace with Massimo, leaned over, taking the suffering woman's hand. "Raquel, how you doing?"

The only reply the chairperson could muster was a blistering scream as her free arm rose, clutched at her abdomen.

"She was suddenly exposed to the full force of the sun so I fed her the amulet," Amy said. "Just like contact did with you, it turned her human."

Massimo had assumed as much. "Yes, but I was not in pain when it happened. What is happening to her?"

"My theory?" Caleb said as they topped the stairs from the ballroom and entered the dining room. "That thing is the reason the corpse didn't have any organs or blood."

Now that he mentioned it, Vega did look pale. It hadn't struck Massimo at first because, as a vampire, she *would* be a little off color... compared to a mortal. But if she was indeed human, and her pounding pulse and flailing as he set her on the dining room table suggested she was, then she was indeed too blanched.

Helsing unbuttoned his jacket and began to shimmy out of it. "We need to get it out of her. Amy, find me a knife."

"A knife?" The huey spit back the word like a curse. "You can't stab it away. You'll kill her!"

"You saw what happened when Massimo lost contact with it. He was back to vampire in a blink. We have to get it out of her before she becomes one of those... things!"

Things? Surely Helsing didn't mean to imply that the "zompires" they'd encountered, that those were vampires who...

The Doge's eyes bulged at the implication. At the edge of the room, a sideboard held service ware, including several sharp knives. It wouldn't exactly be a scalpel, but it would be sharp.

"I will cut it out," the Doge said, pulling a carving blade from a drawer. "I'll need you two to hold her down."

Neither of them argued though Popowitz did herself turn into red and white stripes. For a moment, Massimo feared the huey wouldn't endure the site, that she would again run from the room, or worse, lose the contents of her stomach right where she stood. Only then, something shifted in the huey's demeanor. She squinted, her hands made fists, and she pulled a rapid cycle of breath in and out of her nose. And then, in complete control of her facilities, she put all her weight down Vega's right arm, while Helsing took the left.

No time to lose, and even less time for formalities. Massimo made no request for permission before cutting away the linen shirt and slicing Vega's bra in half, exposing her left breast. The scars were curious. Had she carried those across the crimson line from her human days? *Focus.* He lifted the breast and, to what extent he could, pushed it to the side with his left hand and readied the knife with his right. Seconds from making the incision, a hand wrapped around his wrist, holding him back.

"Not that way." Vega's words wrapped around her guttural, writhing tones.

Massimo caught her panicked eyes, saw the unspoken plea in them, and knew at once what she was suggesting.

And why she had the scar.

"Miss Vega, if I smoke in when you're in this already heightened state, I'm as likely to kill you as save you."

"Not. That. Way." Her head thudded back against the table. "I absolve you..." she huffed, "... but not that way."

Helsing and Popowitz exchanged a look before turning their gazes on the Doge. Massimo, for his part, didn't hesitate.

He took off his robe and let it drop to the ground. "You'll still need to hold her. This may hurt even more than cutting into her."

"I know, and it will." Popowitz nodded. "We'll keep her as still as we can."

"Hurry, Massimo," Helsing said. "I can feel her getting weaker. Don't worry, we'll keep her still."

This time when he smoked inside, Massimo didn't waste time on exploration. He knew where the amulet would be. No sooner had he extended an aeriform finger to her heart than he saw it. Only this time, the amulet wasn't an immutable piece of jewelry. It was a living, thriving thing nested on Vega's racing heart.

It appeared to be feeding directly from her bloodstream. Perhaps that was the first step in this process, and eating the organs came after. The scientific and historical aspects of personality pressed to remain and observe, but the humanity that still lived in his bones said to put an end Vega's suffering as soon as possible.

Concentrating his mass around the insect, Massimo began to thread a very tricky needle. He needed to both reform part of himself physically and not explode Vega's chest cavity in a thousand directions. It did no good to save the patient by killing her.

When again he stood outside the body, his feet material and planted on the floor next to Helsing's, Massimo's hand remained inside Vega, balled into the tiniest fist he could make.

"The moment I pull this out, and she regains her immortality, she will need blood," Massimo said. "A *great amount* of blood."

Popowitz pulled back and began to undo the buttons near her throat. "She can have mine."

"Amy?" It seemed her patron was as curious as the Doge was. "What are you doing?"

"Getting ready to give Raquel blood, obviously." Popowitz grew frustrated by the tiny buttons of her blouse. "She offered hers to me. I'm just returning the favor."

Massimo caught Helsing's eyes and felt the weight of consequence there.

Good, then. The slayer understood the implications of that two-way transaction. Doubtful the assistant did, but that was a discussion for another time.

"Agreed," Massimo said instead. "Ready?"

"No, wait." Helsing pulled up a sleeve and stuck his bare arm over Vega's mouth. "Thanks, Amy, but slayer blood is more powerful. Mine, even more than average. It will heal her fastest."

And without the consequences, although the word may be as strong as the deed.

Arrangements made, Massimo nodded, cupping his free hand above the part of his blood-covered wrist sticking out of Vega's chest. "On three. One. Two... *three!*"

Raquels's shrieks took on an eerie echo as the glass chandelier above the table pulled in the sound and twisted it. Her back arched for several piercing moments. Then, just as suddenly, she fell back on the table, flat, spent... dead? Her heart had stopped, but did that mean she was restored to her vampiric self, or...

He closed his eyes against that possible fate. For the moment, he had to deal with the more immediate threat. The life of a vampiric prince often involved paperwork, but also occasionally required violence. This was not the first time Massimo had had to pull his hand out of some poor body's chest cavity. It was the first time, however, that he did so clutching a living piece of jewelry.

Caleb rolled up his sleeve. "Amy, you know CPR?"

The huey didn't speak. Instead, she mounted the table, her legs folded under her and started chest compressions. "Working where I do? Of course!"

Massimo examined the vitriol on his hand and the tiny little amulet, which had taken to squirming and chasing around, as though it was trying to consume the last elements of Raquel that it could. He searched around the room, desperate for a place to rid himself of the thing before it ran out. It seemed the bug had a taste for vampire. Nearby, the morning dishes left from Portia's breakfast service had yet to be cleared. Thank goodness he'd finally convinced her that cleaning up after herself wasn't necessary, and that his waitstaff didn't arrive until later in the day.

Massimo fetched the coffee carafe with all speed, pressed the button to open the lid, and plunged the chirping golden beetle in, sealing it in. By the time he'd returned to the table, Popowitz was on her second stack of compression counting. Helsing still pressed his bare arm to Raquel's lips, but the vampire had not latched.

Very white lips, Massimo noted. He knew what death looked like on a mortal, and how easily it came. As Doge, it was his duty to ensure the vampiric elements present in his city did not take life. They could feed as much as they desired, either with willing hueys who knew of the supernatural world, or with passing tourists whose memories could be washed by enthralling afterward. He protected his court from the city, and the city from the court, letting predator and prey exist in a balanced ecosystem.

And then, *this* happened under his watch. A vampire with well-known and powerful connections had been attacked by an enemy he couldn't stop, and kidnapped one of his honored guests while creating a situation that was about to destroy another. His reputation would be tarnished once this got out. Worse, his pride. How could he claim to keep those under his rule safe when something like *this* was possible? How could he keep something like this from happening to Portia?

Was he in a place now that he could not protect either?

"It's no good!" Popowitz said, though her actions didn't stop. "She's not responding. What if I fed her her own blood back? Would it help?"

The slayer shook his head. "Doubtful. Massimo, ideas?"

Cynically, his inner voice said, *Call the next of kin.* Did Raquel de la Vega have kin? He knew of her bloodline, but being one based in the Americas, he had limited knowledge of its members. Would her death start a blood feud? Was this the beginning of a new war, after so many centuries of relative peace?

Suddenly, Massimo's thoughts exploded. He agreed with Helsing. Vega's own vampiric blood was unlikely to have any effect. Nor would Massimo's. If vampirism itself could restore her, it would have done so. Maybe a maker's blood, though? And the closest maker he knew of in the city was...

"I will call for Pavlos," he said suddenly, and just as suddenly turned to go.

"Pavlos?" the slayer asked, his faced screwed up. "What do you expect Pavlos to—"

"Wait!" This outburst, from the human.

Massimo spun back to find Popowitz sitting back on her heels, grinning.

"Her heart is beating."

And with the pulse, tiny flecks of blood flew from the hole in the cavity left by Massimo's extraction. But still, the body did not move.

Until, without warning, Vega's eyes flew open, and her jaw clamped down on Helsing's wrist.

"Raquel! Yes!"

Helsing's words suggested relief. No doubt returning home with the chairperson of the board deceased also would have had consequences for him. Though Massimo had to wonder if the slayer would have the same level of concern for his colleague's welfare.

Popowitz took up the vampire's hand in her own, reaffirming that she was a creature of compassion. That, or there was more to her relationship with the chairperson than the naked eye could perceive. Doubtful they were lovers, but that didn't mean there wasn't a comradery. Perhaps one neither was yet cognizant of.

"Raquel," she too said, her voice broken. "Oh my God, I thought we'd lost you!"

Raquel, for her part, said nothing and remained at Helsing's wrist, taking quick, shallow pulls that began to stretch as she came to. With each pull, her pulse grew weaker. In a human, cause for alarm. In this case, it was a sign her vampiric qualities were assuming back control of her body. Massimo watched as the gaping hole in Vega's chest began to close in on itself. He remembered the power of slayer blood. More potent than human, yes, but not a miracle cure. It would take several hours for Vega to recover. Day rest would do her good.

"I will ring my day staff and see that your rooms are reopened." The Doge turned from emergency mode to that of the distinguished host and ruler he was. "Unlikely they've had opportunity yet to reset them following your departure, but you need some time to recover."

"No can do," Helsing croaked as he pulled his wrist back from Vega. "I... have to... find Tina. I... I..."

Covering the marred flesh with his other hand, Helsing stood, moments before falling face first off the table, unconscious.

THIRTY-THREE

T he voices came first. Whispering, hurried twitters that asked questions he couldn't quite hear. Under, a high-pitched buzzing, one that seemed to both assure him he was alive, and aggravate the mind-splitting headache he was suddenly becoming aware of.

"He's waking up!" Amy's hand cupped the side of his cheek, and her face filled in as he opened eyes unto a blurry world.

"Amy?" He wanted to rub the sleep from his eyes but stopped when he went to pull up his arm and something tugged back. "What happened?"

"Raquel drank too much, too fast." She lifted her hand to point at something over his chest. "You passed out from blood loss. Luckily, Portia's a match for you."

A match for him? What the hell did that mean? Portia was already married to Massimo.

Caleb lifted his head just as his vision began to clear and discovered the source of resistance. Beside the bed, a tall metal pole stood, two clear bags suspended from something that looked like an upside-down clothes hangar. From the bottom of one ran a long, thin plastic tube. It spiraled down and onto the bed, before disappearing beneath a patch of gauze strapped to his inner arm.

"Oh, you mean, like blood type." He shook his head. "So we're basically playing pass-the-platelets, huh? Whose great idea was this?"

"Mine." Portia walked into view from the side of the room. "And luckily for you, the *huey* doctor told Massimo it would be a good idea for me to store some of my own blood in case of a medical emergency. No one's sure what getting straight huey blood would do to one of us."

"Based on my experience, nothing but give you a good story to tell about why you needed it."

Both narrowed their glares on the Solari.

Caleb shrugged, as well as one could while lying in bed. "I was young and stupid once."

"Yeah, and now you're only one of those things." Amy rolled her eyes. "Look, the point is, you played hero and saved Raquel, but she almost killed you in the process."

"And she's okay now?" He couldn't believe how much his blood pressure shot up in the moment when he thought she might not be.

But it came crashing back to normal when Amy nodded. "She's going to be okay, just needs some rest is all."

He let out a breath in a slow stream through pursed lips. "And Tina? Any sign of her?"

Portia and Amy exchanged fretted glances before the former crossed her arms and leaned on the foot poster of Caleb's bed. "Our contacts in the police agency say they haven't had any reports of bodies found out in the bay today. They also say no one's reported seeing a thirty-foot tall ancient battleship."

"Yeah, well, I guess overall, that's a good thing." He huffed, closed eyes, and pictured the Greek slayer who'd he'd been avoiding for over a year. "You realize there wouldn't *be* a body though, right? If you put the corpse of a slayer into water, it will break down into some kind of gelatinous goo."

Amy's face screwed up. "Well, as disgusting as that is, I don't think it's the reason we couldn't find her. Personally, I think she's probably been kidnapped, not killed."

Caleb's fists tightened at his sides. "Whoever or whatever it is that took her better be alive, because I'm planning on repaying them, slowly and painfully. Or quickly and painfully. As long as they're dead, I don't care."

"So you think she's still alive, then?" Amy asked.

Did he? His head swiveled in her direction. "You know the hoods and wolves, they can *sense* each other, even their own kind a little. I never thought that was something vamps and slayers had. But somehow I just... *know* she is."

Amy licked her lips and nodded. "Maybe because you're the Solari?"

"I hope not because that would mean I really am the leader of my people, and I have sucked out loud at that."

He managed to sit up. Portia's blood might not be as strong as his, but at least he was ambulatory. "No wonder the board of directors wants to fire me. They should. Yeah, Tina is a pain in the ass, but she's still one of the Reclaimed, and I let her be taken."

He buried a smile as best he could.

"Reclaimed? Funny name, isn't it? Because the only thing I let them *reclaim* was being kept in a tower. I told myself it was for their own protection, but that's a lie. I just didn't want to be bothered by them." He shook his head. "I've got to do better. The whole marriage concept Tina had cooked up in her head is... ridiculous, but she was absolutely right to call me out on my bullshit. I owe them a lot more than I've been giving. Maybe if I'd realized that sooner, Tina wouldn't have ended up in this situation. I'm going to tell her that when we get her back, and I'm going to make sure all the others know it too."

He wasn't sure what he expected when his little speech was done. Caleb certainly hadn't gone off on a soliloquy to impress anyone. Despite that, when he finally looked back at the women, it was to find both wearing smiles.

"Okay, good. So now what?" Amy's voice even sounded a little misty when she spoke. "For the moment, Gabor and the security staff are on high alert. Here, we don't have any leads to go on, and it's not like we can even go back to the scene to look for clues."

"True, but if what you thought was right, and I think it might be, *we* don't have to go anywhere." Caleb turned to Portia. "Is your husband still planning on that ball tonight? The one that was supposed to be in our honor?"

Wide-eyed, Portia's hands dropped to the side. "Um, yeah. *Yes.* As far as I know."

"Good." Caleb threw his legs over the side of the bed. "I plan to be there, and I want *everyone* to know it."

"You think whoever took Tina will come for you." Amy stood. "Caleb Helsing, are you actually planning to use yourself as bait?"

"More than bait. I want to be caught."

The blonde huey's mouth fell to the floor. "You can't be serious."

"I am. Also, I want to see what you're planning on wearing, Barbie. I bet whatever dress you put on will have half of the vampires in the room swallowing their own tongues."

Amy crossed her arms. "Please, it will be a lot more than that."

"We can fit you with a tracker," Portia said.

The 007-inspired statement was so unexpected, Caleb and Amy gaped at her.

"Okay, so yeah, I sometimes wear one if I'm going off to the mainland without Massimo," she admitted.

"So, like, he stalks you?" Amy asked with no little amount of disgust.

"Oh, Lord, no," Portia said. "It was a compromise. I agreed to it in a few circumstances, but Massimo doesn't have the direct ability to see it. Only Pavlos can do that, and he would only look in extreme circumstances."

"I'd normally say no to that, but honestly, I think it wouldn't be terrible this time." Caleb pulled his phone out to check the time. "I need to get ready. I suggest the rest of you do the same."

THIRTY-FOUR

It had taken some time for Amy to wrap her head around the fact that supernatural creatures existed. Her nosedive into that world came thanks to her own near-murder by a vampire. But seeing what Caleb was acting like, she now began to wonder if aliens existed too. What better explanation could there be than assuming her boss had been replaced a la *Invasion of the Body Snatchers*? Who was this responsible man vowing to save the very woman he loathed?

"He *actually* said that?"

Apparently, Raquel had some difficulty swallowing it too. She'd shown up at Amy's door minutes after sunset, asking if she could assist in the huey's preparation for the ball. Little did the vampire know, it wasn't Amy's first. Maybe the first hosted by a supernatural prince and mobbed by vampires, but if Raquel wanted to know what real pressure was, she should try walking the red carpet of the Met Gala at sixteen as the arm candy for some one-hit wonder pop star.

Her father had been so pissed at her.

It had been *fabulous*.

Amy picked up one of her gold shell earrings and worked it through her earlobe. "Yeah, he's planning to get himself taken from the party to find Tina.

Massimo's security, the ones not working the ball tonight anyway, are spreading out across the city so they follow no matter what direction he goes."

"Assuming he goes anywhere they could follow."

Amy pinned the second earring and spun. "What does that mean?"

"It means..." Raquel pursed her lips. "Amy, I have been a vampire for over two centuries. I am well versed in our abilities, traditions, and history, though maybe not to the level of a Varanasi."

Even Amy recognized the name of the vampiric bloodline that served as the archivists for the entire race. In fact, she knew one who was engaged to her best friend's cousin.

"That ship," Raquel continued. "How it appeared out of nowhere... the weather it seemed to cause... the creatures who attacked us... the ability of a little piece of jewelry to make me human, even if temporarily..." Her eyes went unfocused as she looked across the room. "There's always been things about supes that rationality or science can't explain. *Yet,* I've always told myself. Once upon a time, we didn't understand electricity or magnetism. But the things we've experienced since we've been here... even I am perplexed. And these are the forces Helsing will give himself over to? It's not a good idea, no matter how noble the feat."

As though the universe had decided to remind Raquel that she may be immortal, but she wasn't impervious to pain, the chairperson winced and lashed across her ribs.

Amy moved in, cautiously. Even a friendly vampire could be unpredictable. "Raquel?"

"It's... nothing." Her strained voice suggested otherwise. "Only... growing back organs that have been partially consumed by a scarab beetle *is* incredibly painful. If not, I would attend tonight and help."

Amy sat down on the bed next to her. "If you need to take some of my blood..."

"No!" Raquel cut her off with a hand in the air. "I... *cannot* accept *your* blood. Not now. Not now that I offered mine. It would... mean things."

Something caught in Amy's memory, a few words that passed between Massimo and Caleb during the blitz retreat to the palazzo neither of them probably thought she'd picked up on.

"*What* would it mean, Raquel?"

"That you are mine."

Amy swallowed. Hard. "I... you... uh..." She licked her lips and focused on being polite. "Raquel, don't get me wrong. You're... well, hot. You got this whole 'boss bitch' vibe and that hair and those legs of yours... *wow*. But I'm just not that into you... in that way."

The vampire's expression soured. "I don't mean it in 'that way,'" she said, mocking Amy's tone. "I mean it in terms of blood rights. It's unusual for a vampire to offer blood to a huey. More unusual for one to accept. But if the huey then offers back their own blood, it's a type of contract. One in which I pledge to be your protector, and you pledge to open your *vein* exclusively for me. Opening your legs is optional."

"Well, hell, I've gotten less for giving more than just my legs." But then Amy reflected on that. "Wait, I didn't *drink* your blood."

Raquel shook her head. "It doesn't matter. You took it into your possession."

"Oh? Yeah, then, probably best if we keep things static. Though, honestly, having you as my badass sugar mama? Can't say it would be all bad."

"You forget, though, that another might object to it on grounds of a *previous* contract."

Amy's face screwed up. "What does *that* mean? I've never offered my blood to anyone."

"It works differently for slayers."

For a moment, Amy couldn't figure out what Raquel meant. Slayer? She never made any contract with a slayer. Well, except for her agreement with Caleb, but that was only to—

"No!" The huey leaped to her feet. "Absolutely not! I have *never* accepted anything from Caleb. His blood, his... well..." She held up a finger to Raquel's grin. "Okay, we did kiss once. ONCE, a long time ago, and only because he was trying to piss off his ex. I never let his mouth near my... anything!"

"With a slayer, it's the cohabitation that does it," Raquel said. "I think that's why Vlad kept the Reclaimed, the women, anyhow, as a harem and not as prisoners. He wanted it known on both our terms and theirs that they were *his exclusive property.*"

Explanations of supernatural costumes failed to quell the anger burning in Amy's chest. And as it happened, that was the moment a certain slayer chose to knock.

THIRTY-FIVE

The moment Amy opened the door, Caleb wanted to pluck out his eyes.

Not because she was upsetting to look at but because he wanted to do so much more than look. The black dress she wore wrapped up her teasing, taunting figure like a present, one that he very much wanted to unwrap, put batteries in, and spend all Christmas morning playing with. She'd styled her hair to sit atop her head in a swirl of curl and tuck, reminding him of something out of old Hollywood. The cut of the dress allowed her shoulders to be bare, and whatever tape or lingerie she had concealed beneath pushed up her tits in the most delicious way, like two cocktail onions perched on a sugared glass rim. Gods, he wanted to suck them into his mouth and roll them around his tongue for a while.

Luckily, a quick cure for the affliction of "Amy attraction" was Amy herself. No sooner had he become aware that his nethers had gone on high alert and were preparing to launch a rocket than she stepped forward and smacked him full force across the face.

"Ow!" Caleb's body moved with the force of the assault, conveniently hiding his arousal. He rubbed his face as he brought his eyes back up to meet hers. "What the hell? I didn't even say anything!"

"I am *not* your property!"

"No one ever said you were. I was... it was just... gawking!"

Amy stepped out of her room and through the door, a hand raised and a finger pointing into his chest. "When we get home, we are going to have a talk about respect and full disclosure."

"Okay?" Was that all she wanted? *Please be all she wanted* because otherwise, he was clueless.

She stood up and crab-clawed her hips, looking like a woman who still wanted to rip him a new one but knew she didn't have that time. "Well, then, okay."

With that, she stomped past, heading up the corridor. Stunned, Caleb lingered. He had to let the blush on his cheek clear, he told himself. It wasn't untrue, however. The woman walking away, with that fierce *I am woman* strut and the way it made her hips sway...

And then, without warning or reason, he turned to pull Amy's door shut only to find it filled with a grinning Raquel.

"Good evening, Mr. Helsing," she said, straight as a barber's comb.

"Raquel." Caleb nodded, attempting some level of professionalism. "You're, um... feeling better?"

"I am." She looked down to where a suggestive bugle beneath his belt line proved *Slam Helsing* hadn't gotten the clue that this was neither the time nor the place. "It's good to see you still have plenty of blood after what I took."

"I recover quickly." He closed his eyes and let out a steady breath. "And about... *that.* I am male. She is female. I would never do anything to her, but when my lizard brain sees those curves... it's just biology." But then, Caleb remembered what Amy had said earlier about the chairperson offering her blood. His fists tightened at his side as he took a step forward. "But I *will* still protect her if anyone is trying to threaten or coerce her somehow."

"You think I'm feeling out Amy for recruitment, do you?"

"Or feeling her out for... other purposes." He took another step forward. "I don't think I was the only one who noticed how that dress clung to those hips."

"No, you weren't. My interests in Miss Popowitz are... *mostly* professional, however."

Raquel stepped past him, taking a few unsteady steps up the hall before turning back. "If you manage to pull this off tonight, the board will be very impressed."

"Impressed enough to vote for me to stay on as CEO?" he asked.

"Come now, Mr. Helsing, you know I can't guarantee that. But it certainly won't hurt."

"And what if it doesn't work and I don't come back?" He couldn't help but ask.

"Then I can honestly say that you would have made your parents proud."

Portia and the Doge were already in the dining room when Amy and Caleb arrived, the latter a step behind despite the head start. Caleb figured judging himself against the royal couple was fair. When you're at court, you don't outshine the king. From his perspective, Caleb wasn't certain what to think. Though sharply dressed, Massimo's tux was standard issue. Finely made, no doubt, but outside of the forest green vest under the jacket, it kept pace with the slayer's own attire for luxury and appearance.

"Helsing, Miss Popowitz." The sovereign's eyes roamed them both over from head to toe. Though he said nothing, a modest tilted-head nod suggested he approved of their attire.

"Your Excellency, Portia." Caleb kept his eyes distinctly *off* the Dogaressa. At this point, Caleb hadn't been with a woman in almost a week, and the deprivation was starting to get to him. It was bad enough he'd pitched a tent seeing Amy. Portia may be older, yes, but she still had curves all her own. He didn't want to host a whole Boy Scout jamboree in his pants.

Luckily, whatever monstrosity Portia wore prevented any kind of arousal from occurring. The Dogaressa's dress looked like something AI had drawn as a modernist take on a Renaissance gown, rife with lacework and a superfluous amount of cloth that masked her figure.

Amy saved him from embarrassing himself and lying about his opinion. "Oh my God, is that Gucci?"

"Maybe?" The Dogaressa gave herself a quick lookover before pulling blushed cheeks back into view. "I have an assistant who dresses me for these things. The older vampires in court like things that look like they were trendy in their times. But you recognize it, huh?"

"Yeah. My mom used to be involved in the fashion industry. I guess technically she still is, but only resale now. She gets all her society 'friends' to donate their used ballgowns and sells them to raise money for some missing kids' charity."

Portia tilted her head. "She sounds like an amazing woman."

"Not really, but she's had her moments."

Caleb cleared his throat to draw attention away from that social bomb. "Massimo, your security team in place?"

The corners of the Doge's face relaxed. Apparently, Caleb hadn't been the only one set off pace by Amy's comment.

"Indeed," he said. "I have a line who always works the dock and perimeter during one of these functions, but I've called in extra staff tonight. They all have been instructed not to interfere if you are violently or otherwise abducted. Instead, they will throw energy into 'protecting the crowd.'"

Massimo lifted his hands and made twitching bunny fingers. Finger quotes? It was a rare crack in his professional, royal demeanor. It also served as a wink and a nod to Caleb without saying anything that would scare Amy. As tough an adversary as the zompires were, it would take a hell of a lot of them to take on a ballroom full of vampires and have any chance of winning.

Still, they had to keep vigilant. "Don't forget, whatever this thing is, it was able to immobilize *you*," Caleb reminded the vampire. "After our introduction, I'll spin Amy around the floor a few times to maneuver closer to the docks.

I want to make myself easy pickings, and I especially don't want any of your citizens caught in the crosshairs. I'll go without a fight, so there shouldn't be a scene."

"Pavlos is waiting in the security suite upstairs to track your locator and coordinate an invisible tail to follow," Massimo said. "He's also reached out to our contacts in the human authority. They can offer some assistance if things truly go south."

"I never like to go south. Not unless I'm on a date."

Could he blame his blatant return to form on nerves? Or maybe the vampire was so old and stuffy he didn't get the reference.

No such luck. Caleb looked up to see Massimo frowning at him.

"Sorry." Sometimes, his apologizing could give a Canadian a run for his money.

Luckily, the Doge decided to stay focused. "The Dogaressa and I will go in first," he said, holding out his hand to Portia. "We will welcome the court and introduce you, immediately after which these doors will be opened by my staff so you can make your entrance. Miss Popowitz, would you prefer that I refer to you as Mr. Helsing's partner or as his servant?"

Amy's face screwed up. "I'm neither of those things."

"You may refer to her as my fiancée."

"What the fuck?" "She is?"

Portia and Amy's voices crossed over each other, but Caleb knew for different reasons. When he didn't immediately respond, however, the surprise dropped away from Massimo's face and he nodded once.

"Very well then." The Doge offered his hand up, prompting Portia to run hers over the top, giving the couple the classic royalty manner.

"Good luck!" Portia said as the doors opened and the two stepped through.

No sooner were they left alone than Amy rounded on Caleb and punched his arm.

He winced for theatrical value. This time, he'd expected it.

"Fiancée?" she whisper-screamed, perhaps knowing that anything louder might be heard by the supernaturally sensitive ears inside the ballroom. "Are you mental?"

"I don't think it's nice of you to use that term in the derogatory."

"I use it in the accusatory, asshole!"

For good measure, she lapped two more blows into his bicep. He *almost* felt the second one.

"What do you think you're doing, saying we're engaged?"

"After seeing what you look like in that dress, I think I'm keeping you from being hit on by about fifty vampires over the next hour," he said. "Unless you *wanted* to hook up with an Italian undead stallion tonight?"

He didn't need her to give a snappy remark. Her face had gone pale. Amy tolerated vampires. A select few, like Gabor and Raquel, had even won her trust, but she still carried damage from her first encounter with one, when it almost killed her.

"The second we go into that ballroom, they're going to want you. You're a young, well-connected huey who looks like a piece of hard candy in that dress. They'll want to wrap their lips around every part of you and suck until you melt in their mouth."

Despite her open hostility for vampires in general, he smiled when her breath hitched. Ah, Amy. But he also wanted her to know he did have reasons, and it wasn't just because it was fun to see her get a bit flustered.

"Look, if I make it clear at the beginning that you're mine, they won't touch you, even if this plan somehow goes right and I get abducted."

"You seriously think someone in Massimo's court would risk pissing him off by coming after me?"

"I think a hungry vampire isn't that different from a horny man. There's only one part of their body that's doing the thinking."

She passed him a screwed up, even disgusted look.

"Their *fangs*, Amy. They think with their fangs." He reached out and hooked her left arm with his right. "You told me you studied drama at university. Just play this role for the next few hours, and I'll buy you a... a... Mercedes."

"Prada dress."

"You sure? A Mercedes costs more. Gets better milage too. You could sell it and get, like, five Prada dresses."

"I'm not talking about something off the rack, Caleb." She smoothed down her own dress, using it as evidence. "I want a commissioned, custom-designed one-of-a-kind. If you want me to pretend to be your fiancée for *any* amount of time, that's the price."

He swallowed. That sounded expensive. And dangerous to his self-control. "The Mercedes would turn just as many heads if you drive it in the right places."

"Caleb!"

"Fine! I'll get you a Prada dress."

THIRTY-SIX

"You're certain they won't be able to sense me?"

Gone was the unease that Tina had felt the first time gliding down these elegant canals. Now she had no reason to fear the water. Even if she did fall in, her warriors below would see to her speedy restitution. But that question still gave her pause. This attempt to seize Caleb wasn't going to get very far if every vampire in the room knew another slayer was in their midst.

"The goddess has made you invisible to them in that way." Aurelio played the part of both gondolier and escort, pushing along their craft through the queue of those arriving to the palazzo. "Just as you could not sense the *rekhyt*, so shall the vampires not be able to sense you."

That had been one of the first things Tina had learned earlier in the day when she'd agreed to this new cause. *Rekhyt*, not zompires. Truthfully, they were neither halves of that frankenword. The goddess had the power to recall the dead, and in doing so, they were imbued with temporary vampire-like features. But that was just surface level, they *weren't* supes. Not in the way a slayer, hood, or werewolf were.

The gondola slipped into the dock as the one before it cleared a path, giving her the first chance to survey the field. The workers assisting with the unloading of guests were hueys. That didn't surprise her. The sycophantic vampiric population of Venice would all want to be inside, worshippers in the church of their false figurehead. Vlad Tepeş had been the only vampire with a legitimate claim of authority over the rest. Had the Sultan lived, he'd have brought the lot of them under his command, keeping them from running amuck and setting up these false courts in the eddies of his wake. Now that he was dead, however, the rats must be driven from the world.

That was why slayers were born. They were pest control, exterminators. For the last century or so, the few who remained had been driven into captivity or hiding. The vermin had grown out of control. They needed to be culled.

Aurelio managed the dock before the huey attendee could make the approach. For a dead man, he moved with amazing grace, speed, and strength. *Gifts of the goddess,* his voice echoed in her thoughts. *She gives me life so that I may serve her and serve you.* Tina lifted her hand to the level of her eyes, flexing her fingers inside the wrap of her crimson gloves, feeling the buzz beneath her skin. Her solarium lived in her veins, the sun flowing therein eager to leap out. Now, it was joined by other strengths. Gifts of the goddess indeed.

"My lady?"

Aurelio reached down, offering a hand. Tina didn't need his help, but she appreciated that it was offered. She let herself be lifted and placed on the well-worn stone dock.

"You look amazing." He pulled back his hand and bowed when she gained her balance, then offered out an arm. "Helsing will eat himself with desire."

"I'm sure he already does, if he's flexible enough."

She shuttered at the flash of memory of the one night they'd had together roughly two years before. A member of the harem, Tina knew well the intimate arts. Vampires' artificially long life spans allowed them plenty of time to perfect their sensual skills, and she'd been the beneficiary of it on numerous occasions. But when she'd made love with Caleb, there was no substitute for a living body with a pulse pushed by a power that matched her own. She'd known at that moment that she was his, that they had been meant to be together.

Then, when the Reclaimed were freed, Tina had been tossed aside, forgotten, forsaken in lieu of a different huey floozy in his bed, night after night. Her heart had grown hard, but her purpose was undeniable. She was to be the mother of her race as it clawed back from near extinction. Caleb, with his thriving bloodline and awesome power, was to be the father of her children. The progenitor of their *race*. This trip to Venice had been fate intervening, giving her a chance to win back his affections.

It *had* been fate, but she no longer required his heart. In fact, she no longer required even his agreement... though the task would be easier if she could gain it.

The huey attendees had kept their distance, but as they approached the portico, vampiric security agents proved they wouldn't do the same.

"Signor, signore." One of the two guards bowed her head to both in turn. "Potrei vedere il suo invito ufficiale, per favore?"

Aurelio was a native of the city or had been before he'd been called to the goddess. He rambled off a few words in Italian, a language which Tina only picked up when the English or Greek equivalent was a close enough match. Something about *official invites*. Of course, Tina *had* been invited, but that had been when she'd been a guest of honor, one of the beings the ball was meant to honor. There had been no paper given to her.

And now that Aurelio had likely said as much, directly or by consequence, the guards' voices increased in pitch and cadence, if not volume. Aurelio's words became more chastising. He giggled even, and *that* had been the cue. Tina dropped her "date's" arm, raised her hands palm out to face the guards, locked their gazes in hers, and pushed intention through her thoughts and into her words.

"*Be still and quiet.*" Her eyes opened to the miracle and the promise. "It worked!"

The two guards, the male one with his fangs caught in half-descent, stood as statues, like subjects of a photograph frozen in time.

Tina readied her next command. "When I say 'now,' you will realize that you've already seen our invitations and wish us a good evening as we enter." She made sure to keep her voice soft, so the other guests, supes, of course, didn't overhear her. "Now."

The guards snapped back to life. The woman looked over Tina, head to toe, then a quick check on Aurelio's face. "Thank you, *Signori*. Please, enjoy your evening. Next!"

Tina couldn't keep her excitement down. *She* could control *them*? Vampires couldn't even enthrall a slayer, and now she could make one do whatever she wanted to?

Aurelio pulled her in under his arm, giving her a place to bury her grin as they walked through the entry. "That gift is just one of many abilities she may grant you once you've done away with the false solari."

"*No,* Caleb lives," Tina snapped. "I need his seed. Besides, as I told you, our work will be easier if we can still get Helsing to take up his true mantle. Without him, there will be a turf war for the Reclaimed. I will have to win them one by one."

"The goddess knows you can do this."

"There is no doubt, but it will take time," Tina conceded. "I must take Caleb tonight before he has a chance to run back to the Reclaimed and gets in their heads first, or I'll be fighting him on every front. We will serve the goddess together, it may simply take time for him to come around to it."

Aurelio bowed his head in submission before again offering his arm. "When you call for our forces, they will rise up to secure him."

She looked back over her shoulder at the canals, reflecting on how the very thing that had terrified her just a week ago was now the vehicle of her strength.

"Just let me lure him out first."

Inside, vampires stood and chatted, dressed to the nines in clothing both modern and archaic. With few exceptions, Tina observed that the undead preferred fashions that paid tribute to their own eras. "*Formal old fogies,*" her fellow Reclaimed, Keiko, had once said. It was some kind of residual benchmarking to when they'd cared about the trends popular with hueys. It also established a hierarchy at social functions. The woman she passed on her right, wearing a Gilde Age style, had to defer to the one who looked like an Austen heroine.

"It appears that the Doge is speaking on the dais at the head of the room, my lady." Aurelio scuttled just to her right.

She'd noticed that, of course. To the best of her knowledge, the acolyte didn't have the supernatural abilities of slayers and vampires. His one abnormal characteristic was that he'd been recalled from the dead and could communicate with their master.

"I've been listening since the moment we entered." Tina looked around and noted how most vampires, paired off in couples or small groups, kept to low volumes. Their words were foreign to her, but their manner wasn't. A vampire could both listen and speak at the same time, and it wasn't considered rude to do so unless engaged in a direct tete-a-tete.

Luckily, the Doge spoke loudly enough for his voice to rise over all of them, and likely in deference to the guests of honor, was doing so in English.

"... watched as Vlad Tepeş corrupted his influence and power to raise an army on injustice," he was saying as she came to a stop about two-thirds of the way through the room. "The Battle of the Tahquamenon that took place in America two years ago finally rid the world of the corrupt despot. This, you know. But since, the rumor in our community has circled. The victory was assured when a slayer joined the ranks, they say. Tonight, I stand here to attest that this young man, Caleb Van Helsing—"

"It's Victor, actually."

Caleb's interaction brought the whole room to a standstill, most of all the Doge, who probably wasn't accustomed to interruption.

"I'm sorry?" Massimo said, turning toward Caleb. "Have I been calling you the wrong name all this time?"

"No, it's Caleb. But the V doesn't stand for Van. It stands for Victor. In my case, anyway. My dad's middle name was Haim."

Beside Caleb, Puppy Guts rolled her eyes. Embarrassed, no doubt, by the lack of decorum on her boss's part. It wasn't as half as embarrassed as she was going to be when Tina won him over, and he left the thin-boned huey behind.

"Well, then, in any case," the Doge resumed. "That this young man, Mr. Helsing, was the slayer of which the rumors speak. Yes, my people, it is true. They are *not* extinct. In fact, two dozen of them were freed in the final months of the Raven Insurgency, and Mr. Helsing was chosen by them as the leader of their community."

Around her, the groupings of vampires increased in their chattering. Tina could imagine the themes. Surprise, for sure. Perhaps for a few, dismissiveness. Those who were friendly with the Ravens or sympathetic to their cause may have even been approached back in those days about opportunities to *buy* slayer blood. The slayer men kept in the dungeons below Dracula's palace were tapped once a week, and the women once a month. Tina swept the room from under her red-feathered mask and wondered if any here had already tasted her and not known.

"Many decades have passed since a solari walked the streets of our city," the Doge continued. "But tonight, I declare that Venice stands with the Slayers and welcomes them back into our world to take their rightful place. Please, welcome to our court, Mr. Caleb *Victor* Helsing."

A polite round of applause created a clamor over the crowd. Caleb lifted his hand to acknowledge the welcome and began to speak.

"Vampires of Venice, I thank you," he said, sounding uncharacteristically professional. "I know for some of you, I'm the first slayer you've seen in decades. For others, the first you've seen ever. I want to assure you, we're not coming out of the shadows to put you there instead. Our role is to balance out your place in the world and, in rare instances like with Tepeş, to cull extremists whose ambitions or irresponsibility threaten everyone. Slayers have been, and will ever continue to be, friends to vampires. With your support and the support of my fiancée..." he turned and took Amy's hand, bringing her to stand right next to him, "... I know we can work together to bring the supernatural world back into balance."

And with that, Caleb grabbed Puppy Guts by the arms, tipped her stiff-board-of-a-body at an angle, and kissed her dead on the lips.

Tina felt the crackle of power alight on her fingertips before she'd even managed to scream. She'd come here to win over Caleb to the goddess's cause, but maybe she'd just kill him instead.

Thirty-Seven

I t's only for show.

It's only for show.

It's *only* for *show*.

The mantra kept playing over in Caleb's thoughts as Amy's lips opened beneath his and began to suckle at his attentions. He tried to ignore how her pulse sped up, how her hand rose to stroke the side of his cheek, how all of a sudden, the blood he very much needed in his cranium was rushing south to alert other systems in his body.

Okay, that's enough, the last cries of his logic screamed to be heard. *You only needed to suggest to the vamps that she was off the table. You keep this up, you're going to find a nearby table, put her atop it, and start giving them a very different kind of show.*

He respected his assistant, but also low-level disliked her most of the time, what with all her demanding that he "get his act together" and "give a damn about his responsibilities." But, shit, the woman could kiss. The longer this went on, the more Caleb was convinced that coming might be on the table if you allowed for a slight change in the spelling. When he pulled away, it wasn't because he'd done what he set out to do. It was because of the shrill screaming that had broken through his haze of raging hormones.

Caleb, still holding Amy at the angle across his body, looked up in time to see the members of the court had all pivoted. As a group, they focused on something in the back. The slayer narrowed his gaze, trying to pick out in the sea of people the one responsible for the ruckus.

"Caleb?" Amy's voice cracked, and her breath accelerated. "What is—"

No time. Suddenly, the back of the ballroom exploded into light.

Amy hit the floor, the wind knocked out of her lungs, but her body protected as Caleb covered it with his own. Only supernatural speed kept the volley from hitting her square on.

"What..." Amy gulped air. "... was..." harder this time and swallowed, "... that?"

Below in the ballroom, screams erupted, and shouts flew. Massimo barked out orders in Italian nearby. Probably relieving the guards of their posts and ordering them to step into some kind of action. But the guards on duty tonight were all vampires, and if the weapon of choice for the person who had launched an attack was a solarium, they wouldn't stand a chance. Fretful eyes looked to their leader, and the Doge urged calm, first in English, then Italian, he assumed.

And that seemed to work.

Until dozens of zompires flooded into the back of the room.

He had to do something. But first, he had to get Amy to safety.

"Better question is who, and it wasn't me."

"Tina?" Amy's face screwed up. "She's here?"

"Yes, and I'm guessing she wasn't too happy about what she just saw."

Meanwhile, Caleb couldn't be more pleased with himself. Well, not without taking off his clothes.

"You have to get back into the palace." He ran both eyes and hands over the blonde beneath him, inspecting her for injury, and felt a tiny bit of tension ease when he couldn't find any. "Find Raquel. She'll make sure you're okay if this really gets out of hand."

Portia dropped to Caleb's side. "I'll help her."

Caleb nodded once, pulling himself off the trembling blonde beneath him, and cupped her shoulders, pulling her into a seated position before a light push put her in Portia's grip.

"Thank you."

"No problem." Portia pulled Amy to her feet, but she kept the blonde huey from standing up too high as she started guiding her toward the door that connected the ballroom dais with the Doge's residence. "Come on, Amy."

They all stood at the same time, Caleb facing the crowd and presenting his body as a shield, the two women behind him. Below was chaos. Vampires were running in all directions, some in their smoke forms weaving through but turning into swirling eddies as someone else cut through them. At the back of the ballroom, the protective doors connecting the room to the docks had been closed, leaving only an opening the size of a standard double door. A dozen of Massimo's men lined the perimeter. Caleb's heart leaped into his throat when he realized they weren't standing idly by. Twice their number of zompires had somehow gotten into the ballroom before the doors had been closed.

Tina stood among the crowd, observing, all while wearing a shit-eating grin.

"Caleb!"

The solari spun. "Amy!"

He didn't know how or how quickly, but in the few moments out of site, Amy had managed not only to lose her protector but also come under the direct attack of a zompire... who looked particularly fresh. On the floor nearby, Portia had been knocked to the ground. She stirred, telling Caleb she was conscious.

"Caleb, help me!"

"How dare you touch my mistress's lover!" Oh, so zompires *could* talk. English even. Impressive. "You dare to sully him with your mundane touch!"

"Okay, time to go." Caleb grabbed the perpetrator's arm and spun him around, freeing Amy and letting her run away and through the nearby door. Instinctively, his hand started to glow with power. Immediately, however, the higher functions of his brain kicked in, telling him he couldn't chance killing the Doge just a few feet away by lighting up this firecracker.

The thought gave him the smallest moment of hesitation, and that proved enough for the creature to get the advantage.

Caleb stumbled back until his lower back hit the railing of the balcony. The thing's hands... they were so strong. Around his throat, they clutched and tightened. Forget choking to death. Caleb was worried this thing was going to pop his head off.

"Aurelio, no! Not Caleb! He's mine!"

The voice was Tina's, and it carried over the crowd despite the havoc, confirming that the female slayer had new friends who didn't come to party.

Tina's pleas fell on deaf ears. *Aurelio's* grip didn't loosen a bit, and as much as Caleb hated to admit it, the creature might be stronger than him. Unable to pry the fingers off his throat, it had him tipped back far enough that his feet no longer touched. Pulse pounding in his ears, the slayer tried to remember how far the drop from the balcony to the ballroom floor beneath him was. If he could shift his weight, maybe physics would pull him over.

Only then, the most amazing thing happened. Suddenly, Aurelio had a red-headed monkey on his back. One that looked very much like the Dogaressa and whose palms were shining with a bright golden hue.

"Let him go, asshole!" Piggybacking, Portia pressed both hands against the man's face, her arms reaching out over his shoulders. The effect was immediate. Aurelio's hands released as he heaved his body backward, stumbling away from the balcony. Portia kept her grip somehow, skimming her hands down his neck and over his shoulders, leaving a dry, crumbling path in their wake. The zompire screamed and fell to its knees as Portia regained her feet.

Caleb gasped and doubled over but kept his eyes up, watching with amazement as Portia's hands pushed through what had been flesh and plunged into the chest cavity. Aurelio made one last whimper before what remained of his body caved in on itself, and his clothing fell into a pool on the floor.

"Portia!" Massimo suddenly realized his wife had returned. He rushed to her side, taking one look at her, then a wide-eyed look at the cheap set of duds on the floor, and then out to the crowd. He didn't have to say words to state the obvious. Yes, Portia probably just saved Caleb's life, but she'd also given away her secret. The vamps still in the room were running each and every way, but surely, a few of them had to have seen what had just happened on the balcony above.

"No time for this now." Massimo shook his head and pushed Portia by the back toward the door leading back to the dining room. "Get to the panic room. I will come for you when it is safe." He quickly pressed a kiss to her lips before pushing her through the door and swinging around.

"Fuck, Massimo, I'm so sorry. I—"

"Not now, I said." The Doge's hand flew up, cutting off his words. "Do you still hold Tina under your claim?"

Shit, was she? The subtext of the question was obvious. Massimo was asking if he had permission to take lethal measures without regard to her survival. As a slayer in good standing, Caleb was duty-bound to protect her and avenge her if necessary. The last thing he wanted to be doing as the solari was starting a blood war with any of the Italian courts.

Then again, to be rid of Tina...

No, he couldn't think that way. Even if she was a delusional bitch, she was still one of his people.

His head dropped to his chest, and his teeth ground as he spoke. "Damn it, yes, she fucking is."

But to his surprise, instead of rolling his eyes, Massimo just put a hand on Caleb's shoulder. "Then we will take her with minimal harm to her person." There was a tenderness that reassured in his voice, a tone that seemed to say *that was the right answer, even if it felt wrong.* "You must flee as well," Massimo said, pulling back his hand. "My security team and I will subdue her."

"No, I can't let you do that. She'll kill you. Look at her." He pointed to where Tina stood, glaring at them from a distance, her hands loaded with power and ready to drop pain. "You get close to her, she's going to reduce you to human Rorschach. *Vampire* Rorschach. You know what I mean."

"I have faced more than a few errant slayers in my time and always come away victorious," Massimo bragged. "You are one of the last of your kind, and a leader must safeguard himself to remain in power."

"No, a leader must protect the innocent, whether they're his people or not, or what's the fucking point of being a leader?"

Massimo grinned. "There may be hope for you yet, Helsing."

The Doge gathered himself to his feet. Without pause, Massimo jumped down from the dais and pushed his way through the startled vampire crowd.

"Potsia!" he bellowed. "How dare you unleash your weapon among my people without cause! How dare you—"

Caleb jumped over the railing of the balcony and landed on his feet among the vampires below. He had to get in front of this. That was his place. But before he could assume it, something completely unexpected happened.

The Doge froze, not just stopping where he stood. His mouth had frozen mid-word. His right hand remained fixed before him, a finger pointed in accusation.

Caleb regained his feet even as his mind went reeling.

"Your fiancée?" Tina's voice was as wild as her eyes as they found him in a clearing. "I haven't even been gone a day, and you proposed to that tramp?"

"Tina?" Caleb felt two poles in his intentions spring up, pulling him in opposite directions. There was no doubt the solarium had come from Tina and that it had been meant for Amy. But at the same time, his missing lamb had wandered back into the pasture.

In the end, compassion and concern won out. "Are you okay? What happened to you? How did you get back here?"

She tilted her head, the fingers on her hands cracking as she curled them over. "Are you ignoring my question?"

"No, of course not, but Amy and me..." He scooted in closer and lowered his voice, unsure how many of the immortals gawking at the scene before them spoke English. He switched to Turkish, positive that number would be less. "... it's just for show. I didn't want any of these guys..." he pointed vaguely to the right, "... hitting on her. You know Amy's terrified of vampires she doesn't know."

Tina switched her tongue to the one he'd chosen. "That kiss looked like it was about a lot more than a little flag planting." She lowered her tone, but only a hair. "Yes, I'm okay. In fact, better than okay. I only came back here to save you."

"Save *me*?" His face screwed up. "I'm only at this thing hoping whoever or whatever it was that took you would show up to take me too. I was hoping it would lead me to you so I could *save you*. Tina, what happened to you after they took you off the ship and..." he looked around, his eyes wide, "... what the fuck is making *this* happen?"

A devious curl of smile bloomed on Tina's face. "*I* am. I have this power, thanks to the goddess."

A chord struck deep within him. "The... goddess? What are you talking about?"

Suddenly, Tina was a basket of giddy smiles. "She revealed herself to me, Caleb! She's been trying to collect us slayers so we could serve her and her glorious purpose."

Boy, someone had been given a shot of the Kool-Aid, drank it down, and asked for seconds. "You're starting to sound like the little harem girl I met a few years ago. The one who thought the moon rose and set in Dracula's eyes."

"This is nothing like that!" Tina spun as her voice ratcheted up to a scream again. "I'm not imprisoned. I am *free!* She reminded me of who I am, of who a *slayer* is meant to be."

"And that is?"

"It's no great mystery. It's right there in our name. We're not supposed to be here, fraternizing with the enemy. We're supposed to be *out there...*" Tina pointed vaguely over her shoulder, "... fighting them, killing them. We are not wolves and hoods. They are ancient and natural. *We* were created after these monstrous parasites, not to keep them in line but to remove them from existence! Our purpose is to *destroy* every vampire, to cleave them from the face of the planet and render them all dust."

"Destroy all the vampires?" Caleb stumbled back. "You can't be serious."

"Of course, I'm serious! They are a plague, an unnatural creation by a bitter deity jealous of the place hueys had taken up among the pantheons. The goddess showed me the truth that you and all the slayers have forgotten!"

"Well, then, the *goddess* can't be serious. Come on, Tina, think about this! Yes, there are bad vampires, just like there are bad *people*. But vampirism is only a disease, one a lot of them never chose for themselves. Most of them are chill, cool people. Only when one makes trouble do we have a duty to step up."

"There are no good vampires. There are only vampires who haven't gone bad *yet*." She looked at him with a sense of sympathy, like she was sorry he couldn't understand this basic point. "You of all people should understand this. Vampires killed your parents!"

"And other vampires helped me defeat them. I don't get how you can use that argument, but in your mind, Tepeş is some kind of god figure. You do realize it was his generals that murdered my parents, right? It's like you—" His fingernails cut into the heels of his hands. This couldn't be happening. "Look, I don't know who or what this *goddess* actually is, but can't you see whatever radical line of bullshit she's forced down your throat is the same tired tripe Vlad fed you all those years? With despots and extremists, it's always like that: black and white. Their way or the highway, and anyone who disagrees is the enemy. You're not a prisoner anymore. You can choose your own mind and your own way. Don't do this."

"How am I any less of a prisoner back in Chicago? All of us sit in that gilded cage you made for us, waiting. Oh sure, we can come and go as we want. We can read what we want, think what we want. But all we really *want* is to have purpose again, a future, a place. You could have given us all of those, but all you wanted to do was go nurse your broken heart in other women's beds."

"I already told you that when we were on the way to the airport, I realized I screwed up. I'm not going to argue with you. You're right. I was an amazingly self-centered prick, and I promise I'm going to do better in the future. Now, please..." He lifted a hand, offering it to her, as he walked with cautious steps in her direction. "You know this is wrong. You know that—"

He'd just about reached her when it happened. Someone from the crowd got brave enough to play hero. The nameless vamp leaped forward, fangs out, and ready to strike. He got within inches of Tina when she managed to pivot and hold up her hand, the glow already forming.

The vamp became a little pile on the floor as Tina's solarium burned a hole into his gut before fingering through his torso, limbs, face... turning the creature to a pile of ash.

Panic. Ensued.

The vamps who could smoke, smoked. The ones too young or too scared ran for the docks. Tina already had her weapon ready again. Caleb followed her and found the next intended victim at the pointy side of Tina's glare.

"Tina, no!"

Caleb leaped, making a spot-on impression of a superhero as he sailed through the air. But it worked. Seconds before she managed to vaporize another victim, he interrupted her solarium's trajectory. Caleb seethed as the solarium hit him. Its energy dissipated, even if it did sizzle his very nice suit off his body.

"So you *will* side with them?" Tina spoke through gritted teeth. "Then you are no longer fit to be solari. I will find the others, and I will claim them, and together, we will rid the world of all you fang sympathizers and fangs alike. *Rekhyt*, now!"

As Caleb rose and spun, looking for a clue about whoever this *rekhyt* was and whatever he was planning on doing, he found his answer in the mass of animate decaying bodies suddenly falling in on him from all directions.

Zompires. Apparently, the zompires were *rekhyt*.

A slayer wasn't a hood. Even if Caleb's parents had lived long enough to teach him everything they knew, it probably wouldn't have included military tactics or gang warfare strategy. He'd never looked around to assess the wisdom of his positioning when he'd run across the room to Tina, how that had put her back against the exit to the docks, and a dozen vampire guards behind her. On his backside, the zompires, or *rekhyt*, were closing in, their hands all out in front of them in the stereotypical zombie way. There was no denying the stakes here. No matter what Tina had said about the need for all vampires to die, that wasn't her goal here tonight. She intended to either capture him or kill him.

Perhaps the best strategy still was to let her.

"I surrender!" Caleb threw his hands up, recalling the solarium that itched just under the surface.

The rekhyt drew to a stop.

"What?" Tina asked incredulously, her brows furrowing as she blinked rapidly.

"You wanted me defeated, so I'm defeated." Without taking his eyes off Tina, Caleb pitched up the volume of his voice. "Your Excellency, recall your guards."

"Mr. Helsing, do you really think—"

"Your Excellency, *I insist.*" This time, he did pivot, catching Massimo's eye across the room and winking. "I *want* to be captured. *Recall your guards.* I will give into her demands and go with her peacefully."

The Doge was a practiced politician. He gave a nod but no other sign of emotion. "Very well, if that's what you wish." Then, looking at Tina, the Doge added, "Miss Potsia, a week ago, I welcomed you into my home. Tonight, I planned to introduce you as a guest of honor. From this day forward, however, you are an enemy of Venice. If I ever see you in my city again, I *will* destroy you."

"If ever you see me again, my solarium will go straight through your eye before you can blink. *Ahnut rekhyt!*"

With Tina's shrill screech, one of the zompires lurched forward and bowed.

"Tie him up!" Tina's shouts were now for her sickly band of lackeys. "If his hands are bound, he can't throw his weapon at you. Do not think for a moment that you've saved anyone here tonight by surrendering, Caleb. All you've done is delay their deaths a while."

"Sometimes the best we can hope for in battle is to live the fight another day." He shrugged. "Though I kinda think winning is so much better."

"Too bad for you then that you won't be getting that tonight." She lifted a hand to his cheek and stroked it. "Though you may be getting something else."

As the *rekhyt* pulled taut a cord, Caleb identified the material of choice. "Silk rope?" he asked, his smile reaching his voice. "Tina, you little freak. I never knew you were into the kinky stuff."

"Oh, I am," she said, then pulled close to him, her face inches from his. "But coincidentally, silk rope has impressive tensile strength. I think you'll find it *quite* difficult to break, and with your hands cuffed behind you and pointed the wrong way, impossible to burn. To the boat!"

Someone pushed him from behind, prompting Caleb to move. Tina waited for him to pass, allowing the *rekhyt* to form a protective line between them. Smart. Then again, Tina had been educated in the court of a Dracule. It was she who Tepeş had sent in a raid in Istanbul to capture Geri Kline and the others hiding out among the werewolves who called that city home. He guessed, then, in hindsight, that she knew how to handle command shouldn't surprise him.

He only wished he hadn't ignored it—or Tina's potential—for so long just because he'd been embarrassed about their forced tryst once upon a time. If he'd swallowed his ego and found his balls, the *metaphorical ones*, in this case, he probably wouldn't be in this situation right now.

Half-expecting the impressive ancient warship that had collected Tina from the open waters earlier in the day, Caleb was surprised to see the vessel into which he was being loaded was much humbler. The wood-sided cruiser reminded him of Massimo's own private boat, if perhaps a little smaller. One of his captors pushed down his shoulder, forcing Caleb to descend from the dock to the vessel. The dozen or so rekhyt funneled in after him, spreading out and taking points around the deck. Caleb couldn't see into and past the cabin well enough to be able to tell if the captain was one of the zompires or a huey. He hoped the former.

"So, Tina..." He exhaled as the boat eased away from the palazzo dock, making its way towards larger waters and escape. "I feel I should tell you now, I have no plans to join your cult, so if that's what you're expecting, just kill me now."

"Kill you?" Tina settled herself on a bench perpendicular to him and grinned.

"For a moment, when I saw you snogging Puppy Guts, I thought I might. But then I remembered. First, I need something from you."

"Is that what this is, some kind of heist to get money out of WWL?" He shook his head. "You forget, the Board hates me. They'll probably just send you a note back saying, 'Keep him. He's a dickhead.'"

"I don't need money. But you being a dickhead or, more specifically, having one..." Her voice tapered off as her eyes slid suggestively at his crouch.

Normally, Caleb's internal fanfare would go off whenever a sexy woman paid attention to his *not-so-little* friend. This time, attack sirens sounded. He tried to cover it with his normal bravado. They still weren't far enough away from the city's structures. He had an inkling of an idea here, but if Tina and her henchmen threw him overboard, he was done for.

"So you're kidnapping me to be your sex slave?" He shifted his position in the seat. "That explains the silk rope better."

"I don't need to have sex with you. We've already done that, and well, no offense, but having been with seasoned vampires, you didn't exactly impress." She looked at her nails with passing interest. "No, what I need from you is your *seed*. The Helsing line is the most powerful, and I want my children to have every advantage."

"*Your* children, not *our* children?" He clicked his tongue. "And here I thought you wanted to be my Solari Queen or something like that?"

"Drop the Queen part, and that's still true." Tina sneered. "There's nothing in our tradition that says the solari has to be male. We're not backwoods wolves and hoods. We don't have the burden of gender roles."

"Yeah, too bad we can't also self-impregnate, or you could really be full of yourself."

He winced as her hand connected with the side of his face. Caleb's head lashed to the side. Fortunately too, because otherwise, he might not have noticed the blue and white boat marked POLIZIA trailing them at a distance. Good in one way, bad in another. Were they far enough away from small channels of the island and out into open water yet?

"I apologize. That was beneath me." Caleb brought his gaze back to hers and turned on the smolder. "Like you'd like to be."

She raised her hand, preparing to strike again, when his words gave her pause.

"Haven't you forgotten something, Tina?"

Her hand slowly lowered. "How much of an ass you are? No, you *constantly* remind me."

He pressed past the insult and hoped his words distracted her from his hands fidgeting behind his back. "You want to be the bearer of my children because you want them to have my gift. The Helsing Fire, or whatever else you want to call it. I don't blame you. It *is* pretty fucking awesome. The best thing about it is that I don't need my hands to make it happen, and even if I did—"

Her jaw dropped when his right hand, then his left hand, came out in front of him, the latter with the silk rope in tow.

"How did you—" Tina looked like a woman on the edge of a conniption fit. She spun, shook her head, spun back. "You know what? It doesn't matter. We're out in the middle of the water, and my rekhyt vastly outnumber you. Make a move on me, they'll overpower you. Use your *fire*, and we'll both end up in the water... you, as I recall, too spent to swim. You're way too conceited to sacrifice yourself that way."

Caleb stood up and buttoned his jacket. "I really wish that were true."

With a single thought, his body exploded out power.

And a moment later, the boat went up in a ball of flame.

THIRTY-EIGHT

I t had been years since Massimo had imbibed human liquor, but if ever there was a time to do so, it was now.

Too bad intoxication wasn't possible for a vampire. Even centuries later, he could recall the calming lull of drunkenness, especially in the days following the death of his wife and daughter. He wanted to be numb. Too much had happened in too little time, and the consequences had him reeling.

"Surely your court does not blame *you* for the actions of a rogue slayer," Raquel said, sitting across the table. "Especially not since Potsia was defeated."

"We don't know that she's dead." Pavlos, sitting next to his friend, had coordinated with the huey authorities following the previous night's events himself. "The police searched the waters in the hours following the explosion. No body has been found."

"But there wouldn't be a body, would there?" Massimo laced his fingers and placed his hands on the table. "As Helsing reminded us, when a slayer dies, water will dissolve the corpse. The better question is, as Potsia's body was not found, does that mean she is dead?" He leaned back and shook his head. "We cannot know. She may have survived. Helsing did."

"Only because the police were able to find him minutes after the ship exploded and pull him to safety," Amy noted. "If Tina *did* survive, I'm personally going to kill her."

Vega cocked a grin. "That would be an impressive feat for a huey to pull off."

The *huey* in question rounded on the vampire. "Like my friend Geri told me, there are very few things that can survive without a head."

The Doge felt the mood of the room slipping, and he did need this meeting to remain focused. Clearing his throat, he drew the attention back. "All things being equal of what was and what yet may be, for the moment, the moment *is* the focus. Luckily, none of my court were fatally injured in Miss Potsia's attack. These rekhyt are strong, but not gifted in battle. Their only advantage seems to be in numbers. Mr. Helsing's willingness to sacrifice himself, even with our limited damage, has balanced out the hostility that might otherwise have arisen in the wake of the slayers' return. My court is cautious, but open-minded. But..."

He let his words linger. The longer he did not say the obvious, the longer he did not have to acknowledge it. Unfortunately, he'd married a woman who didn't believe in... he believed the term she used was "pussyfooting around."

"They won't accept that your wife is one," Portia completed for him.

And there it was, the truth. Massimo had never hesitated for a moment in loving the woman who'd become his partner in the twilight of his years. The fact that he was supposed to disdain her on standing had never made sense to him. But the members of his court. Nay, even those of his race at large...

Most hueys had progressed to see past old-world boundaries, but vampires in this regard had not advanced in parallel.

"Sire, I will testify against anyone who dares to slander the Dogaressa." Pavlos took to his feet like a man standing to attention. "Our Lady Brunelli is among the bravest and most loyal wives and sovereigns one of the Eight Courts has ever known. I'll take the head of any fool who suggests otherwise."

"I trust that you would do that, my old friend. But then, any prejudices of the court would only be driven further in place. As the next Doge, you must do what you can not to so discord unnecessarily."

"The next—" Pavlos's eyes went to the floor. "Your Excellency, you have never formally named me your heir."

"I name him *now*."

Massimo rose then, a long, leisurely sweep of the room that hung heavy with memory and pride. He'd never had royal ambitions when he became a dark one. He'd merely been seeking purpose beyond losing his family. If he could not find it in the light, perhaps that purpose lay in the shadows. And so it had. It was as if he'd been born to be this city's sovereign. He had loved Venice, and so Venice had loved him back for four hundred years. But as he had one night walked into this room wearing the crown unexpectantly, ready to embrace the next chapter of his existence, so too could he walk away from it.

"It has been my sole privilege and honor to serve this Serene City, but it is time to move on. I have some years yet to live, and I'd like to live them where my wife can see out the full potential of her own being and purpose and where my guidance and experience, for whatever it's worth, can help guide the other Reclaimed and keep this fate from repeating." He took his gaze to the end of the table where Vega and Popowitz sat. "If the offer struck in London is still open, I'd like to close the loop on it."

"Well, we..." Vega turned to Popowitz with a questioning look on her face.

"We'd be thrilled to have you on our team and at our side at WWL." The huey's tone lacked any doubt. "But ultimately, that would be up to our CEO. This is kinda an executive decision."

"It sounds then like I'm supposed to decide something?"

Everyone shot to their feet as Helsing entered the room, looking like a kitten whose mother had licked him up one side and then down the other. The slayer wore pajamas, and wrapped in a thick wool blanket, he might be on his way to a slumber party instead of taking audience with the ancient sovereign of one of the Eight Vampiric courts of Italy.

"Caleb?"

Popowitz was at his side in a second. The lack of a kiss or even a hug told the Doge the romantic theatrics performed before his court really had been a farce. Funny, he'd been fooled for a moment to think real emotions were happening in that display.

"It's okay, Amy." Helsing put his hand up, stopping her advance. "My ears are waterlogged, and I feel ice cold. If someone would have the compassion of a saint and bring me an espresso, I think I'll be just fine."

Massimo's eyes connected with one of the staff always in the room whenever he was present. The man nodded once without the need for further instruction and zipped off to the kitchen.

"So what is it you're asking then?" the slayer asked as he lowered himself into a chair next to Vega. "A deal on Athenian glass? I'm sure we could extend a friends and family discount."

"A kind offer, to be certain, but…" Massimo exchanged a look with Portia, who took over from there.

"We'd like to take up your original offer," she said, pulling the Doge's hand into her own and locking their fingers together. "Massimo and I will join you in Chicago. He, as a mentor. Me, as a student."

"A student?" Caleb pulled a face. "Looked like you handled yourself pretty damned well last night."

"I got lucky. The thing I destroyed didn't know what I was. He was distracted. I'm hoping there's a way for me to learn to… *project* the way you do."

Caleb curled on a smile just as the servant returned and put a cup down before him. He lifted it and raised it as if making a toast. "Sure, sounds great."

"I need a month, perhaps two, to ensure the proper transition of power," Massimo added before things got too far. "In fact, it would probably be best if Pavlos visit the other sovereigns, both to announce his investiture and to tell them what happened here tonight. Rumors will fly. I want them to know what is true, what is fallacy, and why I am choosing to leave when the precedent among the sovereigns is to serve until death or otherwise deposed."

After all, Massimo himself had come to the throne by overthrowing the previous Doge. She lived on for centuries afterward, before having her head removed by the Red Matron just a few years ago, if rumors were true.

Rumors, the current Doge suddenly realized, he could have substantiated if he wanted. Supposedly, Helsing had been in the room when the deed happened. A reminder that, while he was clearly immature and forsaking his duties, Helsing wasn't to be dismissed. The Solari was a warrior, one with powerful friends. Hopefully powerful enough to protect Portia on standing.

"Our research department has made some advances in their understanding of slayer genetics over the last few years," Vega suddenly picked up. "We still have a long way to go to figure out if we can solve the male Reclaimed's fertility problems, but we're not without some advances. It's possible they might have treatments that could bring that part of your makeup into the foreground."

"You mean, like genetic therapy?" Beside him, Portia bristled. "Um, let me think on that, but thanks, good to know."

Popowitz flagged down the servant, pointed to Helsing's coffee, then herself, before turning back to the table. "Okay, then, can we discuss the elephant in the room?" she questioned. "What the hell is going on? Tina is working *with* those zombie vampire things now, but clearly, she isn't the big villain in this situation. Do we have any idea who is, and what they're after other than slayers?"

Helsing notched his chin into the air. "She said something about the goddess destroying all vampires everywhere."

A chill ran down Massimo's back. "I'm a Catholic. I don't believe in *goddesses*."

"And I'm a Jew with a Muslim mother, but when I see reanimated corpses attacking vampires, I'm open-minded to the possibility." Helsing took to his feet and began to pace, espresso cup in hand and a limp in his step. "Look, I'm not saying I believe in random deities either, or just the one big one, frankly. But hueys think we supes are just a story made up to scare little kids. Who's to say there aren't other older, rarer things out there *we* think are just mythic? If they are, we don't have any idea what they're capable of."

"The *Bible* has stories of people rising from the dead," Portia said, and it felt like the comment was meant for Massimo's attention specifically. "So even in a Christian paradigm, it's possible."

Helsing went on, "Like Amy and I said, that papyrus scroll at Schloss Wolfsretter claimed slayers and hoods had something to do with Egyptian gods. These little scarab things that seem to be used to bring the dead back as some kind of minion-monster also had ties back that way. So maybe there really is an ancient so-called goddess out there with a grudge against vampires."

A memory tickled Massimo's thoughts. "Once upon a time, one of your ancestors told me the Helsing line was the most capable and powerful because it was the first. He said the first vampire was an Egyptian priest, and the first *Hem-al Shenmish* was created to defeat him."

Everyone spun on Helsing.

"*Hem-al Shenmish*?" he repeated. "It's not exact, but it's close to how you'd say 'warrior of the sun' in Hebrew. My dad said something about it once too. That our family's legacy stretched all the way back to the time of Moses. I thought he was pulling my leg, but then again, maybe not."

Massimo nodded. "Then as you say, perhaps even us supernatural creatures should put more faith in the things *we* hold as myth."

He stood then, offering his hand out to Portia. "We will be in touch in the coming weeks to make the necessary arrangements and if we should have any development in the search for Miss Potsia, be she this side of the grave or the other. Please travel safely back to Chicago. Anything you need to make your journey easier that my staff can provide is at your disposal."

THIRTY-NINE

"Well, Mr. Helsing, I suppose I should congratulate you." Raquel used the comment as an opportunity to slide into the seat opposite him. "You managed to win over one of the most powerful allies possible in the supe world and convince him to join your staff. That's quite a victory."

Caleb watched the buildings and vehicles and people on the ground shrink away as the plane climbed into the sky. The ice in his glass clinked the edges. He tipped back the whiskey and finished it off. "Somehow, I feel like a failure."

Reaching a hand up to lower the window shade, she pulled his eyes up. "It's understandable that you feel badly for losing Miss Potsia, but it does sound as if she made her own choice."

"No, she made a choice from the limited options my neglect gave her."

He shifted in his seat and looked down the aisle to the rear of the jet, where the bedroom door to the executive suite was closed. He'd given up the room to Amy when he'd seen how dead tired she'd been. Evidently the events at the ball had triggered memories for her, and she'd barely slept a wink in nearly two days.

"Amy was right. In the ways that really mattered, Tina was still trapped in the harem. Her way of getting loose was to align herself with my enemies because she couldn't see me as the ally." He took a sip of the rosé he'd opened shortly after takeoff. "But she still wants to be my baby mama. Is that weird?"

"If not for the need for you to perpetuate your species, I'd advocate for a vasectomy." One of Raquel's eyebrows raised. "But you believe this *goddess* is your adversary?"

"Sure doesn't seem to be my friend, does she?"

Per her usual, Raquel mused a space in silence, showing nothing in her face of what was going on in her brain. Then, without missing a beat, she picked up, "You must at least be relieved that your plan worked. Massimo Brunelli is a good friend to have. He will be an asset to the WWL team and relieve you of much of the... *pressure* you felt as CEO. The board will be pleased with this development."

Caleb cocked an eyebrow. "You knew about my plan?"

"Don't be offended, Mr. Helsing, but I've been around long enough to recognize a bait-and-switch. I might even be guilty of counting on it. You see, I very much think there's a place for you at WWL... once you're done sowing your wild oats and are ready to embrace it. In the meantime, the Doge will help steer our ship with wisdom and experience."

And that had all been the point, hadn't it? If Raquel was ready to accept it, why shouldn't Caleb jump for joy that he'd pulled off what he thought would be a con? It was true. He'd come to rely on Massimo's sage wisdom in the places he himself had none. But even with the fact that Portia was slayer enough to conjure some kind of lethal solarium, Massimo would never... *could never* be the leader of the slayers. And they needed a leader. Watching Tina go so far off track so fast had convinced Caleb of that.

"What if... I wanted to try to..." He shrugged, hands out and palms up, "... be better now, I guess?"

"Be better at what?" Raquel asked.

"I don't know. Running the company? Guiding and teaching the Reclaimed? Maybe just life in general, be a better man?"

"Then I'd say that's a pretty ambitious shift for someone as well rehearsed in self-indulgence as you." She pulled to the edge of her seat, laced her fingers, and put her hands in her lap. "People who try to change too much at once find it's a bigger task than they reckoned for and give up from the weight of the effort. If you want to be a better man, start with trying to be just an okay one first and work your way up from there. Are you sure you're ready for that?"

Caleb nodded, knowing she was speaking the truth. "I have to be. Look, I'm not sure who or what this *goddess* is. Could be a complete fake or just some uppity rogue slayer wanting to build a cult. I didn't know Tina well, but I knew her well enough to know she's dangerous. That's all fine when she was on my side, but now she's not. If this goddess and Tina are operating on an 'all vampires must die' campaign, we have to stop it. That starts by making sure the other Reclaimed know that's not our place. At least, it shouldn't be. I won't have a genocide on my watch, and for all I know, there might be other Reclaimed who, like Tina, don't agree. I need to know who stands for our side and make them stronger, and who doesn't, and make them understand."

"Not all men can be talked out of their own conclusions. Prejudice is the echo of fear. What will you do if one of them refuses to agree?"

Caleb knew this was a test, and he knew what the vampire solution would be— stand with us or die alone. "I refuse to strike down someone unless they're attacking me. If they just think differently, I'll let them go and hope they see the light. You can't change a dead man's mind."

Raquel leaned back in her chair. "Then the Board and I will stand behind you." For once, she grinned. "Assuming that you aren't voted out, of course."

"You're going to tell them I shouldn't be, right?"

Raquel rose from her seat and walked to the front of the plane.

Chances were fifty-fifty that Caleb was about to be hit in the face, but he'd take the risk. His body was spent. His mind was fatigued. Even his eyeballs hurt.

Exploding his most powerful solarium ever and nearly drowning moments had come with consequences.

"Caleb?" Amy's voice cracked as she lifted her head from the pillow and fixed him in her sleepy glare, pinning him in place. "What are you doing?"

"Sorry, didn't mean to wake you." Caleb froze mid-creep. "Hoping I could sleep in the armchair over in the corner in here. It reclines, and the passenger seats in the cabin don't, so I..."

"Uh, is that all?" She turned back over and tucked her head into the pillow. "Take the bed."

Well, that was... fucking awesome, honestly. He stood his ground and waited at least a dozen seconds before saying, "Thank you, but can you move, please? I'm dead on my feet."

Amy's voice was muffled, the pillow pushing into her face. "Clarification, you can sleep here *too.*"

Sleep with Amy. In the bed? With Amy? *Next* to Amy?

Amy?

Suddenly, there were parts of Caleb that were anything but tired. Fortunately, none of those parts were connected to his higher cerebral functions, which knew the only part of Amy he'd be feeling if he tried anything was her knee as it connected with *his balls.*

"That's okay, I'll take the chair."

"You almost died, and you know if you try anything with me, you will." Without turning over and laying on her side, her top arm reached and tapped the empty space at her back. "Lay down and shut up."

Well, you didn't have to tell him twice except, apparently, when you did.

Being as silent as possible, Caleb pattered to the edge of the mattress and slipped off his shoes, jacket, and dress shirt. For a moment, he contemplated leaving his pants on. Then he remembered they were Armani. They joined a pile of clothing he quickly folded and sat on the floor next to the bed. Then, gingerly as a cat, he reached down and started to lift the bedclothes.

"On top of the blankets, Buffy. We both know you don't need them anyways."

True, and an exceptionally good idea, he realized suddenly. He hadn't managed to peel the blanket up far, but why he did left him wondering if Amy was wearing *anything* under there.

He laid down then, on his opposite side so he wasn't facing her, and tried not to think about how sweet her perfume was or how long it'd been since he had sex, or how fucking hot that kiss they had at the Doge's palazzo was.

He tried to think about... the Roman Empire.

"Were you scared?" Amy's words found him somewhere between Gladiators and centurions, but luckily before picturing bacchanals.

"When?"

She turned over, navigating carefully so her body stayed hidden beneath the blankets. "When you went off with Tina? Were you scared?"

He considered lying. Since he'd decided that he did want to be the Solari and try to be the leader he was supposed to be, Caleb had an image to uphold now. He needed to inspire confidence and respect.

He also knew that Amy knew him well enough to call him on any bullshit he threw her way.

"Of course I was scared. I knew the moment I exploded the ship around us, Tina and I were dead. I was more scared that part of me wished she was."

"It's my fault, kind of, that this happened. Ultimately, I'm the one who invited her to come."

Caleb shook his head. "No, you were absolutely right. The feelings she had... they weren't new, and who knows how much those poisoned the others while I was too busy ignoring the Reclaimed."

"I don't think the others feel the same way she does. *Did?*" She closed her eyes and snuggled into the pillow. "I guess we don't really know for sure, do we? Whether she's alive or not?"

"No, probably not."

His body froze as she curled up next to him, inching her way across the mattress to get closer. Caleb stayed that way for a few minutes as her breathing deepened and grew long, afraid to move back or forward.

He'd just about fallen asleep when she muttered something that roused him again.

"Sorry, what?" Caleb's eyes shot open.

"I said. I was scared too." Her eyes stayed closed. "That you weren't coming back. I'm glad you did."

He let his eyes fall close. "Me too, Amy. Me too."

ACKNOWLEDGMENTS

First and foremost, to the readers, especially those of my Facebook reader's group, Kendrai's Keep, who have been getting #AmWriting notifications and teasers from various attempts to write this book for FIVE FULL FREAK-ING YEARS. I appreciate your patience, and thank you for taking the journey with me.

To Chantell Reid, my editor who still came back after all these years because she loves these characters (and I think maybe tolerates me).

To the prereaders and ARC readers who help put the last bits of polish on this book. (Did I mention it took me five years to write this book? Seriously, there are kindergartners learning the alphabet right now who weren't alive when I started this.)

To my writer and real-life friends J.R. Frontera, Kristin Helling, Elizabeth Hunter, and Julia Vee, who helped support my soul and my sanity as I picked up and made a new life half-way across the country, dragging my worldly possessions, a corgi, and ALL THE DRAMA LLAMAS.

To Rod, the other half of my soul, who wouldn't let me give up on myself and supported me in my most self-doubting moments, and who didn't break up with me when I told him I didn't like the ending he wrote on his own book.

I couldn't have asked for a better partner at this point in life than you, and YOU'RE NEVER GETTING RID OF ME.

To the hope that renews and the doubts that die, and all the pain that it took to be here now without it.

ABOUT THE
AUTHOR

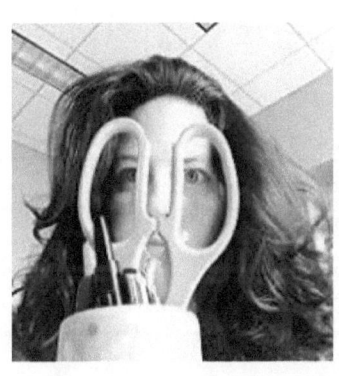

Firstly and foremost, Kendrai detests sarcasm. She became a published author in 2011, dabbling foolishly in romance before wisely turning her talents to science fiction and fantasy. A world music devotee with a love for travel (though she does hate to fly – a conflict, for certain), Kendrai enjoys twisting the extant into the exceptional, often basing works on historical themes or legendary folk tales and mythology.

She's currently based in the Kansas City area, though she leaves it as frequently as possible.

To discover other works, projects, and events Kendrai has coming, visit kendraimeeks.com.

MEEKSOLOGY

*Series complete.

**Title also available in audio

Red Chronicles*

Requited** - Book .5

Reluctant** - Book 1

Relinquished** - Book 2

Ravening** - Book 3

Rebellious** - Book 4

Righteous** - Book 5

Red Origins*
Beauty & the Betrayer** - Book 1
The Wolf & the Watcher** - Book 2
Red & the Restorer** - Book 3

Enter the Kingdom*
Court of Discontent** - Book .5
Mistress of Cinders - Book 1
Freebird (A side story novella)
Isle of After - Book 2

Vampire Sovereigns
Venice Dusk
Medici Moon (coming 2025)

Like romantic reads?

Check out these titles written as Killian McRae
The Lord's Second Chance**
Snapped**
Have Gown, Will Wed
Complements

CATCH A TYPO?

The Crimson Line has gone through several layers of editing. If you found a typographical, grammatical, or other error which impacted your enjoyment of the book, we offer our apologies and ask that you let us know so we can fix it for future readers. To do so, <u>click here</u>. In appreciation, you will be entered into a monthly drawing for a $10 gift card.

Build Edition: 05182025